BITCH
I
PLAY
FOR KEEPS
FINESSED
BY:
NIKKI NICOLE

D1519865

Acknowledgments

Hi, how are you? I'm Nikki Nicole the Pen Goddess. Each time I complete a book I love to write acknowledgements. I love to give a reflection on how I felt about the book. I've been writing for almost three years now and this is my 1st book. When I first started writing I only had one story I wanted to tell and that was Baby I Play for Keeps. I'm so excited to revamp this book to see what you guys think. I appreciate each one of you for taking this journey with me. I'm forever grateful for you believing in me and giving me your continuous support.

This book right here is dedicated to my queens that have been in or currently in a committed relationship or years and you've been blindsided by love for a long time. You've missed all the signs of infidelity, cheating, scheming and his manipulative ways.

Everybody has a breaking point and one day you finally decide to wake the fuck up and realize what the fuck is going on around you and face that shit head on. You've been dealing with a fuck boy and everything that he's doing or had been doing hits you at one time.

Guess what queens I'm unleashing Kaniya Miller she's going to let you walk in her shoes and hop in the passenger seat of her whip with her for a few hours and show you the fuckin' ropes of how to give a FUCKBOY a dose of his own medicine.

Book 1 the realest shit I ever wrote and the only story I ever wanted to tell! If I never write another book again; I don't care because this is the only one, I EVER wanted to write because this message wasn't being conveyed and it's still not 3 years later!

I speak for the strong queens, I rep and put on for you. I speak for the ones that ain't laying down crying over nann nigga! I speak for the queens that ain't scared to buss a man in they shit! I speak for the ones that ain't scared to buss a bitch in they shit! I speak for the ones that got a few replacements and free agents on call! This one is for you! BITCH I PLAY FOR KEEPS

I want to thank my supporters that I haven't met or had a conversation with. I appreciate y'all too. Please email me or contact me on social media. I want to acknowledge you and give you a S/O also.

I dedicate this book to my Queens in the Trap **Nikki Nicole's Readers Trap**. I swear y'all are the best. Y'all go so hard in the paint for me it's insane. Every day we lit. I appreciate y'all more than y'all will ever know. The Trap is going the fuck up on a Sunday. I can't wait for y'all to read it.

It's time for my S/O **Samantha, Tatina, Asha, Shanden (PinkDiva), Padrica, Liza, Aingsley, Trecie, Quack, Shemekia, Toni, Amisha, Tamika, Troy, Pat, Crystal C, Missy, Angela, Latoya, Helene, Tiffany, Lamaka, Reneshia, Charmaine, Misty, Toy, Toi, Shelby, Chanta, Jessica, Snowie, Jessica, Marla Jo, Shay, Anthony, Keyana, Veronica, Shonda J, Sommer, Cathy, Karen, Bria, Kelis, Lisa, Tina, Talisha, Naquisha, Iris, Nicole, Koi, Drea, Rickena, Saderia, Chanae, Shanise, Nacresha, Jalisa, Tamika H, Kendra, Meechie, Avis, Lynette, Pamela, Antoinette, Crystal W, Ivee, Kenyada, Dineshia, Chenee, Jovonda, Jennifer J, Cha, Andrea, Shannon J, Latasha F, Denise, Andrea P, Shelby, Kimberly, Yutanzia, Seanise, Chrishae, Demetria, Jennifer, Shatavia, LaTonya, Dimitra, Kellissa, Jawanda,**

Renea, Tomeika, Viola, Barbie, Erica, Shanequa, Dallas, Verona, Catherine, Dominique, Natasha K, Carmela, Paris B,

If I named everybody, I will be here all day. Put your name here_____ if I missed you. The list goes on. S/O to every member in my reading group, I love y'all to the moon and back. These ladies right here are a hot mess. I love them to death. They go so hard about these books it doesn't make any sense. Sometimes, I feel like I should run and hide.

If you're looking for us meet us in **Nikki Nicole's Readers Trap** on Facebook, we are live and indirect all day.

S/O to My Pen Bae's **Ash ley, Chyna L, Chiquita, T. Miles,** I love them to the moon and back head over to Amazon and grab a book by them also.

Check my out my new favorite Author **Nique Luarks** baby girl can write her ass off. You heard it from me. I love her work! Look her up and go read her catalog!

To my new readers I have six complete series, and three completed standalones available. Here's my catalog if you don't have it.

Crimson & Carius 1-2

Cuffed by a Trap God 1-3

I Just Wanna Cuff You (Standalone)

You Don't Miss A Good Thing, Until It's Gone (Standalone)

Journee & Juelz 1-3

Giselle & Dro (Standalone)

Our Love Is the Hoodest 1-2

Join my readers group **Nikki Nicole's Readers Trap** on **Facebook**

Follow me on Facebook Nikki Taylor

Follow me on Twitter @WatchNikkiwrite

Like my Facebook Page AuthoressNikkiNicole

Instagram @WatchNikkiwrite

GoodReads @authoressnikkinicole

Visit me on the web authoressnikkinicole.com

email me authoressnikkinicole@gmail.com

Join my email contact list for exclusive sneak peaks.
http://eepurl.com/czCbKL

https://music.apple.com/us/album/victory-lap/1316706552

Table of Contents

THE
SUMMER
IS
MINE

PROLOGUE
FEBRUARY 2016

Lucky

Freak hoes Freak hoes

Bounce that ass

And Let Your Knees

Touch Your Elbows

The sounds of **Future's Freak Hoes** were blaring through the speakers of an after hour spot Veno, Quan, and I slid through. I should've taken my ass home on some real shit. I decided to fall through with my niggas just in case some shit popped off. Quan was my little brother. We were two years apart, but we didn't fuck off in these streets unless we were together. It was so much ass and pussy in the building that it was crazy. As soon as we stepped in the building all eyes were on us.

These bitches were choosing, and I'd already chosen. I had way too much shit going already.

Juggling another female wasn't part of the plan right now. Quan and Veno were trying to set me up. As soon as we stepped in the building it was this little freak named Melanie and that bitch was all on me. I told shorty to move around, but every time she sees me, she kept throwing the pussy at a nigga. The devil was on my back heavy telling me YOUNG NIGGA YOU better FUCK something.

Melanie was sexy as fuck. Her skin was the color of a chocolate Heath bar. She had big brown eyes and a cute button nose. She was slim thick. Her ass wasn't fat, but she had enough. It wasn't flat and all back. Her thighs had a little meat on them. I never saw her real hair because she kept a weave, a sew in, or whatever they called that shit. I could fuck with it though. I had a situation and it's hard as fuck resisting temptation. I can look but I promised myself I wouldn't touch or feel.

Temptation is motherfucka, but I had everything I needed at home. She stood right in front of me and bounced her ass to Freak Hoes. Shorty didn't even have no panties on. She wanted me to see her fat ass pussy and my eyes were trained on her. She was to fuckin' fine to be giving it up like this in the club. Every nigga in the VIP sections surrounding our eyes was on her, but her eyes were trained on me.

Quan and Veno tapped me on my shoulder. I looked over my shoulder to see what they wanted. Veno had this sneaky ass grin on his face. I knew he was up to no good. Quan shook his head.

"Aye, shorty got that pussy on a platter, what are you going to do about that?" He asked. Veno was tripping. I wasn't about to do shit.

"Bruh, don't test them motherfuckin' waters if shawty is giving up like that. She's nothing but bad news," he explained. I heard everything Quan and Veno were saying, but if shawty was trying to fuck with me she had to come better than that. If she wanted me to have it, she's fuckin' up by letting everybody see it. I made my way toward Melanie. Quan and Veno tapped me on my shoulder and I waved them off.

"I'm good," I chuckled and explained then approached Melanie. I pushed up behind her and grabbed two-hand full of her ass. I finger fucked her wet. Her pussy sounded gushy as fuck. I whispered in her ear.

"Shawty, you could never fuck with a nigga like me, if you're popping your pussy in this motherfucka for every nigga to see." She looked behind her to see who it was, and she was surprised that it was me. I ran my fingers across my nose to see what it smelled liked and it was clean. It didn't have a stench to it. I headed to the bathroom and she was on my ass. I walked in the bathroom and she walked up right behind me. I stepped in the stall to use the bathroom and she was right behind me. I took a piss and looked over my shoulder and shawty was behind me licking her lips.

"You like what you see or something?" I asked and wiped my dick off.

"Yeah, I just want to touch it. You ran your hands between my pussy. I want to slide my tongue up and down your dick," she stated. I looked at shawty and shook my head. She was crazy and damn near took the dick.

"I can't let you do that. I just wanted to smell it and that's it," I chuckled. I tried to walk past her, but she pushed me in the stall and locked the door. She started tugging at my belt then my pants dropped to the floor. She freed my dick and went to work. I grabbed her hair and fucked her face roughly.

"You a nasty a little bitch, huh?" I asked. I kept pounding her mouth. I felt my dick touch the back of her throat.

"I'm a nasty bitch for the right nigga," she stated and continued to hum on my dick. Melanie swallowed my shit whole. I damn near fell to the ground. I grabbed her head for support and fucked the shit out of her face. She drained the fuck out of my dick.

"Oh yeah, let me see how nasty and wet that pussy is?" I asked. Melanie did as she was told and bent over and tooted that ass up. I grabbed the condom out my back pocket and slid that motherfucka on. Her pussy was wet but not that tight though. I wasn't the only nigga she was fuckin. I beat her pussy out the frame, and she was throwing that pussy back at a nigga trying to make it count for something. She was looking over her shoulders at me.

"Damn, you feel so good. I ain't never felt an orgasm like this," she moaned. I smacked Melanie on her ass and grunted in her ear.

"Shut up and take this dick and stop running from it." Melanie turned around and clamped her pussy muscles on my dick and attempted to drain the fuck out of me. I pulled out, turned her around and shoved my dick in her mouth. Shorty swallowed my shit again. I fixed my pants and attempted to head out. She tapped me on my shoulders and gave me the pouty face.

"What's up?" I asked. "I got to get the fuck up out of here."

"So where do we go from here?" She asked. I was hoping she wouldn't ask that. She wanted to fuck so we did that. I couldn't offer her anything else but that. Kaniya would kill her and I if she ever found out.

"Look, you know I got a girl and it's not a bitch walking that's going to come in between that. We've already done too much because you were persistent. It's nothing I can do for you," I explained.

"I know you got a girl, Lucky. What's understood doesn't have to be explained. I don't mind being number two. I can play my position. Are we going to stand here all night, or can I roll with you to show you what this pussy and mouth really do?" She asked.

"Alright, let's go and the minute you start fuckin' up it's a rap," I explained.

"I got you. I'm not going to fuck up. I promise. I want to be a part of your world Lucky, so if it means playing number two for a while then I'll do it," she begged and pleaded.

"For a while?" I asked. Ain't no way in hell she was moving up to my main. Kaniya held that down and it wasn't up for grabs.

"Yeah awhile. I think I can make you love me and leave her. Give me some time, I'm confident," she smiled. I escorted Melanie to my car.

I sent Veno and Quan a text and told them I was out before I even pulled out the parking lot. Melanie was already unbuckling my pants. Her face was buried between my legs. Veno and Quan were in the parking lot. They flagged me down and I stopped. I didn't want them to see me. They looked in the car and witnessed Melanie topping me off. Quan and Veno both shook their heads.

"Aye, you're playing a dangerous game. Hurry up and drop that bitch off at home and hit me up when you get to the crib," he argued. Quan was tripping for real. I wasn't taking Melanie to my house. I was taking her to my condo in the city. She had to be gone before 9:00 a.m. because Kaniya Williams would be calling by that time.

I made it to my condo in about forty-five minutes. As soon as I pulled in the garage. I picked Melanie up and threw her over my shoulders. I finger fucked her wet and headed upstairs. I tossed her on my bed, and she bounced a few times. She started playing with her pussy. I took off my clothes and undressed her. She bit her bottom lip. It was about to go down. I grabbed a Magnum out my drawer because I was about to take her down through there.

THREE MONTHS LATER

Chapter-1

Lucky

Tonight was a good night. Every nigga and bad bitch in the city were in my spot. I finally got my club, Lee's Palace open. It's been open for over a month and business has been booming. I can't even complain. The bar was paying for itself. The kitchen was making some noise in the city. We had to open at 11:00 a.m. for brunch because everybody was talking about how good the food was. I had no complaints. Life was good, minus the bullshit. Quan, Veno, and I was sitting in our private section. No one was allowed up here but the people we gave the okay to. Our security allowed Melanie in. Quan and Veno grilled me. They knew I was fuckin' with her heavy on the low. We go through shit every night. Melanie walked up on me and wrapped her arms around my neck. She leaned in and gave me a kiss and made herself comfortable on my lap. I like having her around because it was no strings attached.

"Aye Lucky, you're fuckin' up. Our club is one of the hottest spots in the city. Stop bringing her here because one-day Kaniya or her girls will fall through and you're going to get caught up. Guess what nigga, I'm not covering for you," he argued. Veno was tripping. I knew he was looking out, but I got this. Melanie cleared her throat. I gave her a look instructing her not to say shit.

"I got it trust me," I explained. Quan and Veno left us alone and exited our section. We were in our own world. Melanie knew I was thinking hard about something. She ran her hands across my face. I looked up at her to see what she wanted.

"What's up with you? I see you're letting your brother and your best friend in your head. Maybe I should fall back because clearly, you're never going to leave your girlfriend and your people think I'm not good enough for you," she argued and cried. I wiped Melanie's tears with my thumbs. I didn't want her crying behind some shit she already knew the answer to.

"Why are tripping? You already know what it is between us. You wanted this and if you want out, let a nigga know something. The same way you came in is the same way you can exit out," I argued and explained. Melanie stared in my face long and hard while the tears poured down her face. I wasn't wiping that shit again if she wanted to continue to cry. "Stop crying because it's not that fuckin' serious. What do you want from me? You know I'm not leaving her, so we don't even have to address that. Whatever you ask for you get it. I've always made sure you're straight."

"Damn Lucky, do I mean anything to you. We've been fucking around for three months. Twice in three months, I've been pregnant by you. Don't you think it's meant to be? You've been with her for five years and she can't even give you that. I can't continue to do this because I want more from you and I'm tired of this. I can't do this with you Lucky. It's somebody for everybody and maybe you're not for me. I can't change how I feel, but I'm out," she cried. Every other day she was tripping, and it was some shit with her. She's out but her feet haven't touched the ground.

"Melanie, if you want to leave, baby I'm not going to beg you to stay. I can't give you what the fuck you want. I'm not leaving her. You and I both know I'm not the only nigga you're fuckin'. I'm just the one with the bag. I wasn't about to wait until the baby was here to find out if it was mine or not. So, yes, I handled that shit immediately. I did that nigga a favor too, but you can leave because you already know what it is it with me," I argued and explained. It was this bad ass little bitch named Yirah standing outside of my section.

Shawty was trying to fuck with a nigga too. She had my attention because Melanie was tripping. I guess Melanie noticed what had my attention and it wasn't her. She looked over her shoulder to see what I was smiling at. She gave me an evil scowl. My eyes were still trained on Yirah. I wanted Yirah's ass too and she knew it. I'm tired of the flirting.

"Are you fuckin her?" She asked. I looked at everything but her. Melanie cupped my chin forcing me to look at her.

"Not yet. I'm waiting for you to get up so she can shoot her shot. You're leaving right?" I asked and chuckled. Melanie wasn't feeling that. She unbuckled my pants and freed my dick. She was doing too much.

"Aye chill out. What are you doing?" I asked.

"What you mean, what am I doing? She wants to fuck you, why else would she be staring up here. I want her to watch me fuck you right here, Lucky. I'll give a bitch something to look at," she argued. Melanie stood up in a squatted position and squatted on my dick and started riding my shit. I swear this girl was crazy as fuck. I know Yirah left. I rested my hands behind my head and closed my eyes. Melanie was doing the most.

"Aye shut the fuck up and ride my shit. You talk too much." Melanie started sucking' on my neck and shit.

"You wanted me to leave so you can link up and fuck that bitch? I'm not sharing this dick with nobody but Kaniya for now until it's all mine," she moaned. I wasn't even about to address this bitch. "I know this bitch isn't still watching me fuck you. I feel somebody staring at me."

"Melanie, ride my shit and shut the fuck. Stop worrying about whose watching you. Obviously, you want a motherfucka to see you or else you wouldn't be doing it. Hurry up so I can bust my nut,"
I argued. Melanie turned around and looked over her shoulder.

"Lucky, who is that tall foreign bitch that's grilling me? Are you fuckin' her too?" She asked. I tossed Melanie up off my lap and fixed my dick back in my pants. She was doing to much talking and not enough riding. It's only one tall foreign bitch that would've been grilling Melanie and that was Barbie. The last thing I need is for Barbie to catch me with my pants down with Melanie. I curved Melanie and sprinted to my office. I had to play the cameras back to make sure that wasn't Barbie or else I'm fucked. I'm not trying to get fucked. Kaniya leaving me was never a part of the plan.

Barbie

Ugh, why did I have to witness that? I just wanted to come out for a drink and some wings, that's it. I wanted to walk around and check this spot out. I had no clue Lucky owned it. When I asked the bartender who owned this spot, she pointed to his VIP section. I wanted to congratulate him on his new establishment. I couldn't even do that because he was so busy getting his dick wet. Lucky is so fuckin' disrespectful. I stood there and watched him fuck that bitch in the club. I recorded it and took pictures. Kaniya was going to see this. I don't give a fuck. This is not the type of nigga you should commit to.

I locked eyes with Veno and Quan because they knew I was telling on his ass. I'm sick of his shit. My friend is at home in the bed being faithful to your community dick ass. It's not going down like that. You can play any bitch you want but not mine. I couldn't even enjoy myself. He ruined my fuckin' night. As soon as I hopped in my car, I called Ketta. I knew she was up because her shift just ended, and she was headed home. I hit the Bluetooth and the call connected.

"Barbie, what's up? What are you doing?" She asked. Ketta and Kaniya are my girls and I love them to death. I'm the oldest and I'll always look out for them no matter what.

"Girl, I'm just leaving this little new Bar and Grill on the Southside. Let me ask you a question and I want you to be honest with me. If you saw my man fuckin' another bitch in the club would you tell me, or you would rather me find out on my own?" I asked. I know Kaniya would want to know. She would flip if she was out there looking stupid.

"Girl, you know I would tell you in a minute. I don't want to be out there looking stupid. I feel that we're close enough for you to tell me and I wouldn't take it as you are being malicious," she explained. Ketta and I finished talking. We made plans to see link up tomorrow. I hate to be the one to break it to Kaniya but it's time for her to wash her hands with him until he can give her what she's giving him. Kaniya's a good girl and she doesn't deserve this at all. Lucky is so damn trifling. Kaniya ain't told me shit about him owing a club. You're fuckin' random bitches for the world to see. I know I'm not the only one that saw that. I wish I hadn't, but I did and I'm not protecting his sneaky ass.

Kaniya

I'll never forget this day as long as I live. One Friday afternoon my girls and I were about to kick it and my life changed drastically in a matter of minutes. It's been along week for all of us. It's been a minute since we've been able to kick it and catch up with each other, but this weekend there are no excuses. I didn't have any plans for today. My schedule was clear. It's May 1st to be exact. It's May Day Bitch and it's 90 degrees in Atlanta. You know I'm feeling myself. I act with the weather. If it's hot bitch, I'm hot. Anytime me and my girls linked up it's a fuckin celebration. I've been working and busting my ass all week so of course; I was looking forward to the turn-up. I had my clothes ready and in rotation for the weekend, so my best friends wouldn't be complaining about me taking forever to get dressed.

"Ketta & Barbie let's hit these streets," I yelled. I was feeling myself and for some reason, I felt like getting into some trouble. I guess it's something in the air. You know they always say black folks don't know how to act when it gets hot. I'm that black person they were talking about.

"When bitch, what day, and what time?" My best friend Ketta asked. I rolled my eyes at her. She had her hands rested on her thick ass hips. It's safe to say that she's already dressed and waiting for me. I do everything in real time. I started getting dressed early. I already knew they would've been popping off and talking shit about me.

"There you go always talking shit Ketta. Damn, you haven't seen me in two weeks, and you won't even let me have my moment. Is that how you treat your best friend? Maybe I should've taken my precious time. I've been dressed for a minute now. Shit, I'm waiting on y'all. Where's Barbie at by the way?" I asked. We've been best friends for over fifteen years. I wouldn't trade her for anything in this world. We've been through it all together.

"Girl, she's on the phone caking with some trick," she laughed. Barbie kept a nigga with a bag. If she had it, we had it. If he was cashing out for her, then he was cashing out for us too.

"That's my motherfuckin bitch," I squealed. Ketta and I slapped hands with each other. If Barbie was on the phone talking to a nigga, and she was nowhere in sight that was a good thing. She was giving this nigga her undivided attention, so she can begin the finesse. Tell a nigga everything he wants to ear, so he can cut a check.

I went back upstairs to my room just to look myself over in the mirror. I've lost a few pounds this past month and it's not that I was trying to. It's just that my boyfriend has been stressing me the fuck out these past couple of weeks. I've been with Lucky forever. Shit, since I was nineteen. He's the only man I ever been with. He's two years older than me and I know I'm not the only person he's been with, but I'm not tripping off that. He taught me how to be his personal freak. I know we didn't have any problems in the bedroom at all, but lately, he's been switching up and not acting like himself. I asked him about it, and he told me I was tripping so, I left it at that.

I swore I would never stress over a nigga, but I love Lucky. We've been together for so long that I wasn't trying to lose him. I know whatever you do in the dark will come to the light. I'm not going to go looking for anything. If he says I'm tripping then I better be because if I ain't, he better be ready to stand in the fuckin' paint. Let me stop worrying about the wrong shit. I stood in front of my mirror and did a few spins. I feel as good as I look. A bitch finer than a mother fucker and the last thing I should be doing is stressing over a nigga.

Let me introduce myself. My name is Kaniya Miller, but my folks and my closest friends call me K. I live in Atlanta, GA born and raised. I'm twenty-four years old with no kids yet. I'm 5'5 caramel brown skin with red undertones. I have perky breasts that I just got pierced. A fat ass, slim waist, nice teeth, and medium length red hair in an edgy style. I just graduated from college with a degree in Business. I'm thinking about going back for my masters, but who knows. I 'm starting my own staffing company and it'll be up and running in a couple of weeks. I do some other things too, but you'll find that out later.

"Kaniya, bitch, hurry the fuck up. Listen you're not going to look any better," she yelled and clapped her hands. Ketta was doing the most. I think she took a few shots at the bar this morning.

"Let me be the judge of that, bitch. I'm cute and I'm fine," I laughed. I glanced in the mirror loving my look. I had on a pair of ripped white True Religion jeans with a white tank top. My red bob was looking fierce. I touched my hair up a little bit with my flat iron.

I rock my natural face with no beat and gold lip gloss, that's all I need. "I'm coming trick," I yelled while heading down the stairs. "Do you hoes want lunch or nah?" I had plans to cook us a nice brunch before we combed the streets but that never happened because we sat around and gossiped all morning.

I must admit my bitches are bad. I stay screaming Ain't No Bitches Like the One's I Got. Chicks get intimidated when they see us coming. For instance, you got Ketta. She's 5'9, built like Serena, with a 20-ounce coke cola shape, and long pretty brown dreads with red-blonde highlights. She got a big ole ass that you can spot from a mile away. She's a registered nurse and every time we go somewhere, she's stopping traffic. She stays on her designer shit.

Then you got Barbie. That's my foreign bitch and the most real bitch I've met since I lived here. Blood couldn't make us any closer. She's a thick red bone. She's 5'10, real Brazilian hair, a pretty face, and a slim waist. She stays fly and having it her way. She got good game for days.

"Nah, let's grab something when we out," they explained. Say less because that was perfect.

"Okay, cool. Let me lay these steaks out for later. What's the move? What are we getting into today?" I asked.

"The mall, park, and bar hop," Ketta stated. I was down with that.

"Whose driving bitch, because I'm riding. We can take my truck but I'm riding," I explained. Barbie decided to drive so I tossed her my keys. I climbed in the backseat. I started checking my emails and looking at my bank statements, which was looking nice as fuck right now. I'm minding my own business and listening to the music thinking about some shit.

"I saw your nigga last night," Barbie blurted out and stated. We were quiet and the only thing playing was the music in the background. I ignored her last comment because if it's not directed it ain't respected. I looked up and she was staring at me in the rearview mirror. My antennas were up now. Was she talking to me? I gave her my attention now.

"Kaniya, do you hear me?" She yelled while cutting the music down.

"Are you talking to me? You saw Lucky? Did he see you because he didn't say he saw you when I spoke to him this morning?" I asked.

"No, he didn't see me, but his bitch did," she argued. I tossed my purse and phone in the seat beside me. I'm trying to see what Barbies is talking about because I'm the only bitch that Lucky has. My blood started pumping.

"Come again, sis. BITCH? What BITCH? Am I missing something?" I asked. I know Lucky wasn't trying to fuckin' play me. I don't even swear but on everything, I know he doesn't want to play with me. He'll regret it every fuckin' time.

"Sis, you heard what the fuck I said, HE as in LUCKY was with another bitch," she argued and explained. I couldn't even keep my guard up if I wanted to because I'm in front of my girls. I'm comfortable in front of them. I don't even have to hide my feelings from them.

"Oh really, please tell me you took a pic?" I asked. Barbie tossed her phone in the back seat so I could see. One thing about it and two things for sure Barbie wouldn't speak on anything if she didn't have receipts. If her phone was in my lap, she had all that.

"I do? Scroll through my pictures," she beamed with confidence. I opened her picture gallery and I wasn't prepared for what I was about to see. I just shook my head, if he was anywhere near me, I would've fucked his ass up.

"Damn, Lucky is really giving up it like this? This nigga is about to get his rights revoked. He's going to regret the day he ever tried to play me, let alone live to tell about it, but I'm tripping though. Nah, nigga, you're tripping. You got a bitch on your arms that's not me and publicly? He's bold, as fuck too."

"Best friend, are you okay?" She asked. I knew Ketta was looking out. I've never been one to sugar coat anything. I can't even pretend that I'm okay because I'm not.

"Hell no, I'm not okay. I've been with Lucky since I was nineteen and I'm almost twenty-five. My heart is in this and I don't appreciate him taking that for granted. I'm tripping though because I told him if he wanted to do some shit just let me know. It's all good though. He wants his cake and ice cream too, but not with me though. I don't come second hand to no bitch when I know can be first," I argued.

"Calm down, Kaniya," Barbie sighed. I don't even know why she was surprised. You can play with anything Lucky, but motherfucka don't play with me, my heart, and my feelings. Don't let this cute face fool you.

"How can I be calm when the love of my life is cheating publicly and he's still lying next to me? We've been together for five years, how. I'll be good. The best revenge is kept silent. You know me, I'm not in these streets for a reason and it's to spare him and not me," I argued. I swear to God I'm so fuckin' hot.

"Ketta, what's up girl? What's been going on with you? I know you got some tea," Barbie asked Ketta. She was trying to change the subject. The bullshit was still in the air and I won't be satisfied until I can touch Lucky physically.

"Nope, I don't have any," she laughed. Barbie had all the tea and I'm thankful that she was able to expose Lucky. Nah nigga, I was on to your stupid ass. He got this bitch out in public without a care in the world. He didn't give a fuck if somebody saw him or not.

"Barbie, what's going on? I know you got some more tea beside the tea you just gave me," I asked. I don't need to hear anything else. My day was going well until I heard that. I need to re-direct my focus immediately. I started thinking about what I wanted to wear tonight. Maybe I could wear some shorts. I don't want to wear a dress. I know I wanted to wear my Giuseppe Shoes and a cut off shirt. I'm fucking some shit up tonight includ-ing the club, and most definitely some niggas mind. Lucky better be glad I'm not in the streets, but that's about to change and it's all because of him.

I don't go out every weekend. Lucky hated for me to be-cause he didn't want any niggas up in my face. He was always in the club and now I see why. I chill at home a lot and make ap-pearances every now and then, but this summer is fuckin' mine. I'm counting checks and fuckin' up a few niggas mind. I'm trying to build an empire.

We finally made it to the mall. I wasn't even in the mood to shop after the fucked-up news that landed in my lap.

"We're here bitches. Look at these Divos in Lenox," I beamed.

"I hate coming to Lenox because it's never anywhere to park. Why do we always walk in Lenox Mall through Macy's?" Barbie asked.

"I don't know. Just park so we can shop and get the fuck up out of here." Barbie found a parking spot and she tossed me my keys. I hit the alarm and we headed straight in. It was hot as fuck outside. This air was everything. We made it inside of Macy's and we stopped in the women's section thumbing through the dress rack.

"Hey cutie, what's your name?" The salesman asked. I wasn't in the mood to talk, but I wasn't about to be rude. I had some serious shit going on right now and my mind was clouded because of it.

"Hi, I'm Kaniya," I beamed.

"Hi, I'm Mr. Chardonnay. Are you looking for anything in particular? Can I pick you out something? I'm an upcoming designer! I would love to style you," he stated. I'm always open to trying new things. I'll let him do it.

"Okay cool, I was thinking about some shorts and a cute blouse," I explained.

"Nah Boo-Boo, I want to put you in a bad ass dress, so that ass and them titties can sit up like a stallion," he explained. Okay, Mr. Chardonnay might be on to something. I like him already. I was trying to get in trouble. He just added fuel to fire.

"Oh Lawd," I laughed. I needed this laugh right now. I'm glad my energy has been redirected.

"Where have you been all my life, Mr. Chardonnay?" I asked.

"I'm here now, that's all that matters," he explained.

"It's about to be some shit now." We slapped hands with each other. Mr. Chardonnay thumbed through the racks picking me out plenty of pieces that would look good on me. He had me trying on several different looks. I wanted him to grab me some fly accessories and shoes too. I like his style so far. Barbie and Ketta walked up.

"Damn bitch, are you through yet?" They asked and laughed? Nope, we were just getting started. "Keep calm ladies, she's getting slayed by the best," he explained.

"Oh really?" Ketta asked.

"Yes doll," he beamed. "Let me style you ladies too? I'm trying to get my name out there." Mr. Chardonnay got them right together. I took a seat with my bags. He handed me a mimosa to drink while he picked Barbie and Ketta out a few pieces. I sent a text to Riley and my best friend Tiana to fill them in on this nigga.

"Mr. Chardonnay, I'll definitely be using you again," I beamed. We exchanged numbers making promises to link up next week to do lunch and discuss business ideas. I love to talk about business. That's me all day. "Let's stop by the Mac counter and Bloomingdale's and we can head out, cool."

Traffic is lit as we leave Lenox Mall. All you see are Maybach, Bentley's and Maserati's. These young black niggas getting out the mud.

"Barbie and Ketta bump my shit," I yelled. I'm about to fuck traffic up one time.

"What are you about to do, sis?" Barbie asked.

"I'm about to shake this ass that Kaisha gave me. Play **Stick Talk by Future**!" I beamed and smiled. Future's new Dirty Sprite album was the shit. I kept the album in rotation. Tonight, it's going down. I hopped out my truck dancing and rapping. I didn't give a fuck. I was showing my ass today and it's all because of Lucky. Every nigga out here eyes had been focused on me.

Took a Shot of Henny I Be Going Crazy, Crazy

They Say My Whole Got It Under Investigation

You Know They Talk That Stick Talk That Stick Talk.

They Know We Talk That Lick Talk That Lick Talk.

Ten Million Dollars Cash Fuck a Friend.

Loving the attention. I knew I fucked it up. I hopped back in really quick. Bitches were hating and shit blowing the horn. "Fuck you hoe," I yelled to the bitches behind us blowing the horn.

"How are you going to cuss these folks out, when they're watching you dance and fuck up traffic?" Ketta asked.

"Whatever! Oh lord, this nigga in this Bentley Coupe pulled up beside us blowing the horn," I mumbled. "Pull off on his ass."

"Don't get scared now bitch," Barbie laughed.

"Scared for what?" I asked. I looked to the left and spoke to this sexy ass nigga. I wouldn't even be entertaining this nigga if Lucky hadn't fucked me up. It is what it is. I'm single again.

"Hey, what's up?" I asked him. I don't know if I should've spoken to this nigga or not. He was licking his lips and shit. "Pull off Barbie," I laughed.

"Nope bitch, let's see if you still got," she stated and laughed.

"You, what's your name?" He asked. I don't know who this nigga is, but he was handsome and he's a temporary distraction. He was iced the fucked out too. This ain't even me but Lucky has tried my whole fuckin' life. When I met Lucky, I was in the streets heavy, but the moment we made it official I switched up everything for him. He said he didn't want his woman in the streets and out clubbing every weekend. If he wanted to cheat, he could've told me and I could've gotten back to the old me, but he wanted to make a fool out me.

"Kaniya," I smiled and ran my tongue across my lips. Barbie and Ketta were tripping. They knew I was cutting up bad today.

"Oh, I like Kaniya," he stated. I know you do. I don't mean to be conceited but what's not like. I'm every nigga dream. Too bad, I wouldn't be his though. If Lucky was cheating, it's over and I don't even want to work it out. The summer is fuckin' mine. I want to play and do me.

"Do you?" I asked him. Judging by his eyes and his persona he was looking for more than I could offer him. It was time to nip this conversation in the bud.

"Yes, I do. Do you dance like that all the time? Are you a dancer?" He asked. I knew it. He liked to fuck off on stripers. You got to be a real King to get a show from me. Barbie and Ketta were in tears laughing. This is the reason why I wanted them to pull off.

"No, I'm a business owner." I wanted to ask him was his momma a fuckin' stripper but I decided to keep my cool.

"Oh okay, can I get your number Ms. Kaniya?" He asked. I knew that was coming, but it's to my bad my number was one that he wouldn't be able to get access too. I can already tell he's a stalker.

"Let me get yours instead," I stated. He gave me his number and I keyed it in my phone. I forgot to get his fuckin' name.

"Are you going to call me?" He asked. I might call him. A small conversation couldn't hurt.

"Sure, what's your name?" I asked.

"Smitty." I've had a whole conversation with him, and I forgot to ask his name. That's the first thing that I needed to know.

"Okay cool, I'll hit you up later."

"Please do," he chuckled.

"Bitch, if you don't call that nigga I will. You are showing out today." My girls said in unison.

"It's May Day and it's something in the air besides Lucky cheating. I told y'all hoes this nigga don't know how I get down or how I come when I'm coming. Lucky is going to regret this shit. If you don't believe me just watch. Bitch I play for keeps, watch me work shawty. Speaking of which, let me call this cheating ass nigga." I can't believe the one I gave my heart to would do me like this. Hurt people hurt people and guess what I'm going to hurt that motherfucka BAD. Lucky knows he a fine sexy black ass nigga with the perfect set of white teeth.

He's 6'4, a Gemini, and his body is nice as fuck. He's cut the fuck up, twenty-six years old, and his body is tatted the fuck up. His skin is the color of a chocolate Hershey kiss. He has a head full of ocean waves with light brown eyes. He just started growing his beard. My pussy was starting to get wet right now just thinking about him. I wouldn't mind sitting on his face right now.

I love the way his mustache and goatee stroke my pussy as soon as it brushes up against his face. He slangs good dick for days. He's a Balmain junky and he swears he designed that shit himself. Our relationship wasn't perfect, but it was ours and we've made it work for the past five years. It's been just the two of us with no fuckups. We didn't live together because I wasn't living with him if we weren't married. Lucky was a great boy-friend. Just the thought of him cheating rubs me the wrong fuckin' way.

Chapter-2

Lucky

"Aye Lucky, check this shit out. Shawty on this live looks fuckin' familiar," he laughed and punched me in the shoulder. I looked over my shoulder and brushed his ass off. I knew Veno was with the shits and I didn't have time for it. I'm already two hours behind schedule. I didn't have time to see what he was talking about. My day is already long as fuck. I'm in the studio with my right-hand man Veno and my brother Quan. I was trying to make sure I had this beat together for one of my artists. Time is money and I wasn't fuckin' wasting mine.

Veno shoved his phone in my fuckin' hand. I had to look again. I know that wasn't mine out there cutting up showing my ass giving a nigga something to see and she belongs to me. Her shirt raised up and the lucky charms that adorned her stomach gave her ass up. Barbie and Ketta were hanging out the window of the truck I brought for her boosting her up. A nigga pulled up beside of them and she was cheesing all up in his face begging me to knock her fuckin' teeth out. My brother Quan snatched Veno's phone out my hand to see what had my attention.

"Lucky, is that Smitty and Kaniya? What the fuck is up with that?" He asked. For Smitty's sake and Kaniya's, it shouldn't be shit going on if that nigga wants to live to see tomorrow. Kaniya better shut that shit down. She knows what's up. Quan gave me the phone back. I kept my eyes trained on the video. They were talking way longer than they should've. Whoever was recording the video had zoomed in on the two of them. Smitty pulled his phone out. I swear to God if Kaniya gives him her fuckin' number I'll murk that nigga before the sun goes down and I put that shit on her. Veno's phone rung interrupting the LIVE. It was his wife Vanessa so, I tossed him that shit.

"Veno, who's fuckin' LIVE video is this?" I asked.

"Lil Vic mane, he's leaving Lennox. You know how kids are when they see shit, they go live with everything. He told me to tell you Kaniya fine as hell too," he laughed. Lil Vic was Veno's nephew. He knew who the fuck Kaniya was.

"Okay, tell that nigga to send me that fuckin' video if he can and stop looking at my wife," I argued. Kaniya got me fucked up. I couldn't even work. She had better not have given him her number.

Kaniya

☆

We finally made it to my house. I grabbed my bags out the trunk. I still haven't placed this call to Lucky yet. I wanted to go in on him. But I had to play it cool. Normally I'm big on vibes and since when was this nigga doing some foul shit? I just never felt Lucky was cheating. I never got that vibe from him.

"You're to calm sis," Barbie explained. I had to be in order to stop from fuckin' shit up.

"I have to be calm because when I catch this nigga it's going to be hell to pay. I'm saving my energy because I want to catch him in the act." I called Lucky and this nigga answers the phone on the first ring.

"Hey baby, what are you doing?" I asked. I tried to sound like myself as much as I could through the phone. It's hard. Lucky knows me, and he can tell when I'm pissed. I hope he couldn't pick up on my attitude just yet.

"I'm not doing anything Kaniya. I'm working and shit. What's up?" He asked. I could tell he had an attitude and he didn't want to be bothered. I got a fuckin' attitude too, but the only difference is, he won't get to hear it over the phone. I want him to feel it.

"That's what's up." I sassed and sucked my teeth. I wasn't beat for his attitude, but I always gave a nigga what they gave me, and Lucky wasn't excluded.

"What are you doing Kaniya? Do you need anything? It sounds like you got something on your mind. Say what you got to say," he stated. I got a lot to say but it won't be said over the phone.

"Yes, I need some money, I'm catching a flight to Miami at 7 p.m," I explained. I need him to handle that.

"Oh yeah, how much you need?" He asked. If he only knew I was about to tax the fuck out of his ass. He had to pay, and he'll find out just how much.

"6 MOTHERFUCKIN' RACKS BUSS DOWN," I sassed. Lucky knew I was with the shits. Just run me my fuckin' money and we won't have any problems. Ain't no telling how long he's been fuckin' this bitch, but you're going to pay for fuckin' her though.

"Kaniya, what are you about to do?" He asked. Does it matter just pay up? I ain't never needed an excuse for why I need to do anything.

"Have some fun that's all. I'm going to Miami." I beamed.

"Who's going with you?" He asked. Damn, he's asking a lot of questions. Just know I'm going to find me something new.

"Barbie, Ketta, Riley, Tianna, and I," I lied. I just knew Lucky was about to say something smart. I don't know what it is about Barbie, but he can't stand her.

"Barbie?" He asked. I knew Barbie was about to go in on his ass and he deserved it. I placed my face in my hands. I know shit was about to go left.

"Bruh, don't fuckin' play with me," she argued and shot back at Lucky.

"What the fuck are you going to Miami for?" He asked.

"It's a girl's trip," I beamed and lied.

"You know to be good and don't do nothing I wouldn't do," he explained. If he only knew. He should be glad I don't have a nigga in rotation because if I did, I would fuck him just out of spite. Lucky knew he had some extra shit going on. He just wanted to make sure that I wasn't doing him the way he was doing me. I don't have to cheat, and he knows that. I'll leave before I do that. I'm mad because he didn't give me the opportunity to leave because I would've.

"Lucky, you and I both know that you have a good woman, don't you?" I asked. Lucky knew I would never cheat on him. I can't say the same for him. I always knew if we were to break up it'll be on him and not me. He's proven my theory correct. I can't wait to tell him I told you so.

"You're right. I'm tripping, Kaniya," he stated. He knew he was tripping. Just a few minutes ago he acted like he didn't want to talk, but now he's questioning me about everything when I should be questioning his ass.

"You're a cheating ass nigga," she coughed. Barbie is crazy. Ketta was trying to muffle her laugh. I'm hoping he couldn't hear her. The last thing I wanted him to know was that I was open to something. I had to cough to stop from laughing!

"Something got caught up in my throat." I coughed.

"I just wired you the money check your account," he explained. I pulled up my SunTrust app to check my available balance and it was there. Now I can get off the phone with him and stop pretending that I'm going somewhere.

"FaceTime me now, so I can see what you're looking like before you leave," he stated. I ignored Lucky. I wasn't about to FaceTime him. For what? Why do you want to see me so bad and you're cheating? Tell that bitch you were posted up in the club with to FaceTime you.

"Why Lucky? I need to get off this phone because my battery is about to go dead. I'll call you later. Where are you going tonight," I asked?

"Probably Halo baby, or that new spot on the South," he explained. He said Halo to throw me off. I knew he was going to that new spot on the Southside and I'll be there too. I haven't fought in a long time but tonight he can catch these hands.

"Oh okay, I'll talk to you later." I hung up the phone with Lucky so quick. He was crazy because he didn't need to see me at all. I got my money now and I good.

"Girl you're a fool with it. Why did you get that much money from him?" Ketta asked.

"Just because I wanted to. Just wait until I pull up on him later. Sis, do you see how he said your name. He's wondering if you told on him. I didn't even say anything. Not yet anyway." Here he goes texting me telling me to FaceTime him.

Lucky - FaceTime me now

Me - Nigga who the fuck you think you talking to

I wasn't thinking about Lucky at all. I had no plans on hitting the FaceTime button. I threw my phone on the seat. Seeing his face was the last thing I wanted to see. Especially after hearing about him with another female.

I guess Lucky didn't get the picture he hit the FaceTime button and I cleared him out and he called me right back. I decided to answer before it escalated before I had the chance to curse him out.

"Yeah baby, what's up?" I asked. Lucky was fine as fuck. I wanted his ass right now, but I couldn't even down like that because he's sneaky. If he was fuckin' somebody else, he couldn't fuck me. I needed to go checked.

"Damn Kaniya, you look sexy as fuck today. I'm feeling the different shades of red hair. I like it and you're killing it. I want to bend that ass over right fuckin now," he explained. Tell me something I don't know. I look better than the bitch you're creeping with. Looks don't even matter, a nigga will cheat because he can, and a bitch will let him fuck just because.

"Aye, have you been to the mall today?" He asked. What's with the twenty-one questions? Inspector gadget ass nigga for real. Have you been to see your bitch today? That's the real question.

"Yeah, Lenox earlier. Why?" I asked. I could see the angry look on his face. I ain't got time for Lucky's shit. Not today nigga, you already ruined my vibe with the cheating today and even though that shit is fuckin' with my mental I'm not trying to show it. I knew he was ready to argue about some irrelevant shit.

"Stand up for a minute," he demanded. I shook my head no in the camera. I'm not feeling it at all. The fuck you need to see me for.

"Man gone with that shit, Lucky," I argued and sassed.

"When in the FUCK did you start twerking in public and you got my shit on display?" He yelled and asked. I knew shit was about to go left. I noticed the sweat on the brim of his forehead and the mean ass scowl on his face. His eyes had a hint of red in them and they were glossy. I don't know why he was mad, and I haven't done shit.

"When you started cheating," she coughed. Barbie was loud as fuck. I know Lucky heard that shit. I didn't want to accuse him of anything. I wanted to catch his motherfuckin' ass.

"What did you say, Barbie?" He asked. Oh shit, I knew he heard that slick shit. "Is she fuckin' talking to me, Kaniya?" I just shook my head. Lucky was on one, but you know what they say. A hit dog will motherfuckin' holla. He was guilty as fuck.

"I didn't say shit Bruh, I'm on my fuckin phone. I ain't nobody thinking about you. Kaniya get your fuckin' man because I'm not his issue, you are. I don't even understand why he's all up in my fuckin' conversation," she argued and got his ass right together.

"What are you talking about though, Lucky?" I argued and asked. Damn, he's acting all crazy and shit like I'm the one that's fuckin' cheating and I haven't done anything.

"Just know a nigga seen you and that fuck nigga that pulled down on you earlier. Lose his number now Kaniya," he argued. Oh, so this is what this about. He's mad because he saw a nigga all up in my face. He's not the only nigga that's choosing.

"Damn Lucky, for real? What the fuck are you talking about; you know I didn't get nobody's number," I argued. Lucky wasn't buying that shit at all. Technically I wasn't lying. I got Smitty's number but who said I was going to use it. It doesn't feel good if I was to do him how he's doing me.

"Kaniya, stop fuckin' playing with me. I caught you. I'll be by in one minute to smell your pussy with your hot ass," he argued and yelled. Now he wants to come by here and smell my pussy to see if I'm fuckin' somebody. Niggas are crazy.

"How you know I'm at the house?" I asked and argued. Lucky was getting on my last fuckin' nerves. I didn't sign up for any of this shit today.

"I fucking know Kaniya, open the fucking door right now," he yelled. Barbie and Ketta pointed at me and laughed. They made a beeline to the back. Lucky started banging on my door like he was the gawd damn police. The fuck is wrong with this nigga. If he's acting this crazy now, I know he'll be tripping when I fuck around and leave his ass tonight. I swung the door open and was face to face with this lunatic. He pushed passed me and didn't even speak.

"Can I get a hey, how you are doing or something?" I asked. My hands were rested on my hips.

"Follow me Kaniya, with your hot ass. You got me and life fucked up," he argued and pulled me upstairs to my room. He was damn near dragging me. "I'm not the nigga to fuckin' try." I cocked my neck to the side. I'm trying to see who he talking to like he was fuckin' crazy.

"What's wrong with you?" I asked. I folded my arms across my chest waiting on an answer from him. Lucky pulled out his phone and he threw his phone at me. "Aye, you need to watch your fuckin' self because if your phone would've hit me; we would've been rumbling in this bitch."

"This is what the fuck is wrong with me," he argued. He showed me the video of me showing out in traffic. I pressed play on his phone. Lucky was so sexy when he was mad. Where did he get this from? That was the question. "What the fuck are you trying to do, Kaniya?"

"Nothing, I'm chilling and just kicking it and shit," I sighed.

"This isn't even you. If we're in relationship Kaniya, why are you out in public showing your motherfuckin' ass? Showing something that belongs to me," he argued. Oh, now he wants to talk about being in a relationship. He wasn't thinking about our relationship last night when he was out in the club with another bitch.

"I was having fun, that's all. I didn't mean shit by it. I'm not tripping off that nigga, Lucky," I sassed and sucked my teeth.

"No, next time you want to have fun don't be fucking dancing like that. You're my fucking lady and you need to act as such. Take them fucking pants off and let me smell your pussy. No fuck that, I'll take them off. You got me so fucking hot right now, Kaniya. I want to hurt you so bad for that disrespectful ass

"You know it ain't about the money with me, Kaniya. I'll never treat you like you're a hoe but since have I ever had to beg my woman to fuck. Are you fuckin' somebody else since you don't want me to fuck?" He asked and argued. I just shook my head from side to side. I can't believe he's trying to flip this shit on me. I wasn't trying to argue with him. Guilty motherfuckas always like to flip the script. How did we get here, we were together for five years? I could normally sense when a nigga was living foul. I didn't feel it though. I guess I'm off my square or something.

"Grab the condoms out the drawer," I argued. He had an angry scowl on his face. I don't give a fuck. If you want to fuck me. You won't be hitting me raw.

"Condoms? When the fuck we start using condoms?" He asked. I kept my game face on. Lucky hoovered over me. My breasts were touching his chest. He gave me an evil look. You could see the chills all over my body. The blonde hairs that adorned my forearms were raising up.

"Lucky, I haven't fucked you in three weeks. My period was on one week. Since when you go without pussy for 2 weeks?" I asked him. He wasn't counting but I was. We always made plans to see each other no matter how busy we were. I knew that was a bit strange but now I know why.

"I've been busy taking caring of business," he explained. Lucky let the lie roll right off his fuckin' tongue. I knew Lucky was in the streets heavy, but I came before that, so I thought. He was in the process of going legit, so I knew that was a transition within itself. It still wasn't an excuse not to make time for me. I always made time for him. No matter what I was doing.

"We fuck anywhere and everywhere. It doesn't matter the time or place and you know it so, strap up," I argued. I've been so busy I wasn't even paying it any attention but now it sticks out. It's the small shit that we always did and now he's switching up. I'm recognizing it now.

"Kaniya, what you on?" He asked. If he only knew what I was up to. He wouldn't be sitting here with this stupid ass look on his face. He started whispering in my ear. "Aye Kaniya, you know I love you right? Are you trying to give my pussy away?"

"To who Lucky? Stop fuckin' playing with me and fuck me like you miss me," I moaned, grinding and rotated my hips on him.

"Damn Kaniya, this pussy is tight and wet just like I like it," he moaned. Lucky was taking my body to new heights. Each time he would stare at me in my eyes I would look away. He cupped my chin and bit my bottom lip. He slid his tongue in my mouth. The kiss we exchanged was so deep and passionate. It intensified my orgasm. I came so many times I couldn't even count.

"Show me how much you like it," I moaned. He started fucking me like he knew it was going to be his last time, I could feel it. I had to throw this pussy back on him and show him what he was going to be missing He bit my lips and started gripping my ass. Watch this.

"Lucky, let me ride you from the back. Let me sit on this dick and make my ass clap and let you know who the boss is," I moaned. I flipped Lucky on his backside, but he flipped me in a different position.

He had me pinned down face down and my ass was tooted up. He slammed his dick inside of me. I gasped for air. I could never get used to his size no matter how long we've been together. I started grinding my hips and throwing this ass back at him. I made my ass clap.

He pulled my hair and gripped my left ass cheek with his free hand. I sped up my pace. I was in control and I wanted it to remain that way. I stood up and started to squat and ride.

"Damn Kaniya, don't do that," he moaned. Fuck that, I'm pulling out all the tricks tonight. I wanted to fuck the shit out of him. He'll remember this night for the rest of his life because this is the last time, he'll ever be able to get this close to me.

"You got yours yet?" He asked. Of course, I got mine I wasn't about to tell him that. I wanted to drain his ass. Good luck trying to fuck another bitch.

"Nah, not yet baby. I'm getting ready to ride this dick like it ain't no tomorrow," I moaned. I was getting orgasms back to back that I had lost count. Just like I knew it, his toes were curled the fuck up.

"Let me hit you from the back, Kaniya," he stated. Oh, shit here he goes. I ignored him and continue to do me. He flipped me on my backside. He started whispering in my ear. "I like the flowers on your ass cheeks." I like them too. Lucky started picking up the pace. The only sounds you could hear in the room was him pounding me. His strokes were so rough and hard and intense. I knew he broke the condom. Tears fell down my face.

"Slow down it hurts," I cried and moaned. Lucky was so rough and aggressive with me. I couldn't take it. It's like he was trying to prove a point. He was taking the enjoyment out of it.

"I'm trying to make it hurt. You've been a bad girl today and just because you were shaking your ass like that, I must beat this pussy out the frame. Marry me, Kaniya," he said. Ain't no way in hell I'm marrying him. I'm not even about to respond.

"Huh?" I asked. I looked over my shoulder to see if he was serious.

"You heard what fuck I said. If you can what you can hear!" He yelled. I turned back around and ignored Lucky. He pulled my body close to his. He yanked my hair back forcing me to look at him.

"I know you heard what the fuck I said. I want to marry you. I'm not bullshitting Kaniya, I'm ready," he argued.

"Actions speak louder than words," I sighed. I couldn't even look at Lucky. I turned around immediately to avoid eye contact with him. He pulled my hair back and shoved his tongue down my throat and sped up the death strokes. You see ladies this is what good pussy will do to a nigga. You either got that whacker or the snapper. This pussy was snapping. Listen to him begging like Keith Sweat.

"Don't go to Miami this weekend baby, kick it with me and we'll go next weekend," he begged. I knew this was coming after the intense sex session we just had. My eyes were watery because this was the last time that Lucky would have me this wide opened and addicted to his touch. I guess it's true, all good things do come to an end.

"Flight booked already," I beamed. Lucky wasn't feeling that at all. The only flight I had booked was pulling up to the spot and catching his cheating ass later tonight.

"So, I don't give a fuck. Cancel it," he argued. Lucky wasn't feeling me leaving at all. I don't know why he was tripping so hard. I wouldn't even be doing this if he wasn't fuckin' off in these streets, having me out here looking like a damn fool.

"Don't start that shit, Lucky! Let me feed you before I leave. I laid out steaks earlier," I explained.

"Okay." I knew steaks were his favorite. Hopefully, that'll help him change his mind. I needed him to link up with whoever he was with in the picture. I wanted to catch him.

We jumped in the shower together and took a hot shower. I scratched his back up. I was marking my fuckin' territory. Lucky and I finished cleaning each other up. I dried off and applied lotion to my body.

Lucky dried off and put his clothes back on. His phone was ringing off the hook. It was on silent. I could see it blinking through his pants. My eyes were focused on it. I threw on one of his nightshirts and a pair of shorts. He knew I saw his phone going off. He walked up behind me and wrapped his arms around my waist and started biting my neck, so passion marks would appear. I opened the door to my room, and we headed downstairs to the kitchen.

"Damn bitch," Barbie and Ketta laughed and teased me. Lucky and I did the walk of shame. I buried my head in his chest to hide the embarrassment. He wrapped his arms around me and placed kisses on my forehead.

"I had to put this lucky pussy on him," I laughed. I slapped hands with Ketta and Barbie. Lucky was a cocky and arrogant ass nigga. He had a smirk on his face. I just knew he was about to say some shit that was about to make me blush.

"Don't forget to let them know how you were running from this dick and you were begging me to slow down because it hurts," he explained and laughed. I shoved him. I can't stand his ass.

"I wasn't," I sassed. Lucky smacked me on my ass.

"Ouch." I swatted his hands away and rubbed my ass. He knew I hated when he did that.

"Y'all crazy Kaniya," they chimed in.

"Come sit at the island with me Lucky, so I can feed you," I explained. I motioned with my hand for him to come and join me. My kitchen was so fuckin' bad. It was a chef's dream. I had stainless steel everything and a built-in bar and grill. I cut the grill on, seasoned the steaks, cut the onions and peppers, and sautéed the asparagus. Then I put the potatoes in the pressure cooker. Lucky walked up behind me while I was cooking and wrapped his arms around me. I swear everything about this man felt so right. He rubbed his nose against the nape of my neck. It sent chills through my body when he bit my neck.

"Kaniya, you know I love you right?" He asked. I leaned up and rested my head on his chest. I gazed up at him to see if he meant what he said. He gave me a peck on the lips. I swear I love him. Why Lucky would ruin something that we've built?

"Yes," I sighed. He cupped my chin forcing me to look at him. He pecked me on my lips.

"Never forget that."

"I won't." I knew Barbie would never lie to me. I trust her with my life, and I don't trust to many. She provided proof but I wanted to see it for myself. I'm not doubting anything that she's saying, but I want to see it.

"Hey, we're getting married," he blurted out. Ketta and Barbie looked at me. Giving me the side eye. Lucky knew I didn't agree to marry him. If we were married and he was cheating on me, I would kill him first then bitch he was creeping with next. I meant that shit. Don't play with my heart or my feelings because I won't play with yours.

"Congratulations Kaniya and Lucky, that's dope," they beamed. They boosted him up. I wouldn't mind marrying Lucky, but he would have to be faithful. I wouldn't dare say I do just to say we're married and he's out cheating on me. My mother raised me better than that.

"Let me get this, Kaniya. I need to step out really quick and take this call," he stated. I wonder who was calling him that was so important that he couldn't take the call, in front of me? I tried to think positive and not think the worse. I continued to cook my food and focus my energy elsewhere. He was gone for twenty minutes. I fixed his plate and everything.

"Bitch you a fool! You fucked that nigga so good he's talking about marrying you now, and you're about to feed him good. Then you're going to leave him," she laughed. Ketta is crazy. That's the funniest shit she's probably heard all day.

"Sure is, you got one time to play me and it's a fuckin' wrap," I sassed. He'll find out later though. "Ketta, go bring my luggage downstairs to really throw him off." Ketta went upstairs and did as she was told. I knew he wasn't outside handling business. He was probably outside talking to a bitch. He knew better than to talk a bitch in my house. I would've barbecued his ass right on the fuckin' grill and he would've been looking crazy as fuck. If Lucky is cheating on me and I feel he is. He's about to witness a whole different side of me.

"I'm grabbing this to go, baby. I got to handle some business," he explained.

"Okay that's cool Lucky, let me fix your plate to go," I beamed and explained. I played that shit cool. I'm glad he's fuckin' leaving so we can get this show on the road.

"Damn baby, this shit good. You should be a chef or open a restaurant? I got my wife on whatever. I'm out baby, be good. Do you want me to take you to the airport?" He asked. Hell, no you can't take me anywhere. If he offered, he was heading to the Southside and I can't wait to pull up on the Southside.

"No," we beamed and laughed in unison. Lucky was trying to see what we were up to. He'll find out later.

"Okay cool hit me up when you land," he stated. Lucky kissed me on my lips and eased his way out of the house. This would be the last time we see each other, and it'll be this peaceful. I swear Lucky doesn't want to see me act a fool, but it's coming.

"We're straight, keep one eye open these streets a beast," I sassed and sucked my teeth. He looked over his shoulder and headed out the door. I'm so good on Lucky. I hope he's not cheating but if he is, it's a wrap.

"Friend, are you really done?" Ketta asked. She stood by the island in my kitchen waiting on an explanation.

"Yes Ketta, I'm done. Lucky and I will always be best of friends no matter what. We just can't be together. If he can't keep it real about what the fuck he's got going on, then he's not that nigga for me. Speaking of which, let me go pack up all this niggas shit before I go to the club. I'm going to drop his shit off at his crib. I'm riding solo because I want some time to think to myself, are you chicks cool with that?

I really don't even want to talk about this shit no more. Let's take some shots and pregame and get ready so we can set this shit off tonight. I can't worry about Lucky or pacify him. I just can't, ugh. I will miss that long dick and his fuckin' money.

Oh well, the summer is mine," I explained. I meant that shit. I'll get me some toys. I got to focus on me.

Let me go soak in this tub and soak this pussy in Epsom salt. I want to scrub anything that reminded me of Lucky off me. Fuck Him, Feed Him and Leave Him. I had to make that shit clear. Barbie lined up the shots across my bar. She poured each of us three shots a piece. Barbie was in go mode.

Chapter-3

Kaniya

"The night is still young and so are we! Shots, shots, shots! Let's be easy now. We know Patron ain't no hoe," she beamed. Barbie tossed back one shot and slammed it on the bar. Ketta followed suit and I did the same thing. I tossed two shots back to back and slammed both glasses on the bar. I wiped the liquor off my cheek. I was saving my third shot for later. I headed upstairs to my room to get dressed. I stepped in my room and ripped the sheets off the bed.

Let me get all this nigga shit up out of here. I packed up everything that belonged to him. If we break up tonight, I don't want to look at anything that would remind me of him. I'll take his stuff by his house before I hit these mean Atlanta streets.

He won't have any reason to bring his ass back over here. Locks will be changed tomorrow. When I'm through with a nigga I'm through. I never look back. Lucky who? When God made men, he made many.

I got to keep pushing. The first thing I need to do is stop thinking about this nigga. Let me turn these speakers up. As always Future was in rotation. **Future Dirty Sprite 2 Slave Master** was Blaring through my speakers.

Jump Out New Whip Nigga

Like I'm Slave Master

I Pull Two Zips Nigga

I'm Feeling Way Better.

I'm pulling my Corvette out tonight. I had to because I know if I catch Lucky cheating, he's going to run up behind me and do anything in his power to stop me from leaving. I need to jump in my Corvette and pull off on his ass as fast as I can.

"Aye call the Xan man. I want to pop one," I yelled. Hopefully, Barbie heard me. It's a new beginning, no more Lucky and Kaniya. I wonder how long he's been doing this shit. I started getting dressed. Lucky fucked up my hair. Thank God he blessed me with a nice pair of hands.

I could style hair pretty good too. I see what Mr. Chardonnay was saying. I love the way this Tory Burch dress fits. Everything is sitting up just right, and it fits my body like a glove. I paired my dress with a pair of Gold Gucci Sandals. I need these sandals in black too.

No makeup tonight just lip gloss and eye shadow. I'll go easy with the jewelry. I can't leave the house without my gold choker, diamond earrings, and bracelet. I gave myself the once over in the mirror. Jaiuna did the damn thing with this red feathered bob. Kaniya don't kill'em. Let me make sure I got two straps. My 9mm and my 380 and a fresh pair of brass knuckles. I headed downstairs and my girls had already headed out. They didn't say bye or anything. I hope they locked the door behind them.

Let me text these chicks and let them know I'm dropping his shit off and to meet me on the Southside. The text was sent and Barbie and Ketta left my message on read. I grabbed water out the refrigerator and headed toward the garage. I hit the garage button and tossed my clutch in the passenger seat. I'm riding out in my 2016 Chevy Corvette tonight. I'm looking real coupish. Purple and Black, this bitch is too sexy. I had to get her. I got the peddle to the medal riding down I-85S. Let me slow this shit, down its 100mph on the dash. **Young Dro We Be in City** came on blaring through my speakers.

Car Ain't Got No Roof Car Ain't Got No Roof

We Be in City We Be in City

All My Bitches with It

Oh, Where Your Hoe at

Oh, Where Your Hoe at We Be in City

I hope this nigga isn't home and he wasn't. I pulled up in Lucky's garage. Thank you, Jesus he wasn't home. I keyed in and I keyed out.

This is the old Club Ritz. Damn this spot thick. They're always closing clubs down and opening them back up under a new name. I'm valet parking and I see Barbie's Pink BMW X5. Let me text them and let them know I'm outside.

"Kaniya, is that you," someone asked. I looked up to see who was talking to me. It was Dred. Dred and I went to school to-gether. We were close, but he started hanging with Lucky, so I don't hear that much from him anymore.

"What's up, Dred?" I asked. Dred always had a thing for me, but we never acted on it. He was hoe and I couldn't fuck with that. I stayed as my brother.

"What's up, sis?" He asked. Dred couldn't even look me in my face. I don't have time to wrap with him. I'm trying to get inside of this club to see what's up. I got a bad vibe from Dred, so I already knew something was about to pop off.

"Nothing much, working and you?" I asked. Dred was stalling for a reason. He already knows how I give it up. I came here to have a good time and if I got to fuck Lucky and his bitch up then it is what it is. Please don't stop me because I'll fuck his ass up too.

"I can't let you go in there, Kaniya," he explained. I already knew what time it was. Yep Lucky is cheating and I'm about to catch his ass. Damn, I wish I would've worn some shorts, tank top, and AirMax. I would rather be comfortable and fuck his ass up, but it is what it is.

"Look Dred, I already know he's in there with another bitch. It's all good I'm trying to do what he's doing. I'm a mack too and spit my pimping. I'm not going to trip at all. Does it look like I came to fight? I'm dressed to kill baby. I'm trying to do what he's doing and enjoy myself," I explained.

"Are you sure, Kaniya?" He asked. It's loyalty over royalty. Dred was team Lucky, and he can be, just let me in this motherfucka before I move his ass around and let myself in.

"I'm positive. Don't text that nigga shit or let him know I'm in here. You've been knowing the whole time he's been fucking with another bitch and you've been smiling up in my face. At the end of the day, your loyalty is with him and not me. Even though you met him through me remember?" I asked and reminded him.

"Don't say that, sis," he sighed. Fuck Dred. I stopped being his sister the moment he chose Lucky over me. I wasn't his sis when he knew Lucky was fuckin' another bitch and he didn't give me the heads up.

"Oh, it's sis now? It is what it is. I'm getting ready to walk up in here and make my presence known. If he's gone by the time I walk in here. I know you tipped him off. I'll air this bitch out. Bodies and blood will be on your fuckin' hands. Try me Dred, I'm begging you too. The only thing that will be left moving in this bitch; is my bitches that's in there," I argued. I let Dred know what it was off the top with me. Lucky doesn't want to see the side of me.

"For real, Kaniya?" He asked. Does it look like I'm fuckin' lying? I ain't never cheated on Lucky. Now I wish would've.

"Dead fucking serious," I sassed. I had my game face on. My blood was fuckin' pumping. I couldn't wait to catch Lucky. He couldn't give two fucks about me if everybody knows about this bitch. When was he going to fuckin' tell me?

"I'm not gone say shit. You good, Kaniya," he stated. At this point, I don't give a fuck if he says something or not. I'll post up outside on Lucky's car and bust his windows out and wait on that motherfucka to come out.

"See you bruh," I sassed and sucked my teeth and chucked up my deuces. Ketta just text me back. She said she got us a section. Okay, Bitches and Bottles. I sent text her back and told her to be looking out. I made my way inside of the club. I couldn't wait to see this nigga. Let me scan this bitch out. I looked around taking in everything around me.

It's real nice in here. It looks like a small 40/40 Club. The color scheme was plush gray and white. The bar setup was nice, and the dance floor was huge. This might be the new spot. I see some folks I know and some that I don't. It's some eye candy in here! I see some niggas with potential. I couldn't help but to eye fuck each of them. I feel like Trina

Single Again

Back on the Prowl

I Thought He Was Perfect

but I Don't Know How

Bingo there that bitch ass nigga goes. It's about to be some messy shit going on! I'm about to pop me a nigga and bitch. I wish he would put his hands on me.

I swear to God it'll be the last time he uses those motherfuckas too. I shot a text to Ketta telling her to give the DJ $50.00 to play **Fight, fight** by **Project Pat!**

It's about to be some shit now

I'm here now

Anytime I hear that song I'm ready to box a bitch out. Guess what, tonight would be no different. My name ain't Kaniya Nicole Miller if I don't tag a bitch or a nigga. This that real Tennessee shit. Let's get this show on the road. This dumb stupid ass nigga doesn't even see me coming. He's real exclusive with this bitch and this shit is so disrespectful. He's kissing her right after he ate my pussy and shit. Wow! This bitch isn't even weighing up to me on a bad day. I'm cool on him.

"Hey Lucky," I beamed and tapped his ass on his fuckin' shoulder. I damn near punched his fuckin' back in. He dropped his drink. He recognized my voice. He already knew what time was. He's caught now. "Hey Ms. Lady, I'm Kaniya, Lucky's EX. And you are?" I asked and grilled the bitch. If she said the wrong thing, I'm laying her ass out on the floor. I'm begging for a bitch to fuckin' try me.

"Melanie," she sassed and smirked. See I was trying to be cordial, but that attitude and smirk is what's going to get your ass whooped behind fuckin' with this nigga.

"Okay, it's nice to finally meet you. Did this cheater tell you he had a lady?" I asked.

"He did but I didn't care. I don't mind being number two," she sassed and sucked her teeth. I can't be mad at her, but I can beat her ass. Clearly, she knew about me, but she didn't give a fuck. Clearly, my hands don't give a fuck whose face they land on. A bitch can't disrespect me without any repercussions.

"Oh wow, and how old are you? How long have you been fucking him," I asked with an attitude? I swear to God if this bitch says the wrong thing, I'm going to show my ass. I can't be-lieve Lucky. My eyes were trained on him the whole time. He couldn't even fuckin' look at me. I can't believe I loved this type of nigga.

"21 and for the past three months," she beamed proudly. It's was on from there. As if on Que the DJ played my song that's my DJ!

Fight, Fight

It's About to Be Some Shit Now

We Here Now

Lucky already knew how I got down. I punched that bitch so quick in her head. She didn't even see me coming. Straight head shots. Me hitting her and that bitch hitting the motherfuckin' floor.

Just like I knew he would he grabbed her off the floor. I coughed up some spit and spit on his ass. I put my brass knuckles on so quick. As soon as he bent down to pick that bitch up. I knocked his ass dead in the fucking jaw. I kept jabbing him. The club was going stupid now. I heard somebody in the crowd say. "Lil shawty came to play. Ain't shit outta place. She handled hers," the crowd was saying. I'm not with that rah, rah shit, I'm on some boss shit.

"Aye Lucky, run me 12k right now since you been swimming in other pussy. I'm out," I argued. I let him know what time it was. He can keep fuckin' her because tonight was the last time, he could ever fuck me. He should pray to God I don't find a nigga with potential because if I do, I swear I'm going to be the bitch that he loves to hate. I put that on his fuckin' momma. He can play any bitch he wants, but he can't play me.

"Kaniya," he yelled and roared all loud like a beast. I looked over my shoulder to see what he wanted. I gave him an evil look. I know he's not talking to me. Just a few minutes ago he didn't have shit to say but now you want to talk. Nah nigga, is not that type of party.

"Kiss my ass bitch ass nigga," I argued. I flipped that nigga off and made my way to VIP. "NEXT I'm looking for a real nigga. I've been dealing with a fuck nigga for to long." As I approached my section this nigga grabbed me. I looked over my right shoulder and it was Smitty. He wasn't a bad looking guy. I just didn't like how he approached me. I'm good on him. He's thirsty too. Nigga, you don't even fuckin' know me and you're all up on me like you're my man and you're not.

"Damn, it must be fate that I see your ole fine ass twice in the same day," he stated. I looked at Smitty as if he was crazy. I already had an attitude because of what went down with Lucky. I wasn't in the mood. I had to choose my words wisely because I didn't want to come off as a bitch, even though I felt like a bitch.

"Nah, this Atlanta and this is a new spot, that's why," I sassed and sucked my teeth. I didn't feel like being bothered with his ass. As much money as he got, he should be able to tell when a bitch isn't feeling him. I'm sure he curves bitches on the regular and I'm trying to curve his ass.

"Can I get a hug?" He asked. He was pushing it now. This would be the last time he sees me too.

"Sure," I sighed. Damn, he smelled good as fuck. He wrapped his arms around my waist. This wasn't a friendly hug. He was making a statement. Smitty whispered in my ear.

"Damn, you look good as fuck in that dress. I want you right now in the worse way. That nigga fucked up good," he slurred. I could smell the alcohol mixed with mint on his breath.

"Tell me something I don't know? I'll get up with you later," I sassed. I knew Lucky fucked up and he did too. But guess what, it's nothing I can do about it. It ain't no coming back from that. I don't want to hear it. You had another relationship behind my back for three months. He picked the perfect time to fuck up. It's going down this summer and I'm single too. I finally made my way to the VIP section. I locked eyes with Barbie and Ketta. They had the biggest smiles on their faces. I knew they watch me cut the fuck up. I told them I would.

"Kaniya, what happened?" Barbie and Ketta asked. They knew what the fuck happened. They just wanted the details play by play. It ain't really shit to tell. He was cheating and I caught him. I'm good. I just wanted to catch him.

"Exactly what the fuck y'all saw. I saw y'all asses looking," I laughed. Before I got shit popping, I looked toward the VIP section to see if they were looking. As soon as I locked eyes with them, they turned their head. I couldn't even contain my laughter. They're crazy as hell.

"I didn't know you still had it in you," she explained. I gave Ketta the side eye. I can't believe she let that shit come out her mouth. I could never let a nigga or a bitch punk me. I don't give a damn how much I love Lucky. I wasn't letting this slide. If I was cheating, he wouldn't let me slide.

"I wanted to kickbox that hoe, but I had this dress on. Y'all know I'm about that life? I didn't have the energy to read that nigga. He's not worth it. I let him know exactly what it was," I argued and explained. Lucky has me out here looking like a fool for real.

"You done sis?" She asked. Barbie looked at me with sad eyes. It wasn't her fault we broke up. Shit, I'm glad she saw him or else I would still be looking like a fool. She knew I was done because if I wasn't, I wouldn't have come here and done all this.

"Yes Barbie, it's was a wrap," I beamed proudly. I love Lucky and I can't lie, but we've been together for along ass time and he threw all that away. It's cool though, you live and you fuckin' learn. I dusted my shoulders off. I see shit for what it is now. "Let's go to the dance floor. I did what I had to do and it's on now." Barbie and Ketta followed me to the dance floor. I was about to have fun. I wasn't about to let Lucky ruin my moment. The DJ was pipped the fuck up. He played **All the Way Up by Fat Joe feat Remy Ma & French Montana.** I love this song.

Nothing Can Stop Me

I'm All the Way Up

Shorty What You Want

I Got What You Need

He came back with the old **Young Jeezy Trap Star.** Everybody that knows me knows that's my shit. The whole club went crazy. He slowed it down a bit and played **Future Rich Sex**. I love this song. I remember when it first came out. Lucky came over to my house and I had it on repeat. I put on a show for his ass. On everything, I love if Kaisha and Killian didn't have money, I would've been a stripper to pay my way through college. If he was somewhere watching, he knew I was about to cut up. I wasn't about to spare his ass. I made my way to the middle of the dance floor. Barbie tapped me on my shoulder and shouted.

"Bitch, don't get killed in this club." I looked over my shoulder at Barbie and Ketta and I gave them a devilish smirk. I stuck my tongue out and flipped them off. The summer is mine thanks to Lucky.

"Watch this you know me." I couldn't wait to shake all this ass Kaisha gave me.

Baby Lets Go and Have Rich Sex

Make a Lil Love Have Rich Sex

Baby Lets Go and Have Rich Sex

Make a Lil Love Have Rich Sex!!

I started grinding in the middle of the dance floor. All eyes were on me. It was a sexy ass nigga looking like Boosie Bad Azz. That nigga walked up behind me. I took him in, and he took me in as well. He pushed up behind me. I could tell he had a big ass dick. I felt how hard it was on the tip of my ass. I dropped it low. My ass was damn near touching the floor. I was about to bring it back up slowly and before I could come back up good Lucky snatched me up quickly. I looked over my shoulder and gave him a nasty look.

"Why you bitches didn't say shit? Give me my purse," I yelled. Barbie and Ketta set my ass up. They saw Lucky before I felt him. They could've given me the heads up. Lucky was carrying me somewhere. I don't even want him touching me. Go touch your bitch. He carried me outside the fuckin' club. I wasn't ready to fuckin' go.

"Put me down," I argued and slapped the shit out of him. I hate his cheating ass. He grabbed my hands to stop me from fuckin' his ass up

"Can we talk Kaniya?" He asked. Lucky's' stare was very intense. It's like he was trying to speak to my soul. We just made love earlier, but you're hugged up with another bitch a few hours later. I grilled the fuck out of Lucky. You had plenty of time to talk, Why now?

"For what, Lucky? Ninety days ago, did you want to talk?" I asked. My hands were rested on my hips and my fists were balled up. I can't stand him. It ain't shit to talk about. I don't want to hear anything he has to say.

"Let me explain, Kaniya!" He yelled. He was grilling me and mad for what. I haven't even done anything. He fucked up, not me.

"Nah Lucky, let me explain. You had the chance to talk earlier, but you didn't say shit. Real Niggas Do Real Things. I thought you were a real ass nigga boy was I wrong. You already know you got one time to fuck up with me and it's a wrap. I packed your shit and it's already at your house. Ain't nothing to talk about. Let's talk about me leaving you. I'm gone Lucky. You can accept this shit and get the fuck on because I'm out," I argued. I hopped in my Corvette and did a doughnut on that nigga. I'm not going home because I know he'll be there. Let me get a room at the Westin.

I might have to move fucking with him. Nah he needs to let me be or I'll kill his ass seriously. I'm done with Lucky and I mean that shit. I can't believe him. He didn't owe me an explanation. I heard everything I needed to hear and not one time did he correct that bitch and say she was lying. Melanie was comfortable about fuckin' him and letting me know.

Guess what? It's his fault he made her comfortable and she can stay comfortable. Let me turn my speakers up loud. Tonight, was a good night despite the little bullshit. May is starting off really heavy. I need a vacation. Let me text Riley and let her know I'm booking her and Tianna a flight; I need them here like now.

My mind was in a million places and my emotions were through the roof. I had to stand for something, or I would fall for anything when it comes to you. Taking Lucky back overnight was out the question. I can't believe this is how we ended. My heart hurts so bad. I swear to God when I was alone in my room, I was praying that none of the allegations or pictures about Lucky were true. I thought I meant something to you. I guess not. You couldn't find it in your heart to stay true.

Did you ever think about how I would feel if I saw or heard this shit about you? Ninety days you've been cheating and creeping with a bitch that doesn't even weigh up to me. I can't believe he gave another bitch access to him. I can't wait to give another man access to me. He should pray to God that I don't hurt him how he just hurt me.

Chapter-4

Melanie

I've been pacing back and forth in Lucky's office for the past hour. He brought me here and left me here. I knew he went running up after that bitch. I couldn't wait to tell her that I was fuckin' him. I knew who she was the moment she walked up on us. My thing is, why are you mad at me? You asked was I fuckin' him and I told you yes. I know Lucky wanted to put his hands on me.

Oh my gosh, I was so fucking embarrassed. Everybody was looking at me getting my ass beat. When I finally got off the ground the only thing I could see where phones in my face, which means the fight was uploaded to social media. I can't believe this bitch just knocked me out with one punch. I wasn't expecting that. It's on. I can't wait to tell my sister Shaela what just popped off.

I should've just kept my mouth shut, but I didn't like her approach. I hated the way she looked. She was competition. I was aiming to get her man. That was my only motive. Ugh, I couldn't stand her, and I didn't even know her. She had something that I wanted and that was Lucky. I accomplished that. I'm not like the other bitches that he's used to fuckin'. I'm not keeping quiet to pacify her feelings. I'm tired of being number two. Lucky told me from the jump that he had a fiancé. I told him straight up what does that have to do with me? I was looking to fly for this bitch to put her hands on me. I told that bitch straight to her face I didn't mind being number two and I didn't care that he was with her. That was the truth and to be honest I think Lucky was feeling me too.

I think I grew on him. It started out as just casual flirting. I kept trying to throw the pussy at him and he wouldn't take it. So, I had to show him what this mouth did. That's all it took was for me to wrap my mouth around him one time and suck the soul out of his dick and I had him. I still pursued him and then we were fucking every day. I've been pregnant by Lucky twice and each time he's made me have a fuckin' abortion. He sat in the clinic with me to make sure I had it done.

She should've kept that shit moving and took the loss. Baby girl your nigga ain't shit. He's for everybody. Lucky's name is ringing bells out here in the streets. Everybody knew that nigga had it and for the right bitch, you might be able to fuck him. Guess what? I was that bitch and I was in his pockets. I never expected Kaniya to pop up on him and me.

My sister Shaela told me that she didn't go out. She was a college girl. I thought I was going to talk shit and argue all day. I was prepared to do that. Nothing more nothing less. It's true what they say, never judge a book by its cover. I followed the bitch a couple of times. The only places she went to where the nail shop, Books A Million and the mall. Basic shit. He was available now so; shit I was in the first place.

Not one time did he tell me to shut the fuck up when I was talking? So being the messy bitch that I was born to be, I kept going. As far as I could see, we can be a couple now since she knows about us. I couldn't wait to see her again because it was on. I need a rematch. I need to find Lucky. He just up and left me to go chase after her like I just didn't get knocked out.

He needs to cater to me. I could have a concussion; I have this huge knot on my forehead. I heard a knock at his office door. I went to open it to see who it was, and it was Veno. He was the last motherfucka that I wanted to see. I know he didn't care and that's cool, but I wasn't going anywhere today. Lucky told me to wait here for him and that's what the fuck I intended to do. I folded my arms across my chest to see what he had to say.

"Aye Melanie, it's time for you to clear it. Lucky told me to tell you, your ride is out back, and he'll slide through later," he explained. Veno couldn't even look at me. I wasn't going any fuckin' where. I came with him and I'm leaving with him.

"I'm good Veno, I'm not leaving this club without him and you can tell him I said that. His bitch will leave before I do," I argued.

"Look, Melanie, I'm not trying to be in your business but since my nigga put me in it, I'm in it. You're the side bitch, play your fuckin' position. If he tells you to leave, then you need to fuckin' leave. Kaniya comes first and you come second. You agreed to it and that's on fuckin' you. Take your ass home and go clean your fuckin' face-up. The last thing you want is for her to come back here and see you. Judging by the big ass knot on your head you don't want another one," he argued and explained while gritting his teeth. I wasn't even about to argue with this nigga. I grabbed my purse and slammed the fuckin' door. Kaniya or Veno doesn't put any fear in my heart.

Lucky

I fucked up and I don't want to admit it, but I did. For the first time in a long time, I don't know what to do. I knew losing her wasn't a fuckin' option. Kaniya was never supposed to catch me with Melanie. I thought she was going to fuckin' Miami. What the fuck did I give her $6,000.00 for, just to see her in my club? She was taxing me. I had to give her an additional $12,000.00. I didn't have a problem giving it to her. If I could have a moment of her time.

I heard Barbie came through the club last night, but I was low key. I know she didn't see me. Kaniya knew I was cheating but why didn't she say shit? If she would've asked me, I would've denied it. We could've talked about it and she wouldn't have to see any of this shit. No wonder she wanted me to wear a condom. I made the condom break on purpose. I had to send Melanie's ass on her way. I ran my hands across my face. I'm a nigga that doesn't even stress, but this whole situation was fuckin' blowing me.

"Dred and Veno, I fucked up," I explained. Veno looked at me and shook his head. I knew what he was thinking, but I didn't want to hear him say it. Dred worked for me, but Veno was my fuckin' business partner besides my brother Quan. I trusted

Veno with my life and I knew he would never stir me wrong. Veno knew I was fuckin' off on Kaniya and he didn't like that shit at all. He's been married to wife Vanessa for a minute. They've been together since high school.

"You did bruh!" He argued and yelled. I was looking at Dred like he was crazy. I wasn't feeling his tone at all. I'm looking at him sideways anyway. I met him through Kaniya. I kept that nigga close because I know he wanted her. The only nigga that had the right to speak on shit was Veno. The only reason why Dred was even in here is that he works the fuckin' door.

"She'll be back," he chuckled. I mugged the fuck out of Veno. He thought this shit was funny, but it wasn't. I remember a few years ago before he said I do; I was covering for his ass when he was fucking off on Vanessa. "Stop cheating on her Lucky, before you fuck around and lose her. Kaniya is a good girl. You don't want to lose that fuckin' around with these hoes out here, like the one that just left."

"No, she won't. She's stubborn as fuck look at my damn jaw," I argued and pointed at my jaw. Kaniya fucked my shit up. She rocked the fuck out my jaw. It took everything in me not to slam her ass in the fuckin club, but I knew she had that little ass dress on.

"Damn Lucky, she fucked you up good. I knew she was crazy," he stated and laughed. Veno thought this shit was funny and it wasn't.

"She better be glad I didn't put my hands on her. Niggas in the club were looking at me sideways and shit. I let her get hers in with me because she was upset. Roll the tape back Dred. Kaniya doesn't even know I own this club, that this my shit," I argued. How did she know to come here? Somebody dropped the fuckin' dime on me.

"Why are you cheating on her if you know you don't want to lose her?" He asked. and I sized him up. Dred was taking it personally as if Kaniya was his bitch and not mine.

You know they say keep your enemies close. He was an enemy and he didn't know it. I saw how he looked at her. Dred, Veno, I watched the tape. Dred fucked up when he let Kaniya in here, and he knew I was with another bitch. Everybody that worked here knew not to let her through those fuckin' doors but that nigga went against the fuckin' grain.

"I don't know. You know how it is when you have a shit load of money, hoes come with the territory. Some I can resist and some I can't. You know what Dred? I don't even know why I'm explaining myself. Fuck that pussy ass nigga. Why in the fuck did you let her in here? Dred you watch everything coming and going and you set me up. A nigga can't set me up and live to tell about it," I argued and explained.

"Lucky, she told me she wasn't on no bullshit. I swear to God I wouldn't have let her in here if she was. She already knew you were in there with Melanie. Look she told me if I tipped you off, she was going to air this bitch out with her Desert Eagle. Bodies and blood would be on my hands and the only thing left moving up in this motherfucka would be her and her bitches," he explained. I looked at Dred like he was fuckin' crazy.

"Nigga, I fuckin' pay you not Kaniya. I'm the only motherfucka you take orders from. I don't give a fuck what she knew. She still wasn't supposed to see it. You know you fucked up right? She told you that, and you fuckin' listened?" I asked. Veno and I were laughing at Dred. I hope he wasn't that fuckin' dumb. Judging by his actions he wanted Kaniya. That's why he let her in.

"Kaniya." I ain't saying Kaniya won't cut up but I knew she wasn't about to shoot this club and hurt all these innocent people to get to me.

"You believed her," Veno and I asked.

Dred shook his head yes. "I'm going to show you how real this shit gets pussy ass nigga. Since you wanted to set me up and let my wife catch me on some creep shit. You're gone be the last nigga or bitch that wants to try me or stand in the way of me and mine," I argued. I pulled out my Glock 40 loaded the clip. I screwed the silencer on and emptied the clip in Dred. "Call the cleanup crew, Veno. I want this shit spotless ole of this soft as nigga. Let me go to her house. She got me fucked up thinking she's going to leave me and it's not any repercussions." I'll get her back if I got to kill every nigga, she thinks she's going to be with. I'll do it if she's not with me. I'll be damn if she's with any-body else. I'm not throwing five years away. The next nigga that must go is Smitty. That bitch ass nigga been hating on me since middle school. He can never be me.

I've been wanting to kill him anyway. Keep coming close to Kaniya and death will hit him sooner than he can blink his cock eye. When did she start wearing dresses and shit? I don't have a choice, but I got to get rid of my lil shawty Melanie.

She was talking way too fucking much. I'm surprised Kaniya didn't beat her ass some more. I was feeling her, but can't no bitch walk around here that will interfere with me and mine. Let me wire her $12,000.00 as she requested. That's my I'm sorry gift. Barbie ole big mouth ass, I can't wait to get rid of her or I'll never get Kaniya back. Kaniya is her fuckin' lifeline. That's the only reason she's going to live.

Chapter-5

Ketta

Man when I say Kaniya showed her motherfuckin' ass in the club, she showed her ass. We knew that Lucky was cheating, but I didn't want her to see it. You never want your friend to see something that would fuck with her mentally and physically. It's important that she knows. I hate that Lucky was so fuckin' sloppy with it. I was praying that he wasn't here when we pulled up, but that's too much like right. We just saw you and you were bragging about the two of you getting married and you're in the club caked up with someone else why your girlfriend of the past five years is at home.

He knew I was disgusted with him after he drug her off the dance floor. We locked eyes with each other, and I just shook my head. I know she did that out of anger. Kaniya and Lucky have been together for a long time. Even though he fucked up I was still rooting for the two of them. I know my girl is hurt and I'm hurting because she is.

I know Kaniya and she'll hurt Lucky just because he hurt her. I don't want Lucky to see a side of Kaniya that she's kept hidden for so long. I feel a storm coming and I don't know if they'll be able to weather it. Barbie and I left the club. The only reason why we went was to support Kaniya but since she was gone it was time to keep it moving. I had to meet up with my baby Don in a few. Damn, I can't wait to see him. I haven't seen him since this morning. I looked at my phone and he sent me a text asking me when I was pulling up. Barbie hit the unlock on her truck. I slid in and got comfortable. Tonight, was one for the books.

"Where the fuck did Kaniya go to?" I asked. I checked my phone and I didn't have any missed calls from her. I hope she's okay. Even though she appears to be so strong on the outside she's still human. We all hurt and have emotions but I'm sure she's wearing hers on her sleeve.

"I don't know. You think she left with that nigga?" She asked. I looked at Barbie and laughed.

"Hell no," we said in unison. Kaniya was to mad to leave with Lucky. If she did, I wouldn't judge her. She's not the first person to be in a relationship with somebody and caught them cheating and she went back to them.

"I'm glad she left his ass in Kaniya fashion. That nigga has been living foul. Ketta, I always see him out on some sneaky creep shit. His name ring bells out in these streets and when the bells ring these hoes come. I just got tired of seeing him entertain different bitches, so I let it be known. I don't give a fuck if he's mad at me. That's my lil sister," she argued and explained. I heard everything Barbie was saying. I'm not in the club so I would never catch him. If I'm not at work, I'm laid up under my man. If he's giving it up like that, I'm glad she shed some light on it. I can't believe Lucky. That nigga always had money but Kaniya wasn't with him for that. I hope he wasn't dumb enough to make a permanent decision on temporary emotions. He knows better than that.

"The night is still tender. We're looking to fly to babysit the couch," I explained. Don wanted me to meet up with him and Julius. I didn't mind. I just didn't want to be the only female, so hopefully, I can get Barbie to come with me. Julius has been trying to get up with her for a minute. I told him she wasn't cheap. He said he pays like he weighs.

"Mr. Chardonnay did that. I'm feeling you in the nude color shorts Ketta. I wish I had those legs, and that ass. I'll be a stripper caked the fuck up," she beamed and gloated. Barbie had me blushing. I really need to go home and change because if Don saw me, he would be tripping hard. My body is for his eyes only.

He knew I was going out with Kaniya and Barbie. He just didn't know we were going to the club to catch Lucky up.

"You're Barbie, you bad as fuck too. You're looking fine as fuck in that jumper. I love it and the Chanel sandals are too cute. They make your legs look extra right and stout. Your ass is peeking out that jumper. Denim is your color," I mentioned. Barbie was killing it too.

"We're definitely going to use Mr. Chardonnay again. I'm feeling myself and I can't even lie. Where to?" she asked.

"The Blue Fucking Flame. The west side is the best side," I yelled and beamed. I was to hype. I couldn't wait to see my baby. "What you know about Don, Barbie?" I hope Barbie doesn't mind me putting her in Julius path. I told Don I was against, but he told me to let the cards fall where they may. If it's meant it's meant and it's nothing, we can do about it.

"Don from the East side?" She asked. Yes, that's my Don. The one that all these bitches are lusting behind, but I Ketta, stake claims to all that.

"Yep," I beamed proudly. Every time I thought about Don, he brought a smile to my face.

"He drives a black Porsche Cayenne on 28's. I don't know much about him. He's a sexy red nigga tatted up like the subway in Harlem with his New York ass. He's built nicely with all those damn muscles and green eyes. Yes Lord," she beamed and laughed. Barbie described Don to perfection, and he was all mine. If you wanted to know something about someone Barbie was the person to see or ask. If she knew something about Don, she wouldn't hesitate to spill the tea. Thank God he was a real one and he wasn't out here giving females hope.

"That's my boo," I beamed proudly.

"Word? Damn, I got to find me a nigga. Y'all look good together. Put that pussy on that nigga and give his ass a few babies," she stated. Don and I haven't discussed having children yet, but I'm sure that's coming. I just graduated from nursing school. I'm open to having a child with him, but I'll have to be certain that he's the real thing.

"Bitch, normally I wouldn't do this, but I need you to hook me up or plug me in with his friend Julius," she stated. If they're both feeling each other then why are they playing games?

"Barbie, are you checking for him?" I asked. Long as I've known Barbie, I've never known her to talk about a man let along watching her face beam talking about Julius.

"The question is, is that nigga checking for me too? Every time we see each other we eye fuck. No words were spoken but it's a stare off," she beamed proudly. Julius and Barbie are playing games with each other, but why? It's obvious y'all want each other.

"I got you Barbie, I'm going to hook you up," I beamed and explained. Huh, little does she know Julius wants her in the worst way. He's been begging me to hook him up with her. He didn't even need my help. He just needed to say something.

"Please do," she beamed.

"We're going to New York tomorrow. Ride with us. I'm always the only girl and Julius is coming," I explained. Julius and Barbie both needed to settle down because they're one in the same.

"Oh yeah, let's make an appearance really quick. You know it takes me forever to get my stuff packed," she explained. She wasn't lying at all. Don and Julius wake up at the crack of dawn and as soon as they get up, they handle their hygiene and they're ready to pull out.

"Cool because they're in The Flame. I'll ride back with Don and Julius can ride with you," I beamed and mentioned. I hope Barbie didn't catch that but I'm sure she did. My man is already in there waiting for me. We were about five minutes away from The Flame. I didn't want any surprises before we got there.

"Julius is with Don in The Flame? Bitch, are you trying to set me up or some shit?" She asked. Yep, Barbie was feeling his ass, she was panicking, and she didn't need to be. I hope he locks her ass down, but we'll see.

"Barbie, relax." I laughed. I can't believe she's doing all this. I can't wait to tell Kaniya, Barbie tripping off a nigga. It looks good on her.

"Okay, we're here. Let's valet park. I can't park this BMW X5 anywhere. You know when bitches see this Pretty Pink truck, they be on some fuck shit. Damn, it's lit in here. Snake knows me so; we're walking straight through. Barbie tossed the valet driver her keys. I checked myself over in the mirror one time. I wasn't trying to impress anyone because Don was waiting on me. I couldn't wait to see him. We headed inside of The Flame and it was packed as fuck. Tonight, was a good night. Money was being thrown in the air. Drinks were being poured. The smell of loud as weed hit my nostrils. I scanned the club looking for the only thing that had my attention. I locked eyes with Don, and he threw his hands up telling me to come to see him.

"Damn, this bitch piped up. It's nothing in here but ass, niggas and money," she beamed. We slapped hands with each other. I agreed. I don't ever think I've seen this much money being thrown.

"Let's go to the bar and get some shots. Don and Julius got a VIP section already," I stated.

"Bitch, are you sure you didn't set me up? How come nobody's in there but them two," she asked and panicked? I put it on everything I love, I ain't never seen Barbie act like this behind nann nigga. I know Julius is the one if he has BARBIE tripping.

"Hush and be glad damn. Don already knows not to have a bitch in my space. Let's take these two shots and enjoy our night. Cheers to new beginnings," I beamed.

We tossed our shots back we headed to the VIP area where Don and Julius were waiting for us. As soon as we stepped inside Don approached me and pulled me into his arms. He hugged me so tight. I damn near wanted to fuckin' melt. His hands roamed every inch of my body. My panties were fucked up instantly. He bit the nape of my neck and started whispering in my ear.

"Damn Ketta, you look good as fuck tonight. I've been waiting on you for a minute. I wanted to chill for a minute but now the only thing I want to do is undress you and suck every hole on your body," he slurred and explained. I had to squeeze my pussy because the faucet that was between my legs was dying for Don to quench it. He grabbed my left ass cheek with his hand. He had a devilish smirk on his face. He knew what he was doing.

"Baby, can you please stop you're fuckin' up my panties," I pouted and whined. Don wasn't playing fair at all. I couldn't take it. I wanted to get out of these clothes so fuckin' bad.

"I can't help myself. You know what it is with me. I'm ready to go home because my dick is hard as fuck right now. I need to dive in that pussy and make a fuckin' mess," he slurred and explained. He was tipsy and I could smell the liquor mixed with mint and weed on his breath. Don grabbed my hand and placed it on his dick. I looked at him and my eyes got big as fuck. He was hard as fuck. It was time for us to blow The Flame. Don's dick was long thick and wide. It touched the middle of his thighs. The last thing I wanted was for a bitch to get a glimpse of that. I ran my tongue across my lips. I couldn't wait to taste and feel him. We probably wouldn't even make it home because as soon as we got in the car, I was coming up out these clothes.

"Baby, I'm ready to go home too. What about Julius and Barbie?" I asked. I looked over at Barbie and Julius. A small smile appeared on my face. He was in her personal space and his hands were wrapped around her waist. The two of them were in their own world.

"What about them, she's in good hands and he is too. Our security is airtight in this motherfucka. Ain't shit gonna happen to my brother. We got moves to make in the morning anyway so if he sees us leaving then they're out too," he explained. Don sent Julius a text and told him we were out. Barbie and Julius followed suit. Don escorted me out of VIP and to his car. As soon as he opened the door for me, and I slid in his leather seats. It was going down. Thank God his tent was dark.

Chapter-6

Kaniya

Lucky called me all night and I didn't answer. I wanted so bad too, but I couldn't. I wasn't giving in. I wasn't the type of woman that you could cheat on and come back to like nothing didn't happen. It's nothing that he can say to me that would make me change my mind. I said what I had to say, and he never apologized. He didn't even have a reason to cheat. He cheated because he wanted to cheat. I had to go hide out at Sonja's house to get away from him. This is my safe haven and he'll never find me here. He thinks I'm crazy. I know he's at my house. I want to be there tonight or tomorrow. Just leave me alone and let me be. If I'm ready to talk to you then I will but it'll be on my terms and not yours. I'm not ready to talk to him.

I sent a text to Riley and Tianna to let them know I booked them a flight down here so be at Tyson McGee Airport at 8:30 a.m. ready for takeoff. "Sonja, what are you doing?" I asked and beamed? Ms. Sonja is my favorite Auntie. She's forty-two and she doesn't look a day over twenty-five. That's Sonja the Body. Buffy ain't got shit on her.

She's a bad bitch with long jet-black hair and caramel complexion. I hate going places with her. Niggas stay stalking my auntie. These young hoes don't have anything on Sonja the Body.

"Sit down, Kaniya. What happened and don't leave shit out?" She asked. Sonja wanted all the tea since I called her last night. I wouldn't dare call my mother to let her know what went down because she would be going in. My mother liked Lucky, but she saw right through him. She knew he was too good to be true.

"First show me around. I see you've redecorated. Let me find out you got you some new young nigga up in here that's straight caking you. It looks good, everything's rust brown and gold. It's not much to tell. He was cheating for ninety days with some little young girl. I packed his shit up took it to his house before I pulled up on him at the club. He was looking so dumb when I approached him. Believe it or not, I was cool. I saw what I needed to see. I lost it until she said she didn't care that he had a woman. I punched that little bitch so hard in her head. It was a wrap after that," I explained.

"Don't take no shit off no man, Kaniya. You're too young to be committed. I wish I knew what I know now back then but I didn't. If I did, I would've left your uncle Kanan a long time ago. Don't lose yourself over any man. Stick to what you believe in.

I'm proud of you though. A lot of women would stay and ignore that shit. I stayed and I don't ever want you to go through what I went through," she explained. I knew Sonja went through a lot with my uncle Kanan. I just don't know how much. She never goes into details.

"You schooled me a long time ago. Trust me, everything you taught me I never forgot. If he wanted to test the waters, he should've said something. You won't have your cake and ice cream with me unless we're going to Cold Stone Creamery to get it. I'm about to have me some fun. I don't feel like being bothered with Keith Sweat," I explained. I gave Lucky the last five years of my life and he took that for granted so know I'm about to live my life.

"Who Is Keith Sweat?" She asked. I started laughing. Sonja was looking at me like I'm crazy. Lucky had been begging me since I left his ass to answer the phone and talk to him, but I didn't have anything to say.

"Lucky. He has called me over 100 times between texting and calling," I laughed and showed her my phone. Sonja was having a field day reading through the text messages and listening to the voicemails but I'm tripping though. Now he's tripping. Sonja and I finished talking and she fixed us some breakfast and a nice cup of coffee. I needed something strong.

I had to shower and handle my hygiene so I can pick up Riley and Tianna from the airport! The shower felt so good. The temperature was just right. Now this shower has some good head! Let me hurry up and dry off and put my clothes on. I'm thugging it out today. This Bath &Body Works Sheer Cotton Lemonade Pure Shea Lotion was made just for me. It just kisses my skin. I don't even need perfume when I wear this. Here he goes again calling.

"Yeah, Lucky!" I yelled through the phone. The only reason why I answered is that I didn't want him to keep calling my phone. His calls and text messages were killing my battery itself.

"Are you through running?" He asked. I started to hang up the phone. I'm not running from him. I just don't want to be bothered with him. I didn't want to makeup. I just wanted to enjoy our breakup.

"Are you through cheating? I ain't never ran from a nigga or a bitch. So, what are you saying?" I asked. I don't even want to hear why he did it. He can keep doing him and leave me the fuck alone so I can do me. He'll hate me, in the end, I can promise you that.

"Where are you?" He asked. We're not together so he doesn't need to clock my moves. Clock the bitch who you were posted in the club with.

"On my way home to switch cars and head to the airport," I explained. I knew he was waiting for me at my house, but it'll be a while before he sees me, and I meant that shit. If I see Lucky now, I'm liable to fuck his ass up. Smacking him was minor. He had me out here really looking like a fool. As if I was the side bitch and she was the main bitch.

"Are you going somewhere?" He asked. I rolled my eyes as if he could see me through the phone. His voice fuckin' irks me.

"Why?" I asked. I could hear him huffing and puffing in the background trying to get his words together. He knew I didn't want to have a conversation. I don't even know why he's trying.

"Can I come?" He asked. Lucky was trying to run game. He must come better than. Getting back in my good graces won't be that easy

"No, let me be. Go tend to your girlfriend. I'm single and so are you," I explained. I swear it hurts just to let that escape my lips which means it's real.

"Why can't we talk?" He asked. I said everything I had to say last night, and I don't want to talk about it anymore. I need him to respect that and let me be single.

"We did earlier, remember? I got to go to, Lucky." I couldn't stay on this phone with him any longer. Now, all suddenly he wants to talk. I don't have anything else to say. I heard it and I saw it and I've seen it with my own two eyes. I'm good.

"I love you, Kaniya," he stated. He doesn't know what love is. Love should've told him to walk away if he wanted to cheat. What we had didn't matter, so everything I'm about to do is about to shatter his world.

"I like you to," I beamed and laughed. I hung up the phone and disconnected the call. He fucked up and it'll be a long time before he hears me say that again.

I booked Riley and Tianna a flight here this morning. I told my girls what happened. I needed them and they were on their way. No questions asked they're coming to see about me. That's the bond we have. I'll drop whatever for them and I'll drive 100mph on the highway to make sure mine are straight and vice versa. It's always been that way.

We're going to have some fun this weekend. I got them on whatever. It ain't no limit. I finished getting dressed. I stayed in the guest room that Sonja allowed me to stay in. I had to leave to make my way toward the airport. I didn't want to be late picking them up.

I made my way to the airport. I just got the text their flight just landed. I'm on my way. Atlanta traffic is so bad on a Saturday. Where the hell are all these people going? Lucky really won't get the picture. I'm done and I mean that shit. Here he goes on his Keith Sweat shit again begging and texting me. Why now? You didn't think about the consequences if I found out and left you. Deal with that shit.

Lucky - Can I see you today?

Lucky - Where did you stay at last night?

I just talked to this crazy fuck 20 minutes ago. I can't wait to find some potential. I made sure my read receipt was on. No response. Riley and Tiana walked out of the airport. I tooted the horn so they could look in my direction. A smile instantly appeared on my face. There my bitches go right there. They headed in my direction. I hit the unlock on the door and they hopped in.

"Hey, I missed y'all," I beamed. My bitches are bad I swear; looking like they're fresh off the runway. When you see

Riley her pores reek with class. It's levels to this shit. As she says; she's tall brown skin with long brown hair with blonde highlights. She's real classy. She's a model. She's a Chanel junky. If it isn't Chanel, she isn't fucking with it. She's slim thick. Don't let the class fool you. Her shape is bad. I see why half of the Instagram models are mad.

Last, but not least I got Tianna the Don Dada Tennessee's most wanted. She's really petite light brown medium length hair with a big ole butt. She's cornbread fed and she can dance her ass off. She stays dressed to kill and anything she puts on she SLAYS. Riley and Tianna threw their bags in the back and I pulled off. It's going down this weekend and I can feel it. I needed them here because Barbie and Ketta dipped headed to New York.

"What are you doing girl with all that?" I rapped.

"Ew, nothing," she chuckled. Tianna was silly as fuck. She laughed at anything. I knew tonight was going up since she's in the building. Every time we see each other I hit her with that. Riley was busy texting on her phone. She wasn't paying us any attention.

"Riley Nicole, I'm sorry you had to leave your dick idle, but I needed you more," I beamed and explained. I didn't mean to be rude, but it was the truth.

"Shut the fuck up with your messy ass. The Boss is on the way. He couldn't let this pussy be to idle for too long. He'll be here in a few hours. We're going to stay for a week," she explained. Riley met her a real boss and her relationship is fresh, so I understood where she was coming from but BITCH, I need you just for a few days. I'm glad she came.

"What the fuck happened last night," she asked. I knew Tianna couldn't wait to pry to see what happened and I couldn't wait to fill her in on all the details.

"Your girl came to play last night, and I fucked shit up! He was looking so dumb, I wish y'all would've been there. The lil bitch said she didn't care that he had a bitch and she didn't mind being number two." I argued and explained. I couldn't wait to show her what being number two felt like.

"What you do, Kaniya?" She asked. Tianna was laughing with her silly ass. She couldn't even keep a straight face. She already knew I cut the fuck up. She just wanted me to confirm it.

"I showed that bitch how it feels to be number two. I punched that bitch so hard in her head she fell to the floor," I explained. I had to. She wasn't even fighting back.

"That's your style TKO," they said in unison and slapped hands with each other.

"He had the nerve to pick that bitch up off the ground. I put my brass knuckles on so quick I bust that nigga in his jaw about five times." Lucky was going to feel me one way or the other.

"He must don't know how gangster this shit gets," she asked. Lucky forgot I could show my ass. I've changed but I'm still me. I'll never let a nigga, or a bitch disrespect me.

"He doesn't have a fuckin' clue because if he did, he would've done better," I explained. "So, what y'all want to do? I need to get my nails and feet done and then it's on."

"Are we going to the same spot we always go to," Riley asked. She loved Best Nails, of course, I was headed there.

"Yep, Best Nails it is," I beamed. We're catching up and shit doing what girls do. Having it our way. Every time we link up, we have a ball. "I'm taking y'all to the mall. Everything on me, straight balling. Tianna, we're going be hot today. I want to go to Mozley, or Maddox Park off Bank Head since Riley is booed up!" I haven't been single in a while. It's time for me to let my hair down and test the waters since Lucky is testing new waters. Two can play that game I'm with all the get back shit. I got to get that nigga back.

"Bitch you were just in a relationship 24 hours ago," she mentioned. I flipped Riley off and gave her the middle finger. Who told her to remind me of my yesterday?

"It's not packed. Come on before the hoes flock in here." We hopped out my truck. I locked the doors and made our way in. I signed our names on the book. "Sue Young you remember these two? Give them the VIP treatment," I beamed.

"Okay Kaniya," she responded.

"Where's Tina," I asked.

"She's coming give her a few minutes," she explained. I took a seat in the corner waiting on my nail tech to come in. I'm scrolling through my emails on my IPAD checking the shipment on the furniture. I ordered for my Staffing Company **Work Now Atlanta.** I heard the door open and I looked up. I know this isn't that hoe Melanie. She done strolled her lame ass in here. Is this bitch following me? I have never seen her in here. I'm dressed down today Pink Outfit Air Maxes and fitted hat you know it's on. I sent a group text giving my girls the heads up.

Me - That's Lucky's lil bitch Melanie that just walked in. She must be following me around

Riley - What you want to do?

Tianna - What you want to do?

Me - I want y'all to stay in here she probably thinks I'm by myself. Her friends outside. I'm getting ready to box this hoe out. Look at her. She's not even getting anything done. If one jumps in y'all know what to do

I exited the door of the nail shop. I got my brass knuckles on. I'm ready to TTG this bitch. Just like I thought, she followed me out. Lucky had to be fuckin' with this girl heavy if she's following me and clocking my moves. I'm not even trying to fight her again because I could've sworn, I handled that bitch yesterday, BUT today is a new fuckin' day. She fucked up by rolling up on me at the nail shop. She got the right fuckin one today. She can have Lucky because I'm so through with his ass

"Fuck this shit I'm out. I'm on my way outside. Tianna come on they got mine fucked up," she yelled. I knew Riley wouldn't let me handle this on my own or by myself that's not how we roll. I knew she was coming outside. I gave a stern look to inform her that I had it. This is my battle and let me handle this bitch and her bitches according. I put it on my momma if one bitch jump in I'm setting this motherfucka off like the 4th of July.

"Riley trust me she got it, that's Kaniya you're talking about," she explained. Tianna had to assure Riley because she knew I was ready to put in work by myself. Yesterday I took it easy on the bitch because I had on a dress but TODAY, I'll stomp a bitch out. Lucky was sloppy with his shit.

"What's up, Kaniya?" She asked. Bitches like Melanie kill me. Today you want to be cordial but yesterday you had so much bass in your fuckin' mouth it was ridiculous.

"Hi Melanie, are you following me!" I asked. I wanted to know why she was here. Lucky couldn't have told this bitch how crazy I was? Yesterday it was about him, but today bitch it's about me.

"Don't get scared now bitch! I'm about to beat your ass for last night," she explained. I busted out laughing. She was silly as fuck and she'll never win fuckin' with a bitch like me. It took me a long time to get to this point here. Oh, she came to fight, and she better be prepared to lose or die depending on how I'm feeling.

"You got a lot of mouth little girl. See I'm not with all that talking and going back and forth. I'm going to handle mines straight up. Watch me work because I play for keeps and I'm not talking about Lucky. You better ask about me. You'll fuck around and die fuckin' with me and I mean that shit literally. A bitch will never fuck my face up," I argued and explained.

"Beat her ass, Melanie," they yelled. I looked to my left. This bitch had a gang of bitches with her. I shook my head. Her cheerleaders were hyping her up to get her ass beat.

She's about to get sent straight the fuck out. I'm a savage with these hands. Let me take these brass knuckles off, so I can show this hoe.

"Run up on that bitch," they yelled. Her cheerleaders were still talking shit.

"Come on Melanie you heard what your friends said," I laughed. I was done talking a few minutes ago. I walked up on that lil bitch. I hit her dead in her fucking eye. I lost it after that. I beat her like a fucking rag doll. I gave her straight headshots. I picked her up and slammed her on the concrete. The niggas from the barbershop next door came out and started recording. She started crying.

I kicked this dumb bitch in her head. I put my foot on her neck applying pressure. I pulled my 9mm out and pressed it to her temple. I told that lil bitch. "Give me one reason why you shouldn't be the next bitch on a RIP tee shirt?" I asked. I took a picture of this bitch, just like this and sent it to Lucky. I'm sick of him and his bitch. Leave me the fuck alone because I'm not bothering you at all.

"I'm sorry, please don't kill me," she cried and begged for her life.

"I never came for you. You came for me. I don't play with kids. Find you something safe to do and get the fuck out my face. Melanie, playing with a bitch like me is dangerous and that's not a threat it's a fuckin' promise." I argued. "Stop hanging with them bitches over there. They're not your friends. My bitches standing over there they would never let any bitch get the best of me," I explained and pointed to Riley and Tiana. I walked back toward the nail shop where Tianna and Riley were standing. Tianna handed me a water bottle. I went inside to take my seat. They were right on my heels. They stood in front of me and grilled me. I didn't want to talk about it.

"I told y'all I had it," I argued. Riley grilled me. I wish she would sit down and get her nails and feet done. I didn't want to talk about me and what I just did. I'm over Lucky and his bitch. I swear he's going to regret it.

"I don't care! I don't trust these hoes," she explained. I agree with Riley but if she wanted to keep getting her ass whooped than that's on her. The next time I'm shooting a bitch. I don't give a fuck.

"Go get your nails done and get cute," I beamed trying to hide how annoyed I was.

"Kaniya, you are crazy. Were you going to really shoot that girl?" She laughed and asked. Tianna was crazy she'll laugh at anything.

"I was but Lucky isn't worth it. I'm not catching a body behind him. What if I didn't know he was cheating, and this hoe caught me off guard? Ugh, I'm so sorry to bring y'all down here in this mess," I argued and explained. Once again Lucky has me out here looking like a fool. I haven't fought a bitch in a long time. Trust me Melanie is going to hates that she's the one that brought me out of retirement.

"It's not your fault," she stated. All three of us were sitting in the spa chairs getting our nails done. I need a vacation after the night and day I've had. We sat back and relaxed and I called Lucky.

"Did you get my picture," I asked. I held my hands over my mouth to stop from laughing. I know he was about to flip out.

How are you right by your phone and not checking your messages I've sent? I guess he was too busy messaging somebody else.

"What picture, Kaniya?" He asked and argued? Lucky had an attitude and he shouldn't. If anything, I should have the attitude. He fucked up and not me. I'm the one out here fighting in the streets behind his stupid ass.

"Lower your voice Lucky, I should be mad not you. Check your messages," I argued and laughed. I knew he was pissed off about something but oh well. Keep your dick in your pants and you wouldn't even have a reason to be in your feelings. I can't even get in mine, because I'm still fighting a bitch that you're fuckin' that doesn't even weigh up to me.

"What the fuck Kaniya, you didn't?" He asked and argued? I looked at my phone because I knew he wasn't questioning my moves behind a bitch he was creeping with. I cut him off before he could say anything else.

"Tell your bitch never follow a savage if she isn't prepared for how real shit gets. I can't wait to find a nigga who's worth fuckin'," I argued and hung up on him. I cut my phone off. I don't have time for the back and forth shit. I'm over Lucky and everything that's coming behind fuckin' with him. I made an appointment with my OBGYN to make sure I didn't have anything. Melanie was trash if you ask me. Ain't no telling who she's fuckin' if she's willing to be number two.

Chapter-7

Tianna   ☆

I've been in Atlanta for a few hours now and I'm ready to make some moves. I'm on my good bullshit. I couldn't wait to see Quan. The same bitch whose ass Kaniya beat was the same bitch he lied and said was their cousin. She just so happens to be the bitch Lucky is fuckin'. I knew her handshake didn't match her smile. I don't get down like that. Quan and I have been beefing for a week now because some bitch he used to fuck with called him after 1:00 a.m. You know ain't nothing open after 1:00 a.m. but legs and mine were already up. We argued about that shit all night and I left. He didn't want me fuckin' off with another man, but he was fuckin' off with another female.

Kaniya had no clue Quan and I was fuckin' around heavy. I was kind of scared to tell her because the William's men are crazy. Kaniya caught me by a few hours because I was just about to hit the road and smack the fuck out of his ass. Quan and I have been fuckin' around heavy for the past few months and I been living with him for the past three months. Quan was trying to be smart and not answer his phone. I shared my location with him. I wanted him to know that I was in the city. As soon as he saw my location, he was blowing up my phone. I cleared his ass out and the texts started coming back to back. Keep that same fuckin' energy.

"Okay, its Saturday bitch, and I didn't come down here to mope around. I came to party and bullshit. I want to go to the park and go out tonight. I want to shake my ass until my feet tell me it's time to sit down. The same energy you had when you were mopping the floor with that bitch that's same the energy you need to have now. We're looking for replacements and free agents. Let's get dressed and have some fucking fun," I beamed. I meant that shit. Lucky and Quan are brothers and they're together every fuckin' day. I don't put anything past Quan, but he's so fuckin' fine and handsome. For his sake and not mine, I hope he isn't doing what Lucky's doing because I will kill his ass in his fuckin' sleep. I love him and I'm not trying to get my heart broken loving him.

"Riley, are you down or do you and Boss have plans tonight?" Kaniya asked. I knew she had plans for us but as soon as I see Quan it's a wrap. He's not going to allow any of that to go down. If Lucky's with him Kaniya can forget about that shit.

"We have dinner reservations later at Scales 925, but I'm going to the park with you guys," she explained. Riley was the only one not having a problem with her man. I can't even be mad at her. If Boss was following her all the way to Atlanta that speaks volumes. I'm happy for her because deserves it. Shit, we all do.

"Okay cool, do you guys want to grab lunch before we head to my house, or do you want me to make us some Grilled Chicken Club Sandwiches and Waffle Fries?" She asked. I looked at Riley and she looked at me. Kaniya knew we wanted her to cook for us. I wish she would open up a restaurant and stop fuckin' playing. I don't have time to be sitting in a restaurant for an hour when I can sit at her house and be comfortable.

"You can cook, bitch. I'm ready to get to your house and shower," I beamed. I couldn't wait to show my ass. The only clothes I packed were ones that showed my ass. I knew Quan was at the park playing basketball because he does it every Saturday. If I catch a bitch in his face, I'm showing the fuck out. Every ounce of class I have is going out the window.

"You live too far away, Kaniya. Why did you move?" Riley asked. I agree with her. It seems like we've been driving forever just to get to her house. Damn, I'm used to pulling up to her Condo in the middle of the city. Who wants to drive out here from clubbing? You're begging to get a DUI.

"New scenery and I wanted to be close to Work Now Atlanta," she explained. I understood that she moved to be closer to her business. It makes sense.

"How long we got?" I asked. I swear we've been driving for a long ass time. I'm ready to eat the fuckin' food she made plans to cook for us.

"Not long. We're almost here," she explained. I grilled Kaniya. If she says we're almost there one more time I'm going to fuckin' scream and I mean that shit. I feel like those kids in **Are We There Yet.**

"I was about to say it seems like Jeezy CD went off and came back on," I laughed. I'm not bullshitting that CD has repeated itself twice.

"Whatever bitch stop lying. Look we are pulling up right now," she laughed and sassed.

"Damn Kaniya this shit is nice and ducked off," Riley explained. I agree with her. This house was nice as fuck. Kaniya has always had good taste. She gets it honestly from her mother. She pulled in the garage and we hopped out. She had a few whips in her three-car garage.

"Damn bitch, when did you get this Corvette?" I asked. Lucky and Quan both had it. I know he was taking good care of her not that she needed him to. I know for a fact he brought her the Range Rover that we're riding in.

"A couple of months ago," she explained.

"I'm driving that tonight. I got a date," I beamed. Kaniya isn't the only one keeping secrets. I know I've been out of the loop, but she didn't tell me she finally copped one of those. I remember when we test drove one of those. I told Quan I wanted one and he brought me an Audi instead. He said I didn't need anything that fast because I would fuck it up.

"A mess already, Tianna," Kaniya beamed and laughed. She knew I was up to no good. I need to tell her about Quan and me sooner than later. We're always open with each other and I don't want to keep a secret from my best friend.

"Yes, I have a piece of Chocolate Candy in the A that's been waiting on me," I beamed and sassed. I sucked my teeth just thinking about Quan. He was so fuckin' sexy. Tall, dark and handsome. Quan was tall, he stood about 6'4, 230 pounds solid, and pretty white teeth. He rocked a bottom grill. He had shoulder length dreads that adorned his head.

"I heard that, plug me in. Does he have a friend? Maybe we can double date," she asked. Kaniya was serious too. I could tell by the expression on her face. It too bad Lucky has fucked that up. I can't stand that cheating conniving son of a bitch.

"He has a brother, but you wouldn't like him," I laughed.

"How do you know?" She asked.

"Trust and take my word for it."

Riley

It feels good to be back in Atlanta despite the circumstances. I knew it had to be serious if Kaniya booked us a flight. To hear about the fight is one thing, but to see my girl beat ass again over the same nigga is crazy. Lucky is wrong for that shit. Kaniya and Lucky were relationship goals. On the outside looking in I would've never thought he was cheating. He seemed so perfect for her. Judging by old girls' actions she was feeling him something serious if she popped up on Kaniya. I could understand her wanting a rematch but bitch you need to sit the fuck down and take that L.

Getting your ass whooped comes with the territory of being a side bitch. Stay in your fuckin' place because you fuckin' agreed to it. Kaniya has come a long way. I hate that bitch and Lucky brought her to a place that it took her a long time to come from. I'm here as long as she needs me to. I've been through a few breakups. If anybody knows how she feels it's me. She loves the fuck out him. We finally made it to her house, and I was so glad because the shoes I was rocking wasn't comfortable at all. I kicked my shoes off immediately.

"This house is huge. I would be scared to sleep in here by myself. What do you need a big ass house like this for and it's just you?" I asked. Kaniya didn't need this much house. We always talked about living in big houses but neither one of us has had any kids yet. I don't want to be the first one elected.

"When I have kids and kidnap you bitch and get custody of Aubrey, Kirsten, and Natalie," she laughed. Kaniya would be a great mother and I can't wait until she makes me a Godmother.

"Show us around. It's beautiful," I beamed. I love the way she has it decorated even though she didn't ask for my touch. Interior design is my profession and it's missing my touch to really make things extravagant.

"Here's the living room. You can take your own detour, you guys are family," she mentioned. I am looking around and it was beautiful. I am proud of my best friend. She's done well for herself.

"White and gold everything, hmm? I love this color scheme. I like the cathedral ceilings and oversized sofa and love seat. The plush white rug and fireplace setup are nice. This dining room is bad as fuck. Grey and marble green. I love this antique look. Oh my gosh, I fuckin' love this kitchen, damn. How many bedrooms?" I asked.

"Four bedrooms and three bathrooms," she beamed. I love everything about this house. It's dope and it's a cute little setup. I can't wait until she fills it up with babies.

"I swear if you got a pool I'm moving in this summer," Tianna asked and laughed? She was crazy as hell, but she was dead serious too. I got to see what's up with her lately. She's been missing in action and I haven't been able to catch up with her. These past few days is the most I've seen of her in the past few months.

"That's cool. I'm going upstairs to my room to shower and get dressed. I'll cook our lunch soon as I'm finished. It's a bathroom down here and one upstairs. It has towels and soap in there and a towel warmer," she explained. Kaniya was so damn extra. It's crazy, a fuckin' towel warmer. I made my way upstairs right behind her. We couldn't even get upstairs good because the hallway was flooded with red and white roses. We both looked at each other. I couldn't even get to the guest room because it was so many roses. It had to be over 60 dozen red and white roses. Somebody was sorry. I followed Kaniya in her room and it was covered with roses and a big ass I'M SORRY CARD.

"Kaniya, look at this shit. Tianna come here right quick and look at this shit," I beamed and yelled. Tianna marched her ass right upstairs. Kaniya looked at everything but the roses. I'm nosey. I wanted to know what the card says.

"Bitch look at all these roses," Tianna beamed. She was just as excited as I was. I never have seen so many roses in my fuckin' life. Lucky was pulling out all the stops to plead his case.

"What does the card say?" I asked. My eyes were trained on Kaniya and she refused to look at it. I want to hear what he has to say. If he's coming this hard, he had to put some thought into the card.

"Do I have to read it?" She asked. I rolled my eyes at Kaniya. What type of question is that?

"Yes bitch, read it," we beamed. Tianna and I both wanted to know what the card said.

"Not now, please. If he wouldn't have cheated, he wouldn't need an I'm sorry card. I don't want to read it," she argued. Kaniya is so stubborn. She stomped in her bathroom and closed the door. I'll leave her alone for now, but I wanted to know what the card said.

Chapter - 8

Kaniya

I knew he came here last night. I'm glad I made the decision not to come home last night. I want my keys back. Lucky can no longer have access to me. His side bitch knew too much shit about me, and I wasn't feeling that at all. My house filled with roses and a big ass card and a teddy bear is not enough for me to take him back. He made a fuckin' fool out of me. I'm over him and all his fuckin' lies. I guess I'll read the card before I trash it. I opened the card to see what it said.

Kaniya Williams,

Baby, I'm sorry. I know I'm sorry isn't enough. I swear to God I am. I'm man enough to admit that I fucked up. I never meant to hurt you or stray away. I slipped up and I made a big mistake. Please don't throw away what we have over one mistake. Please, can you find it in your heart to forgive me? What can I do to make it right and right my wrongs? I got beside myself and fell for the trap. I love you so much. I'm fucked up Kaniya because I hurt you. I'm hurting too because I don't want to lose you. My heart hurts just to know that I've hurt you and I might lose you. I can't live without you. Please Forgive me Please, Kaniya.

Lucky

"Here he goes with his Keith Sweat stuff," I sighed. The card was nice but it's not enough. I don't trust him and probably never will. It's too late for this. He should've been honest in the beginning. He wanted to lie until he got caught. I can't forgive him that easily. He wanted to test the waters so, it's time I test some too.

"Kaniya, you're so damn crazy," Riley laughed. I looked at her and laughed. I had to laugh to stop myself from crying. I wouldn't wish the pain and betrayal that I feel on my worst enemy and he wonders why I wanted him to strap up and wear a condom. He's selfish as fuck. He can keep her because I don't want him.

"Whatever I'm not thinking about Lucky. I just want to have fun, be free, get Work Now Atlanta up running, help my people get to work and provide for their families that's it.

If I meet a nigga in the process, oh well. Let me go ahead and get dressed so we can eat and be out. I want to go to The Shops of Buckhead in Atlanta if we have time," I explained. These past twenty fours have been crazy. I would've never seen any of this coming. I'm not going to worry and keep thinking about it. I'm just going to pray on it and let God work. I stepped in the shower and made sure the water adjusted to my liking. Damn this shower feels so good. Love and Sunshine Body Wash from Bath & Body Works smells so good. It lathers great.

I must make sure my snapper down there is always clean. I feel so much better since I prayed on this situation and gave it to God and let it go. I have too much going for myself and things I'm trying to accomplish to be in these streets fighting over a nigga that doesn't want to be kept. I'm not trying to keep a nigga that don't want to be kept.

This shower feels so good and this afternoon head from this shower is amazing. Let me get out this shower before I run all the hot water out. I cut the water off and stepped out the shower. I dried off and wrapped a towel around my body. I thumbed through my closet. I had a million things to choose from, but I wanted to be cute. What should I wear? I'm thinking about this Nude Guess maxi dress that shows my stomach. It clings good to my hips and ass, yep that will do.

Diamond studs set my ears on fire and my Diamond Bracelet had my wrist on beam. Nude lip gloss coated my lips. I looked myself over once in the mirror to make sure I'm good. I'll touch up my hair and we out. I flat ironed my hair and feathered my bob. I applied an extra coat of Caramel creme nude NYX lip gloss. I needed an extra pop so; I applied a little mascara to my eyelashes to make them pop. I slid my toes in my nude Guess sandals. I sprayed my Dolce & Gabbana perfume on and headed downstairs to meet my girls.

"Look what the cat blew in, about fucking time. I'm hungry, Kaniya," Riley pouted and whined. She was doing the most. I don't even feel like cooking if I start now, we'll miss all the action and I wasn't trying to do that at all. I'll make it up to them.

"About that girl, I looked too good to be in the kitchen cooking. We can grab some food off a food truck, or I can call a chef to pull up on us and bring us some food. You chicks look too cute and smell too good to go somewhere smelling like chicken club sandwiches.

Damn Riley, you're looking sexy in the pencil skirt and crop top to match. Royal blue and gold, that's your color. Your spiral curls and those royal blue sandals, you're slaying that shit," I beamed. My girl was killing it. Boss better hurry up and pull up before we hit the scene.

"Thank you, this old thang," she beamed and lied. I couldn't wait to buss her ass out.

"Bitch stop lying. I can smell new Versace a mile away," I beamed and laughed.

"Kaniya, you're crazy," she beamed and laughed. I know she just popped the tags that outfit. It's a part of their new Spring Collection but it's old. Riley never wears the same thing twice, but it's old. Girl stop, I know you better than you know yourself.

"I know New Versace when I see it. Tianna, bitch, look at you're showing out today. You should've told me you were wearing some short ass shorts and a crop top. I would've put my dukes on too. You're straight killing it. I wanted to let my ass hang out too. Why didn't I get the memo? You got your legs and that ass out. You're killing those stilettos. They're setting your outfit off right. Those niggas about to go crazy and there are some bitches who are about to be mad," I beamed. We slapped hands with each other. I told y'all my bitches were bad. When we pull up and hop out all eyes on them. "Come on let's go. Who's going to be the DJ, or should I play Pandora or Sirius XM?"

"Play Pandora," Tianna blurted. I looked at her like she was crazy. I fuck with Pandora but I'm a Tidal and Apple Music junky. Sirius XM is cool, but they talk too much.

"Okay, what radio station?" I asked. I swear I don't want to hear any fuckin' slow music. The last thing I fuckin' need is anything that'll remind me of Lucky. If that's the case they'll be listening to Jeezy and Future, all day and I don't care.

"Bryson Tiller," she blurted. I rolled my eyes at Riley. I know she wanted to listen to some slow shit. I wasn't with it, but his new album was on point.

"Buckle up bitches, let's get this Saturday started off right. No drama, I'm looking for replacements and free agents," I beamed and cheered. Lucky better pray I don't run into Mr. Right, because if I do it's a wrap and I'm feeling lucky today. A redbird sat in my window seal for a few minutes and I made a wish. I hope it comes true.

"That's my bitch, that's the Kaniya we know," they cheered and slapped hands.

We were cruising the city making our way to the West Side. Bankhead Mozley or Maddox Park is where we were headed, whichever one was popping the most. Traffic was smooth and that's surprising which means everybody must be parked and posted up. Soon as we hit Donald Lee Hollowell it was going down. My antennas were already up. I'm ready to park this truck and hop out.

"Look Kaniya, if a nigga tries to holla at you go for it okay. Live a little," Riley explained. She knew me better than that. If a nigga had potential, he could get some of my time. Had I known Lucky had hoe tendencies we would've never made it this far. You live and you learn this time around. I'm choosing to live.

"I got this. Did you forget how I used to be? Girl you haven't seen anything yet. Watch me work." Riley and Tianna knew how I gave it up. I'm not in the streets or clubs heavy to spare Lucky because I used to be. It's thick as fuck at Mozely Park. Cars were wrapped around the block and down the street. It's going down up in this bitch. It's going to be a great day. Free agents and fucking replacements, that's my motto. Let me find somewhere to park.

"Let us out," they yelled. I looked to my right and Riley had the biggest smile on her face. I looked over my shoulder and Tianna were smiling too, but I could tell that smile was masking how irritated she was.

"Nah, we're getting out together," I yelled. I wanted to get out too and be seen and pull a few niggas, fuck that. We came to-gether let's hop out together.

"Nah, fuck that. I'm hopping out this truck right now. I see something I like," she beamed and sassed. I cut my eyes at

Tianna. I looked over my shoulder again to see what Tianna was on. She was on some good bullshit. It was a nigga out here that had her attention. I put my feet on the breaks so she could step out. I didn't want anybody to say that I was holding them back because I wasn't.

"Oh lord, I'm not going to be a cock blocker. Get that ass out and bring these niggas to the yard. Bring one for me too," I beamed and cheered. I meant that shit. She was about to break her damn neck trying to hop out my damn truck. I didn't want her to scar her legs up being fast in the ass. The last thing we need is for her knees to be bloody.

"I sure will. Hurry up and park the Range Rover so we can get this shit popping," she explained. I threw my Range Rover in park. She grabbed her clutch and bottled water and did her thing. The moment her foot hit the pavement I could hear the catcalls.

"It's popping out here today, and I'm not playing fair. It's whatever. I'm back on the prowl. I'm not sparing no nigga or bitch feelings. The summer is mine, just watch," I explained. I found a spot right on the left. I looked over my shoulder so I could back in. It's perfect, right across from the courtyard. Some-body must've just pulled out. Let me call these impatient chicks and let them know where I'm parked at, shit. I want to be seen too. I feel like I missed something since I had to go park. I hit the

Bluetooth and called Riley and she answered on the third ring. See this is the shit I'm talking about.

"Hey, where y'all at? I'm up the hill by the courtyard where the grills at," I asked and explained. I could hear some niggas in the background and Tianna laughing. See we should've caught a fuckin' Uber. It was my fuckin' idea to even come here and now I'm missing out. Ain't that about a bitch.

"We're on the way. I found us a nigga that's going to give us a ride. I'm not walking in these heels," she argued and sucked her teeth. I hung up the phone in Tianna and Riley's face because I already told them that. I wasn't walking around this park with some heels on. It'll be just my luck I'll end up fighting some dummy again. I stepped out of the truck and observed the scenery. I rested my hands on the hood of my truck. It was still warm. I stood in front of my truck posted up. For some reason, I felt uncomfortable. It felt like somebody was starring a hole in me. I turned around to look and see if I notice anybody, but I didn't see anyone. Maybe I was tripping but I didn't feel like I was.

Ms. Eula pulled up in front of my truck with her frozen daiquiris cart. She told me she runs about $10,000.00 on the weekends out here. She's balling and daiquiris ain't the only thing she's selling. She had appetizers, some bomb ass wings, nachos, fruit bowls, and cake slices.

"Hey Kaniya, how many frozen daiquiris do you want?" She asked. I need to eat before I start drinking and getting fucked up. I haven't eaten since earlier. I need something on stomach bad.

"Give me four daiquiris. Two mango pineapple and two strawberry and kiwi mix," I explained. Ms. Eula fixed my drinks and handed them to me. I peeled off two twenty dollars bills. She threw me a cake slice for free. I appreciate that.

"I saw you're fine ass man out here earlier. You better be glad I'm old enough to be his momma or else I would take him from you," she laughed. Ms. Eula always fucks with me about him. Any other time I would let her have it and express how much I love him to her, but not today. I hated Lucky's ass with a passion.

"I'm single Ms. Eula," I sighed. I hope she minds her business and doesn't ask why but that's too much like right. She loves Lucky's black ass and he loves her too. Every time he sees her, he always gives her weed to smoke for free.

"Oh, okay Kaniya, let you tell it. When I asked him about you earlier, he didn't say shit about the two of you not being to-gether. What the fuck did he do? I'll beat his ass when I see him," she argued and explained. Ms. Eula was good people. I appreciate her looking out.

"I'm looking for some free agents and replacements." I beamed. It sounded good coming from my mouth but only time would tell if I'm able to live up to the hype.

"I hear you baby girl, be easy," she stated. Ms. Eula strolled off with her cart. She had to make her money. Tianna and Riley pulled up on the back of some niggas motorcycle. As soon as they stepped off the motorcycle everybody was looking. I noticed Quan was walking toward this way. I don't know if Tianna was still talking to him or not. I hope his brother is nowhere in sight.

"About time y'all pulled up," I sassed. I thought they were never going to show their damn faces.

"This shit live like how Chestnut used to be back in the day," Riley stated. I knew she would love the vibe out here. It's cool. I grabbed my big face Chanel frames out my armrest. It was so many niggas out here. I couldn't wait to eye fuck them behind this eye tent.

"Girl, don't bring up Chestnut. I'm too cute to fight today. Here get your drinks. I got y'all a daiquiri to sip on," I laughed and explained. I handed Tianna and Riley a drink. I reminded them to slip slowly because even though this drink is fruity, it'll have your ass tipsy.

We're having so much fun catching up and kicking shit. It's so many niggas out here trying to holla it's ridiculous. Niggas in Atlanta don't care. They can be with their wife and still try to holla and eye fuck a bitch. I'm good at that. It's a real car show out here. It had to be at least over a hundred Dunks, Camaros, Corvettes, Challengers, and Mustangs out here. It's not even Stunt Sunday. Your name and it's out here. Damn it's a nasty purple and black Chevy Dunk drop top on 28's. It's clean as fuck. I didn't want to stare too hard but damn his candy paint was fuckin' dripping. He was shitting on niggas out here. Every nigga out here was hating, and every bitch out here was trying to catch that niggas attention.

"Damn who is that, Kaniya? He's playing **Plies Shawty** and shit. You can hear his music from a mile away," she beamed. Her guess was good as mine. I wanted to know too. He was raising the bar for these niggas out here.

"I don't know but it's clean. Stop him when he comes through," I stated. I knew Tianna would do it because she didn't give a fuck. Oh lord, this man done got out the car. To my surprise, the nigga driving the dunk pulled right in front of us. He came to a complete stop and hopped out. I turned my head because I didn't want to look at him. It was too many thirsty bitches out here and I didn't want to be one of them. Tianna and Riley didn't give a fuck. I shouldn't but currently, I did.

"Aye shawty, red come here," he stated. I wonder who he was talking to because Riley and Tianna said nothing. They were on mute. They kept ignoring the guy like they didn't hear him.

"Kaniya Nicole Miller, I know you hear me fuckin' talking to you?" He argued and asked. I was scared to turn around. I didn't know who this man was to be calling me by my government name. I felt him walk up on me. I refused to turn around. This nigga is out here making a scene. His cologne already has my pussy leaking, and his voice is sending chills through my body. It sounds familiar that's why I'm scared to turn around. He shouldn't be out of jail now.

"Bitch, who the fuck is that?" They asked and whispered? Riley and Tianna were both grilling me looking for an explanation. I knew he was talking to me, but I'm scared to turn around and find out if it's him.

"I don't know," I whispered.

"Shit he knows you," she laughed. I turned around to see who it was. I bit my bottom lip by accident. I had to play it off.

Damn this man standing before me is fine as fuck. He always matched my fly with 6'2 caramel brown skin. Long dreadlocks adorned his head. They were neat and freshly twisted. His teeth were white as coke. He had two gold fangs with diamonds. Our eyes held a private conversation with each other. His eyes were hiding behind his Gucci frames and mine were hiding behind my Chanel frames. We knew each other well. His Gucci Guilty Cologne molested my nostrils. He was so fuckin' sexy. He was draped in all white YSL apparel. I had to play shit cool. He closed the gap between us. I took a step back. Anytime I was in his presence I felt something between us.

"What's up, Kaniya?" He asked. I swear he doesn't want to know the answer to that.

"Tariq, is that you?" I asked. I knew it was him. I just didn't want him to know that I knew it was him. He removed my Chanel frames off my face. He cupped my chin forcing me to look at him. He wrapped his arms around my waist. I could feel all eyes on us.

"Yes, it's me in the flesh. Why are you acting like you didn't know a nigga?" He asked. I'm glad he's home, but that wasn't the case. I just didn't want to be like every bitch out here that's lusting after him. Tariq was fine as hell. He always has been.

"When did you get out?" I asked. He stared at me very intensely. I knew I wasn't going to like what he had to say. I just spoke to him a few weeks ago and he didn't mention anything.

"Thursday, I was going to hit you up. Can I have a hug?" He asked and bit his bottom lip. Tariq was keeping secrets. I hear from him at least twice a week. I wonder what he's been doing since Thursday. I find it funny that Sonja didn't say shit. I'm in my feelings and I shouldn't be.

Hell yeah, he could have a hug. It's not that I had a choice. His arms were already wrapped around my waistline. I rested my arms around his shoulders. Our eyes started having their own conversation. I gave him a hug. He had his face buried in the crook of my neck. Damn, I missed him. He whispered in my ear. "Damn you smell good. Ride with me?" I wanted to so bad, but I couldn't.

"I can't. I'm out here with my girls and they're from out of town," I pouted and whined. Tariq wasn't buying that at all. Had I known he was out, and Lucky was on some bullshit. I wouldn't have called them. I really enjoyed his company. Tariq and I never judged each other, and we were always open and honest.

"Give them your keys. I'm sure that Range has GPS in it. They can get to wherever they need to," he explained. Our eyes were still trained on each other. I had to get myself together quick because I was so wrapped up in him. I'd lost my train of thought quickly. I had to get away from him fast.

"Where are we going?" I asked. To be honest I didn't give a fuck where we were going. I just wanted to be in his presence. He wasn't taking no for an answer.

"To the mall. I want you to pick me out something to wear tonight and dinner if you hungry," he explained? I was open to that. Tariq was always looking out. He freed me from his embrace. Tianna and Riley's eyes were trained on me. I tried to avoid contact with them as much as I could. I knew they had questions, but I didn't want to answer them.

"Hey, I'm going to ride with Tariq, here are my keys," I explained. I tossed my keys to Tianna and walked off quickly. She was giving me the side eye. I would explain to them later how I knew him, but not right now. I wasn't ready so, let me have my moment.

"You got some explaining to do," Riley laughed and sucked her teeth. I was expecting to hear something from Tianna but not Riley. It wasn't much to tell.

"He's cool. That's Sonja's nephew," I explained. I walked back over to Tariq's car. He opened the door for me like the gentleman that he was. I slid in his leather seats, buckled my seat belt, and he pulled off. Tariq and I couldn't be alone together because both of our minds would be in the gutter.

"Dang Kaniya, you done got thick as fuck on me. You grew up some since I saw you," he explained. We both have grown up some. Tariq begged me to send him some pictures while he was in jail, but I wasn't. I remember one of the girls I went to school with was dating someone in prison, and she sent some pictures of herself. Her pictures were being passed around in jail and her phone number. I knew Tariq would never do that. Tariq was fine as hell and I can't lie. He kept catching glances at me as he drove. I tried to avoid it. I couldn't even hide my smile even if I wanted too. It's like he was trying to read my soul and I didn't want him too. I cleared my throat and he looked at me.

"Thank you, Tariq. You don't look so bad yourself. How did you know it was me?" I asked. I wanted to know how he knew that was me. I for damn sure didn't know that was him. Raven hasn't told me anything either, now that I think about it. I had no clue that was him.

"How could I forget you?" He asked. He grabbed my thigh with his right hand. I swatted his hands away. He grabbed my hand forcing me to look at him and I couldn't hide my smile. Tariq brought that out of me. He had a smile on his face too. I was addicted to his smile.

"Whatever, Tariq." I sighed and smiled. Tariq squeezed my hand. I looked at him to see what he wanted. I hated to look in this man's eyes because he was doing something to me. I tried to fight it, but I couldn't because he wouldn't allow it.

"Stop playing with me, Kaniya. You know I mean that shit," he argued. I knew he was serious, but we could never be. More of the reason I couldn't be around him because he tempted to cross the lines and we couldn't.

"Stop Tariq, you're making me uncomfortable," I pouted. I didn't want to be around him for this reason alone. The conversation would always be about us.

"It's whatever now. You heard what the fuck I said. I don't care, maybe you need to be uncomfortable. Are you still with that fuck nigga?" He asked. I don't know why Tariq never accepted my relationship with Lucky. Lucky wasn't a fan of Tariq's either. He always said that Tariq wanted me. I denied it every time to keep confusion down because I knew I would never act on it. I knew he would love what I was about to say next.

"No, I'm single," I sighed and looked away. Tariq was staring at me very intensely. I guess he was trying to see if what I was saying was true. I had no reason to lie.

"Really, Kaniya?" He asked. Tariq knew I wasn't a woman that told lies, so I don't even know why he was questioning it. I really didn't want to talk about it. "Kaniya, do you hear me talking to you?" I looked over my shoulder and instead of him focusing on the road. He was staring at me.

"Dead ass," I sassed. Tariq squeezed my hand. I looked at him to see what he wanted. I gazed in his eyes. He had a smirk on his face.

"I want you, Kaniya. Can you give us a try?" He asked. I knew Tariq meant every word he said, but we couldn't be together. Sonja was his aunt and Kanan was my uncle and we were raised as family. They both wouldn't allow it. Raven was my sister. I didn't want to fuck our family up. Tariq didn't give a fuck about that. We had this conversation several times. We weren't blood, so I wasn't his family. I was fair game to him.

"I just got out of something not even twenty-four hours ago. It's the summertime and I'm not trying to be committed or tied down.," I explained. Tariq gave me an evil glare. I don't care. I said what I said. I'm single and I want to continue to be.

"Obviously you weren't in anything serious if you're out already," he argued. No matter what I said Tariq didn't want to hear it. I took my relationship seriously. We were together for five years.

"What about Shaela?" I asked. I knew if he was out that bitch was somewhere in the background lurking. He couldn't talk because he was with that bitch for years and the moment, he caught a case she was gone.

"Fuck Shaela," he argued. Niggas love to say that but end up running back to the same bitch that did them wrong. I wasn't buying it.

"Yeah, okay Tariq, I hear you," I laughed. I couldn't fuck with Tariq because I would hurt Shaela's stupid ass. That bitch is ignorant, and I'll hurt her feelings fuckin' with me behind him. I'm not the bitch for it. She never liked me, and I never liked her.

"What's wrong, Kaniya?" He asked. I'm good. I don't know why he asked that.

"Nothing, I'm good." I beamed proudly. Shaela wasn't fuckin' with me period. None of the bitches he entertained did. They couldn't stand me.

"You look good," he mentioned and pointed out. Tariq had me nervous and my thong was in a bunch. I'm praying when we reach our destination a wet puddle wasn't visible on this dress because the color is so light.

"Thank you, Tariq." I know Riley and Tianna were wondering who's this nigga, and where he come from because I'm moving on fast. Tariq, he's Sonja's nephew. Well, you can say it's her son. She has raised him since he was five when his mother passed. Our chemistry has always been strong. I could never cross that line because of Sonja and Lucky.

It was this one time when Sonja had one of her famous Sunday dinners. She was staying out in East Lake a little over five years ago. Lucky and I had just started dating. Tariq had a problem with it. I don't know why when he was with Shaela. I was there of course and so were they, but she left early.

For some reason, Sonja couldn't stand Shaela. I don't know what it was about her, but she didn't like her. Now that I think about it, I think Sonja and Tariq set me the fuck up. Tariq claimed he was sick, and he didn't feel good. Being a good friend that I am, I helped him to his room upstairs. Even though earlier he was giving me nothing but his ass to kiss. He asked me to help him out of his clothes. I did down to his boxers.

He wanted me to see that big ass telephone pole dick that he housed between his legs. I shook my head. He was walking around with too much dick. I knew why Shaela was acting crazy now. As soon as he got in the bed good and I was walking away. He grabbed my dress with so much force and bit his lip. I knew then I shouldn't have agreed to come up here. I looked over my shoulder to see what he wanted. He motioned with his hands for me to come here. I told him no to stop because I didn't want to get sick.

He grabbed me with so much force. He picked me up and sat me on his face. I tried to get up, but he begged me to eat it. I told him that we shouldn't be doing this, but he didn't give a fuck. He raised my dress up over my head. He smacked me on my ass. He ate my pussy like his fuckin' life depended on it. He started sucking on my pussy so good. His tongue, his fat ass tongue had its own rhythm. I was squirting in his mouth for what seemed like an eternity and my legs wouldn't stop shaking. I swear that was one of the best orgasms I've ever had. Sometimes when I can't sleep, I reminisce about that shit.

Ever since that day I swore I could never be alone with Tariq because I knew what would happen. He took advantage of me that day and he knew it. After he was finished, he laughed. I was so hot and bothered. I was so embarrassed to walk back out and join everybody else. I snuck out that back door and flew home. I prayed Lucky wouldn't come over that night. Even though we didn't fuck, I still cheated because that shouldn't have happened.

"Why don't you have any panty's on?" He asked. I knew his mind was in the gutter and I'm not even surprised. I'm glad I wore some. His hands were already massaging my thighs.

"What makes you think I don't have any on?" I asked. I turned around to face him. Tariq thought he knew it all, but he didn't.

"All I saw was ass poking out from the back. I want to taste that pussy. I wonder if it's still sweet like a pear. I want you, Kaniya," he explained.

"We can't, Tariq. You already set me up," I explained. I couldn't be around him. It's too much chemistry that should've been history.

"You didn't stop me," he chuckled. I tapped him on his shoulders because he knew that wasn't the truth. He was persistent as fuck. He wasn't taking no for an answer.

"Do birds turn down bread?" I asked. He shook his head no. I'll take that shit to the grave with me. It happened over five years ago. I wanted to forget all about that. Every chance he gets he wants to discuss it. He got locked up a few years later for a weapons charge. We remained cool but I wouldn't let him suck on me anymore. That's cheating. I would've just left Lucky alone if I had the tendencies to cheat. The only ties me and Tariq have is the $200,000 he asked me to hold for him. It's sitting in a savings account and $220,000 now. I need to get to the bank and get him a cashier's check.

"Kaniya, what are you thinking about? You 're acting weird now," he asked and explained. He knew what I was thinking about. He just wanted me to say it. Guess what? It would never happen. My answer was cut and dry. How was I acting weird because I didn't want to share my thoughts with him?

"Nothing Tariq," I sighed. I guess he didn't get the answer he was looking for.

"You must be thinking about how I sucked on that pussy years ago," he stated. He was thinking about it. He was so fine and freaky.

"Whatever," I sighed. I broke the stare between us. I couldn't look at him for too long because I would come up out my clothes because of him.

"I knew it! I still remember how you taste," he explained. I'm sure he does. It's written all over his face.

"Take me to SunTrust, Tariq," I explained. I needed to give him his money. It's time for him to take back his possession.

"For what?" He asked. I need him to ask fewer questions and do as I say.

"So, I can give you your money," I argued and sucked my teeth. He knew why I needed to go to the bank.

"Do you have any panty's on?" He asked. I felt like fuckin' with Tariq. I raised my dress up to my thighs exposing my legs and my pussy. I slid my thong down my legs and tossed it in his face. He had a devilish grin on his face. He snatched my thongs and sniffed them. "Aye, you better stop before you find yourself in an uncomfortable position."

"Are you satisfied now?" I asked. Tariq looked at me and gritted his teeth. He thought I didn't have any panties on so now he knows.

"Nope because I want to do more than smell your panties. We can get the money later," he explained. It's too bad he won't be able to do that. He can forget about it. I want him to be just as bothered as I am. " I'm glad you still have it. That shows a lot about you and our future."

"Whatever, Tariq? Why do you need me to come to the mall with you?" I asked. I need to get away from him before I end up doing some shit that I have no business doing. It's tempting as fuck with my current situation. I can fuck him without any worries because I'm single as fuck. I just want to do it on my time.

"John and Mack are throwing me a Welcome Home Party. I need you to come with me so you can match my fly," he explained. I cocked my neck to the side. He was having a whole party and I didn't know.

"Are you telling me or asking me?" I asked. I don't know who Tariq thinks he is, but he's not running shit.

"I'm telling you," he stated. I looked at Tariq to see if he was lying and judging by the facial expression he wasn't.

"How do you know I don't have plans for tonight?" I asked. I did have plans tonight and they didn't include him. He's making plans for me and he didn't even tell me that he was getting out. Now we got plans with each other.

"If you do Kaniya, them bitches are canceled. Your fair game now and I can get at you and show you off. You're mine now. We can take it as slow as you want but you mine. I'll give you some time to think about that," he explained. Tariq is crazy. I'm not his I'm single as fuck.

"I have plans to show my ass and be hot in the ass this summer. I'm not trying to be tied down. I've been there and done that," I explained. I'm dead ass serious too. I wanted to enjoy being single too. Tariq is cool but I'm not looking for a relationship. I want to keep my options open.

"I see, but you can be hot when you die," he explained and laughed. Fuck Tariq, he was cockblocking. He knew I was about to shut the park down today. That's why he's doing all that shit. I probably couldn't even pull a nigga over there now because they're going to remember what the fuck he did. My phone went off. I had a text came through from Lucky.

Lucky - You been fuckin' that nigga. Keep playing with me and I'm going to send that bitch ass nigga back to jail.

Lucky is stupid as hell. I guess word traveled fast about me and Tariq. Why is he mad though? I just beat a bitch ass a few hours ago because he couldn't keep his dick in his pants. I had an evil scowl on my face. I wasn't giving him any more of my energy. He was just about to die when he thought I shot Melanie in her fuckin' head. I guess Tariq sensed I was pissed. He grabbed my thigh and I looked at him to see what he wanted.

"Is that fuck nigga texting you, is he making threats? I know he's coming for me on some fuck nigga shit. It's cool because I don't give a fuck. May the best man win because I plan on it," he explained.

"I'm not thinking about him. He was yesterday's trash. I'm focused on today and right now. Tariq, you're crazy. Why did you pull up on me like you were Plies and shit embarrassing me," I asked? We were wondering who that was, and it turned out to be him. I can't lie he had me blushing like a schoolgirl and shit. I was feeling it. Motherfuckas had to been talking if Lucky was already known and he was nowhere in sight.

"That's what a man does when he sees something he wants. He lets that shit be known. I knew that was your favorite song. You liked it Kaniya, just say it," he stated. I wasn't even about to respond because what's understood doesn't need to be explained. He does have a bitch smiling right now. My phone went off again. Riley sent me a text.

Riley - Your EX just pulled up looking for you and I told him you were with your FUTURE.

Me – RIGHT. No wonder he texted me on some bullshit

Fuck Lucky. I'm not thinking about his ass. He wasn't thinking about me and my feelings when he was cheating. He needs to get used to me being with someone else. This is his new reality. He wasn't thinking about me until he heard another man was in the picture. I sent Riley the screenshot so she could see all the crazy shit that was coming out of his mouth.

"Kaniya!" He yelled. I looked over my shoulder to see what he wanted. Tariq has never raised his voice with me. I'm curious as to why he changed his tone. He had my undivided attention I didn't like his tone and I wasn't trying to get used to it.

"Yes?" I asked. I looked over to see what he wanted. He was staring at me very intensely. Tariq was grilling me. I wanted to know why his behavior changed.

"Can you cut your phone off, please? You're on my time," he asked and explained. I thought he was about to say something serious. He was tripping and probably thought I was texting Lucky, but I wasn't.

"Okay Tariq," I mumbled. I cut my phone off. He wanted my attention and he could have it.

"Give it to me," he said. I looked at him like he was crazy. I wasn't comfortable doing that. I'll cut my phone off but giving you my shit was out the fuckin' question.

"For what?" I asked and argued? I turned around to face him. My arms folded across my chest. I knew he was lying.

"Listen to me Kaniya, damn," he argued? Tariq was angry and pissed but for what? He threw my phone out the window. I like the way he commanded my attention but damn you didn't have to do that. I cut my phone off. He was tripping for real.

"You're buying me another phone," I argued. I just brought the iPhone 6s plus a few months ago shit this phone was brand fuckin' new.

"Glad to and I'll get you a new number also," he argued and explained. Tariq grabbed my hand as we headed to Lennox and Perimeter Mall. He wasn't even my man and he was calling shots like he was. I snatched my hand from him. He grabbed my hand back and held it to his lips and kissed it.

Chapter-9

Tariq

Kaniya Miller, I think Kaniya Harris would sound better. I'm working on that. It's only two women in this world that I wanted. Tamia Raye Carter was the first one. I had that and I fucked that up years ago and my life has been bad ever since. Kaniya Nicole Miller was next in line. For some reason, Kaniya's the only one that I wasn't able to get because time was never on our side. If she was single for the first time in five year's I was about to change that. I heard what she said but I wasn't hearing that. Lucky knew I was a threat. I wasn't a fan of his and he wasn't a fan of mine. He didn't deserve her at all. I was about to show her why.

Today I was happy and content with the way things were looking up. I was fresh out the state pen, but I was still on parole though. A nigga wasn't behind bars anymore or caged in. I've been out for two days and imagine to my surprise when I decided to crash at my Auntie Sonja's house the other night, I laid eyes on my future wife. Yes, I said future. I wanted Kaniya in the worst way. The only thing that was standing in between me and her was that fuck nigga Lucky. Shit, I wanted to jump in the bed with her and hold her all night.

The only thing that stopped me was my Auntie Sonja and this chick named Gabrielle that I brought over for a smash session. The lil bitch was begging for the dick. I served her ass to. I was knee deep in that pussy and throat. I had to beg Sonja not to tell Kaniya that I was here. I didn't want to her to see me on some straight dog shit. I should've hit her up to let her know that I was out. I had to handle my business. I'm a nosey ass nigga too. I woke up and went out the back to drive Gabrielle home. When I got back, I heard Sonja and Kaniya talking. I was ear hustling like a motherfucka. She said something about she caught Lucky cheating and she was done.

I swore that was music to my ears, shit. I was free to get at her without stepping on that nigga's toes. I wanted her and I had to get her. Shouts out to that dumb ass nigga because his old lady was up for grabs. I was about to get her and pull down on her and come correct like a real nigga should. It was just my luck she was as at Mozley Park looking right. I had to step to her. I was watching her from afar and she was on her fly shit. Her ass was sticking out begging me to grab it.

She's riding shotgun with me right now where she belongs. I'm taking her to my homecoming party tonight I know the streets are going to talk. Oh well, it is what is. Truth be told, she's the only female that can keep my attention. I promise you; something was telling me that she was the one. It's a certain type of feeling that I get when I'm around her and I want to keep it.

If she gives me a chance, I promise I won't hurt her. She's all I thought about when I was in prison. I would write to her every blue moon and she would write back. Shaela didn't do shit. The fact that she flipped my money and didn't take any of it speaks volumes. So yes, she was the one. Lucky need to fall back and move on. His time was up because it's my time now.

We finally made it to Lennox Mall. I found a parking spot. Kaniya was trying to open the door, but I stopped her. I grabbed her hand and we headed inside the mall. She was hot about that shit. When she's mad that shit turns me the fuck on. I loved getting her hot and bothered. I'm a man before anything and it's my job to do that. I slid her thong in my back pocket. It took everything in me not to take her back to the crib and bury my seeds deep in her fuckin' guts.

She was teasing the fuck out of me. I had to straighten my dick just thinking about it. John and Mac were throwing me a home coming party. I told my niggas I wanted everybody draped in all white. I had an appointment at 4:00 p.m. at Versace to get fitted for my tux. I wanted Kaniya to get fitted for her dress. Kaniya rolled her eyes when she looked at me fixing my dick.

"What I do?" I asked. Kaniya sucked her teeth. She tried to remove her hand from mine. I grabbed it tightly. She was making a scene all eyes were on us. She knew I loved attention and that shit wouldn't work out well for her in my presence.

"Playing with your dick in public. You're out here putting on a show for these people to see," she argued and sucked her teeth. Her cheeks were red as fuck. I stopped walking and cupped her chin forcing her to look at me. All eyes were on us. I leaned in as if I was going to kiss her. Our lips were touching. I could feel her gasp for air.

"I don't give a fuck about none of these motherfuckas watching us. Are you mad at me baby? If you want this dick it's yours. Stop playing hard to get," I asked and laughed? She punched me in my shoulder. I wrapped my arms around her waist and bit down on her neck. I whispered in her ear. "You know I care about you, Kaniya. I love you and I want you." I felt her body tense up. I meant what I said.

Chapter-10

Riley

Kaniya is sneaky as fuck. I wanted the tea on Tariq, Sonja's nephew. That bitch ain't never said nothing about him. She left anything that had to do with him out. He wanted her ass. I hate to admit it, but Lucky fucked up at the right time. Tariq was feeling the fuck out of her. I'm happy for her. She needs a fine ass distraction and he was perfect. I know Quan called Lucky because he pulled up directly in front of us looking for her. I wanted to ask his stupid ass where the fuck was, he at when she was beating his side bitch ass, but I killed him softly. I told him she's with a real man. Kaniya and Tariq look good together, I can't even lie. When his hands were wrapped around her tiny waist, he had me blushing wishing that was me. He's a gentleman and I like that for her.

"Tianna, did you peep that shit?" I asked. I know Tianna wasn't up on game because we both were shocked. All three of us were wondering who the fuck was that nigga that was driving the Dunk. It just so happens to be a nigga she knows. She was acting like she didn't know his ass. I should've known better. Her hot ass knows everybody. It makes sense now as to why she was scared to turn around. It was because she knew it was him. In all my years of living, I've never met a nigga or been in the presence or in contact with one that had my bitch shook. I'm giving Tariq his props. He was the first one to ever do that.

"Riley, who do you think you're talking too? You know I peep everything. Kaniya got some explaining to do. Tariq or whatever his name I, he's more to her than just Sonja's nephew. Look at the way he pulled down on her and approached her. He's in love with her. He was her Plan B if Lucky ever fucked up. Stevie Wonder can see that shit," she sassed and explained. We slapped hands with each other. I agree with her and I felt that shit. Kaniya would be lying if she didn't too.

"Yes bitch, you can't deny the chemistry they got," I beamed. Lucky had some fuckin' competition and guess what, I am rooting for Tariq's ass. I can't get down with the shit he pulled today. At first, I was like they can work it out. One fuck up but they can move past that. Lucky's bitch didn't know her place. Lucky never checked her or told her right from wrong. Kaniya shouldn't have to tell a bitch twice.

"They done fucked before Riley, I don't care. He had to sample a piece of that pussy because he was doing too much," she laughed. I wasn't going to put that out there, but damn they were comfortable with each other. She didn't stop him one fuckin' time when he wrapped his arms around her waist. I knew then it was more to it than what she claims. She was showing all thirty-two of her fuckin' teeth. She had these hoes on Bankhead mad as fuck behind him. All these bitches out here wanted him.

"Girl you stupid," I laughed. I needed Tianna to be quiet I don't want to put our girl's business out in the streets. I don't know who's lurking out here.

"He didn't give a fuck. He let that shit be known he was choosing. Every bitch out here wanted him, but he was checking for Kaniya. Lucky who? He said fuck that nigga too," she laughed.

"Speaking of Lucky did you see how he pulled up? He was looking stupid when he didn't see her. It took everything in me not to laugh in his fuckin' face. Girl, he either has somebody out here watching her every move, or he has a fucking tracker on this truck. This is the first thing she needs to get rid of, if she's through with him," I stated. Lucky wasn't moving right at all and something was different about him. When he spoke to us, I wasn't feeling his ass at all.

Tianna and I pulled off from the park. Kaniya left us so there was no need for us to still be out here. It was still thick, and more people were pulling in as we were leaving out. Tianna knew her way around here better than I did so she was driving.

"You're right, Riley." She stated. I knew somebody was out here watching. I felt like whatever happened shouldn't be talked about. I was acting on that. I wouldn't give a nigga the drop on my bitch. His niggas wouldn't give us the drop on him.

"It's going to be a hot summer. I don't see Lucky just letting her go that easy. That's a crazy chocolate motherfucka," I explained. I've seen him cut up on numerous occasions if somebody was just to speak to her. I knew with Tariq in the picture he would be showing the real him soon.

"Oh, trust me I know. I think Tariq can handle his," she stated. I hope so because Lucky doesn't play fair and the last thing, he wants to see is her with someone else.

"What are your plans for tonight," I asked. I knew Tianna was bullshitting. I knew her and Quan had something going on. I could feel the energy between them. It was dangerous and I didn't like it.

"I thought we were going out, but Ms. Replacements and Free Agents have dipped. Let's call this trick," she laughed. Tianna dialed Kaniya's number and it was going straight to voicemail. "Isn't that a bitch. Her phone going straight to voice mail. She must have those legs up or she's face down, ass up."

Tianna and I slapped hands with each other and shared a laugh at the thought itself.

"I have a date with Boss tonight. You can drop me off at The Westin," I beamed. I couldn't wait to see my baby. I missed him and I'm having withdrawals and shit.

"I guess I'll get up with Quan," she sighed and mumbled. I knew it. I bet he was the one that called his brother. Tianna was so full of shit that it's crazy. She knows that's her fuckin' man. She doesn't have to put on for me. I see right through all the bull-shit.

"You aren't slick either bitch, that's why you hopped out the truck earlier when you saw him," I explained and pointed that out. She wanted to look at everything but me.

"Nah, he saw us pull up and he wanted me to get out. I had to show him how I was coming when I pull up and he was sick. It's not a game. The sooner he figures that out the better we'll be. He had Big Bird with him," she laughed and explained. I rolled my eyes at her. She damn near hopped out the truck be-fore Kaniya had the chance to throw it in park.

"He was so fuckin' disrespectful. He didn't care that she was with him," I laughed. Niggas don't give a fuck and bitches will accept anything. I'm just saying it couldn't be me. I'm glad I never ran across a disrespectful ass nigga.

"She's just something to do until I make up my mind if I want to be in a relationship or not," she explained. I gave Tianna a hard stare. She knew she wanted him more than what she's claiming right now. It was something about The William's brothers and I didn't want any part of it. Lucky's friend Veno was trying to get at me a few years back and I curved his ass. He had whole bitch named Vanessa and she was messy as fuck. That bitch called my phone and played on my shit more than him. I couldn't fuck with it. I like Quan for Tianna. He brings something out of her that I haven't seen before.

"Stop playing with that man," I argued and sassed. Tianna and Kaniya were one and the same and it's probably the reason they ended up with brothers. They were both hot in the ass and always with get back games and shit.

More of the reason why I was hoping Lucky was done with the bullshit and him and Kaniya could work past their shit. I know Kaniya and I know her well enough to know the games haven't begun yet. She'll get him back and it ain't no other way. She won't let that shit ride at all. The same way he gave it is the same way she's going to give it.

"I am today, maybe." She sassed and lied. I just shook my head. I wasn't about to go back and forth with her. She knows everything.

"Drop me off, please. Boss just sent me a text that he's here already," I beamed proudly. I couldn't wait to see my man. It hasn't even been twenty-four hours, but I missed him. I couldn't wait to lay up under him.

"Don't make any babies, Riley." She laughed. It's too late for that. I'm grown and practice makes perfect. I want a few babies by his ass. He's not like these other niggas. It was deeper than material shit, sex, and money. We're building something solid.

"We're trying. He's the one. My heart beats for him. He speaks to my soul. It's like he was made for me," I beamed and explained.

"I'm happy for you! You deserve it. I can tell you're happy. It shows all over you," she explained. That's what happens when you're fuckin' with a boss. I stop fucking with boys a long time ago.

"Tianna, listen to you sounding all grown and mature like somebody's momma," I laughed. I couldn't believe she was talking like this. Somebody's growing up. It's about time because we're not getting any younger.

"I just like to have fun but I'm about to settle down and chill out," she explained. I looked at her with wide eyes and cocked my neck to the side. I was all ears now. As long as I've known her I've never known for her to talk like this.

"Tianna, are you high?" I asked. I had to make sure that she was feeling okay. She swore she would never commit to one man because men weren't committing to women nowadays. Everybody always had some extra shit going on.

"No can I speak some truth?" She asked. Hell, yeah, she could. I want to know what's going on with her. What truth did she need to speak on? I banged my fist on the dashboard and clapped my hands. I wanted to hear what she had to say.

"You sure can spill it." I sat back in my seat and folded my arms across my chest. I'm all ears because I wanted to hear this.

"I'm pregnant by Quan. I'm 6 weeks to be exact, and he wants me to move out here. He bought us a house a year ago. It's fully furnished. It's nice and I love it," she explained. and put her head down. Damn, that's a lot to put out there. Kaniya and Tianna are both sneaky.

"Hold your head up, bitch. When you're riding his dick, you're not holding your head down. You can keep a secret Tianna, you know that right? It makes sense now. No wonder I would ask Kaniya all the time has she seen you. You would be out here, and she was always clueless. She never saw your ass because you were at your own house. I can't with y'all two. You guys are driving me crazy. I'm happy I'm going to be an auntie. Y'all some sneaky pussy bitches. Sneaky pussies always get caught up too. We need to have a sit-down, you and Kaniya, and I." I explained.

"We will soon. Please don't tell her. Let me do it," she begged and pleaded. I wasn't going to tell Kaniya. I wanted to but it's not my business to tell.

"No, because you were the main one screaming that hot shit about free agents and replacements when you pregnant by Quan," I laughed and teased. She wasn't about to do shit.

"Riley, you better not," she argued and sucked her teeth.

"Watch me Tianna and thanks for the ride. Are you going to your home? The house Quan bought for you guys, right?" I asked and laughed. I had to fuck with Tianna. She's pregnant and talking all that shit. I can't with her at all.

"Bye Riley," she sighed and stated. I always loved staying at the Westin Hotel because it's so nice. Tianna dropped me off and headed home I'm assuming. I'm looking forward to this sit-down.

"Check in please," I beamed. I was so anxious to see Boss. I couldn't wait to jump on him. I could already tell I was about to check this attendant. She was rude as fuck and I wasn't feeling it at all.

"The last name," she asked. The front desk attended at The Westin was taking her time. Boss had a suite here. I needed a key to access the floor. It never took this long for me to get the key.

"Hollis." I beamed and smirked. I noticed she cut her eyes at me. I had to count to ten to keep my composure.

"Room 1027," she sassed and sucked her teeth. I swear she was rude as fuck to be a front desk attendant. I will be reporting her ass in the morning. I looked at her name on her badge.

"Thank you," I beamed proudly. I strutted to the elevator. I could feel her watching me. Bitch, you couldn't walk a mile in my shoes. I would love to fuck Boss on the rooftop in this hotel. Let me get my mind out the gutter. I'm sure he would be open to it. I finally made it to our floor. I used his key to access the suite. I smelled him, but I didn't see him.

"Hey baby, I'm here, I beamed and yelled. Where was he? I couldn't find him anywhere. He came from the balcony. I bit my bottom lip. I had the biggest smile on my face. He swaggered through the suite like the true boss that he was. He approached me taking me in. He walked around me, making me nervous.

"Damn Riley, you look extra sexy today. I love the way my money looks on you. I got to make sure I get you pregnant to-night," he explained and slurred. I could tell Boss had a few drinks in him. I knew it was about to go down. I could smell the alcohol on his breath.

"Hush Boss," I beamed. He stuck his finger in my dim-ples. His hands roamed my body. I must admit Boss is so damn handsome. He's very easy on the eyes. He's 6'3, built like a foot-ball player, bald head, and fine as fuck. He's clean cut and doesn't have a hood swag. He's on his grown man shit. He doesn't mind getting his hands dirty. He'll rock some Jordan's and a fitted hat on a low-key day.

"Come here and sit on daddy's lap. Give me a kiss Riley, and make it extra wet," he said. We started tongue fucking. He had me so fuckin' hot and bothered. I wanted him to handle this ache between my legs.

"Are you ready to get up out of them clothes, Riley?" He asked. He didn't have to tell me twice. I was ready for whatever.

"You know it," I sassed. I ran my tongue across my top lip. I started squirming in my seat because my pussy was wet, and I could feel my juices touching my legs. I'm done fuckin' with him. I'm hot and bothered.

"I'm going to make you wait for a little," he explained. I wanted to rape him. I don't want to play at all. I hate when he does this. I knew he was tripping because I left this morning.

"Why? I want to fuck now Boss," I asked and whined. I stood up and rested my hands on my hip. If we weren't fuckin' I had to go shower and relieve this orgasm myself.

"You left me early this morning and caught a red-eye flight to Atlanta. Did you think about waking me up to bless me with some pussy before you left? How was your day Riley?" He asked. I feel where he was coming from, but my girl needed me so I'm out.

"Babe, it was so fucking crazy. You don't want to know the half," I explained.

"You right I don't. I do want to know why you're walking around Atlanta looking so sexy?" He asked. I didn't have the answers he wanted. Boss stepped in my personal space, took my crop top off, and tossed it on the floor.

"Riley, oh my. No bra Riley, really?" He asked. He sucked both of my breasts one by one. "You are being a very bad girl." I shook my head yes. I wanted to be really bad for him. He removed my skirt and my ass was exposed. He grabbed a hand full of it. "No panty's Riley, really?" He smacked me on my ass so hard. "You know what? You're straight playing me and being very disrespectful. I must apply pressure to this pussy," he argued. He was squeezing it really hard, juices started to drip out. "Riley, put that pussy on my face." He didn't have to tell me twice.

"Say no more. Your wish is my command." I wrapped my legs around his neck. Jesus Christ! Boss and his tongue. His lips were gripping my pearl so good. He was squeezing my ass and sucking my pussy like a lollipop. Oh my God, cum was dripping out of me like a faucet. His tongue was covered. I shoved his head deeper between my legs.

"Riley, do you want to try some new shit?" He asked. I'm down for whatever. When it comes to him. He has me so wide open.

"I'm tired, Boss." I sighed and yawned.

"I'm not through with your grown ass. Let's make a movie," he explained. He carried me out to the balcony. I was naked as the day I was born. I don't know what he was up to. He must have read my mind. Atlanta was beautiful at night. I loved the way the lights lit up the whole city. The sun just went down. It was perfect. Hopefully, nobody's out here. I didn't want anybody watching us out here fuckin' and we fuck around and make TMZ and The Shade Room.

"Get up there," he instructed. I looked at him with wide eyes. He gave me a stern look. I knew he wasn't playing with me. I did as I was told. I sat on the rail of the balcony. Boss stood in front of me. I tilted my body back a little bit and he shoved his dick inside of me. I tried to match his rhythm praying I wouldn't fall. He fucked my life away. The wind blowing and the tears flowing down my face. I knew Boss was the one if I trusted him to fuck me on the edge of the balcony and I'm afraid of heights. Long as I'm with him I didn't care.

Chapter-11

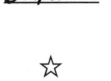

Kaniya

My day started off fucked up, but as soon as Tariq and I laid eyes on each other things were looking up. I forgot all about the bullshit that happened earlier. I haven't stopped smiling since we linked up. Sonja is going to kill me. I already know. She always knew it was something going on between us, but she didn't know what. I don't have my phone, but I wasn't tripping because I knew Lucky would've ruined my moment. I wouldn't have been able to give Tariq my undivided attention and right now I'm glad he had that. He was on to something when he tossed my shit out the window. I know I'm in good hands. He wouldn't let anything happen to me and I wouldn't let anything happen to him. I've been with Tariq since we saw each other earlier.

I've been trying to go home ever since but he's refusing to let me do that. I didn't have a problem being his date. I was very open to that because I'm single as fuck and Tariq is something to fuckin' look at. I just wanted to go home, get dressed, and blush a little tell my girls about my date. That's all I wanted to do. He thought I was trying to get away from him, but I wasn't. Tariq was a real fuckin' boss. I'm not saying that Lucky wasn't because he was. Tariq was that nigga that was cashing the fuck out. He wouldn't let me pay for any of my stuff. I pulled out my debit card, he snatched it right out of my hand and dropped it back in my purse. After we tore down the mall we went and had dinner. It was nice just to catch up and reminisce about old times. We couldn't keep our eyes off each other.

I'm glad Tariq is finally free. I can't lie and say that I'm not enjoying the attention he's giving me because I am. He's always so affectionate with me. He was determined for me to get dressed at his house. Every excuse I had he had a rebuttal. I called Jaiuna to pull up on me to do my hair. I could've done it myself but since Tariq had everything tailored I wanted my hair freshly done. I also wanted my make-up on point. I took a shower before Jaiuna pulled up because I didn't want to mess my hair up. Jaiuna just left and it was time to get dressed because Tariq's party starts in about an hour. I didn't want him late to his own party.

I'm sitting in Tariq's guestroom about to put my clothes on. I dropped my towel to the floor and slid my panties on. I heard the door open. I didn't even bother to turn around because it was just us here. I knew it was him.

I felt him walk up behind me. Damn Tariq's dick was long and thick. I felt it through his slacks. He wrapped his hands around my waist and bit down on the crook of my neck. His hands massaged my breasts. I wish he would stop because the juices from my pussy were dying to be freed. I tried to free myself from him, but he wouldn't ease up. This is one of the reasons why I couldn't be alone with him. He was coming on too strong and some shit would happen that didn't need to happen.

"Tariq, can you please stop. This is why I wanted to get dressed at home. You don't know how to keep your hands to yourself," I sighed to keep from moaning. He was turning me on in the worst way and the last thing I wanted him to hear was a moan escaping from my lips.

"I can't keep my hands to myself because they're meant to be on you," he stated and traced his tongue on the side of my neck. I swatted his hands away. Tariq will fuck around have me bent over taking all the dick that he has to offer and right now I don't need that.

"Please stop or we're never going to make it too you're home coming party," I sassed. Tariq wasn't listening because he was still trying to have his way with me.

"We're going to make it. I just can't keep my hands off you. You know I've always been attracted to you. Even though I used to shoot my shot, you use to always curved me. You gave that nigga a fair shot but not me. It was supposed to be me and you a long time ago.

I'm not going to hold that against you but I'm telling you now I want my shot this time. It ain't no excuses because we're both single," he argued and explained. Tariq was doing too much. I understood where he was coming from but damn, he knew my uncle and Sonja wouldn't want that because we raised as family even though we weren't blood.

"I hear you, Tariq." I sighed.

"I know you do, but are you listening?" He asked.

"I am," I sighed. I heard everything that Tariq was saying but damn, Lucky and I just broke up yesterday. The thought of us not being together is still fresh on my mind.

I'm not even trying to think about that right now. Tariq removed himself from behind me. He grabbed my bra off the bed and fastened it on me. I know he wanted a free feel. I looked in the mirror and his eyes were trained on me the whole time. Tariq was so fuckin' fine. I tried to break the stare, but he stopped me.

I turned around to face him. We couldn't keep this up. I folded my arms across my chest. "Can you stop Tariq, just for a minute so I can get dressed?" I asked. Damn, he was going to fuck around and make me come up out these fuckin' panties and bless his ass with some pussy.

"Kaniya, I'm helping you get dressed? What's wrong with that? If I want to look at you in the process, it's nothing that you can do about that. Come here and slide this dress on so we can get out of here since I'm making you uncomfortable and shit," he laughed. I punched Tariq in his shoulder. I slid my dress on and zipped it up from the back. I slid my feet in my heels. I sprayed a few dabs of perfume on. I looked in the mirror one last time to make sure I was on point. Tariq pulled me into his arms, and we sized each other up for a minute. Neither one of us broke the stare. "Kaniya, you're perfect."

"Thank you." Tariq leaned in and gave me a kiss. This time I didn't object. His hands roamed every part of my body. Damn his touch alone felt so good. Tariq finally broke the kiss. I swear it felt like I came up for air. He grabbed my hand and led the way out of the house. I was in my feelings because for some reason I didn't want him to stop. I slid in the passenger seat of his Wraith. He closed the door to make sure I was in safe. He jumped in the driver's seat and pulled off. He grabbed my hand and I refused to look at him. He gave my hand a tight grip and I looked at him out the corner of my eyes. Our eyes had their own conversation. We both wanted each other but neither one of us spoke on it. In a perfect world, we could be together but just not this one.

We finally made it to Tariq's welcome home party. It was held being held at Prive'. Judging by the outside it was already packed to capacity. Tariq pulled up to valet and he threw the attendant his keys. He walked around to the passenger side to scoop me. He grabbed my hand and we headed toward the entrance. We couldn't even make it in because photographers were everywhere snapping pictures of us. We finally made it inside the venue and it was nice. Everybody was draped in all white. Tariq made sure I walked in front of him the whole time. I could get used to this. All eyes were on us.

As soon as we stepped in his VIP section Shaela was looking at us. He wasn't my man, but he wanted to be. I promised myself I would be on my best behavior, but I swear to God if this bitch says the wrong thing to me, I'm busting her in her shit. Tariq must have sensed that I was about to spas because he squeezed my hand. Shaela walked over and approached us.

"Welcome home, Tariq." She beamed. She kept her eyes trained on me. He didn't even acknowledge her. He threw his hands up and we moved around her. We headed over to where John and Mac were sitting and snapped a few pictures. Tariq and I finally took a seat. I wanted to sit beside him, but he made sure I sat on his lap. He was whispering sweet nothings in my ear. I was grinning like a schoolgirl. A female approached us, and my eyes were trained on her. I was having a good time and the last thing I needed was for a bitch to kill my vibe. Tariq looked up and spoke to the female.

"Yirah, what's up? How you been?" He asked. It was something about this bitch. I can't put my finger on it but it's something up with her. Her smile didn't add up. She was talking to Tariq but for some reason, I felt like she was focused on me.

"Welcome home Tariq, I'm good," she beamed. She fucked him with eyes. Maybe I'm tripping or maybe I'm not. I had two shots and Apple Martini. I'll never get drunk because I never know when I'll have to box a bitch out real quick.

"That's what's up, Yirah. I want you to meet my girl Kaniya. Kaniya, this is Yirah. John and Macs' sister," he explained.

"It's nice to meet you, Kaniya. Tariq, she's a good look for you," she beamed and smirked.

"Tell me something I don't know, Yirah. It's not a bitch in here that's weighing up to her," he chuckled. She was throwing shade but if it ain't directed it ain't respected it. I'm glad he checked her because I was about too. She wasn't even weighing up to me. Please don't let this face fool you. Tariq introduced me as his woman all night. I didn't even bother to correct him, but it is what it is. John and Mac joined us and a few other of his homeboys and the photographers snapped a few more pictures. I was so tired of taking pictures.

Tariq wanted us to take a picture together posted up in VIP. I was sitting in his lap and his head was rested in the crook of my neck. His arms were secured around my waist.

He whispered in my ear. "You're all mine forever and a day. This shit we got going on could never be erased." He sent chills through my body. The party was almost over but Tariq and I wanted to leave before everyone else. We were standing out front waiting on the valet attendant to pull around with his Wraith. We were hugged up. I was tired as fuck and I just wanted to go home and lay in my bed. The Valet attendant finally brought Tariq his car. We hopped in and he pulled off.

"Tariq, can you take me home?" I asked. He looked at me out the corner of his eye. We stopped at a red light. I knew he was about to trip.

"I can but I want you to stay with me. I promise I'll be on my best behavior. I just want to hold you. Can I do that?" He asked. Tariq was so fuckin' sexy. How could I say no? It was late anyway, and I didn't have shit to lose. What's the worst that could happen. Lucky has been fuckin' off on me for three months now and I had no clue. As far as I'm concerned, I'm not cheating because we're not together.

"Yeah and you better to be on your best behavior," I sassed. I'm tired and the only thing I want to do is close my eyes and get some sleep.

"Bet," he chuckled. Tariq pulled off in the direction of his house. He stayed about thirty minutes away. I closed my eyes and enjoyed the ride.

I felt the car come to a complete stop. I guess we made it back to his house. I wiped my eyes with the brim of my hands and a soft yawn escaped my lips. Tariq opened the door, picked me up and carried me inside the house. It was freezing in here. He finally sat me down. I didn't have any night clothes. I wanted to take a shower because I smelled like smoke and I hated that.

"Tariq, can you give me a shirt and some boxers? I want to take a shower," I explained.

"Yeah, go ahead in there and I'll bring it to you. I need to cut the air down," he explained. I headed to the guest bathroom. I cut the shower on and adjusted it to my liking. It was hot and I didn't give a fuck about messing my hair up. If it curls up oh well. I handled my hygiene, cut the water off, and stepped out the shower. Tariq was sitting on the toilet waiting for me.

I looked at everything but him. He knew he shouldn't be here. I reached to grab a towel and he snatched it out of my hands and dried me off. His touch was so rough and passionate. My nipples were erect, and he was tracing them with the tips of his index finger. I didn't want this man to explore my body. Finally, my body was dry. I slid into his boxers and threw his T-shirt over me. I headed toward the guest room and he stopped me. I looked at him with wide eyes.

"Stop playing, Kaniya. My room is this way," he explained. I wasn't even about to go back and forth with him. He led the way to his room. I climbed into his bed. It was so fuckin' comfortable. I face the other direction. Tariq scooted up from behind me and wrapped his arms around my waist. He started kissing on my neck. I felt him tug at my boxers. They were halfway down my legs.

"Tariq, can you please stop. I thought you said you were going to keep your hands to yourself," I asked. His hands started massaging my pussy. I was wet instantly. I tried to say a quick prayer, hoping I wouldn't fuck up his sheets.

"I can't help myself. I want to eat, can I do that?" He asked. I knew him keeping his hands to himself was too good to be true.

"Do I have a choice?" I asked. I knew it didn't because Tariq's head was already underneath the covers. The boxers found their way on the floor. My shirt was being raised up over my head.

"Not really but I wanted to ask you anyway," he stated.

"Why do you want to make things complicated?" I asked and sighed. He ignored me. Tariq started sucking my toes. His tongue slithered up my legs. His mouth finally landed between my legs. He sucked the soul out of my pussy. I couldn't even ride his face like I wanted to because I had so many orgasms. I couldn't keep up. His tongue fucked my pussy to perfection. His tongue had it's on melody my hips couldn't stay on beat. I grabbed a handful of his dreads because I couldn't take it. I needed something to hold on to. Tariq finally looked up at me. I bit the inside of my jaw because I didn't want him to see my fuck faces.

"Kaniya, can I make love to you? I promise I'll be gentle and take my time with you," he asked the explained. Tariq grabbed a condom off his nightstand and tore the wrapper open with his teeth. It was sexy.

"Sex complicates things Tariq, and you know it won't end here. We shouldn't," I moaned. He wouldn't let me get another word out. He pushed me back on his bed. He started sucking on my nipples. His dick found my hole and he was trying to fit his dick inside of me. I opened my legs to give him more access. Finally, after a few attempts, he was able to get inside of me. I couldn't move because his dick was so big. I could feel all of it. He threw my legs over his shoulders and started sliding in and out of me. Tariq hit me with long and deep passionate death strokes. The only sounds you could hear were my juices coating his dick. Grunts and moans were escaping both our lips.

I raised up and wrapped my arms around his neck. I started doing squats on his dick. His eyes rolled in the back of his head. We were in a stare off. His tongue traced my bottom lip before it finally found its way inside of my mouth. Our mouth and bodies were in tune with each other. I matched him stroke for stroke. Our kisses intensified my orgasms. I came so many times. I stopped fuckin' counting. Sex with Tariq was so fuckin' amazing. It's everything I thought it would be and some. We made love until the sun came up.

Chapter-12

Tianna

Damn the cat is out of the bag. I've never been the type to keep secret's, but this relationship shit is new to me. The last thing I want for myself is to be claiming a nigga as mine and he's out here doing him. I know every nigga isn't the same but the majority of them are. I'm not saying that Quan is, but Lucky is his brother and the two of them are together every day because they're close. Quan is real about his shit, that's why we click. He told me he had a bitch with him at the park. He knew I was going to trip. Kaniya is going to be pissed when she finds out how long I've been in Atlanta.

Kaniya and I have never been on a double date with Quan and Lucky. Lucky knows Kaniya and I are best friends. I don't like the company that Lucky and Quan keep. They own a club and they're in the studio a lot late at night. You know hoes love a nigga that raps and are upcoming artists. I was moving with caution. When I thought about it, the bitch Kaniya beat up came to the house before with Lucky. He said it was his cousin and he was giving her a ride home.

That's a lying ass nigga and that lil bitch was dumb. She was agreeing to what the fuck he was saying. I'm glad she got her ass beat. My house was not too far from Kaniya's. It was about thirty minutes away. I wanted to be close to her unless something happened. I can't wait to see Quan and jump on him. Quan is so fuckin' sexy to me. Tall, dark and handsome. He's built really nice, solid muscles, and tattoos that cover his whole body. He's a real Atlanta nigga born and raised. A Robin Jeans junky.

Quan knows he's fine. He's a cocky nigga. That's why I made sure when he saw me I knew he would've been hotter than fish grease. I told him when I was pulling up not have any bitches in his face and his shirt better be on, and we wouldn't have any problems. That's too much like right for him and he did the complete opposite. That's why I hopped out the truck so quick just to let him know. I wasn't fuckin' playing. He had a smirk on his face until he seen my feet touch the pavement and what I had on. He saw those niggas and his niggas was checking for me.

I already know it's about to be some shit when I get home. Quan and I are just alike. Both Scorpios. He's petty and so am I. We must grow up for the sake of our child. I finally pulled up to the home we shared.

I dreaded going in because I already knew we were about to be at each other's neck. To make matters worse this nigga beat me home. Oh wow and he's standing in the door. I could tell he was on one. I could feel the tension just by his stare and gaze. He walked up to the truck to meet me halfway. So much for pulling in the garage. He snatched the door open.

"Hey Quan," I sighed. I knew it was about to be a long night. I was scared to get out of the truck. He snatched the keys out the engine and grilled the fuck out of me.

"Don't fucking hey me, Tianna. You got me so fucked up right now. Why in the fuck do you have this shit on and you pregnant with my seed?" He asked and argued. I was about to respond but he cut me off before I had the chance to. "Talk Tianna, dick got your fucking tongue?" I jumped out of the car instantly because he wasn't about to be talking to me like I'm fuckin' crazy. I wasn't having that shit at all. I didn't even grab my purse because if he says the wrong thing, I swear to God I'm going to forget that he's my child's father and slap the shit out of him. I know he's mad but calm down.

"Hold up Quan, watch your fucking mouth. I'm not that big bird bitch you were with earlier," I argued and sassed. He got me fucked up. He can't handle me the way he handles his other bitches. He laughed in my face pissing me off even more.

"I never said you were Big Bird, you said that not me. What I will say is watch how the fuck you talk to me while you are carrying my child. Don't ever in your life come to Mozely

Park with my shit on display. The moment I put my seed in you Tianna you became mine. I saw you cheesing in that fuck niggas face then you climbed on his motorcycle. You know I'm crazy as fuck. What if I would've murdered that nigga in broad daylight? You know I don't give a fuck, right? I ain't with that friendly shit. I'm done with the fuckin' games," he argued. I stepped back a few steps. He closed the gap between us and invaded my personal space.

He grabbed my thighs and he unbuckled my shorts. His hands massaged my pussy. I'm not trying to do this while we're outside in front of our house. I tried to swat his hands away, but he had a death grip on my pussy lips. The strokes of fingers went from slow to fast. I felt an orgasm coming. He plays too much.

"Quan, can you please stop?" I asked and moan. I hate when he thinks that sex solves everything between us, and it didn't. I grabbed his dick and started stroking it. He stopped thank God.

I made my way toward the house. We didn't need to be outside of the house like this. I took a seat on the sofa and he stood in between my legs. He cupped my chin forcing me to look at him. I held my head down because I wasn't about to do this with him.

"Look at me when I'm fuckin' talking to you. You wanted my attention, Tianna. You for damn sure got it. You tried me for the last fucking time. I'm tired of this back and forth shit with you. Either we're going to be together or we're not. I'm not going to keep doing this shit with you. I'm handsome as fuck. All these bitches out here going wild behind a nigga like me. I can have any bitch I want to but I choose you. I'm not going to keep waiting. So, what is it what's it going to be?" He asked and pointed at my heart? Did this nigga just read me?

"Why does everything have to be on your terms Quan? What the fuck did I tell you about having your shirt off and cheesing in a bitch's face? If you want me, you have a funny way of showing it. Do you know how many niggas are checking for me? You're not the only one with fuckin' options. Can you be faithful and commit to just me?" I asked. Quan and I were in a stare off. I was searching his face for a lie and any deceit. I swear he doesn't want to fuck over me, and he's knocked me up on purpose.

"I'll get rid of the bitches, but my body I got to show it off until you stop playing games," he explained. I stood up from the couch and smacked him in the face. Stop fuckin' playing with me. I swear he so fuckin' petty. He knows how to get under my skin.

"You know what Quan I feel the same way about showing my ass and breasts off," I sassed and sucked my teeth. I gave him a devilish smirk. He was hot now because I hit a nerve.

"What are you trying to do, Tianna? Do you want me to body a nigga, huh?" He asked and argued. He can do what he wants. That has nothing to do with me. "Is that what you want Tianna? You want my son to grow up without me?" Of course, I didn't want that, but he was the one playing games.

"Did I say that? Don't put words in my mouth." I argued and sassed.

"Act like it," he argued. He stood in between my legs giving himself easy access. He started finger fuckin' me wet. My eyes rolled in the back of my head. His touch alone felt so good. He yanked my shorts off.

"Stop playing with me, Tianna. I swear to God you will get a nigga killed looking at you and just thoughts of fuckin with you," he argued. He grabbed my pussy and I gazed up at him. "This right here is deadly. Answer my question, Tianna. What do you want to do? Are you cool with being my baby momma?" He asked.

"I want to be with you Quan," I sighed. I love Quan and he's the only nigga that I've dated that I didn't get bored with. I can be myself with him. We're not perfect but we can be for each other. Neither one of us wanted to see the other with anyone else.

"About fucking time. Big Bird made you step your game up. Get over here and ride this motherfuckin' dick," he argued. He was fuckin' stupid. He didn't have to tell me twice. Quan and I fucked and sucked each other all night long until the sun came up. Neither one of us was ready to tap out. We both had something to prove. He carried me upstairs to our bathroom and placed me in the tub. He joined me and washed my whole body up. I was sore as fuck. He fucked the shit out of me. I rested my head back on his chest. He leaned in and kissed me.

"I'm happy, Tianna. I'm glad you're at home where you belong. I love you and I want you to be Mrs. Williams soon," he explained

"Awe, I love you too, Quan." We started back kissing each other. I heard the doorbell ring, and somebody started banging at the door. I looked at Quan and he looked at me. I swear to God it better not be a bitch at our door looking for him. It had to be about 5:00 a.m. If a bitch came here looking for him at our home, it was about to go down.

"Quan, who is banging on our door. Is that Big Bird, you got me fucked up? You just were pouring your heart out now some bitch is banging on our door like she's the fuckin' police," I argued.

"Chill out baby. I would never do that or bring anybody to where we lay our head at. Stay here I'm going to see who it is," he explained. He a motherfuckin' lie I wanted to know who was at my door this time of morning and they just interrupted our make-out session. I had some words for their ass.

"Fuck that, I'm riding shotgun with you," I argued. I jumped out of the tub. Quan grabbed my robe and handed it to me. We grabbed our straps and headed for the door.

"Kaniya, I know you hear me," he yelled. Those are the only words we could make out as we approached the door. I looked at Quan and he looked at me and I headed right back upstairs.

I wasn't beat for Lucky's shit. He's looking for Kaniya and she isn't here. Lucky' s dumb ass was banging on the door. I guess Kaniya didn't go home last night. I wondered where she stayed. I hope Tariq buried his dick deep between those thighs last night.

"Baby, I'll let you handle that," I sighed. I walked back upstairs toward our room. I stood by the staircase. I wanted to hear what Lucky's dumb ass had to say. Kaniya got Lucky looking bad out here in these streets pulling up at people's houses and shit.

"Lucky, what the fuck nigga? What the fuck are you doing banging on my door this early in the morning like you're the fuckin' police?" He argued.

"Yo Quan, what the fuck is my bitch doing at your crib?" He argued and asked. Lucky was drunk. I could see and hear it. He needs to lower his fuckin' voice when he's talking to my man. Brother or not I'll cuss his ass out. I don't give a fuck. That's what he gets for cheating. It doesn't feel good when just the thought of your girl fuckin' somebody else.

"Lucky, you're crazy as fuck. Kaniya isn't here. Tianna's driving her truck. You're crazy as fuck and I mean that shit. Bruh do you have a tracker on her truck?" He asked and laughed. I wanted to hear what he had to say.

"I do," he argued and slurred. I fuckin' knew it. Lucky was crazy as fuck. Tariq was smart as fuck because Lucky was out in the streets looking for Kaniya. If he wasn't home, she was with someone else.

"Lucky, bruh, let that shit go, she'll be back," he argued. Quan was trying to calm Lucky down, but that shit wasn't working at all. I hope Kaniya doesn't take Lucky back since Quan is so sure of it. Not my bitch not right now anyway.

"Tell Tianna to call her phone for me because she's not answering, and she didn't go home last night," he argued. I tiptoed back in our room and acted as if I wasn't listening. I wasn't getting in the middle of that. He already put me in it when he brought that bitch to my home and lied about who she was. I would never break bread or share a meal with a bitch that was fuckin' my girl's man. I don't give a fuck.

"I'm not doing that Lucky, we're on some us shit right now. Kaniya can handle herself. If she calls Tianna I 'll make sure she calls you," he explained. I would make that nigga sweat since he fucked up.

"Alright Quan, good looking out," he stated. I don't know why Quan lied. I wasn't looking out for his ass. Fuck him and the bitch he was fuckin'. Quan made his way in our bedroom, stripped naked and climbed in the bed behind me.

. "What did he want?" I asked. I knew what he wanted. I just wanted Quan to tell me.

"Kaniya," he laughed. Niggas ain't shit. They fuck up and get mad when you're doing what he was doing.

"Ugh, he needs to move the fuck on. I'm telling Kaniya to get rid of that truck too. His sneaky ass has a tracker on it," I argued. It's not fair he can keep tabs on her, but she can't keep tabs on him.

"How you know," he asked. I knew before Lucky confirmed. I just wanted him to confirm it.

"I just do. He's crazy, ugh, and I can't believe he's your brother. Let me ask you something, Quan," I explained. I wanted to see if he would lie to me or not. I'm sure he would cover for his brother because I would cover for Kaniya.

"Go ahead," he stated.

"Did you know that Lucky was cheating on Kaniya? It's funny the same bitch he brought to the house and said was his cousin he was fuckin'. She's the same bitch Kaniya had to box out earlier," I argued. I could feel Quan's body tense up which confirmed my suspicions.

"I don't know what Lucky has going on. I don't want us involved," he explained. I wasn't about to stress it at all. I just hope it doesn't come back and bite me in the ass.

Lucky

☆

Kaniya got me fucked up. Yes, I fucked up but don't go out and do what the fuck I'm doing. I swear to God if she fucked that nigga I'm going to fuckin' hurt her and kill him. You can't do what the fuck I do. Stay in your place and let me right my wrongs and make that shit up to you. I want to beg for her forgiveness and spoil the fuck out of her. I'm your fuckin' man no matter what. It ain't over until I say it's fuckin' over. I was posted up at her crib until the wee hours in the morning and she never came home. It's the second night in a row I've been here, and she wasn't. Where is she laying her fuckin' head at? I've been calling her phone since I heard she was hugged up with that nigga at the park and she hasn't answered or responded. I know she's mad, but she still needs to answer to me. It ain't no excuse because we're not throwing way shit.

My phone alerted me a text was coming through from Yirah. Shawty was texting my phone all night but I wasn't re-sponding because I was at Kaniya's and that shit is disrespectful as fuck. A nigga wasn't even trying to do that at all. I haven't even pulled off from Quan's street yet. I stopped at the stop sign to see what she wanted. I looked at my phone and damn near lost it. It was several pictures of Kaniya, and Tariq hugged up. I'm going to fuckin' kill her because she knows better. I'm trying to see why this nigga is so fuckin' comfortable hugging on my fuckin' woman and we're together? A nigga can't dap hands with me and try to take my bitch. It's not going down like that. It's the perfect way to sign your death certificate. I don't give a fuck what Kaniya told that nigga. It wasn't going down like that at all. I grabbed my phone to call Yirah. I never used shawty's number until now. We always flirted through text and DM'S.

"What's good shawty, you've been blowing me up all night. What are those pictures about? Where did you get those from?" I asked.

"Good morning to you too. I thought you would call me. I guess you saw something in a few of those pictures that piqued your interest," she sassed. I knew Yirah wanted to fuck with me and I wanted to fuck with her too, but I couldn't. Melanie already ruined something by not staying in her fuckin' place. The last thing I want Kaniya to think that it's over and she's free to flaunt another nigga in my face and she fuckin' can't. I don't want her to think that I don't give a fuck about fuckin' up our relationship because I do.

"Yeah I did, but you already know that. That's why you sent it. Cut the bullshit and let's get straight to it. Where the fuck were you last night? Why were you snapping pics of my girl?" I asked. I heard Yirah let out a little smirk and she sucked her teeth.

I never took her as the type to be ghetto and shit but hey a bitch will reveal thier true colors when dick is a possibility and they want something.

"Lucky, why are you so mad? I don't like your tone. I was just looking out for you. I guess I should've kept the photos to myself sorry. We were at Tariq's Welcome Home Party. John and Mac are my brother's and they're Tariq's best friends. I was under the impression that you were single because Tariq introduced Kaniya as his girlfriend and not once did she correct him. She asked me to take the photos of them," she explained. I don't even lay hands on female's, but I swear I will fuck Kaniya up. I swear I'm going to fuckin' hurt her when I lay eyes on her. She wanted to break up so she could be with that nigga as soon as he got out of jail. It's not coincidental.

"I appreciate the drop but I'm going to hit you up and get up with you later," I argued. I ain't got time to be yapping on the phone with Yirah. I got to find Kaniya's ass.

"Wait Lucky, hold up. I'm sorry I shouldn't have done that because I know what she means to you and the last thing I'm trying to do is fuck up your relationship. Let me make it up to you please. I don't want you to do nothing crazy because that'll be on my conscience," she explained.

"Oh yeah, how do you plan on making something up to me?," I asked. I knew Yirah wanted me, but I had a situation. Unlike Melanie, Yirah was a good girl and I didn't want me to ruin her.

"I'm going to send you my address and you'll have to find out and see," she cooed.

"Your address? What I would need that for?" I asked. My phone alerted me that I had a message.

"Check the message I just sent you and see," she cooed. I checked my iMessage to see what Yirah sent me and it was a video of her playing in her pussy. I could hear how wet that motherfucka was. I just shook my head. Gawd damn. "Lucky did you see it?" Hell, yeah, I saw it.

"Yeah, I saw it. You're giving it up like that huh?" I asked. I never knew Yirah was a freak.

"Umm huh I want you to take all your frustrations out on me and not her," she cooed.

"Aiight, bet. I'm going to pull up and handle that."

"I'm waiting," she sighed.

A FEW WEEKS LATER

Chapter-13

Kaniya

BAby, when I say I was feeling Tariq something serious. I couldn't stop thinking about him. He was always on my mind. I don't know what this man was doing to me, but I don't want him to stop. I like it because it feels different. Every morning I woke up to a Good Morning Beautiful text. Every other night I was waking up in his arms. If I'm dreaming someone needs to catch me. Breakups are hard and I'm not even going to lie and say I haven't thought about Lucky because I have. He's the reason why I ended up here. I think about his ass every day. I wonder what drove him to cheat. Was it me? What would make him do that to me?

Being with Tariq is different. I wasn't trying to compare the two, but Lucky could've been honest about what the fuck he had going on instead of having me out here looking like a fool. If you can't keep it real with yourself about what's going on, then you can't keep it real with anybody else. I'm good on Lucky. I haven't seen him nor heard from him. Tariq and I have been kicking it heavy since we had our link up at Mozley Parks three weeks ago. I bit my bottom lip and squeezed my legs tight just thinking about him.

We've been kicking it strong at least three days out of the week. He makes time for me every week. I was feeling that. Yes, we've made love and it was amazing. I'm keeping that on the hush and to myself. I haven't told a soul and I'm taking it to the grave. Tariq wants to be more than just friends. It was amazing how he's been blowing my back out every week. I swear he has my mind gone between his affection, the head, and his dick alone. I've been busy with Work Now Atlanta and anything else to keep my mind off him.

The night we went to his Welcome Home Party his only focus was me and it has been ever since. He didn't give a fuck about anybody being there. He was showing out because he wanted everybody how much he loved me and how much he was into me.

This man got my head gone for real, and that's real talk. I never doubted that Tariq cared about me or loved me because he's always been that way. Now that Lucky and I aren't together he doesn't have to mask it and he's out in the open with it. Lucky is the only man I've ever loved and been with besides Tariq. Sometimes you can't help who you're attracted to, but I can't deny the chemistry we have is something serious. I tried to hold back but damn he was too irresistible and I wanted it. I needed it. Temptation is a bitch but I wanted to take it there with him. It's not that I was vulnerable. I wanted to experiment with Tariq a long time ago. I wanted to see if he could work the pipe that's lying between his legs. He could very well. He had me doing shit I never thought I would do.

Lucky didn't give a fuck about cheating so why should I give a fuck? I can do what I want if we're not together, but damn I know it no coming back from that. Men can cheat and expect women to forgive them. As soon as a woman treats a man how they treat her it's a fuckin' problem. It is what is. I'll just have to deal with the consequences. I dealt with them in the club when he embarrassed me. His friends and mine knew he was cheating. He was out in the open for everybody and their fuckin' momma to see. I was still being tagged on Instagram and Facebook reminding me of the fight.

What am I supposed to do? I don't want to be judged for dick hopping so soon, but damn I could see myself being with him. I've only been with two men in my life and that's Lucky and

Tariq. Sometimes you must let shit be and whatever happens, happen. I was scared at first because I knew I would like that shit too much. Oh my gosh, I had to squeeze my legs together and fan my pussy just thinking about our intense sex sessions. I got hot instantly just thinking about him. My pussy is going to get me in trouble. Tariq wants me to spend the night with him tonight, but I can't because these legs will be open all night. I wish Barbie and Ketta were here. I can't believe those two heifers fuckin' left me. I wanted to go to New York my damn self. I wanted me a nigga from Up top. I haven't gotten a text, Facetime, and I miss you Kaniya, video or nothing. I can't complain though.

I see how it feels when bitches are booed up and shit. I need to text those tricks and see what they're up to. I need to fill them in on my dilemma. I hope they bring me back a few bags and a couple of pairs of shoes. That's the least they can do. I need to send a text to Tianna and see what's up with her. Riley told me that she was pregnant by Quan. She also stated they had a house down here. Tianna failed to mention any of that to me. Sneaky ass. I wanted me a nephew anyway. I'm glad she locked Quan down. Lord knows he's fine.

Lucky ☆

I wish I could say life's good minus the bullshit but it's not. Melanie, she's getting on my last, fuckin' nerves and Yirah's cool. I've been kicking it with the two of them lately. I haven't seen or heard from Kaniya in a few weeks. It's safe to say that she's been dodging the kid. I know she's been back staying at her house. I had one of my partners follow her home a few nights ago. I knew she had blocked me because all my calls were going straight to her voicemail. We needed to have a serious conversation. I'm tired of not speaking about what the fuck is going on between us. Today was the day. I knew she was at home and I had planned on catching her ass early this morning to see what the fuck she was up too.

I looked at the time on my Rolex and it was a little after 7:00 a.m. I knew she was still asleep. Kaniya was screaming that she wanted her keys back. I wasn't giving shit back. Kaniya and I stayed about thirty minutes away from me each other. I was pissed when she brought her first house because I felt that we should live together since we've been together for so long but

Kaniya refused to move in with me if we weren't married. I understood what she was saying but I wasn't ready to marry her. I'm not trying to go down that road yet.

I pulled up to Kaniya's house and I could tell she's been home because her blinds were pulled back. That only meant she was already up, or she forgot to close them last night. I unlocked the door and I didn't smell any breakfast cooking which means she's still asleep. I headed upstairs to her room and she was asleep. I stood in front of her bed and watched her. I stripped down to my boxers. I pulled the covers back and climbed in bed right in front of her. I always loved to watch her while she was sleeping. This morning would be no different.

Kaniya was tossing and turning in her sleep. She was naked as the day she was born. I wanted to taste that pussy for breakfast. My head got lost between her sheets. I threw her legs over my shoulder. I wanted to finger fuck her wet, but I wanted to wake her up with head for breakfast. My head found its way between her legs and I licked her pussy slow. She started to ride my face. Kaniya was wet as fuck. She must be having a wet dream. I heard her laughing in her sleep. I raised up from under the covers and she had the biggest smile on her face. I ran my tongue across her lips.

"Tariq, stop." She cooed. A frown and scowl instantly appeared on my face. Oh, she said the wrong motherfuckin' thing. The only thing she said right was to stop. She shouldn't even be dreaming about this nigga period. I slapped Kaniya in her face. It wasn't hard just enough to wake her disrespectful ass up. I didn't even leave a mark on her and I should've, but I didn't. I swear I didn't even come over here to fight. I wanted her attention because she for damn sure wanted mine. I smacked her again this time adding a little pressure to it. She was waking up.

"Kaniya wake your motherfuckin ass up," I argued. She jumped up instantly. I pressed her body back down on the bed so she wouldn't fuckin' move. She grilled me with an evil glare.

"Lucky, you better get the fuck off me right fuckin' now. Let me go. Why are in my fuckin' face? Keep your hands to yourself. Whatever bitch you've been laying with for the past couple of weeks go sneak in her fuckin' bed and get the fuck up out of mine," she argued. "Love doesn't fuckin' live here anymore." She argued. Kaniya got me fucked up. She couldn't even look at me while she said that shit. I cupped her face roughly forcing her to look at me. Our eyes locked with each other.

"Kaniya, you know I love you and only you. I did some fucked up shit. I'm sorry but what the fuck you do you mean love doesn't live here anymore? I put in to much time to just say fuck it and move on. If it's that easy for you to leave you never wanted to be here in the first place. You were just wasting my time so, you could be with Tariq when he got out? It's funny as fuck that we broke up and the next day you're on this niggas dick like you don't fuckin' belong to me. Have you fucked him Kaniya? You're mad as fuck because I woke you up from your wet dream.

I swear to God had I known you were at his Welcome Home party I would've murdered that nigga and made you and his niggas fuckin' watch. It's levels to this shit and guess what? That nigga doesn't want to get on my fuckin' level. A nigga can't shake hands with me and attempt to fuck you without any repercussions," I argued and pleaded. If Kaniya fucked Tariq I'm going to hurt her ass and kill him.

"Lucky, I'm not going to tell you anymore. Leave and leave my key while you're at it. Why should I care? I said what I had to say a few weeks ago and I'm done talking. You didn't give a fuck about our five years. You fucked a bitch for three months and I didn't know. You were out in the open showing her the same affection you showed me. Melanie didn't owe me any loyalty, you did.

Tariq doesn't have shit to do with you and me. If you're mad at anybody, be mad at you're motherfuckin' self. I'm single and so are you. You're free to fuck any bitch you want to. You have been doing it so, don't stop now because I found out about it. Cheating is only fun when the motherfucka you're cheating on has no clue. I don't have to do what you did," she argued. Kaniya flipped me on my backside and jumped out the bed. She grabbed her robe and tried to cover up her body. I was right on her heels. "Put your pants back on Lucky and your shoes. You ain't got to go home but you have to get the fuck up out of here," she argued. I grabbed Kaniya by her arm and she snatched it from me. I backed her in the corner of her room. She folded her arms across her chest. I don't give a fuck about her being mad.

"You said what the fuck had to say, now listen to what the fuck I got to say. You can take it how you fuckin' want too. Did you fuck him? Answer that. You act like I'm not sorry about what the fuck I did, but I am. It ain't no fuckin' breaking' up. I'll break your fuckin' neck before I let that happen," I argued. I cupped her chin roughly. "Did you fuck him, Kaniya?" I wanted her to answer that question. That's the only thing I fuckin' wanted to know.

"No, and get the fuck out my face before I shoot your motherfuckin' ass. Keep your hands to yourself. I put it on your fuckin' momma if you touch me the wrong way again you won't be able to use your hands to touch another bitch. Try me I'm begging you to. I'm sick of you. I swear to God I am. A person's true colors always come out when they're guilty," she argued and pushed me in my fuckin' chest. "LEAVE LUCKY, I hate you," she cried. Kaniya saying she hates me fucked with my heart. I ain't never heard her say no shit like that before. I grabbed her fist to stop her from punching me. I pulled her into my chest. I rubbed her back and removed a few strands of hair. I whispered in her ear.

"I'm sorry, Kaniya. You may not believe me, but I am. I fucked up and I want us to make up. I love you and these bitches out here don't mean shit to me. You know you got my heart and you know that one day I plan to make you my wife. Stop crying, please. I'm going to get right."

"I need space, Lucky. I was fine before you came here. I was able to cope with us not being together. Actions speak louder than words. Can you please leave. You're making things even more complicated," she cried. I wiped her tears. I swear that shit was fuckin' with me. Kaniya and I have had plenty of disagreements but none of them have led us here to fussing and damn near fighting.

"I can't leave you like this, Kaniya. I'll give you some space. I fucked up and I get it but it's my job to make sure that you're straight," I explained. Even though we're going through our shit. I never wanted Kaniya to cry and hurt because of me.

"I'm fine and the longer you stay here the more it hurts," she cried. I swear I didn't want to leave but she wanted me to, and I wasn't going to beg her to stay. I wasn't giving her my key back. If she said she didn't fuck Tariq, I'll take her word for it. It better not come back that she did because I will murder his ass. I kissed Kaniya on her forehead and made my way out the door. Hopefully, the next time we see each other it won't be like this. I love Kaniya. I really do but I still have some playing to do. I got to tighten up. She was never supposed to find out about my infidelities.

I know she's going through some shit because we've never been in this type of space. I wish I could help sort through our bullshit, but she doesn't even want me around. I'll give her a little space. Maybe a few more days but that's fuckin' it. The next time I come around I don't care about her crying or none of that shit. She can cry on me. I hate to see her daydreaming about another man that's not me.

Chapter-14

Ketta

Barbie and I have been in New York for almost a month now. I'm glad she came with us. I loved coming to New York because the vibe was always cool. Don and I always had the best dates while we were here. I only had two weeks for my vacation, and I've maxed that out. I told Don that I had to get back to work, but he wasn't trying to hear that at all. Don didn't want me to work. He was a real boss and long as I've been with him, he's always stated that he didn't want his woman working for anybody but herself or working with him to establish a business. I heard him but I wasn't trying to hear him.

I still had bills to pay and I didn't want to depend on him. Don paid everything and told me to stop tripping. My savings was nice, so I wasn't tripping about that. I liked working for Emory hospital because it's one of the best hospitals in Atlanta. I work with some cool ass doctors. I miss being at work and handling my business. I loved being with Don every day too. I guess I couldn't have both. Barbie and I were sitting out on the front of Don's Brownstone while **Destiny Child I Need A Soldier** was playing on **Pandora Radio.** Barbie and I started singing along right with the music.

"I like them boys up top from the BK," I sung in my Beyoncé voice. Barbie and I slapped hands with each other. I had Don and she had Julius. We could both stake claim to that. Julius and Barbie were really vibing.

"I'm so glad I came to New York, Ketta. You put me on in a major way. Julius has been bussing down on any and every-thing. He's not even checking the price. He's my type of guy. I can get used to this. He told me if I play my cards right the ball was in my court," she explained. Don and Julius were brothers and if he was feeling her and fuckin' with her though he's not go-ing to put a limit on anything.

"New York is cool though. Don and I come here twice a month," I explained. I'm glad Barbie was here because I'm al-ways the only female when Don and I are here. He's always run-ning around handling business. It was a business trip, so I under-stood that he had things he needed to handle. I was never coming in between how he eats.

"Damn, you guys are going strong Ketta, with your secre-tive ass," she stated. I beamed proudly. Kaniya is my best friend and I met Barbie through her. She's cool so we clicked instantly.

Since she's going to be around I don't mind giving her the details on my relationship. Judging by the looks of her and Julius she's not going anywhere.

"Yes, we've been together for a little over six months," I swore I wasn't keeping count, but I was. Don and I are taking it one day at a time. One day at a time has led us to the best six months of my life.

"You've been keeping secrets, bitch." She laughed. It wasn't a secret because if you ask Don who he's with he'll gladly tell you and it's the same way with me. My circle is small so I'm never going to boast about us but when you see us, you'll know what it is.

"Whatever but do you see him when you're out?" I asked. I never got the vibe that Don was a cheater but after the stunts, Lucky pulled you could never be sure. I hate to compare Lucky to Don, but it is what it is.

"I do but it's the same way he was at Blue Flame. He's always solo if he's not with Julius that's how he always is. Trust me if I had I wouldn't hesitate to let you know. I've never seen him on some creep shit like Lucky's trifling ass. I think you have a good one. He might even be your husband," she explained.

"I hope so because he wants me to move in with him," I mentioned. I always wanted to live in New York. I love everything that New York has to offer. I just never thought it would happen. I love Don and I've been thinking about it. He's always willing to compromise for me so it's only right I do the same for him.

"You're probably already living with him," she stated. I knew Barbie was looking for a hint.

"I am," I beamed and advised. I hated sleeping without Don at night. When he was out hustling in these streets, he wanted me at home waiting on him. I was his purpose for making it home.

"I need a Xan fucking with you. Please don't throw any more shit on me tonight, ok." She laughed. She asked if I was just being honest with her. "What bar are we going to?"

"This spot in Tribeca." Tribeca is an upscale spot that Don and I have eaten up there a few times.

"What should I wear?" She asked. Barbie brought tons of clothes and we've been shopping every day. Shit, I feel like Keri in sex in the city.

"Get clean bitch. We're out of town, in New York might I add."

"Okay, I'm going to wear this red fitted Kate Spade New York Open Mini Dress and pair it with my Black Louboutin Zoulou strappy sandals. Then I'll flat iron my hair bone straight," she explained. Barbie could dress. I'm sure she's about to fuck it up tonight.

"Okay Bitch, I see you. I'm wearing a white BCBG High Low Dress and pairing it with a fresh pair of Christian Louboutin Gold Nicole Mesh Cage Red Sole Sandals. Do you mind putting rods in my hair? I want the wand curl look and doing my make up?" I asked.

"You Know It. Tonight It's going to be a Zoo-vie," she beamed. Barbie could do hair and makeup like no other. I wish she would open a hair and make-up bar. Let me text Julius and give him Barbie's colors she's wearing tonight. He wanted to match her fly. "Yass Bitch Yass! Let's pregame a little bit before we leave so I can get my nerves in check. Let's take a couple of shots. Grab the Don Julio." Barbie filled the glasses to the brim. We both tossed one back and I poured up another round. I was feeling good.

"Okay, it's getting hot in here. It's been a change of plans, you can ride with Julius and Don and I are going to ride together," I explained. Barbie looked at me with wide eyes. Don and I had a separate date.

"Girl, what car does Julius have? We've been riding with you guys everywhere," she asked. Julius has plenty of cars. He just picks and chooses what he wants to drive.

"The purpose of the trip was to pick up his car," I explained.

"Oh Okay, let me go ahead and get dressed so I can do your hair and makeup. I'll see you in a few," she explained. I needed to do the same. I wanted to be ready when Don pulled up. I missed him so much.

"Don't take forever," I stated. I'm so glad Barbie came out here with me. It's cool to have a female you know out here. She's going to kill me if she finds out that Julius doesn't have any plans to let her go back to Atlanta. He wants her to stay in New York. She always said she wanted to leave Atlanta, but I don't think a permanent move to New York was in the equation. He's crazy as hell, seriously. I knew that he liked her, but damn don't force a bitch to be with you. She's going to go fucking nuts when she realizes what the fuck he's trying to do. She wanted me to hook her up with him. I did what she asked me to do and Julius is playing for keeps.

Chapter-15

Barbie

New York was cool. I loved being here. The vibe and atmosphere were different. Ketta and I are having a great time. I can't even lie. Every day we're doing something that I never thought I'd be doing. The shopping and eating at different restaurants were minor. The bonus is I haven't had to pay for anything. Julius covered everything. He's been spoiling me like crazy. He's everything I thought he would be and more.

We've been spending a lot of time together. I just wish we would've acted on each other a lot sooner. I've never been afraid to approach any man before or go after what I wanted. Julius was a different breed. I just wanted to move a little different with him. We both felt the same way about each other. We came to that agreement a few nights ago. We haven't had sex yet but it's tempting.

I finished applying the final touches to my hair and makeup. After I finish with Ketta's hair and makeup I'll put my clothes on. I threw on one of Julius shirts and a pair of shorts. I didn't want my clothes smelling like hair. I headed out of Julius room to search for Ketta.

"Ketta, are you almost ready so, I can do your hair and makeup?" I asked. Ketta didn't take as long as I did to get dressed so I'm sure she's almost done.

"Yes, I'm putting my lotion and perfume on," she explained. I laid out all my accessories because I wanted to be ready when Julius pulled up. I haven't seen him all day. I missed him.

"Okay, let me know when you finish. Julius sent me a text and he said he'll be here in a few," I explained. More than likely he was already in route.

"I'm ready, you can come in now. I have the water hot," she yelled. I entered Ketta and Don's room she looked so fuckin' pretty. Don was in love with Ketta. I loved how he looked at her. I knew she was going to be his wife. They complemented each other well.

"You look cute Barbie," she beamed.

"Thank you, you look cute too. How do you want your make up?" I asked. I wanted to add some colors to Ketta's face because she always went with a nude or natural look.

"I have on white and gold. So just give me a natural nude beat. Gold eyeshadow, of course, makes it pop. I want a little length to my eyelashes. You should really open your own Make-up Bar. I'm tired of hearing myself talk. You do make up good as fuck," she explained. I might do it since she believes in me and she wants to see me get it done.

"Thank you, but you know I don't like people though," I laughed and explained. I love make-up, hair, and fashion but I don't like being bothered with motherfuckas. Maybe I can change that. I love doing make-up and it's nothing wrong with getting paid for something that you love.

"How could I forget?" She asked and laughed. Ketta was silly as fuck. She knew if a bitch said one thing wrong to me that I didn't like I'm liable to pop off and beat a bitch down. I finished beating Ketta's face and it looked good. Her skin was the perfect shade of almonds.

"Your make up looks good. Turn around so I can put the rods in your hair. I know the curls are going to make your dreads really pretty," I stated. Ketta did as she was told. I covered her dreads with the rods. I dipped each one of them in hot water and sprayed them down with Coconut sheen. I patted them dry with her towel. I removed the rods from her hair and they turned out really pretty.

"My bitch slays in everything. Girl, I don't know if I'm going to get nasty tonight. I'm looking like a million bucks fresh off the runway. A Cover Girl model isn't fucking with me. Oh shit, somebody's ringing the doorbell. Get that Barbie while I put my shoes on," she beamed. I got the door because I knew it was Julius. As soon as I opened the door damn, he was looked so fuckin' good. I bit my bottom lip. I knew he caught all that. I couldn't help myself.

"Hey Julius," I beamed. He pulled me into his arms and felt me up. Damn, he could get the pussy tonight if he fuckin' wanted it. I was ready and being with him every day and lying with him every night was a fuckin' tease.

"Hey sexy, you look good ma. You're matching my fly," he stated. I hadn't had the chance to take him yet. I stepped back a little to observe him. Yes, we were matching, what a coincidence.

"Thank you." I beamed. Damn, Julius was so sexy to me. I was so intrigued by him. He was Puerto Rican and black. Everything mixed with Melanin was beautiful. He stood about 6'1, caramel brown, pretty teeth, and bedroom eyes. He has a Caesar haircut and a long beard. His physique was amazing because he lived in the gym. He didn't have many tattoo's, but he had a few.

"Are you ready for tonight?" He asked. Of course I was. I've been waiting on him all day. I knew Don and Julius had to handle some serious business today because normally we have lunch together every day, but they opted out on it. Ketta said it was an important meeting they had to attend.

"I sure am," I sassed. Julius and I haven't put a title on what we having going, but it's something. I liked being with him. When I first laid eyes on him months ago I wanted to fuck with him because I knew he had that bag. It's not even about that now because I don't have to ask for anything. Every day before he hits the streets with Don, he gives me wads of cash because he didn't want me spending anything. So yes, I could get used to this.

"Let's roll," he stated. He didn't have to tell me twice. He wrapped me in his arms around my lower back gripping my ass in the process. I swatted his hands away but he didn't give a fuck. I just didn't want to be hot and bothered.

"Okay Julius, let me tell Ketta bye and we're out.," I explained. I couldn't just leave Ketta and not tell her I was gone. She needed to come downstairs and lock the door.

"Cool," he stated coolly. Julius was a cool ass nigga period. I loved the way he carried himself.

"Bye sis, we're out," I yelled. I hoped she could hear me because my voice wasn't that loud.

"Bye girl," she yelled and beamed. It felt good outside, the weather was perfect. It felt like spring with a winter chill. I knew Julius had money, but I wasn't for sure if he was riding like this.

"Damn Julius, is this you?" I asked. I knew he was getting money, but I had no clue he was getting like this. I guess the less I know the better.

"Yep, you like it?" He asked. Of course, I like it. What type of question was that? I knew this man was getting paper but damn a 2016 Bentley Continental GT. Yeah, he's definitely getting it.

"I love it. I test drove one at the International car show a few months ago. It's a Bentley GT right?" I asked and beamed.

"Do you? I want you to show me how it's supposed to be driven," he explained. I had no problems doing that. I wanted to show him more than how to drive it.

I wanted to show him how it feels to get fucked and sucked in a Bentley GT but he's not ready and neither am I. Let me get my mind out the gutter. I hope he didn't see the smile on my face. I could feel him starring a whole in me.

"Tonight, I will," I beamed and added a little sass to it. Julius has no clue what I would do to him when given the chance.

"It's a bet," he stated. He pulled off fast as hell ugh. I hope my liquor doesn't come up. Julius was whipping the fuck out of this Bentley. He drove fast but he knew how to handle the steering wheel. I wasn't afraid of his driving.

"What do you like to do?" He asked. Julius always asked me that. I like to do a lot of things and spending time with him was cool also. We always had deep conversations. I'm sure tonight would be no different and I'm looking forward to it. It's a many of nights when we were laid up I wanted to fuck but I could tell he wanted more than that from me. He was different and I was wrong about him in every sense.

"Travel, shop, live life and have fun," I explained. I love catching flights instead of feelings. Love and relationships were foreign to me. I live out of a suitcase. I'm always moving around.

"Why are you single?" He asked. I'm single by choice. I have plenty of options. I wasn't ready to settle down yet. I haven't met anybody that's worth settling down with and if I have there's a chance that I overlooked them.

"What makes you think I'm not taken?" I asked. I turned around to face Julius because he had my undivided attention. I wanted to see what he had to say.

"I don't see a ring on your finger," he explained. What does that have to do with anything? I better not see one on his, with as much wining and dining we've done these past few weeks.

"Are we playing twenty-one questions?" I asked. Julius let out a slight chuckle and stroked his beard. He was so full of himself and it was crazy, but he had every right to be.

"We can if you want to. I'm just trying to get to know my future that's all," he explained. His future, that has a nice ring to it. I'm just taking it one day at a time.

"Really?" I asked. Julius nodded his head yes. I needed more than a head nod.

"I want you all to myself. I had Ketta set this up if you must know," he explained and pointed his finger between the both of us. I looked at him with wide eyes. He could've just approached me. I'd be lying if I didn't enjoy this little thing we have going on.

"Really?" I asked. I can't believe Ketta set me up. She could've given me the heads up. What happened to Black Girl Magic? I can't wait to see her ass soon as we get back to the spot.

"I always get what I want," he explained. Julius was cocky as fuck. I could say the same thing, but I chose to hold my card until I decided to play them.

"Let me ask you something since we are playing twenty-one questions," I stated. It was my turn to put Julius in the hot seat he got me fifty shades of fucked up.

"Go ahead," he chuckled.

"You've seen me in traffic plenty of times. You see me at the park and mall all the fucking time. Why you never approached me?" I asked. I wanted to have this conversation the other night, but he shied away from it. I hope tonight would be the night that he wouldn't hold back.

"Ma, let's keep it real. Every time we see each other we eye fuck. These past few weeks have been heaven to a nigga. Our eyes have had plenty of conversations but these past few weeks and today I'm going to say everything I need to say. Forget all the formalities. Do you want me Barbie like I want you? I see you blushing and shit, Ma. I'll give you a minute to think about what I said. Are you good, do you need a minute, we're here now?" He asked. I can't believe he just threw that out there. I couldn't get the smile off my face if I wanted to.

"I'm great, let's do it." I beamed. Julius valet parked his Bentley GT. He threw the attendant the keys and told the attendant, "Don't scratch my shit up or change my station or it's your Italian ass." I just shook my head. He was crazy.

"This place is nice. I thought it was a bar?" I asked. I'm glad Ketta told me to dress up because she was onto something.

"No Racine's NY. It's a French Restaurant but they have a great wine selection." Julius said.

"What do you suggest?" I asked. I didn't really have an appetite. I had a big lunch earlier.

"I have something else in mind that I would rather eat and it's red and tender. I'm not talking about a two-piece chicken dinner," he chuckled with his eyes trained on me. If he wanted to eat this pussy, I didn't have any problems with him doing so. Every time he licks his lips, he turns me on.

"Oh really?" I asked. He shook his head yes and ran his tongue across his bottom lip. He bit his lip and stroked his beard. I wanted to sit all on his face. Ketta will hear me screaming his name tonight and I don't give a fuck.

"You heard what I said. I didn't fuckin' stutter. I'll get me a shot of Remy for now and I'll let you eat. Nah fuck that, let me get something to eat also." Julius said.

"I want to see what that mouth does," I explained. I needed a dick report asap. I couldn't be with him if his dick was whack. He had everything I wanted and I needed him to slang good fuckin' pipe too. He's too fine not to.

"When are you ready?" He asked. I'm ready now, fuck dinner let's get straight to it. I wanted to feel him between my legs.

"Let's eat first and then it's on. Flag the waiter down because I'm ready to order," he chuckled. My face turned into a frown instantly. He knew I was ready. I kicked my shoes off and placed them in his lap. I was trying to rub my feet across his dick to see if I could feel how big it was. He grabbed my feet and started massaging them both. Shit, it felt good too.

"Talk is cheap," I sassed.

"It is but I can back my shit up, ma," he chuckled. The waiter brought us a drink. I needed to take a few bites and then I was ready to leave.

Julius

I've been interested in Barbie for a long time. I wouldn't say that I was scared to approach her, but I wanted to move a little different with her. She was different than all the females I've ever been with. She knew that I had been established but she never threw herself at me. Neither one of us made the first move. I believe in perfect timing. I wanted to get at her since the first time I laid eyes on her. I just didn't know that she ran with Ketta and Kaniya or she would've been mines months ago. If she plays her cards right, we'll have a bright future ahead of us.

I wasn't just any street nigga. I was the connect. I never wanted anybody to know that. I'm low key for a reason. I'm a little flashy but not too flashy. I was the man that moved and provided the work. I supplied North Carolina, South Carolina, and the whole Augusta region. I wonder if she can handle being with me. I can tell that she's feeling me, and she wants to give us a shot, but can she handle the shit that comes with fuckin' with the connect. I know she's used to lavish shit and getting up and going when she wants too. When you're fuckin' with the connect you can't travel domestic or international. You have to travel on my jet so my security can be with you at all times. She likes to travel, shop, and make moves when she wants to, but can she move on my time? That was the real question.

Being a man in my position I was looking for a wife and I saw those qualities in Barbie. I was ready to settle down. I've done enough dog shit in my life. I was good on these females. I only wanted one. I knew she was ready to go back home because she's been here for about three weeks. Don and Ketta are about to move into their house. I wanted to bring her to my house and to-night was the night. I wanted to see where her mind was about staying in New York a little longer. I wanted to get to know her some more.

I took her passport and license. I know y'all think I'm crazy but I'm feeling this chick something serious. I wanted more from her than just casual sex and dates. She was my future and I wanted her to see that. My parents always told me when you find that one you'll know and feel it in your heart, and that's how I feel about her. It's one of the reasons why I'm doing what I must do to secure it.

I'll never do anything to hurt her and that's a promise. I got her a promise ring that I'm going to give to her tonight. I want her to promise me that she'll give us a real shot and thug it out with a nigga for a while and see where this goes. I'm taking a chance and I want her to be willing to take a chance with me also. I believe in luck and hopefully, it's on my side.

Chapter-16

Ketta

Barbie left, thank God. I didn't know how long I could keep a secret, but damn it I did it. I'm sure I would hear her mouth later and I'll just deal with the consequences. I thought I heard Don pull up, but I wasn't for sure. I had a few more things do before I was completely ready. I heard footsteps and I looked toward the door and it was him. Every time I looked at him, he brought a smile to my face and he was all fuckin' mine. Don walked up behind me as I was standing in the mirror. He wrapped his arms around my waist and buried his face in the crook of my neck. I was so fuckin' weak for him.

"Babe, what are you doing? What's taking you so long?" He asked. Don must have pulled up as soon as Julius and Barbie left. I thought that was him. I put a little pep in my step. I looked at the time on my watch and it was after 8:00 p.m. our reservations were scheduled until 9:30 p.m.

"Not too much. I'm trying to make sure I'm picture perfect," I beamed and explained. I didn't get dolled up just because. I knew he was taking me somewhere special so, I was dressing for the occasion. He knew I was going to clean up nice. Every time we go out somewhere we always run into somebody from his neighborhood or someone he was cool with. Oh, and let's not forget about the women he used to fuck with, they hate that he's with me and not them.

"You're always perfect," he stated. Don always said the right shit. I appreciated him for always complimenting me.

"Where are we going," I asked. I knew Don would never tell me. He always wanted to surprise me. I don't know why I even asked. I'm sure today would be no different. I love the surprises but damn I wanted a hint.

"Where ever you want to go," he explained. I turned around to face him. I rested my hands on his chest. I cupped his chin with my free hand. I gave him a peck on the lips. I tried to pull back, but Don grabbed the back of my head and deepened the kiss. I swear he was romantic as fuck.

"Don, you are so sweet," I blushed. I swear I was blessed when I met him. I couldn't ask for a better boyfriend.

"You bring that side out of me. Let's ride and I'll lock up," he explained. Don was heavy in the streets. I knew he was a ruthless ass nigga, but he was never like that with me. He was always a gentleman because his mother and father taught him how to treat a woman.

"Ketta, were you waiting for me? I told you to go ahead and get in the car," he asked and explained. Of course, I was waiting for him. It's some ignorant ass motherfuckas out here. I knew Don could handle his own, but he's my man and I got him. All of him.

"I always got your back and your front forever," I explained. We locked eyes with each other because I wanted him to feel me. I wasn't losing him period. I know we all have an expiration date but if I had to bust at a nigga to save my man that's what the fuck I'm going to do.

"See, that's why I knew I loved you," he stated. I love him too and that's one thing he'll never have to question. I'm riding for him. A good man is hard to find and I found me a real one at that. No baggage, no kids, or no crazy exes popping up. Don and I hopped in the car and pulled off. I loved riding with him. I'm his Bonnie and he's my Clyde. I feel like I'm on top of the world when we're together.

"Ketta, when are you going to move to New York with me?" He asked. We came to a stop light. I turned around to face Don to see if he was playing. Our eyes were trained on each other. I knew he was bullshitting. I never thought about moving to New York but he's my man and I wanted to be with him no matter what.

"What about my job?" I asked. Don grabbed my hand and I looked at him to see what he had to say.

"You know how I feel about that. I prefer for you to work for yourself than someone else. I want you to be your own boss. You can transfer up here to a hospital if you want. I have a better suggestion, how about you open your own Children's Urgent Care facility? I'll help you do that personally. I want to buy us a house and your name and my name will both be on the deed. What you think?" He asked. I didn't have to think twice. If he was doing this and he wasn't my man I can only imagine what it's going to be like if he becomes my husband.

"You know what baby, let's do it. We only live once. Please don't make me regret it. I'm willing to take that chance with you," I explained. I didn't have any doubts when it came to him. We've been at it for six months strong. I want to keep counting.

"I'll never do that babe because I love you too much. I don't want you to regret anything. I want to show you something before we go to dinner. Be my DJ, ma." He explained. Don leaned in and gave me a kiss taking his eyes off the road just for a second. Things were looking up. This New York Trip was everything so far. I never thought I'd be living here. Wow lights, camera, action! This is better than anything I would've imagined and

I'm happy though. Don keeps me smiling. I've never had a dull moment with him. He lights up all my days. I played **Plies Hotter Than the Street Lights**

Hotter Than the Streets Lights

You Want to Get Did Right

Hotter Than the Streets Lights

You Want to Get Did Right.

I don't know why, but I wanted to hear this song. I love riding through New York at night because it's beautiful. It was something about New York at night. Everybody was moving around with their significant other enjoying what the city has to offer. I wonder what's next?

"Why are we stopping here?" I asked. Don knew I didn't like frequent stops. It's not that I was scared. It's just that you could never be too sure. I always move with caution.

"I need to grab a water, you want anything?" He asked. I looked at Don out the corner of my eyes. He gave me a faint smile. I don't trust his ass. This nigga is up to something. He walked in the corner store and grabbed a few things. He came out with something; what the fuck is in his hands. That's not just water.

"Turn around baby and put this blindfold on. I have a surprise for you. I don't want you to see it," He explained. I looked at Don like he was crazy because I didn't want to put a blindfold on at all. I didn't like the way this night was turning out. He could tell that I was a little skeptical.

"I don't like blindfolds or surprises," I argued and pouted.

"Trust me, baby, I got you. I wouldn't do anything to hurt you. I promise," he explained. I could've sworn I heard Don let a small laugh. He got me fucked up, I swear. I'm not with this shit at all.

"How can I be the DJ Don, if I'm blindfolded?" I asked. Don grabbed my hands to calm my nerves just a little bit. I like to be aware of my surroundings at all fuckin' times.

"I have a little mix we can ride to," he explained. I sucked my teeth and rolled my eyes as if he could see them. I wasn't even about to respond. "Trust me Ketta, I got you, babe." We sped off into traffic. Don started driving like a fucking maniac. He knows I hate that shit and I have a blindfold on. I'm not feeling this shit. He was getting a kick out of this shit too. He was laughing. I wanted to know what was so fuckin' funny. I assumed we were headed to whatever he needs to show me. **Cupid by 112** was playing.

"Turn that up Don," I said. I had an attitude but I would never let that show.

Cupid Doesn't Lie but You Won't Know

Unless You Give It a Try.

True Love Won't Lie

But You Want Know Unless You Give It a Try.

"This used to be my song," he stated. He grabbed my hand and placed a kiss on it. It was my song too. When Don I first made love, this song was the first song that came on the playlist.

"Tell me something, baby," I stated.

"Yes Babe," he responded.

"Is the blindfold really necessary? I like to look at you when we're driving. I wanted to give you some slow head while you drove," I explained. I propped my foot up on the dashboard and started playing with myself. I knew I was getting Don hot and bothered. I just wanted this fuckin' blindfold off. He knew we always got in when we're in the car.

"You're bull shitting, Ketta? I can direct you to do that right now. Be patient, we're almost there. On our way back from your surprise you can give me some slow head while I drive," he explained. Don wasn't fuckin' budging at all.

"I really want to taste it now," I pouted and whined. I started grabbing dick.

"Stop Ketta, before you make me wreck. Damn you're impatient as fuck. Just play along. It's going to be worth it, I promise you. You're bugging for real. You almost fuckin' tempted me. You won't even relax for a few minutes, nosey ass. We're here lil impatient lady, now get your ass out the motherfuckin' car. You better not touch shit and this fuckin' blindfold is staying on. I swear I'm dead ass serious, Ketta." He argued. Don isn't talking about shit. I'm not trying to hear that shit at all. Long as we're here I'm good.

"Open the door Don, and don't let me fall out this fuckin' truck since you want to surprise me," I argued. I like surprises but don't use a fuckin' blindfold. I'm not feeling it at all. I heard the door open. Don snatched me out the truck. I damn near fell. He was doing too much.

"Babe, stop with the theatrics," he chuckled. He grabbed my hand. I put my handprints up to something and it sounded like I heard the door unlock. Where are we? I wanted to see where we're at so fuckin' bad. The scent of the place smelled good. Don ran his hands across my ass and bit the crook of my neck.

"Hey babe, are you ready?" He asked. Of course, I'm ready, who wouldn't be. Don should be glad I love his ass and I'm not trying to start an argument over something small.

"I been ready," I sassed. He took the blindfold off me. I looked around this house. It was beautiful as fuck. I love it. "Awe this is nice! I love it Don, whose place is this?" I asked.

"Ours. I hope you love it. I brought this for us. I knew how much you loved Glen Cove, New York so, I wanted to buy us a house here," he explained. Damn, Don was everything. I feel so bad that I was doing all this complaining. The only thing he wanted to do was surprise me and I was being ungrateful.

"Baby, stop playing. If this was the surprise, why does this furniture look like mine?" I asked. I knew my furniture and color schemes and pictures from anywhere. How was he able to pull this off?

"Thank Kaniya for that. I had your stuff packed and shipped up here. Your place was nice, and you just purchased the majority of your furniture. It was to brand new to throw or give away. I thought it'll look great in here," he explained. Don knew me so fuckin' well. I can't even complain though.

"I'm guessing that's why you didn't want me to go home?" I asked. Don had this shit planned out to perfection. I should've known something was up.

"Yep," he chuckled. I punched him in his shoulder. He could've given me the heads up.

"What if I would've had said no?" I asked. I had to ask that because Don was so damn full of himself that it's crazy. He knew me better than I knew myself. Maybe he was my soulmate.

"I knew you would've said yes because saying no wasn't an option," he explained. Don gave me a hard gaze. He was digging in my soul searching for any uncertainties. I wanted to be with him. Nothing or no one could change that. I love him and I love this thing that we have going on.

"You don't think we're moving too fast?" I asked. We've only been together for six months. I've been staying with him for the past three months anyway but now it's official.

"No, I don't. When you want something you don't put a time limit on anything. You make that shit happen," he explained. I guess he cleared up any doubts that I had.

"What if I get lonely?" I asked. I knew that would never happen because Don always makes time for me. I come first and the streets come second. He was never too busy me. He always made sure that we did something once a week.

"I'll never leave you lonely. I didn't bring you this far to not be by your side. I want to wake up to you every day and come home to you every night," he explained. Don pulled me into his arms and cupped my chin. He leaned in and gave me a kiss. I couldn't even come up for air.

"I'll miss Kaniya," I sighed. Glen Cove is a long way from Atlanta. I can't believe Kaniya agreed to this shit. How dare she help him pack my shit up without consulting with me or giving me any hints.

"FaceTime her. She can come and visit," he explained. I can't wait to FaceTime her and give her a piece of my fuckin' mind. Damn, Don and I are about to do this shit. I wouldn't want to take this journey with anybody but him. I can't even complain.

"Give me the full tour baby, this is amazing. What about my car?" I asked and squealed. This house was too big for the both us. It had to at least have about six bedrooms. It was a fuckin' mansion.

"We'll catch a flight to Atlanta, and we'll drive it back up here. I want you to check out the formal dining room," he explained. Don ushered me to the formal dining room. It was lavish as fuck and amazing. Our house looked out on a lake. Don had outdone himself. He had a nice candlelight dinner setup. The table was filled with steaks, lobsters, oysters, chef salad, fresh fruit, and stuffed potatoes.

"I love it," I beamed and blushed.

"Sit down so we can eat," he stated. Don pulled out a chair for me and he sat in front of me. He grabbed my hand and we said grace. He fixed my plate and loaded everything he knew I would love on it. I poured us both a glass of Dom Perignon. I promise you I love this man so much. I wouldn't trade him for anything in this world.

This moment right here, I prayed for. I knew my time would come. I wasn't looking for love, but I was open and I was patiently waiting for it. I can't really explain the feeling I get when I'm around him, but it warms my soul. Don is everything that I ever wanted and needed. He supports me in any and everything I do. His family loves me, and my family loves him. If this is what forever feels like I hope it never ends.

A FEW DAYS LATER

Chapter-17

Sonja

I'm so glad my nephew is finally free after doing a two-year bid. Tariq is my heart and I love him and his sister Raven to death. I promised my sister on her death bed that I would take care of her two children and protect them like they were my own. My sister Tyra died at the age of twenty-five by the hands of a fuck nigga that wouldn't let go. I don't ever want a man to love me that much that he has to kill me. He beat her so bad she was unconscious. She had fluid on her brain, and it was so much trauma that she only lived six days after that.

Tariq and Raven are both grown now. Raven attends UCLA in California. These past two years I have been living my life to the fullest. Tariq refuses to move out permanently and into his own home. He crashes here at least twice a week. He thinks he needs to watch me, but I'm grown. I'm going to need him to get out of here because he's twenty-seven not seventeen. I like to walk around my house nude with my man Deuce. I'm having a family dinner today and I need to let Tariq and Raven know that I'm about to get married.

We're also inviting Deuce two sons Lucky and Quan. I met Lucky a few times through Kaniya. She has no clue that I'm dating her boyfriend's father. The family dinner can either make or break the family. Kaniya has no idea that I've been dating Deuce for two years' because some things are better left unsaid. I dated Kaniya's uncle Kanan for fourteen years. I didn't want her involved in my love life and shit. I love Deuce and this shit is official. I remember the first day we met and it's been a blessing ever since.

I'll never forget the day we met as long as I live. I was hosting Ladies Night at Houston's with Mechelle. Our lady's night event was about to come to an end. I started walking toward my car and I dropped my purse and all the contents fell out.

I was so fuckin' pissed because it was late, and this is the last thing I needed. You never know if somebody was out here lurking trying to rob you because you were in a fucked-up situation. I grabbed my things as fast as I could. This man walked up behind me and started helping me. I had an evil scowl on my face. I locked eyes with him, and he was so fine. My scowl instantly turned into a smile. Deuce stood about 6'4, hazel eyes, and he had a light skin complexion. Normally I like my men dark. I couldn't hide the attraction between us. Dreads adorned his head and he had a few tattoos. He introduced himself and I introduced myself. He helped me pick up my things. He asked me would I come back inside to have a drink. I did and the rest was history. We've been together ever since.

I had one problem poking me in my side. I hate even thinking about it. Kanan Miller was his name and my ex-fiancé. He was the craziest and deadliest man that ever graced this earth in my opinion. He was due to get out in a month or so and we needed to have a conversation. I wish I could skip town, but Deuce would become suspicious. Let me focus my energy somewhere else. I forgot to call my niece Kaniya to invite her over to my dinner. Anytime I have a dinner or a party she's always welcomed to my home. I haven't heard from her in a few weeks so, I called her phone.

"Hey Kaniya, how are you?" I asked. I love Kaniya. She's a product of her mother and father.

"I'm good Ms. Sonja, what's up?" She beamed and laughed. I could tell Kaniya was up to some shit because I can hear it in her voice. I hope she's been on her best behavior. I haven't heard from her since her breakup and I hope it won't be any hard feelings when she sees Lucky again. I hope they could work past their disagreements.

"Nothing much, I'm having Sunday dinner at my house today, and I wanted you to come," I mentioned. I knew Kaniya would bring her ass without a hassle. She was the only one that I was inviting from Kanan's family.

"Oh lord, you and these Sunday dinners. Do I need to bring my fuckin' strap, shit? It's always some shit at your house with your famous fuckin' dinners. I hope I get the chance to eat," she asked and laughed.

"No Kaniya, I'm not in East Lake anymore child with your crazy ass. Keep your god damn straps at home. I know you're coming with your straps any fuckin' way. It wouldn't be you if you didn't," I sassed and laughed. I swear she acts just like her fuckin' mother. Kaisha ruined her.

"Do you want me to bring anything besides my gun?" She asked and laughed. I swear she gets on my damn nerves but that's my baby and the daughter I never had.

"Make two fuckin' strawberry shortcakes damn it," I argued and laughed. I swear Kaniya's a fuckin' trip for real.

"Okay I'll be there by 6:00 p.m.," she explained. Kaniya and I finished talking. I had a lot of shit to do before everybody arrived. I wanted things to be perfect. I met Lucky before but not Quan. Deuce walked up behind me and wrapped his arms around my waist. He grabbed a handful of my ass. I rested my head on his chest and gazed up at him. He leaned in and gave me a peck on the lips. God, I love him.

"Deuce, baby, what should I cook?" I asked. On Sunday's I throw down and today wouldn't be any different.

"It doesn't matter baby, you don't even have to feed these niggas if you don't want to. I'll cater to you tonight. If you want me to wine and dine you or whatever, I'll do it. We're just letting my kids, your niece and nephew, and a few people that you're close to knowing that we're about to get married," he explained. I swear Deuce was perfect and I love everything about him.

"I'll get some fried chicken from Cajun in Ingles, and I'll bake some macaroni cheese, stuffed mashed potatoes, cabbage, and yeast rolls. Kaniya is going to bring the strawberry shortcake," I explained. Kaniya could bake her ass off. Kaitlyn's old miserable ass taught her a few things.

"That's cool Sonja, but can you let me eat your strawberry shortcake before all these people get here?" He asked. I wanted to say no but saying no to Deuce wasn't an option. He hates when I deny him anything. I really needed to get everything set up before our family comes over.

"You're too much Deuce," I beamed and laughed.

"You like it," he stated proudly. Hell yeah, I liked it. I fuckin' loved it. Deuce and Kanan were night and day and it was no comparison. Kanan was evil and cutthroat and Deuce was loving and attentive but cutthroat at the same fuckin' time.

"I love it," I beamed and blushed. Deuce was the freakiest man I've ever been with. The shit he does to me amazes me. He picked me up and sat me on the island in the kitchen. He undressed me from my head to my toes. He started sucking on my toes and worked his way up to my pussy. He sprayed whip cream between my legs. He pushed my legs up above my head in an angle like the letter V and held them still with his hands.

He smacked me on my ass and started finger fuckin' me wet and I came instantly. He dropped his head between my legs and I grabbed his dreads for support. He started sucking on my pussy like a dog eating his last meal. I couldn't take it. I tried to ride his face, but I couldn't keep up. My legs were shaking something serious. He removed his face and slammed his dick inside of me. I backed up instantly. I wanted to run from the dick but he climbed on top of the island and started nailing my pussy the cross.

I couldn't control it. My juices were flowing with the orgasms I got back to fuckin' back. I don't know if I'll be able to cook dinner. He insisted on fucking me in this same position. God be the Glory, this man was hung. He was blessed between his legs and his pound game was serious. Deuce and his tongue game were crazy. All he wants to do was eat me for breakfast, lunch, and dinner and you best believe me, I fed him every fuckin' time.

He couldn't just eat my pussy and be done with it. No, he had to eat my ass too and suck on these breasts like he was my newborn baby himself. He couldn't go a day without being breastfed.

"Deuce, baby, that's enough. I must get this food ready," I screamed. I needed him to stop immediately.

"Okay, I'll ease up for now but later we're picking up right where we left off," he explained.

"Thank you," I sighed and moaned. I had to still get my dishes together. I prepped the Mac n cheese earlier. I still had to fry fish also. The mashed potatoes, cabbage and yeast rolls were the last few things I needed to do. Deuce was going to pick up the chicken from Ingles. Raven was the first one to come. Thank God Deuce and I finished having sex before she came.

"Raven, can you watch this food while I go shower, and change clothes. Your brother should be here shortly and the other guest," I yelled.

"I got you, Auntie," she yelled. Soon as I went upstairs, I heard the doorbell ring again. Damn, they're coming early. Normally black folks are always late. I guess these motherfuckas wanted to eat.

"Hey Tariq," she beamed. I knew Raven was glad to see her brother. It's been a few years since they last n each other. I wish Tyra could be here to see here babies.

"Hey sis, I didn't know you were in town," he stated. I knew Tariq was going to trip when he saw her because she's grown so much. He wants her to be his baby forever.

"I'm here for the summer, I missed you," she stated. Raven loved her brother. He's all she has as far as she knows. She has other siblings that she has no clue about and for her sake and mine, I would like to keep it that way.

"I missed you too youngin," he stated. Tariq and Raven finished talking. I could no longer hear what was being said between the two. I heard a voice that I didn't like. I know damn well Tariq ain't got this bitch up in my fuckin' house.

"Hi Shaela," she stated. I told Tariq about fuckin' with her but he didn't listen. I can't tell him who to date but I knew she wasn't good enough for him. The moment he went to jail that bitch was gone and fuckin' on the next nigga. I couldn't wait to tell him I told you so. The only bitch that stood by him was Kaniya. Till this day I wonder why she did it, but hey we were family and that's what family is supposed to do.

"Hi Raven," she sassed. Ugh, I couldn't stand Shaela for anything in this world. She irks the fuck out of me. Nothing about her is genuine. She only wanted Tariq for what he could do for her. If you asked me, he should've stayed with Tamia. But nope he was a young nigga getting money, too much pussy was being thrown at him, and he didn't know what to do. He should've stayed true to her.

"Raven, where's Auntie?" He asked. Tariq was so damn protective of me it was crazy. I couldn't piss without him wanting to know where I was going.

"The food is almost ready, and Sonja went to shower," she stated. Raven kept everybody intact. Ten minutes later the doorbell rang again. I wonder who that was. I had to make sure I was perfect before I stepped out. The announcement for my engagement was special to me. Deuce put the North Pole on my damn finger.

"Hey, we're here for Deuce," he stated. I knew Lucky's voice so that had to be Quan. I finished putting the final touches on my fit. I took the flexy rods out of my hair and I ran my fingers through my hair. I applied a matte red-purple to my lip and gave myself a once over in the mirror. Yeah, I was still that bitch. These young hoes ain't got shit on me. Sonja the fuckin' body. That's what the niggas in the streets used to call me. I made my way downstairs to entertain our guests.

"He went to the store he'll be back shortly," she explained. I kissed Raven on her cheek and whispered in her ear.

"Thank you. I'm Sonja it's nice to meet you. Deuce should be back in a minute. You guys can have a seat," I explained. Tianna was looking at Tariq crazy. I wonder what that was about. I knew all of Kaniya's friends. I had no clue that Tianna was dating Quan. I swear these kids can keep fuckin' secrets. Tariq and Quan made idle chat. They hit it off good. Deuce finally pulled back up. Tariq knew Deuce already and they made idle chat. The girls came into the kitchen to help me. The doorbell rang again and I sent Raven to the door to see who it was.

"Hey Kaniya, I missed you," she beamed. Kaniya and Raven had a great relationship. Kaniya always treated Raven like her sister and I appreciated her for that. Raven needed that more than she would over know.

"Hi Raven, I missed you, sis. I didn't know you were in town. Hi everyone. I'm headed in the kitchen. Hey Sonja," she yelled. I could hear the aggravation in her voice. I knew something was up. I hope she doesn't start any shit. I'll ask her about that later.

"You made it," I beamed and smiled. I pulled Kaniya in for a hug. She was so pretty, looking like her damn momma. God Kaisha and I had to beg Killian to let her date, but he wasn't going for it. I noticed Shaela was mugging Kaniya. I wonder what that was about. I swear to God Shaela didn't want any smoke. The last thing she wants to do is come up in my house and fuck with my niece. I swear she wouldn't make it out of my house alive and that's a fuckin' promise.

Raven

I'm Raven I'm Tariq's baby sister and I'm twenty-one. I'm a sophomore at UCLA in California. My major is English Literature. I could tell something was going on between my brother and Kaniya because their faces told it all. Tariq has been in love with Kaniya for as long as I can remember. I think she loves him too. It was only one problem, she was already taking. He had something going on with Shaela. So, they remained friends, stayed cool and never crossed that line from what he told me. I never asked her about it.

Kaniya was always the sister I never had, and I was the little sister she never had. She always looked out for me. She always took me shopping and to get Mani and Pedi or to get my hair done. If I ever needed her for anything, I could call her, and she would drop whatever she was doing to come and see about me. No questions asked. I would forever be loyal to her.

I never had a relationship with Shaela. It's not that I didn't like her, I just didn't get that sister or genuine vibe from her. It's like everything was forced. She would only speak to me when Tariq was around. I just never got a good vibe from her. I was curious to know why she was here because Tariq told me while he was locked up that she got her number changed. No calls no visits or anything. The only people that held him down was our auntie and Kaniya.

I just didn't understand what her purpose was because she showed her true colors two years ago. That's on him. I wouldn't be playing buddy, buddy, with her if she left me as soon as I had to do my time. I will always root for him Kaniya, to be honest. She's my sister rather her and Tariq works out. I prayed for them too. I think they will be great for each other. I hope it happens.

I could've sworn Sonja told me it was going to only be a few people coming over. She lied because I've been running back and forth to the door like crazy. I had plans to ask Tariq what was up with them two. I'm nosey and I want to know. I would ask Kaniya but judging by her facial expressions she wouldn't disclose it. I could tell she was pissed.

Chapter-18

Kaniya

S omething told me to stay at home. I should've trusted my first fuckin' instincts but I knew Sonja would've been mad. I can't believe Tariq brought this bitch up in here and I've been lying up with him for the past three weeks. I swear he ain't got shit to say to me. I'm glad I brought his check with me. He can get his money and leave me the fuck alone. I knew he didn't want me to give him his money. I tried to keep my composure for as long as I could, but I couldn't. I wanted to take my plate and leave.

I shouldn't even be catching feelings behind this nigga but I am. Tianna's here and she looked as if she was surprised to see me. I wonder what's up with that. I knew now wasn't the time to air everything out, but we needed to talk. I wanted to know why she was so comfortable keeping a secret and her pregnancy from me. I stood right beside her and grilled her.

"Hi Tianna, what are you doing here? I see you're keeping more secrets, huh." I asked. She gave me a deadly look begging me not cut up. Fuck that, I can't hide my feeling or emotions for shit.

"Don't start Kaniya, please," she begged and laughed. I can't even promise that because it's been over three weeks and she still hasn't told me she's pregnant by Quan or living with him. Yeah, I'm feeling some type of way on top of Tariq's shit. I needed a reason to go off. I could feel Shaela staring a hole in me. I swear she better tread fuckin' lightly. I'll beat her ass up in this motherfucka and then I'll slap Tariq just because he tried me and flaunted this bitch up in my face. I focused my attention on her.

"Hi Shaela," I sassed and sucked my teeth. That's the only explanation she'll get from me.

"Hi Kaniya," she sighed and sounded dry. I didn't have to speak. The only reason I did is that Sonja was begging me to clear the air. She gave me a stern look, so I know I needed to address the elephant in the room. I don't even know why Sonja was doing this, It's not like she liked the bitch, or did I miss something.

"Who pissed in your Cheerios?" I asked. Shaela chose not to respond, and I didn't have a problem with it. I knew she was salty behind Tariq. "I'm hungry Sonja, let's eat." I walked toward the formal dining room. Raven and Tianna were right on my heels. The doorbell rang again. Damn, Sonja invited a lot of people. I knew I had to go because I just felt some shit was about to pop off.

"Get the door," she yelled. Deuce got up to get the door. I wonder who that was.

"It's Lucky and Melanie. Come on in guys, we're in the dining room," he explained. I cocked my head to the side. It's about to go down. Jamel Lee Williams got me all the way fucked up. I'm glad I was standing my ground and not taking his ass back. Just a few weeks ago you were sneaking in my house just to eat my pussy, but here you are today with the same bitch you said you didn't give two fucks about, but she's meeting your dad. I swear I'm so sick of niggas. It was time for me to go before I turn this bitch out and get live quick at Sonja's house. Tianna kicked me up under the table. I'm looking at my phone to hide the anger and aggravation on my face. Tariq sent me a text me trying to explain.

"But you stand up a nigga though. Fuck you and the bitch that's with you," I argued. He knew I was fuckin' talking to him. He needs to stay away from me. I wish I could un-fuck him.

"What Tianna?" I asked. I looked up and it's Lucky and Melanie. This can't be life right now. Let me be cordial for the sake of Sonja. "I'm not biting my tongue and I'm not about to spare no bitch or nigga feelings." I don't give a fuck. I meant what the fuck I said, and he knows it.

"Fuck him," she mumbled. Lucky locked eyes with me. It's so much tension in the room that you could feel it. Lucky's mad because he got caught up again. Melanie looked scared as fuck.

"I'm not going put my hands on you little girl," I argued. I beat your ass twice. I wouldn't fight you a third time, but I'll fuck Lucky up for the second time. Tariq's mad at me because he's caught up with Shaela. "Why are we all here anyway? Is dinner ready because I'm starving?"

"Kaniya, come in the kitchen with me for a minute, what's wrong?" Sonja asked. She knew I was pissed, and I really didn't feel like giving her an explanation.

"Lucky's here with his lil bitch; the ones whose ass I beat twice, and Tariq's here with Shaela but we've been kicking it for about three weeks," I argued. Sonja looked at me with wide eyes. I knew she had something to say about the last statement.

"I'm dating Lucky's father Deuce and we're getting married. I wanted to tell everybody," she beamed and smiled. Sonja deserved to be happy, but I know my uncle Kanan isn't going for that shit. If she was getting married, I wanted front row tickets. If her wedding was happening, she just signed Deuce's fuckin' death certificate.

"You sure can keep a secret but I'm happy for you! You deserve it," I beamed and smiled. I meant it. Shit, I wanted to be happy too even if it's not with those two niggas.

"I knew Lucky would be here, but I didn't know he was bringing anyone," she explained.

"It's cool Sonja, but it's funny because I've been with this man for five years and I've only met his father a few times. I've never shared a meal with his father or been in his presence longer than an hour before, but he brings this bitch to meet him? It's a trip, but I'm good. This is a special moment for you and I'm not going to ruin it because it's not about me, but you. Let me get out here so I won't kill these hoes," I beamed proudly. Soon as I walked back out to the dining room all eyes were on me. I couldn't share a meal with Lucky and his bitch. It's not happening. I'll turn this bitch out before I do.

"Everything smells so good. I'm hungry let's say grace so we can eat," Raven stated. She was my baby. I know she was trying to keep the peace. The food was being passed around. Everybody was filling their plates to the brim but I lost my fuckin' appetite a few minutes ago.

"I have an announcement everyone. The reason we're all here today for this dinner and meet and greet is that Deuce and I are getting married," she beamed proudly. I'll toast to that and take my plate and fuckin' leave.

"Congrats Sonja and Deuce," everyone cheered and beamed. I stood up from my seat and grabbed my purse. It was time for me to turn a fuckin' corner. On my way out I was stopped by Sonja and I gave her a kiss on the cheek. She knew I couldn't stay here without turning this motherfucka out.

"I'm happy for you Sonja. I'm going to take my plate to go, is that cool?" I asked. I knew she would agree. She could look at my face and tell that I didn't want to be here.

"It's fine, Kaniya." She stated.

"She needs to go," she argued and sassed. I turned around and cocked my head to the side. I know this bitch wasn't talking to me. I tossed Sonja my purse if Shaela wanted war, she can for damn sure get it.

"Speak up, Shaela. You got some motherfuckin' pressure on your chest? It ain't shit for me to air that motherfucka out. You better ask that bitch that's sitting next to you what this fuckin' pressure is all about. I ain't the one bitch," I argued.

"Next time you fuck with my sister, I'm going to beat your ass," she argued. A bitch can't threaten me and live to tell about it. If she wanted to fight, I'll gladly pass the hoe a fuckin' ass whooping.

"Word? Who's your sister?" I asked. She was steady talking and I was walking up on her ass ready to pass that bitch these motherfuckin' hands.

"Melanie," she argued and sucked her teeth. I laughed so fuckin' loud and hard. She was funny as fuck. Her sister couldn't have told her how I dusted her motherfuckin' ass.

"Look, I'm not trying to be conceited but y'all niggas keep jocking me. They keep on jocking me. Melanie if you know what's good, you'll put your sister in her fuckin' place. You were fucking my nigga, I wasn't fucking yours. Obviously, you're where he wants to be, just tell him to quit stalking me. You know what here are the keys to this Range he brought me, you can have it. I don't want anything to do with him, I'm cool on him. I done had him and guess what bitch I don't fuckin' want him. Let me call an Uber," I ain't got time for this shit. I threw my keys at Lucky.

"I'll take you home, Kaniya." He offered. I wasn't fuckin' with Tariq either. He can't take me any fuckin' where.

"No the fuck you won't," she argued and stood up. I tried to be a low key as possible at Sonja's house, but this bitch has tried me one too many fuckin' times. I don't tolerate disrespect at all. I'm about to slide this bitch these hands one time so she can shut fuck the up and speak when she's spoken to. I stepped in her face and she blinked twice. I rocked the fuck out of her face. Raven and Tianna pulled me off her. I pushed them off me. She had to fuckin' get it.

"What's your issue with me? You're mad because your nigga is checking for me? Check him and not me. See that's why you hoes got the game wrong, check that nigga and not me.

If a bitch ever tries to check me behind a nigga that's not mine, I'll rock a bitch to sleep and as you can see Shaela you ain't fuckin' excluded. You come out better playing the lottery before you attempt to play with a bitch like me. I'm cool on you too, Tariq. A bitch once told me you either share the dick or have none, at all," I laughed at the hoe again. I hit a nerve because Lucky was hot now. I don't give a fuck. Lucky ran up on me.

"Are you giving my pussy away, Kaniya?" He asked. He hadn't said shit to me all night since I caught him with his bitch.

As soon as I said something, he didn't like he finally had to say something. I wasn't even about to respond. He grabbed my arm with so much force. I snatched it away from him and I had a mean ass scowl on my face.

"Lucky, the only pussy you need to stake claim to is the one you came here with. You and I are done. It ain't no coming back. Picture another nigga fuckin' me how you used to. The summer is fuckin' mine. Stay out of my fuckin' face," I argued. He tried to tackle me to the floor. Deuce and Quan grabbed him off me. I meant what the fuck I said. I opened my purse and gave Tariq the $220,000.00 cashier's check. "Here's your money Tariq, let me be okay. I'm cool on you too. I'm going outside to wait on my Uber."

"Tariq, my nigga, why are you giving my woman fuckin' money?" he argued. Lucky was still trying to get at me and Tariq not answering him was only making shit worse. I had to get up out of here.

"We'll take you home," Tianna and Quan offered. I didn't want to ruin their dinner because of me. I'll catch an Uber and I didn't want to talk about any of the shit that happened.

"I'm good. This is a family moment, enjoy it," I beamed and smiled. I'm good because I laid hands on a bitch. I sat outside on the porch waiting for my Uber. I felt somebody walk up behind me. I knew it was Tariq because I could smell his cologne.

"Kaniya, can we talk?" He asked. I'm done talking. I said what the fuck I had to say.

"About what, Tariq?" I asked. He knew I was mad at him.

"Why does everybody want to talk when they get caught up? When you were being sneaky and still fuckin' on Shaela you didn't want to talk then. I'll respect you more if you keep it real about what you got going on. I can't do shit but respect it. I'm not playing number two.

I'm nobody's side chick. You got me out here looking like a fool too. You're good, trust me. All this bullshit I'm going through it's a lesson, but my blessing is coming. There's my Uber. Bye Tariq, nice knowing you and have a nice life," I argued.

I was so glad when my Uber driver pulled up at Sonja's house. I'm pissed. I couldn't catch a break between Lucky and Tariq and all this extra bullshit. To top it all off, when the fuck did Sonja start fucking with Deuce? My uncle is going to go fuckin' nuts when he finds out she's about to get married. Kanan and Sonja were together for years before he went to the feds. I'm not going to say anything, but he gets out on June 16, 2016.

He'll find out sooner or later. I don't want any parts of what the fuck they got going on. I'm not explaining shit to anybody.

I finally made it home. This is the slowest Uber driver I ever FUCKIN' rode with NEVER AGAIN. I approached my door and let myself in. I have a nice house. I never really get to sit back and enjoy the fruits of my labor and the hard work I put in. This 3300 square feet home is decked out. Let me unwind for a few. I need a glass of wine. I didn't even get to finish eating my food. Let me warm this shit up so I can eat. I wish Tariq and Lucky would quit texting me.

Tariq - I'm sorry. It's not what you think. I haven't fucked her. Shaela knows I want to be with you. She asked me and I told her the truth. That's why she had an attitude. Can I come over?

Lucky - Are you at home I need to drop your truck off?

I wasn't about to respond to either one of them. I'm hungry and I couldn't wait to taste this food. It was good as always. Sonja doesn't need to throw any more ratchet functions. I can't wait to tell Killany about this shit. That's my best-kept secret. She is going to die laughing. I finished my food up and wiped my kitchen counters off. I set my alarm clock and made my way upstairs.

I ran a nice hot bath. The roses Lucky sent me two weeks are still holding on and smelling great. I added some Milk and Honey Bubble Bath and Bath Salts to my water. I lit, my candles and cut my iPod on. This felt so good. I couldn't even enjoy this bath because my alarm system was alerting me that someone was trying to come in uninvited. I got movement and I wasn't expecting anyone so I jumped out the tub.

I don't give a fuck because whoever is attempting to bring their ass up in here got me fucked up. They'll meet their fuckin' maker tonight. It's too many home invasions to be unprepared. I grabbed my AK-47 out of the closet and threw my bulletproof vest on. I cut the scope on. I wanted a headshot.

I approached the stairs sat down on the fourth step. I heard someone fucking with the locks. A motherfucka was really trying to break in my fuckin' house. Finally, they entered my house. I think they noticed I had the red beam on their forehead. I didn't even bother to hit the fuckin' lights. If a nigga brought their ass in here, they weren't making it out of here alive.

"Drop that shit motherfucka before I fuckin' drop you," I yelled and argued.

"Kaniya, it's me, baby. Why are you naked and wet holding an AK-47. Put that shit down baby? Damn, that's a sexy sight to see. If a motherfucka was about to break in, why are you letting them see my pussy?" He explained and asked. I hate Lucky. Why is he even fuckin' here? I need my fuckin' keys and I mean that shit. Leave go back to wherever you fuckin' came from.

"I thought somebody was breaking in," I argued. I headed back upstairs to my room. I don't want to be bothered. I had enough of his ass earlier.

"Kaniya, you were really going to shoot me?" He asked. Hell, yeah I would've shot his ass if I didn't know it was him. He needs to leave before I decide to do it anyway. I'm sick of his lying cheating ass. I can't believe I gave this nigga five years of my life.

"I will. I'm not sparing no nigga or bitch," I argued. Lucky walked up behind me. He tried to wrap his arms around my waist. I swatted his arms away. I didn't want him touching me because my body was reacting to him. I swear I hate his fuckin' touch because I still had feelings for this nigga, no matter what he's done to me these past few weeks.

"Drop the fuckin' gun, Kaniya. I swear to God you look so fuckin' sexy holding that iron like that. You're turning me on in the worst fuckin' way. Can we talk?" he asked.

"Talk," I argued. I headed back upstairs to my room. I threw the vest on the bed. I hopped back in my tub. I wasn't about to let him ruin another fuckin' moment of mine. I was relaxing just fine until he showed up. I don't want to hear shit Lucky has to say because his mouth says one thing and he does the total opposite. It's nothing he could say that could change my mind. He just wanted to know if I fucked Tariq or not, that's it. He kept a secret for three months, so I'll hold mine too.

"Can I join you?" He asked. I wasn't even about to respond because no matter what I said he was getting in anyway. I don't even want him near me because I've caught him with the same trifling bitch twice. It's something about her that he likes because he keeps lying to me about it. He doesn't even have to lie about it to pacify my feelings.

"Do I have a choice since you're already undressing?" I asked. Lucky ignored what the fuck I said and got in anyway. I knew he would do that. I got something for his ass. I don't even recognize his ass. I know he's fuckin' this bitch. He can't even lie. What would make him think I want him near me and you're openly fuckin' a bitch and you keep lying about it? Lucky was a lot of things, but a liar has never been his trait or maybe I didn't know him as well as I thought I did.

"Why do you have this water so fuckin' hot?" He asked. I wanted to cleanse myself of him and Tariq. What are the chances of that, Melanie is Shaela's sister? No wonder that bitch kept looking at me crazy at his going away party. She was probably the one who told Lucky I was with Tariq. I don't understand why he's so worried about me and you're still fuckin' off.

"That's how I like it. You're free to get out," I argued. Lucky climbed in right behind me and started massaging back and shoulders. He bit the crook of my neck and started whispering sweet nothings in my ear.

"I'm sorry, Kaniya. Can you forgive me? Tell me what a nigga got to do to make shit right between us," he asked. I shook my head. I couldn't believe he had the nerve to ask me that. You're not even ready to be in a fuckin' relationship with me anyway. Lucky knew I wasn't dumb. I don't even know why he fuckin' trying me at this point. I turned around to face him. I wanted to look him dead in the face because he needed to feel what I felt.

"There's nothing that you can do at this point. Actions speak louder than words. You claim that bitch doesn't mean shit to you. We wouldn't be here because of what you fuckin' did nigga. You're parading this bitch in my fuckin' face, but you care about me. You couldn't because you wouldn't continue to fuckin' hurt me. How is that she's shared a meal with your father before I did? I have been with you for five years.

Do you know how I fuckin' felt Lucky? Deuce and Quan both know this bitch, which means you're comfortable as fuck with her to even let her meet them. it's cool though because you can keep that bitch. Let me live a little. Let me sample some new dick," I argued and explained. His whole demeanor has changed. His nose flared up. He grabbed me and pulled me into him. We both were breathing heavy. I had some more things that I wanted to say but I've said enough.

Veins appeared on his neck and forehead. His blood pressure was high. I don't give a fuck. Oh well, I guess he wasn't expecting me to say this shit, but I don't know what the fuck he thought. Lucky knows he's one sexy black nigga and he can have any bitch he wants, but he can't have me and multiple bitches. I don't give a fuck how fine and sexy he is. I'm one bitch that's not settling. He can have that and any bitch that's willing to accept that. Lucky used to be so fuckin' perfect to me. I couldn't help but stare. He wasn't the same man I fell in love with.

His waves and his whole physique were intriguing. His teeth were white as coke minus the two gold fangs he had at the bottom. His eyes were light brown and threatening. His eyelashes were long and thick. Black is so beautiful. My pussy was moist as fuck now looking at the monster that lived between his legs. I need to calm down.

"Cat got your tongue?" I asked. I knew Lucky wanted to lay hands on me. I could tell, but if he did, I would drown his motherfuckin' ass in this tub and drag his ass to my fuckin' trunk and get rid of his body.

"I fucked up one fuckin' time Kaniya, and it's a mother-fuckin' wrap huh? Don't ever in your life let me hear you say you want to sample some new fuckin' dick," he argued. He made his way closer to me. He was all up in my face. I stepped back a little bit allowing space between us. He closed the gap and wrapped his arms around my waist. He leaned between and bit my bottom lip. I kept trying to break free from him. He had a death grip on my hips. "Kaniya, do you think I'm some sucker or a pussy ass nigga? You know it ain't shit pussy about me." He pushed me against the tub and bit my nipples and grabbed my pussy. I wasn't about to fuck him period so, he can stop with the free feels.

"Stop Lucky," I argued and sassed. He wasn't hearing me though.

"Is that what you think Kaniya? I'm not about to stop shit. Talk that tough as shit now, motherfucka. What's up with that tough shit now? You got me fucked up.

You've been disrespectful as fuck lately. Two wrongs don't make a fuckin' right. Listen to what the fuck I got to say and I'm not going to fuckin' repeat myself twice. You can either be with me because I put it on your life you don't want to know what it's like to live without me. It's not a threat, you'll die by the hands of me before I let you be with any of these pussy ass niggas. This shit right here," he argued and pointed between me and him. "It's forever. This shit is not a fuckin' game. I love you. I will die chasing you and making this shit up to you.

I'm going to fall back though, but if you even think about trying to be with Tariq. Sonja will be burying that bitch ass nigga and that's a fuckin' promise. I see what it is. I will make your life a living fuckin' hell. Don't ever in your life think you are going to give a bitch some shit I done gave you. Your truck is outside where it belongs.

That bitch doesn't mean shit to me. Yeah, I fucked her a few times, but that's about it. She doesn't come before you and you fuckin' know that. Stop acting like you know everything. It ain't what it fuckin' seems You can never get rid of me," he argued and explained. I hate him. Tears were in the brim of eyes. I wiped them with the back of my hand. He stepped out the tub and dried himself off. I can't believe him. He had the nerve to flip this shit on me.

He got me in my feelings, and I shouldn't be. It's like I'm in the wrong and I'm not. I wasn't the one cheating, shit he was. I need to lay my ass down and finish reading **Cuffed By a Trap God**, Sphinx was the truth. I wish Barbie and Ketta hurry up and bring their hot asses back from New York. I wanted to go out tonight. I need to get my life back on track. Lucky can't stand Tariq because he knows that's his competition. I'm feeling Tariq though and I can't deny it. Our chemistry is amazing. I know I'll have to beat the dog shit out of Shaela again. She's mad about her sister. Girl, I wish my sister Killany was here. I swear a bitch didn't fuckin' want it. Killany my twin sister, yes we're identical. No one knows about her but my immediate family.

Our father Killian Miller wanted it that way; he knew that we would cause hell together. We always have since the womb. Our grandmother raised her. She always wanted a daughter. She said I use to holler too much so she wouldn't keep me, just Killany. She's coming real soon. She finally texted me back.

Killany - Bitch you're lying. I can't wait to pull up. Your life sucks right now. I miss my sister. I'll be paying her a visit real soon. I needed her more than she would ever know.

Lucky

I'm trying to make this shit right between me and Kaniya but she isn't trying to forgive me at all. I fucked up and I told her that. Can we move past this shit? I know her and Tariq had something going on. He looked at Kaniya the same way I did. If she gave that nigga my pussy, I swear to God I'll kill her and him. I'm ready to go war with Killian behind the consequences. I swear to God had I known that my father was dating Sonja, Tariq's aunt, I would've never brought Melanie to the dinner. I was just sliding through. I had no fuckin' plans on meeting everybody. I didn't even pay Kaniya's Range any attention and I should've. I wanted to turn around when I saw her, but it was too fuckin' late.

I got to quit fuckin' with Melanie because I'm not trying to lose Kaniya behind her ass. She's not fuckin' worth it. I know we're going through our little bullshit right now, but we'll move past it. I haven't caught a body in a few weeks and Tariq doesn't want to be the next nigga on my hit list. I knew it was something going on between him and Kaniya. I could tell by how he looked at me when I came in. I wanted to knock Kaniya's fuckin' head off when she smashed the fuck out of Shaela's face behind that nigga. She was out here fighting over him.

Melanie was blowing up my phone. I had plans to fuck Kaniya into a coma, but she wasn't having that. If she wanted to be single then, she can be. She just better not be out in the open with that shit. Yirah was blowing up my shit too. I'll fuck around and slide through there and get my dick wet and slide right back out. Quan was hitting my shit now. I knew he had some slick ass shit to say.

"Talk to me nigga? What's the fuckin' move? Are you getting out tonight or you're lying up?" I asked. I could hear him chuckling. Tianna had his ass on lock. I knew he wasn't going anywhere. Thank God Tianna didn't drop the dime on me with Melanie's ass.

"Nah nigga, I'm in for tonight and you should be too. You should be tired of getting caught up. In all my years of living, I swore you were a smooth as nigga but for some reason, Kaniya keeps on catching you. Nigga slow your fuckin' roll and try to work that shit out with her. Tariq is moving in. I saw some shit that I shouldn't have," he explained.

"I'm trying nigga. Trust me she's not feeling me. I'm going to get right though. She knows what it is between us," I explained. I finished chopping it up with Quan.

I pulled in Yirah's garage and cut my phone off. Yirah was a good girl and she was always playing her fuckin' position. Whenever I slid over here, she always had that pussy hot and fuckin' ready. I didn't even have to tell her twice. Her spot was always clean and neat. I made it upstairs to her living room and she was sitting on the couch in a pair of lace boy shorts. I hovered over her and ran my tongue across her lips. She started unbuckling my pants instantly. I like a bitch that knows how to act.

"Slow down shawty, I'm going to give you what want. Be patient with a nigga. You missed me or something?" I asked. I couldn't keep my hands off Yirah. I slid her boy shorts off and reached for the Magnum out of my back pocket. Yes, I will be fuckin' these hoes but I'm not fuckin' these bitches raw. I could fuck Yirah raw because I knew I was the only nigga she was fuckin'. I had the keys to her spot and I've only been fuckin' with her for a few weeks.

"What type of question is that, Lucky? You know I missed you. I'm always at home waiting for you. Sometimes I wonder would I ever be more than just a creep to you," she asked. I like Yirah. I ain't gone lie because she never nags the fuck out of me. I cupped her chin and she was looking at me trying to figure out my next move.

"Look shawty, you know my situation. Kaniya and I aren't together right now but I fuck with you the long way. Keep playing your position and keep your legs and mouth wide the fuck open. When I ask you to and you'll go far. I can promise you that. It's not all about the pussy with me, that's a bonus. I see something in you, and I like what I see. Keep fuckin' with me and we'll see where it leads too. I like you Yirah, a lot," I explained. I leaned in and stole a kiss from her. She pulled back a little.

"Lucky, for some odd reason I trust you. You're the type of nigga my mother and brothers warned me about, but I like you a lot. I want you and I want to be more than just your number two. I know it's too soon but I'm feeling you. I'll hold you to your word but please don't hurt me," she sighed. I leaned in and deepened the kiss between us. I attempted to slide the condom on. I wanted to knock the frame out of Yirah's pussy. "Lucky, can I feel you please without the condom," she begged, moaned and pleaded. I shook my head no. Yirah pulled the condom off and tossed it on the floor. She started bouncing on my dick. I bit her collar bone. This shit felt good as fuck. I matched her stroke for stroke. She could barely catch her fuckin' breath.

"You want me to murder the fuck out of this pussy?" I asked. Yirah nodded her head yes and leaned up and gave me a kiss.

A MONTH LATER

Chapter-19

Kaniya

I'm really dreading going to Miami with Sonja and her new family. I should've said I had something to do because I wasn't trying to see Tariq or Lucky. I wasn't trying to fight any of the bitches that they're entertaining. Normally I would've been all in about hanging out with Sonja because she's cool as shit. I didn't want to be anywhere around her if some shit was about to pop off. I felt a storm coming. My Uncle Kanan called me a couple of times in the past few weeks inquiring about her and her new man. I knew he heard something because he's never on my line.

To make matters worse he started going off on me like I hooked her up with Deuce and I wasn't feeling that shit at all. I didn't want to be involved at any cost. The last thing I needed was to hear my father's mouth about the company I'm keeping.

My uncle said he was due to get out in a week or so. I wouldn't put it past him he's probably already out. He assured me that he would see what the fuck Sonja had going on. I haven't seen my uncle in years since he's been in the FEDS. Speaking of the devil herself, she's calling me now. Damn, I wish I wouldn't have agreed to go with her. I feel some shit brewing in the air and I always trust my instincts. She didn't even give me the chance to say hello.

"Kaniya, are you still coming? I was calling to make sure. Everything will be fine," she explained. Sonja sounded as if she was unsure of the trip herself. I'm big on tones and vibes and she sounded nervous as fuck if you ask me.

"Hey Auntie, I'm good. I'm bringing my friend JD with me to the party, is that cool? I'm not worried about Lucky or Tariq. My only focus is Work Now Atlanta. I'll be there in a few minutes. I'm getting my stuff together," I explained. I haven't heard from the two of them and I was cool. I'm living my life and they can live theirs too.

"Let me ask you a question Kaniya, is JD a boy or girl?" She asked. I looked at my phone. Sonja knew I was bringing a nigga with me. I wasn't bringing a bitch.

"A guy of course," I laughed and explained. My mother always told me the best way to get over a nigga is to get you a new one. Speaking of my mother I need to call her. I've been avoiding her for a few weeks now. She wanted to come and visit me because she knew I was going through it with my little break-up. I couldn't deal with Kaisha right now.

"Girl, you like playing with fuckin' fire," she laughed. I wasn't playing. I'm single and so is Lucky. What the fuck can he say? He made me single. He's dating why can't I date?

"I know you're not talking. Let's talk about Kanan, that's supposed to be getting out in about seven days. Hell, he might be already out. What the fuck are you going to do?" I asked. I looked at my phone and the call dropped. I bet she hung up in my face on fuckin' purpose. The reason why we were going to Miami was that it's Deuce birthday and Sonja wanted to throw him a birthday party. We're all going to be there for four days. He paid for a driver to charter us down there in a Stretch Range Rover.

I'm sure Tariq and Lucky brought them a bitch to tag along with them. It's cool, that's why JD was meeting me down there. I wouldn't say we were dating but we're cool and hang out often. He's fine as shit. He stood about 5'10 and his skin was the color of a caramel kiss. His hair was cut low with deep waves running all through his shit. A nice trimmed mustache and goatee adorned his face. He's built nicely as fuck too. His teeth were perfect. He's from Miami. He knows about my ex. I told him to bring his strap because that nigga is on some fuck shit. I see now what type of nigga Lucky is. He wants to do his dirt, but he doesn't want me to do anything.

I got JD because he has nothing to do with Lucky and I not being together. Lucky needs to get used to seeing me with someone that's not him. I hope Lucky can act civilized. I swear if he even thinks about getting on that bullshit, I'm going to spas out. I wasn't passing up a free trip to Miami. JD and I are going to drive back. He caught a flight down to Miami because he needed to pick up one of his cars from down there anyway, so he was cool with me going down there to chill with him.

Ocean Drive Miami, these niggas will know my name this weekend. I sent Barbie a text and told her to pull up. KOD here I come. I brought some bad ass swimsuits. I'm feeling myself already. I can't wait. I made sure I was extra cute today. I was rocking a cute pair of white True Religion shorts and boy are they short. I have a white True Religion shirt on to match with my shorts. It's see, through and it shows my stomach. I'm not sporting a bra. I changed my nipple rings, they're gold now.

I paired it with my Gold Giuseppe peep toe sandals. Yes, I'm killing it. I got a new tattoo sleeve on my leg and it's bad as fuck. I had a rose bush with roses and butterflies. It was so cute. I'm to turnt this weekend and I don't need nann nigga raining on my fuckin' parade. Hopefully, it'll be dope and drama free. I checked my bags twice. I had to make sure I had everything I didn't want to leave anything. I locked up and threw my bags in my back seat.

I'll make it to Sonja's house in about twenty minutes according to my GPS. Traffic was heavy. I was bobbing and weaving through traffic. I will be driving so fast in this Corvette I'm surprised I haven't gotten a ticket yet. I sent Sonja a text. I had to let her know if Shaela pops off, I'm busting her in her shit again, straight up. I finally made it to my destination. I guess I was the last one to arrive. Save the best for last. I grabbed my Louie Duffel Bag and locked my car up. This is a nice stretch, Range Rover. Let's get this show on the road. I knocked on the and door the passenger side opened. I walked up to the stairs and threw my big face Chanel frames on.

"Hi Kaniya, we were waiting on you," Deuce stated while he greeted me.

"Hey, Deuce, what's up? Traffic was heavy," I beamed and lied. I was taking my time because I didn't want to fuckin' come but I couldn't let Sonja down. I made my way to the back.

"Hey Raven," I beamed.

"Hey Kaniya," she beamed and spoke back. I saw Tianna and Quan I waved at them. I locked eyes with Tariq. Ugh, look at him. I hate he's so fuckin' fine. He was really with this bitch Shaela. He's looking hard as fuck.

"Pick your face up Tariq, it's just me," I sassed and sucked my teeth. I'm messy as fuck and I don't give a fuck. Let's not mention I locked eyes with the last motherfucka I wanted to see. Lucky. I walked right past him. I can't believe his bitch is not in tow. I guess he knew better. I heard Lucky coming behind me.

"Back up and go sit back in your seat," I argued. He needs to go back up front to his seat. I'm not with that bull shit today. He walked up on me and wrapped his arms around my waist. He felt me up a few times. I knew he was doing that to make Tariq jealous.

"I just want to carry your bags for you," he explained. Lucky hasn't grabbed one bag. The only thing he was grabbing was me. I swatted his hands away a few times. I didn't want him touching on me and he's been touching on someone else. I'm territorial as fuck.

"Yeah right," I sassed and sucked my teeth. He knew I wasn't fuckin' with him. Lucky couldn't keep his hands to himself. He was already putting his hands in my shorts. I squeezed my legs tight. I prayed my pussy wouldn't get wet for him. "Go on Lucky no free feels over here we're through." He started kissing me on my neck and whispering sweet nothings in my ear.

"You like that shit. Stop playing, Kaniya." I wasn't playing. I was dead serious. I put my luggage up. I wanted to toss my purse in the free seat I had beside me. Lucky took it upon himself to sit down. He picked my purse up and placed it with my luggage. He pulled me down and sat me on his lap and bit my shoulder.

"You feel that monster, Kaniya? He misses you and he's extra hard for you right now," he explained. I'm sure he does. A nigga always misses something that he can't have.

"Look Lucky, I'm not doing this shit with you. I know you're fuckin' somebody else so, you and I can't do that. I don't give a fuck who misses me," I argued. I grabbed Lucky's dick and he looked up at me and smiled. "I can't fuck you because you're fuckin' somebody else you should've kept your dick in your pants." I raised up off Lucky and he pulled me back on his lap. He insisted on feeling me up. I kept removing his hands.

"We used to, Kaniya." he sighed.

"We used to do a lot. You used to be faithful. We're not together, Lucky. The last time we fucked was our last time two month ago. I'm getting up now," I explained. I don't want to talk about us.

"No, you're not, just sit here. I want to hold you please," he begged and pleaded. Lucky and I have never been broken up before since we've been together. This is a first for us. We've had plenty of disagreements and we wouldn't talk for a few days but nothing this extreme.

"How long are you forcing me to sit here?" I asked. I folded my arms across my chest. I didn't want to be here with him. I wanted to focus on having a good time.

"The whole ride," he stated.

"Ugh, let me get comfortable," I pouted. Lucky was adamant about not letting me bust a move. We got comfortable. Lucky was lying down and I was lying on top of him. His hands roamed my body. This shit feels so right but I'll never tell him that. We used to do this all the time. Why did he fuck up this?

"Lucky where's Melanie?" Shaela asked. I warned Sonja. She wanted to be messy. If I smack the fuck out her people will say I'm wrong but she needs to mind her business and not mine. I told Sonja what time it was.

"Do you fucking see her, Shaela?" I argued and asked. I got up off Lucky and walked up in her face. When you see Melanie let her know Kaniya is occupying Lucky's time. Go run and tell that bitch. Be messy and tell your sister that shit," I argued.

"Fuck You," she argued. I punched that bitch dead in her mouth. Her shit was leaking now. "You got some pressure on your chest. Pick up your mouth bitch. Why are you so worried about Lucky? Tariq is right next to you. Worry about your own nigga."

"He isn't yours that's the problem," she argued.

"See that's where you're wrong bitch, Lucky will forever be mine. Your sister is just something to do. She will always be number two and she cool with that shit just like you," I argued.

"Tariq, I don't want to disrespect your girl at all. Can you please tell her to stay out of my business and don't talk to me about shit? Ask Melanie why she's not here," he argued.

"Let me find me another seat," I explained and got up to walk off. I had to go because bitches don't know their fuckin' place. They're always worried about me.

"I'm sorry, Kaniya." He explained. I'm tired of hearing Lucky say I'm sorry. He has yet to prove that he was. One of the reasons I came on this trip was to forget about everything that happened in Atlanta between the two of us. My past has followed me here. I know I had to face Lucky and everything we've been going through. I just didn't want it to be today with Tariq being here.

"You're good, let me move though," I pouted. Lucky wasn't trying to hear anything I was saying. He wouldn't let me leave his side for anything. I appreciated the gesture, but it was a little too late for that. I just wanted to enjoy myself and not talk about us.

"No Kaniya, you don't have to move. Fuck her, she's just miserable. I want you right here. It's the only fuckin' place I want you. Let's talk right here right now because it's long overdue," he explained. Lucky cupped my chin forcing me to look at him. I closed my eyes. A small smile was etched on my face. God, I used to love his touch and I hate that my body still responded to him. I miss the fuck out of him. He leaned in and stole a kiss. I opened my eyes. Lucky and I starred at each other and he gave me that sexy cocky smirk that I once love and adored. I'm not about to do this shit with him.

"Okay talk Lucky, I'm listening," I sighed. I wonder what he had to say that would be different than anything that he's said in the past?

"I'm sorry Kaniya, I am. You might not believe it but I am. I want to change and I'm trying if you would allow me to. I know I've done some dumb ass shit but you're worth fighting for. I refuse to throw away five years for a couple of fucks. Fight for US, Kaniya. I made one mistake in five years. This right here feels so right. This is how we're supposed to be.

Can we get back to this; give us another shot. This past month I've been sick without you and you know it too. I Love You, Kaniya. It's not a bitch out here that's weighing up to you. All these bitches out here know how much I fuckin' love you. I fucked up. Give me another chance and I swear I won't fuck up. Tell me what I got to do to make shit right between us," he begged, pleaded and explained.

"I love you too, Jamel." I beamed. I love Lucky and I can't lie. We've been together for five years and you just don't stop loving somebody overnight. We've been apart for a month but I still wasn't ready to take him back. He'll have to do more than talk. I'm judging his actions, not by the words he puts together. My phone went off alerting me that I had a text. I looked at my phone and it was Tariq.

Tariq - Tell that nigga to quit begging

Me - lol

"What's so funny?" He asked. I exited out my messages quick. I know Lucky wanted to know who was sending me text messages, but it was for me to know and not him.

"Nothing, just a text," I explained. He snatched my phone out my hand. Lucky was going directly to my text messages. I knew he was about to read the text Tariq sent. Thank God I didn't have anything on my phone to incriminate me.

Lucky's face was snarled up and I could feel the flames dripping from his pores. I was scared. I knew he saw some shit that he probably didn't agree with. The last thing I needed was for Lucky and Tariq to come to blows behind me. Lucky needed a reason to get at him. He's always the topic of our conversation. Lucky knew we had something going on. He just didn't know that I've had sex with him. To be honest I didn't want him to know that either.

"Tariq, I will die begging my nigga. I know you want Kaniya but keep wishing MOTHERFUCKA because it's not going down like that. It's fuckin' MURKIN' season and I mean that shit literally. I'm begging for you or any nigga to fuckin' try me," he argued. Oh God, I hated when Lucky got in his feelings because he would go on and on. Tariq wasn't one to back down either. I knew he wasn't about to let what Lucky said slide.

"Shut up Lucky, please," I begged and pleaded. Tariq got up and walked toward us. I looked at him with threatening eyes begging him not to feed into Lucky, but he wasn't with it. He was going to do what he wanted to do regardless.

"Lucky, I ain't never been your nigga and you ain't never been mine. I'm not with the bullshit. It's always fuckin' murking season with me. I'm not beefing with you behind nothing or no one that doesn't belong to me yet," he argued. I can't believe Tariq said that. He was making shit worse. Lucky stood up and pushed me behind him.

"Oh yeah, YET? Is that what the fuck you think? Whatever the fuck you think you and Kaniya got going I suggest you dead that shit if you want to continue breathing and living in the land of the living. I don't make threats. I make good on all my fuckin' promises," he argued. Deuce and Sonja came back to the back to keep confusion down. Sonja just shook her head. It wasn't me this time. I didn't even do shit. Sonja ushered Tariq back toward the front. Deuce was trying to calm Lucky down. Lucky pulled me on his lap and bit my shoulder.

"Can you please calm down," I begged and pleaded.

"Cut your phone off and give it to me? We're trying to work on us right now and the fuck nigga interfering." I cut my phone off to keep confusion down. I wasn't giving him my phone. Fuck that.

The last thing I needed was for Lucky and Tariq to fight and it slips that I've been fuckin' Tariq. We wouldn't make it off this bus alive and I was to fuckin' fly to die. The niggas and Miami haven't even seen me yet. I wasn't wasting these bathing suits, fuck that.

"Do you think we're going to be able to work on us in eight hours?" I asked and sighed? It's the beginning of the summer and I haven't been single in a long time. I just wanted to have fun, enjoy my summer, date and flirt a little.

"I think we can," he explained. I know Lucky loves me and I love him but he's not ready to be with me and only me. If he can hide a bitch for three months without me knowing, that nigga can hide any fuckin' thing. I wasn't ready to be in a relationship again. I wanted to get myself together without him.

"I forgive you Lucky, but I will never forget. Was I hurt? Yes, I was and I still am. Will I continue to throw it in your face every chance I get? No, because even though I want to, I'm not because I'm not petty and I don't want to block my blessings. Am I ready to take you back right now? No, I'm not. I need more time to myself," I explained. I wasn't jumping back in a relationship with him. He fucked us up and that's some shit he must deal with. He has to work extra hard to get me back. It ain't easy getting back in my good graces.

"I can respect that. Can we be friends with benefits?" He asked. I knew Lucky wanted to fuck me because I wasn't fucking him. He wanted to make sure I wasn't fuckin' anybody else but him. Thank God it's been a few weeks since Tariq and I made love. Hopefully, if we did cross that line, I would feel the same to him. I know Tariq stretched me wide open. His dick was long and thick.

"No, we can't have sex," I explained. I craved for Lucky plenty of nights. I wanted to call him so bad so he could break me off, but I knew he was fuckin' somebody else and I wasn't ready to go there with him. I was holding out. I was nobody's fool and I for damn sure wasn't dick silly.

"Who you been giving my pussy to?" He asked. I knew he wanted to know that so bad. I couldn't tell Lucky that I fucked

Tariq because he would beat my ass and my gun is in my purse. I would have to shoot him. Lucky is the type of nigga who can't take what he dishes out. I laid my hands on him for fuckin' off. I knew he would lay hands on me for doing the same thing I accused him of.

"Nobody. I don't slang my pussy like you slang your dick. I don't give my pussy away to everybody. I should've found somebody else to fuck. Move let me get up," I argued and pushed him out my way. I attempted to get up. He tugged at my shorts. I swatted his hands away.

"Damn Kaniya, what the fuck did I do, where are you going?" He asked. He wanted to ask me all the questions about who I'm fuckin' because he's fuckin' somebody else. The last time I saw him. I went to his house and guess who never came home. Him. I knew he fucked somebody that night. I felt it but he's so fuckin' worried about me.

"Away from you, Lucky," I argued. I shouldn't even be this close and cozy with this cheating ass motherfucka.

"What I do? I'm sorry, Kaniya. I miss you that's all. I love you," he explained. He started feeling and rubbing on my stomach. "I'm going to put one in you. I'm ready for you to have my baby." I looked at him as if he was crazy. I wouldn't dare have a baby by him and it'll be just my luck I would have twins. Shit, my father is a twin. I have a twin and my father's mother has a twin. I'm sure twins wouldn't skip my ass. He moved his hands to my breasts and started massaging them.

"Why don't you have a bra on Kaniya?" He asked. I wasn't even about to respond to him, because I do what I want, and I don't have to consult with him.

"I don't need one on," I sassed. He moved his hands in my shorts. He started playing in my pussy. I started to ride his fingers just to bust a nut, but I'll pass. I swatted his hands away. He was doing too much. He finally stopped and brought his fingers toward his nose. He looked at me and smiled. Lucky was a real freak and he taught me how to be his personal freak. He licked his fingers clean.

"Why the fuck you don't have any panty's on. You gone make me fuck you up. She misses me, Kaniya." He asked and explained? I did miss him but I wouldn't let him know that. I missed everything about him. I missed what he was holding between his legs. I'll continue to fight temptation before I slide on that.

"No she doesn't miss you and she'll be alright," I beamed proudly.

"Let me taste her?" He asked and begged. I knew Lucky wanted me to sit on his face. He's been asking me since he's been back here. I was not about to do that on the bus. He just wanted to fuck with Tariq.

"Nope, we aren't doing this? That's why I don't need to be sitting back here with your freaky ass." I sassed and laughed. Lucky was trying to rip my shorts off. He was trying to take something and prove a point. We're not on that level so he can't be doing this.

"You want it, Kaniya." He stated. Lucky was so rude and aggressive. He knew he was turning me on in the worst way. He grabbed my hand and placed it on his dick. I ran my fingers across the tip and it was leaking with pre-cum. It was hard as soon as I touched it and it started jumping.

"I'm cool," I laughed. Lucky wasn't having it. He backed up against the window. He grabbed my face roughly and shoved his tongue in my mouth. I wouldn't kiss him back even though I wanted too. Lucky and I kissing would lead to us fucking right here on this bus. His hands roamed every inch of my body. He knew I was addicted to his fuckin' touch.

"Stop playing, Kaniya. You know I don't give a fuck. Come on up out them fuckin' shorts and put that pussy in my face. I need to salute that diamond between your legs," he argued and explained. He was so rough and aggressive. He roughly pulled my shorts down and laid me down on the seat. He threw my legs over his shoulders and went to work. Lucky had something to prove. He was sucking the soul out of my pussy I wanted to scream. I bit down on his collar bone to muffle my screams. I knew for a fact I just fucked this seat up.

I had an orgasm so big my whole body started to shake and my legs wouldn't stop shaking. Lucky's phone started ringing. I grabbed it and looked at it. I started to throw it at his head. I shook my head. It was Melanie. I cut my eyes at him instantly. Why is she calling his phone? I started to shove his ass in his head while he's between my legs.

"Your phone ringing Lucky and its Melanie," I argued and sassed. Lucky raised up from between my legs and his mustache was drenched in my juices. He knew I was mad as fuck.

"Answer it," he argued and buried his face back between my legs. I answered his phone.

"Hey Baby," she beamed and smiled through the phone. I couldn't wait to bust this bitch's bubble. She was feeling the shit out of Lucky too. I didn't have a problem putting a bitch in their place and guess what, this hoe wasn't excluded. She was going to learn today. Lucky had this bitch to comfortable.

"Hey Melanie," I sassed and sucked my teeth. I could hear her huffing and puffing in the background. I swear I got fuckin' time today. I already busted your sister in her shit. I can guarantee you she doesn't want to be next.

"Put Lucky on the phone," she argued. I looked at the phone and let out a soft moan. I was trying to keep it classy. Normally if a bitch has beaten your ass twice you would know to stay in your fuckin' place, but see Melanie was dick dizzy and it's all Lucky's fault. My momma always told me you should never have to check a bitch twice. If you do, shoot the bitch dead in her head to make sure you'll never have to check her again. I live and die by that shit.

"He's eating and his mouth is full," I sassed and sucked my teeth. I could hear her huffing and puffing in the background. I started riding his face even more and moaning in her ear.

"He can talk," she argued. I started laughing loud as fuck in her face.

"He can't talk because my pussy is in his mouth and it's too good to talk," I moaned. She hung up the phone. I knew she would. A small smiled appeared on my face. His phone started ringing again. Oh lord, she hit the FaceTime. I guess she wanted her feelings hurt. She has the right one today. I picked the bitch up and hit that green button. I had to let her see Lucky was eating this pussy. I flipped the camera around so she could see he was eating my pussy. I smiled at the bitch showing her all thirty-two of my teeth. Tears were running down her face.

"Melanie, if this is what it feels like to be number two it sucks to be you right now," I laughed. This bitch was livid. I had to laugh at her stupid ass, she was a dumb little bitch. "Lucky you're petty as fuck." I don't know what Lucky was telling these bitches but I would never agree to it.

"I don't care. This shit is real between you and I. I don't care about that girl. Kaniya, you got my fuckin' heart and you know that. Let me put the tip in," he begged. I wasn't about to fuck him. I don't care that he proved a point. That bitch was dumb as fuck.

"No Lucky, why do I always have to give up some pussy after you eat my pussy?" I asked. He can't just eat my pussy and go on about his business. It's always stipulations with it that's why I didn't want him to eat my pussy in the first place because I knew he would be demanding to fuck me.

"Why are you being difficult Kaniya, damn? I should've been done raped your hot ass. I don't know why you keep fuckin' playing with me. Let me stick it in. It's been my pussy for years. I'm going to pull out I promise. I know you're not going to leave me hanging? Nobody can judge us. It's always us against the world. Jamel and Kaniya 'til we die, baby, you know it," he explained. He started sucking on my neck and playing with my pussy getting me hot and bothered.

"Whatever Lucky, hurry up," I moaned. I hope I don't regret this. "Grab a condom Lucky, I'm not fuckin' you raw." Lucky grabbed a condom out of his back pocket and slid it on. He kept grilling me while he was putting it on. I don't care. He doesn't have those type of privileges anymore.

"Thank you. Damn this pussy feel good as fuck. If this shit was loose I was going to choke your this shit out of your ass. I can just fall asleep in it. Ride your dick. Damn, you just don't know how bad I want to bust up all up in your pussy right now. You can be mad all you want to. I want you to get pregnant and have my son. I don't care. I'm ready for us to have a child," he moaned and grunted.

"Lucky, I don't want to be trapped with a child right now," I moaned.

"Well, I want to trap my future, my wife. I feel like you're trying to leave me and never look back. It ain't no breaking up. Tell me what a nigga got to do to make shit right between us. Slow down you're about to make me bust a nut," he grunted. I knew Lucky was on the verge of cumin. I started riding his dick like I was riding a horse. I could feel Lucky's dick get harder and harder. He sped up his strokes.

"I'm cumin', Lucky." I moaned and whispered. I didn't want anybody to hear us.

"Get yours, I want us to cum together," he moaned and grunted. I came all on his dick. I knew he got his because I got mine. Lucky and I were both trying to catch our breath. We were both spent. I needed that. I heard some footsteps. Lucky and I both played like we were sleeping.

"Y'all some nasty motherfuckers. Y'all will fuck any-where. Deuce seen y'all. That blanket isn't doing y'all any jus-tice. All we saw was ass rocking. Y'all couldn't wait," Sonja asked. I was so fuckin' embarrassed. I buried my face in Lucky's chest.

"Kaniya Nicole Miller I know you hear me fuckin' talking to you," she laughed. I peeked from around Lucky to look at Sonja and she was shaking her head and smiling at me.

"Auntie Sonja I didn't do anything. That was all him. Can I take a shower?" I asked and smiled. A blind person could see that Lucky and I just fucked. We both had something to prove. He missed me just as much as I missed him. If we were together I wouldn't even care what people thought be we're not.

"It's a shower on here," he explained and pointed toward the back. Sonja and Lucky talked for a while, as I made my way to the shower. I felt a pair of eyes on me. I looked over my shoulder to see who it was. It was Tariq and he was making his way toward the bathroom. I knew he had some shit he wanted to say to me but I didn't want to hear it. I locked the door as soon as I stepped in and slid down the door. I turned the shower up on high I wanted the water as hot as possible. I grabbed my toiletries out of my bag. I could hear some commotion outside the door.

"Tariq, you need to back the fuck up. My lady in there handling her fuckin' business. Give her a minute," he argued and explained. Tariq was really trying to get up in here.

"I got to piss real quick. Kaniya doesn't have nothing that I haven't seen before," he argued. Tariq was doing too much. He was still trying to make his way in the bathroom. I could hear him messing with the door handle. I'm glad I locked it.

"Do you want to fuck my bitch pussy ass nigga," he argued? I knew Lucky was looking for a reason to fight Tariq. I hope Tariq doesn't say the wrong thing to provoke him. I said a quick prayer to my ancestors hoping they would hear me out.

"I do want to fuck her," he argued. Fuck my life, Tariq. Why did you fuckin' say that? I could feel my blood pressure getting high all of a sudden. I swear I don't want to be in a fucked up situation. Tariq wanted the world to know that we've been fuckin' and I wanted to keep it a secret. What's understood doesn't need to be explained.

"Why in the fuck did you say that shit? Deuce break this shit up," she yelled and argued. I could hear bumps and knocks up against the door. Lucky and Tariq had to be fighting and going blow for blow. I swear I don't want to go back out there.

"Quan get your motherfuckin' brother," he yelled. I knew that was Deuce. I knew I should've stayed at home and this is the reason why. I swear I didn't want to leave this bathroom but it would only make me look guilty. I dried off good and applied a little almond oil and lotion to my skin. I brushed my hair up into a messy ponytail.

"What's going on, what's wrong Lucky?" I asked. I walked out of the bathroom into a fuckin' danger zone. Lucky and Tariq's eyes were both trained on me and I didn't like it. I kept my eyes trained on Lucky. I couldn't look at Tariq because Lucky would suspect that something was up.

"This fuck nigga tried to come in the bathroom while you were in there," he argued. I tried to play it off and changed the conversation.

"Oh, why are y'all fighting?" I asked. I really didn't want to know. I'm glad they're not fighting now because I would have to pick a side and I didn't want to do that.

"He wants to fuck you that's why," he argued. Deuce and Sonja tried to calm Lucky down. I attempted to go back to my seat, but Lucky wasn't having that. He grabbed me by arm and pointed to the seat where we were sitting. "Have a fuckin' seat right here and if I find out you fucked that nigga I swear I'll fuckin' hurt you and that nigga." I knew shit was about to go left. It was written all over Lucky's face.

Chapter-20

Lucky

I can't wait to get to Miami. I'm not staying at the beach house. Tariq wants to fuck my bitch bad. Guess what, he'll fuck around and die and I don't give a fuck. A nigga can't openly disrespect me about my bitch and live to tell about. I'm not that nigga and you can never try me as if I am. He is too pressed for some of Kaniya's pussy. I think he might try to take something. I need to ask her has she fucked him. This shit isn't adding up. He was wearing his emotions on his sleeve and willing to die behind something that doesn't belong to him.

She's not staying at the beach house either. I don't trust him. I don't give a fuck, I'll kill Tariq. There ain't no way around it. Kaniya tried to act as if she was sleep, but I knew she wasn't. I could tell by the way she was breathing. She can't fuckin' run game on me. She should try running it on another pussy ass motherfucka but not me.

"Kaniya, wake your motherfuckin ass up," I argued. I tapped her on her shoulder hard as fuck. I'm not playing with her ass.

"What's up?" She yawned and stretched her arms. She was looking at everything but me. I knew she was hiding something from me. I just wanted her to be honest.

"Have you fucked that nigga?" I asked. I wanted her to say the wrong thing so I can beat her fuckin' ass for trying the fuck out of me and having a nigga she's fuckin' sitting in my fuckin' presence trying me like I won't kill his fuckin' ass.

"Come again, Lucky?" She asked and argued? I knew Kaniya had some shit that she was trying to hide because of her tone. I know Kaniya. I've spent five years with her. She was defensive for a reason I can tell she has some shit that she wants to say but she's scared to say it because she knows it's going to be some fuckin' repercussions.

"You heard what the fuck I said, answer my fuckin' question. You must be guilty of some shit," I argued and explained. Kaniya was beating around the bush. I don't even put my hands on women because my father raised me better than that but if she fucked Tariq or did anything with him I swear to God I'll fuckin' hurt her ass.

"I haven't fucked Tariq, but he has eaten my pussy that's all," she stated in a matter of fact tone. She got me fucked up. I snatched her motherfuckin' ass up. I grabbed Kaniya by her neck and choked the fuck out of her ass. I threw her up against the seat of the bus.

"Kaniya Miller I will fucking kill your dumb ass. BITCH don't you ever in your fuckin' life think you can fuck with a nigga that's less than fifty feet away from me and I won't do shit. You got me fifty shades of fucked up. I will fuckin' hurt you for real. You can't do what the fuck I do. I knew you did something with his ass. We haven't even been broken up that long and you got my pussy in the next nigga's mouth. You out here acting like a whole motherfuckin' hoe," I argued.

I looked over my shoulder. I heard somebody coming and was Tariq. I swear to God he better not interfere with what the fuck we got going on. I will handle his ass the same mother-fuckin' way. I knew he heard me. I wanted him to. Tariq tried to get me off Kaniya. Soon as I felt Tariq touch me. I shoved his ass off me, and he pushed me back. Tariq an I started going blow for fuckin' blow. Nobody broke it up.

He wanted to fight me and play captain save a hoe behind my bitch and I'll beat his ass every fuckin' time behind my bitch. It's levels to this shit and my bitch is off fuckin' limits. That shit goes for Tariq or any fuckin' body. My father and Quan finally broke the fight up between us. Tariq and I both spat blood on the fuckin' floor. Tariq was about to say something. The only thing he needs to do is stay the fuck up out business before I silence his ass for good.

"Lucky you're mad for what though? You and Kaniya aren't together. The two of y'all have both showed us that y'all ain't. I got mad respect for her because she kept it real. She didn't lie about what we've done. I'll never let a nigga put their hands on her while she's in my fuckin' presence," he argued and explained. Tariq was feeling Kaniya for real. I couldn't let anything he said slide. Basically, he was saying that he didn't give a fuck. I pushed my brother out my way and got to Tariq again. We started going blow for fuckin' blow. My dad pushed me to the back. I felt a huge punch to my head. I looked over my shoulders and it was Kaniya. I tried to grab her ass so fuckin' quick. My dad and my brother were both blocking me from getting at her.

"You know what Lucky, see the difference between you and me is that I can keep it real about what the fuck I do, but you can't. You want to continue to lie, but I'm far from dumb. Why are you mad at me because I'm moving on? How many bitches have you entertained that I don't know about tell me that?" She asked and argued. I wasn't about to go back and forth with Kaniya about shit because she already know what it is between us. I told her those bitches don't mean shit to me and she needs to stop focusing on them.

"Fuck you Kaniya, and don't say shit to me. Keep fuckin' talking and I swear to God I'm going to fuckin' hurt you. I'm begging you to fuckin' try me. I wish this nigga would try to play Captain Save my Bitch again and watch what the fuck I do," I argued and explained.

"You caught me slipping one fuckin' time, Lucky. I promise you if you touch me again I'll shoot you dead in your fuckin' head on this fuckin' bus. I'm sick of you and all your bullshit. Leave me the fuck alone. I don't give a fuck how many witnesses is on this motherfucka I'll air you out and send you back in a fuckin' box to your fuckin' momma and I put that shit on me. If you ever fuckin' touch me again. I hate a jealous ass nigga. You want to fuck everything but you're mad at me. Keep fuckin' these bitches because I don't fuckin' want you. Let me get my shit from back from your stupid ass. Give me my fuckin' phone back," she argued. Kaniya tried to snatch her phone out my pockets. I grabbed her phone so quick she wasn't getting this motherfucka back. She was too fuckin' sneaky.

"Shut the fuck up and sit the fuck down," I argued. She rested her hands on her thick ass hips and held her hand out for her phone. She wasn't getting it back. Kaniya wanted to be single so she could be hot in the ass but I'm not the nigga for it.

I love Kaniya. I swear to God I do and my actions may not show it but damn shawty you didn't have to get a nigga back like that. You don't go out and give yourself to the next fuckin' man because I fucked up trying to get over me. She gave Tariq more than hope and it's not over between us until I say it is.

Chapter-21

Kaniya

I'm so fuckin' livid right now. Lucky and I can't be anywhere around each other if we're not together. This trip went from bad to worse in a matter of minutes. Tariq being here only made shit worse. I shouldn't have said anything because Lucky didn't even deserve the truth from me because he hasn't even kept it real with me. I couldn't wait to get off this fuckin' bus and get away from the two of them. Lucky threw my phone at me damn near hitting me in my fuckin' head. He's doing too much. He wanted a reaction out of me, and I refused to give him one.

I didn't want Lucky and Tariq fighting over me. I cut my phone on. I had a ton of missed text messages. A smile instantly crept up on my face. JD sent me a text to see what time I would make it. He was cool as shit and a breath of fresh air. He can pick me up soon as I make it and we can pull off. I wanted to get as far away from everybody as possible.

I'm over this whole fuckin' trip. The text message that stood out the most was from Tariq. He still wasn't letting up. I was mad as fuck at him and he knew it. I've seen him on two occasions with Shaela, but he claims he's not fuckin' with her. It's something because he's keeping the bitch around and he can continue too.

Tariq - You so disrespectful. How are you fucking this nigga on the bus and giving my pussy away? I should smack your ass.

Me – Whatever. Aren't you with Shaela? Tell her to bust that pussy open? That's why you're mad. I'm not turning down head and you know that. Leave me alone Tariq. Thank you for earlier. I appreciate you 😘😘

Tariq was cool. We just couldn't be together. He had some shit going on and I did too. I wish we would've never crossed that line but it's too late and it happened. I heard someone approach the seat where I was sitting. I looked over my shoulder to see who it was, and it was Lucky. I turned my head quickly because I wasn't beat for any of his shit today, I've had enough. I looked at my neck in the mirror and it was red because of his crazy stupid ass.

He placed his hand on my shoulder. I gave him an evil scowl. My gun was sitting between my legs. I meant what the fuck I said I would kill his stupid ass.

"Scoot over," he argued and smiled. I can't stand his motherfuckin' ass. What would make him think that I wanted to be bothered with him after he just tried to beat my ass because I moved on because he cheated. Lucky made room for his mother-fuckin' self. I folded my arms across my chest. I could feel him staring a hole in the side of my face. I refused to even look at him. I'm sure he could tell that I was uncomfortable because I fuckin' was. He tapped me on the shoulder.

"Go on somewhere please. I'm not dealing with you," I argued. I thought he would've left already, I guess not. "You couldn't wait to text that nigga," he asked. I looked at Lucky as if he was crazy. Every action doesn't need a reaction. Lucky snatched my phone. I don't know why he was so fuckin' determined to read my text messages. I could've gone through his phone but I wasn't about to hurt my fuckin' feelings. I already know he was up to some shit. That's why I wasn't even taking him back. He wasn't even moving the same. He cupped my chin roughly forcing me to look at him.

"Kaniya, let me ask you a motherfuckin' question and I want you to fuckin' answer me. Why does he think your pussy is his, because it isn't, tell me something Kaniya? The way he's acting is if you let him fuck or something. When did he eat your pussy?" He asked. My heart dropped to my fuckin' stomach.

Lucky was doing to fuckin' much. Why does he want to know so bad if it's only going to get him upset? Lucky and I couldn't have a conversation like a civil couple that's broken up because he wanted to throw hands immediately.

"The same reason you think it's still yours and it's not because we're not together. Why does it matter when he ate it?" I asked. Lucky needs to learn to live his life without me because I've been doing it. He wasn't even thinking about me until he saw someone sniffing up behind me. I hate to admit it but it'll be a long time before Lucky, and I will ever get back together.

"I know it's mine and you fuckin' know that too. I'm sorry for putting my hands on you. I mean it. I should've walked away but I couldn't because he was testing my fuckin' gangsta. He told me he wanted to fuck you. It's not a nigga walking that will tell me that to my face and not get fuckin' touched.

The only reason he's still breathing is that my fuckin' pump is underneath this motherfuckin' Range Rover. I just wanted to let you know you're not staying at the beach house with him," he argued and explained. Lucky was full of shit. I swear I'm starting to hate his motherfuckin' ass. I wasn't staying there anyway. I couldn't wait to bust his fuckin' bubble.

"It's cool I booked me a room anyway. I wasn't planning on staying there." I sassed and sucked my teeth. It's nothing. Sonja and Deuce could say anything to me to make want to stay there. Lucky and Tariq already showed their ass on the fuckin' bus. I already know it's going down at the house. I'm just here for the free fuckin' ride. These motherfuckas won't even see me after I touch down. "You got us a room?" He asked. A soft laughed escaped my lips because Lucky was funny as fuck.

"There is no us. I'm single. Do you see a ring on my fuckin' finger? Lucky, we're in Miami, enjoy yourself because I will," I sassed and smirked. JD had a lot of shit planned for us and I was looking forward to that. At this point, I didn't even want to go to Deuce's party. I need a getaway and Virginia Beach is looking real nice right about now. I think I'll pay Killany a visit in a few days. I miss her so fuckin' much. I needed an escape from Atlanta from all my bullshit.

"Kaniya, don't fuckin' disrespect me while we're out here. That's all I ask? I'm not fuckin' playing with you," he argued. I had some shit to say.

"Lucky, how can I disrespect you if we're not together? Again, you're single because you cheated and I'm single because I refused to be with you, and I know you're living a double fuckin' life. What I do is my business and not yours," I argued.

"You heard what the fuck I said, Kaniya. I'm begging you to fuckin' try me. I can't wait to make an example out of one those pussy ass niggas. I guess Tariq is the first motherfucka I'm going to lay down. How much do you want to fuckin' bet?" He asked, argued and explained. I swear I'm sick of his ass. I thought our little break up was cool because we haven't seen each other but Lucky couldn't take me being with the next man. He could dish out all the bullshit, but he couldn't take it.

Finally, we made it to Miami. I swear it felt as if we were never going to get here, about fucking time. I couldn't wait to get off this fuckin' bus. This trip didn't start out how I thought it would. The only good thing that happened was I got me some bomb ass dick.

Lucky broke me off proper before he attempted to break my fuckin' neck. I should be good for another month or so. I couldn't even get off the bus good. Lucky saw Tariq about to approach me and he was about to fuckin' lose his mind. He can't stand to see me with another man or doing me. I've seen him plenty of times with Melanie on numerous occasions.

Did I trip? Fuck no, do you. But when you watch me do me don't get fuckin' get mad. Don't get your blood pressure high.

I didn't want to stay at the beach house no way. I'm Ocean Drive Miami all fuckin' day. He knew I was about to show my ass. And everything that Kaisha fuckin' gave me. I can't want to hit Collins looking so fuckin' stout.

Tariq know he's a standup guy he told that nigga to his face that he wanted to fuck me. He had my pussy hot as fuck when he said that shit. I couldn't wait to sit on his face and let him take me down through there again. I was smiling just thinking about it.

"Come on Kaniya, bring your hot ass on. I swear to God it feels like history is repeating itself. Your mother used to be on the same shit with your father before she had you and Killany. Kaisha with a K was a hot ass fuckin' mess and she's passed everything down to you," Sonja explained. She always told me I acted just like my mother. I knew Killany acted more like my father. She was his favorite and he would lie and say he didn't have any, but I knew fuckin' better.

"What did I do now," I asked. I didn't even do nothing from the moment I stepped on the bus and it was a fuckin' problem. Shaela started her shit and I fuckin' finished it. Tariq was mad because I wasn't giving him any attention. Lucky was made because he knew Tariq was choosing and I could choose too because we're not together. I knew he was still fuckin' with Melanie because she kept blowing up his fuckin' phone. I don't even give a fuck about her watching him eat my fuckin' pussy. She chose to be number two so deal with the fuckin' consequences. She willingly signed up for this shit.

"On some real shit Kaniya, and I'm telling from your mother's point of view. If you are going to be with Lucky, be with him and stop playing fuckin' games. That goes for you and him. Leave Tariq the fuck alone. Please, that's my fuckin' nephew and I'm not trying to lose him behind some pussy that he knows he shouldn't even be sampling.

I don't want my stepson and nephew beefing over you. I don't see this shit ending well. To keep everybody alive please leave Tariq the fuck alone and I'm going to tell him the same fuckin' shit," she argued and explained. I understood where Sonja was coming from, but I didn't fuck up my relationship he did. I'm just leveling the fuckin' playing field.

My momma always fuckin' told me never to wait around on a nigga to get his shit together. Move around and get yourself together with the next fuckin' nigga. Why the fuck are you waiting the whole time you're at home sad and fuckin' lonely and he's laid up with the next bitch. Guess what, Kaisha Miller ain't never told me a fuckin' lie. Her word is fuckin' law.

"Whose team are you on?" I asked. Sonja was in the middle period because she has a connection with all three of us. Her fuckin' stepson. Bitch please, if she knew like I knew, she'll leave Deuce right where she fuckin' found him at because my Uncle Kanan ain't going out like that. He's worse than Lucky. It was funny just thinking about it.

"I'm team Kaniya all fuckin' day," she beamed proudly. She better be because I wasn't beat for her shit either. I only came on this trip for her. I should've kept my fine ass at fuckin' home.

"It takes two Sonja, give Tariq the same speech," I laughed and explained. I don't think I could stay away from Tariq if I wanted to. I'm in too deep and I'm infatuated with his ass. it's one of the reasons why I won't take Lucky back. I'm still curious ass fuck about him. We finally made it to the house. I grabbed my bags and walked toward the house. The house was nice as fuck. It sat right on the beach and I knew Deuce paid a nice grip for it. It's too bad I won't be able to enjoy it.

I sent JD a text and gave him the address on where to pull up. I needed to grab me a room quickly so I can shower, change clothes, and get ready for my date tonight. I didn't want to smell like Lucky around JD. I found a room that was empty. I was about to dip into the room before I felt a damn football player damn near tackle my fuckin' arm off. I didn't even have to look over my shoulder because I knew who it was. I stopped in my tracks.

"You're hard-headed as fuck. I told you that you couldn't fuckin' stay here, let's go," he argued and explained. I snatched my arm away from him. I wanted to laugh in his face so fuckin' bad he was losing his fuckin' mind trying to run everybody off.

"Lucky, I'm good. I just wanted to shower and change my clothes. My ride is on the way," I argued and sassed. He had no clue I didn't want to be here as bad as he didn't want me here.

"Kaniya, do you want to fuck Tariq as bad as he wants to fuck you?" He asked. I wasn't even about to respond because Lucky is making everything about Tariq. I'm just saying if you're doing all of this why did you fuckin' cheat? You opened the door for the next fuckin' nigga.

"No," I argued and walked in another direction. He was still on my fuckin' heels. Why because I'm leaving.

"I can't tell because you're so fuckin' determined to be over here. Fuck that this shit, it isn't up for discussion, Kaniya. I don't know why I'm explaining myself to you. Bring your moth-erfuckin' ass on, I'm tired of fuckin' tell you," he argued and ex-plained. I heard two bitches talking and I knew it was Shaela. I swear to God if that bitch says the wrong thing to me I will murk her ass right here and Lucky will clean this bitch up. That's a fuckin' promise because beating ass ain't enough for these hoes.

"Here he goes Melanie," she argued. Shaela and her sister were so fuckin' stupid. He didn't want me to stay here because his bitch was here. I hate I fucked his trifling ass today. You live and you learn a nigga only has three fuckin' times to show me who he is. I'm done fuckin' with him. Lucky has struck the fuck out, stupid ass clown. Melanie had the nerve to smile at me.

"Bitch, you just watched him eat my fuckin' pussy and you weren't smiling at that. Thank God I'm saved by hoe number one and two. I'll let you explain to your lil bitch what you got going on. I'll see you around shawty." I sassed and sucked my teeth. I jumped at Melanie and Shaela and they both backed the fuck up. Lucky knows he's a jealous ass nigga. He doesn't even want me to be around Tariq or anybody else. He's so selfish. He's acting like I cheated. Nigga I caught you. You can never catch a bitch that's not doing anything. Him forcing me to be with him isn't going to work.

I walked toward the beach and sat in the sand. I'm waiting for JD to pull up. I had so much shit on my mind and listening to the ocean was perfect. Tariq walked up on me and started massaging my shoulders. He sat behind me and scooted up behind me and wrapped his arms around my waist I wish he would stop. He already got this nigga acting retarded.

"You shouldn't be over here," I argued and sassed. Tariq wasn't trying to hear that. He wanted to talk because we haven't spoken since the first time I caught him with Shaela's ass. I cut his ass off. I missed his company and affection, but he would never know that.

"What are you thinking about?" He asked. If he only knew how heavy he was on my mind. In a perfect world, we could be together. We were rooting for us, but everybody was against us.

"Nothing that I care to share," I sighed and whispered hoping that he couldn't hear me.

"Since you got an attitude, think about us," he argued and laughed. I always thought about us. Every time I thought about us it always brought a smile to my face.

"You're an asshole, Tariq." I sassed. He knew he was with the shits. At least he was able to show his feelings. I had to hide mine to spare the next niggas feelings. That shit isn't fair at all.

"You love me, Kaniya?" He asked. Of course, I love him. How could not? What's not to love about him? He's sexy as hell and romantic as fuck. I love everything about him, and he accepts me flaws and all.

"I got love for you always," I beamed proudly. I felt it too.

"I didn't ask you that. I asked you do you love me?" He asked.

"Yes, I love you, Tariq." I finally said it and I meant it too. My head was lying on his chest. He cupped my face forcing me to look at him. We were gazing at each other and neither one of us broke the stare. We were reading each other souls. He was searching my face for a lie but I wasn't telling one.

"Tariq, Tariq!" She yelled. I swear between her and her fuckin' sister. I was done. Shaela was yelling and running her dumb ass down here to see what we were talking about. I wasn't for the drama at all. I'm sick of it. Lucky and Tariq sure do know how to pick them.

"I'll holla at you later. Your situation is coming. Go meet her halfway, because if she's coming over here to talk shit, I'm busting her in her mouth again," I argued. Damn JD come on.

☆

JD finally pulled up and we pulled off. I was so fuckin'
ready to get the fuck up out of there. Lucky was all in his feelings. To make matters worse, this nigga had the nerve to put his
fuckin' hands on me. That was the ultimate no-no. Tariq caught
me off guard asking me did I love him. I got love for Tariq, lord
knows I do. That past couple of weeks we spent together was so
much fun. We could never be together if Sonja and Deuce get
married. It would be too much, but I would miss the insane sex
sessions and bomb ass head he was serving me.

"What's up, baby? How was your day?" He asked. I was
hoping that he wouldn't ask me that. If he only knew the fucked
up day I had. I swear this day goes down as one of the fuckin'
worst. I couldn't catch a break.

"Man, you don't even want to know. The bus ride was
long and Lucky was tripping hard," I sighed. I can't believe
Lucky cut up as bad as he did.

"I'm sorry you had a bad day. I should've got you a flight.
Where to? Where did you book your room?" He asked. I couldn't
wait to go to my suite and kick back and relax. I had an ocean
view room myself. It felt so good outside I'll change clothes and
lay on the beach and get a tan.

"Fontainebleau Miami Beach on Collins," I beamed. It's one of my favorite hotels to stay at. Lucky and I always booked a suite here anytime we vacationed here.

"What would you like to do while you're here?" He asked. I really didn't have too much I wanted to do. I wanted some bomb ass food, shop a little, and lay out on the beach.

"It doesn't matter as long as I'm with you, I'm cool," I explained.

"Kaniya, you need to stop playing with me. I know you're not ready to be in another relationship but damn your wife material. You're so fucking perfect. I'm willing and prepared to wait it out with you. I understand what you're going through, and I'll help you through it. I feel like you're worth it," he explained. I liked JD but I wasn't ready to be in a relationship yet. The fun hasn't even begun yet. I wanted a stable full of niggas in my pocket.

"Awe you're so sweet. I'm glad you think of me that way," I beamed and lied. I wasn't looking for love. I just wanted to have fun.

"Have you heard from your sister. Is she still coming?" He asked. Barbie was supposed to meet me down here. I haven't heard from her in a few days. Ketta and Barbie are booed up with some fuckin' bosses. I need to ask Don does he have anybody for me.

I haven't heard from her today but let me text her. I had my phone on airplane mode. I took it off and I still haven't received a text from Barbie but Lucky of course. I wish he would leave me the fuck alone and take his ass on. Go and tend to your bitch. Stop worrying about a bitch that's not worried about you.

Lucky - Your so fuckin' disrespectful, what nigga picked you up? You gone make me put my hands on you and my foot in your ass

Me- Sis are you coming?

Barbie - Sis I need you to drive up here. This nigga took my passport and license. Everything. He refuses to let me leave. Bring them two girls with you

Me - Oh hell no. I'll be there on Wednesday. He got you fucked up

"She's not coming. I have to go to New York to pick her up Wednesday." I kept it short with JD. I didn't need to go into that much detail. Trust me when I pull up it's about to be some shit. I kind of figured something was going on. She's been gone damn near the whole month. I knew Ketta wouldn't be coming back because Don wanted her to move out there. Of course, she said yes. My sister would've been back by now. That nigga must be crazy. I knew she wouldn't miss the Miami turn up for anything. Oh lord, here goes my phone again going off. It's Tianna. I wonder why she's texting me because she hasn't said shit to me all day. I expected her to pull Lucky off me. I guess Quan didn't want her getting involved.

Tianna – Bitch, you got Lucky so pissed right now! Who did you leave with?

Me - The one and only JD

Tianna - Bitch you play all year

Me - Hardly

Lucky is going to dig himself an early grave worried about me and what I'm doing. I'm having fun and living my life. No need to stress about what he's doing, fuck that.

"Kaniya, what's up with Work Now Atlanta?" He asked.

"It'll be open in about four weeks. The building has to pass inspection. I wanted the commercial carpet out of there and hardwood floors all the way through. I have some contractors putting that in now. I signed the contracts already with the companies that I would do the direct hiring for. We're almost up and running. I might have a small Grand Opening Party. Nothing too big."

"Can I be your date? Do you need me to do anything." He asked. Damn JD, let's have fun. He's too clingy I just want to kick it and have fun.

"You can definitely be my date. The only thing I need you to do is don't stop being you," I explained. I don't want a date to my grand opening.

"Let me ask you a question Kaniya and I want you to be honest with me? Do I have a chance with you yes or no?" He asked. I swear if he asks me something that has to do with me one more time I going to scream just go with the damn flow.

"You have a chance. I've been in a relationship for five years and I gave it my all. So, the next relationship I have I can't put a time limit on it. What's meant to be will be. I'm just going with the flow," I explained and lied. Damn, can I be single for a few months without somebody wanting to lock me down?

"I respect that. I'm glad you won't hold back," he explained. I'm holding back for as long as I could. I don't want to be tied down no time soon.

"We're here, baby? What time do you want to have dinner? I'm sure your tired and want to get some rest," he asked. If he keeps asking about me and him, he won't ever have to worry about seeing me again. I'm serious.

"9:00 should be fine. I'll make sure I'm ready before 8:30," I stated. I gave JD kiss on his cheek. I grabbed my Louie luggage and made my way into the Fontainebleau and checked in. As soon as I grabbed my room key and made my way on the elevator, I had to think for a minute. Is this fuck with Kaniya's head day? I like JD but damn I'm not ready to jump back into a relationship yet. Just go with the flow. Not to mention I'm still thinking about the shit Tariq said. That's heavy on my brain.

Me and Tariq can't be more than friends. I can't deal with Shaela. That bitch will be dead fucking with me. I'm a Miller and a killer so don't push me. I need a nigga with no baggage. I entered my room and laid on my bed. I'm so tired. I need to call Killany and tell her about my day. My daddy called me earlier I missed his call. I need to call him back.

I didn't even have a chance to go out on the balcony and look at the ocean. Sleep took over me soon as I laid down. I slept for about two hours. I really needed the rest. I checked my phone and I had tons of missed calls and text messages. The only people that I was calling back was my mom, dad, and Killany. Everybody else was on the back burner. I called my dad first to see what's up with him. My dad swears he's an OG. Listen to how he answers the phone.

"Talk to me, baby girl. What's good, where are you? I've been by your house," he asked. My father checks up on me at least three times a week. I should've stopped by his house before I left so, he wouldn't be worried about me.

"I'm in Miami," I yawned. I was still sleepy.

"You must be with Sonja and Deuce," he stated. I looked at my phone. My dad knew everything. He knew I was with Sonja then why ask a question he already knew the answer to.

"How you know daddy?" I asked. I knew he wasn't about to tell me.

"Kanan," he sighed. My father and Kanan are night and day. My father is calm and Kanan is the hot head and doesn't give a fuck. That's what I love about him. He doesn't think twice about shit.

"Oh lord, how he knows we down here?" I asked. If Kanan knew we were here that means trouble and I know Sonja and Deuce ain't ready to go to war with a nigga like him.

"Kanan knows everything Kaniya, he's down there on some good bullshit. Please don't let a motherfuckin' thing happen to my fuckin' twin brother. He just got out the Feds," he argued and explained. If Kanan knew he just got out of the FEDS, why would you bring your ass to Miami looking for trouble?

"What is he coming down here for? Its Deuce birthday, that's all," I asked. Please don't ruin this man's party behind Sonja. I don't even know why Sonja was even entertaining Deuce knowing damn well Kanan ain't playing with a full deck.

"He wants Sonja to come back home," he explained. I figured as much. I don't understand why my father didn't warn Sonja what would go down. Hell, she fuckin' knew she couldn't move on with another fuckin' man after dealing with a Miller.

"I can't be bothered with this shit," I cursed and sassed. I don't want any parts of Kanan and Sonja's bullshit.

"Stop cursing Kaniya, you ain't grown. Take my partner's number down, you might need back up fucking with Kanan," he explained. Back up, the fuck I need back up for.

"What is he planning on doing?" I asked. I wish my father would stop talking in fuckin' circles. Poor Sonja, she was all up in my shit and a lunatic has followed her to Miami. If Kanan was in Miami it was about to go down. She needs to get her ass back on that bus and go home.

"Look, baby, you know your Uncle Kanan is crazy. Just be ready. He's ready for some good bullshit. I'm texting you the number now. I love you," he explained. My father rushed off the phone as quick as hell.

A FEW DAYS LATER

Chapter-22

Kaniya

I had so much fun these past few days with JD. It was breathtaking and that's big coming from me. I guess lady luck was on my side. JD was a great distraction to keep my mind off Lucky and Tariq. Don't get me wrong he's a real street nigga but I love his softer side more. He's a gentleman and I like that about him, and I love how he handles me. He's so fuckin' attentive and charming that it's crazy. He's catered to all my needs every day and showed me around his city. I've been having a great time just the two of us with no bullshit or strings attached.

We had breakfast and dinner on the beach, it was so fuckin' romantic. I could get used to this shit. JD was husband material if I were looking one. He was exposing me to some different shit. I never had to plan anything. He took care of everything. I even met some of his friends. They were cool and down to earth. We had fun racing each other on Jet Skis. He taught me how to fish. I cooked dinner for us at his condo. He was a breath of fresh air and I was feeling him. I can't even lie. I stayed with him last night at his condo.

Temptation is a motherfucka or I was in heat. Last night I was lying in his bed. His 5,000 thread count sheets felt so good against my skin. I kept some space between us. He scooted up behind me and I felt his third leg tapping me on my ass all night. I was ready to hop on JD's dick and see what that thick motherfucka do. I would turn around to face him and he would be smiling at me. I had to hide the big ass blush I had on my face because he was tempting as fuck.

My pussy was so hot I had to fan myself a few times down there. JD might be the one. I hope all this shit he's doing is not a front. You know how some niggas do everything to get you and once they get you shit changes. I'll leave your ass just as quick as shit starts to change up.

You better ask Lucky. I just can't take any bullshit off any man, for what? If I don't give you any bullshit than don't give me any in return. That's Law. I'll continue to take it one day at a time. I appreciate him for showing me around to different parts of Miami that I haven't been to. We had to get ready for this cookout Sonja was having at the Beach House. Thank God it was Saturday because if it was Sunday I probably wouldn't be going. Deuce's birthday dinner was tomorrow. It was an all-white affair at Prive.

I was on the edge about everything because I know the moment I showed up Lucky was going to trip. It didn't matter if Melanie was with him not. He's been blowing up my phone like crazy, but I haven't returned any of his calls. He only wanted to know what I was doing because he couldn't see it. He knew I was with a nigga, but he didn't know who. The only reason why I was going to Deuce's fuckin' party is because of my dad. He said Kanan was somewhere out here lurking around about to pull up on Sonja and Deuce. He wanted me to have his back.

This shit can go two ways. He can say fuck Sonja and go on about his business or he can be with the shit. I know Kanan and he's with the shit. I can feel a war brewing and I know it won't end well. I think Sonja needs to tell me what happened or what's going on. I don't like being in the dark about shit. My father is fuckin' tight lip about everything but he wants me to have Kanan's back. I know it's always shoot first and ask questions later but damn.

I knew some shit was about to go down if my dad wanted me to hit up one of his friends. They were orchestrating something and I really didn't want to be involved because if something happened to Deuce, Lucky and I would be in a fucked up place. It'll be worse than our current state. I swear when its rain's it pours. Now I wish I would've stayed at home.

JD

I would be lying if I said I wasn't feeling shawty because I was. Kaniya was a cool ass chick from the Eastside. I met her one morning running. I was running into Starbucks to grab my assistant an ice coffee. Shawty was the baddest motherfucka in the barista. She stood the fuck out. She had my attention the moment she opened her mouth and placed her order. I knew she was to fine to be single but shit a goon like me had to shoot my shot. I knew she wasn't ready for a relationship but whenever she was, I wanted to be first in line.

"Baby, are you ready?" I asked. I walked up behind Kaniya and placed my arms around her waist. I rested my nose in between her neck and inhaled her scent. Damn, she always smelled like heaven. I looked in the mirror. I liked the reflection that was looking back at me. "We look good together, what do you think?" I wanted her opinion to see if she saw what I saw.

"We do," she beamed and smiled showing all thirty-two of her teeth. Kaniya stayed with me last night, so we could leave on time. She was matching my fly. For some reason, my text messages wouldn't go through on her phone. I don't know what was up with that. I sent her a few text the other day and she claimed she never gets my messages. I would have to always call her.

Last night she said that she sent me a text asking me if I could come over. Hell yeah, I would've pulled up quick but I never got the message. She called me instead. I knew something was up with her phone. I told her it was cool she can come and stay with me. She thought I was blowing her off, but I wasn't. I need to take her by the Apple Store to see what's up with her phone.

"I'm ready JD," she stated. I grabbed Kaniya's hand and led her to the car. We'll make it to the Beach house in about thirty minutes. I'll stop by the Apple Store because it's in route. I loaded the drinks and ice in the car. I made sure Kaniya seat belt was fastened before I pulled off like a bat out of hell. I drive fast. I knew she hated riding with me especially when I'm driving one of my sports cars. I just got the Challenger Hell Cat. I wanted to hear this motherfucka purr like a cat. I like the rush sometimes, but damn I try to drive normal, but I can't.

Kaniya

My morning has been perfect so far, I can't even complain. I was dreading going to this fuckin' barbecue. I can feel the bullshit coming and I haven't even stepped in the fuckin' room. I'm going to let Sonja know I don't want to ruin the cookout, but if any of them BITCHES are in their feelings please check them. I don't want to beat any ass, but if I have to then I will do those two bitches so fuckin' dirty they'll never forget me. I'm putting stamps on bitches head. I understand that's your sister, but she was fucking my man, it's not the other way around.

She knew she was a side chick, so she should've behaved as such. Shaela should know after I busted her in her fucking mouth to shut the fuck up talking to me. Let that bitch keep on playing tough and watch these hands beat the breaks off her stupid ass. Guess who ain't going to break it up, Tariq. Tianna already recorded the shit. She should be glad I didn't put her ass on World Star. She's one of those bitches that talk shit but can't back it up like her fuckin' sister.

Finally, we made it to the Beach House. I guess everybody was waiting for us to arrive. We were bringing the drinks and the ice. Oh well, they'll be alright. JD locked his car up and grabbed our stuff. Damn this house is nice as fuck. I couldn't help but admire this home. It was beautiful to bad I couldn't enjoy the amenities that it had to offer. JD walked around to the passenger side and opened the door up for me.

"Let's get moving and beat your pretty as feet," he stated. JD was always complimenting me. He kept a smile on my face, and he was cool as shit and sexy as fuck. JD pulled me out the car and pulled me into his arms. He wrapped his arms around me and we stood still for a minute. I swear I didn't want him to let me go. I love being wrapped up in his arms. JD pulled back and grabbed my hand. We walked up toward the house. I knocked on the door and Raven opened the door. She took the drinks from JD. We made our way in the house.

"Hey Kaniya," she beamed and cheered. Sonja must have been in a great mood judging by her tone. She looked at me and looked at JD. She had an aggravated look on her face like she was crazy. I already knew what that was about. Why can't I bring someone with me if Tariq and Lucky have someone with them? That's not fair at all.

"Hey y'all! What's up, this is my boo JD," I beamed proudly. If looks could kill. I would be a dead bitch judging by the looks on Tariq and Lucky's face. Fuck them. They need to mind their business and not mine. Everybody was smiling and having a good time until they saw me. Now they have the sour face. JD doesn't give a fuck. He already knows what time it is. He's a savage too and a real street nigga. He's from Liberty City. He made sure his hands were rested around my waist and his face was in the crook of my neck.

He had his pistol was on display. He wanted these niggas to know that he was holding. They both got bitches with them. Melanie and Shaela who's mad, and clearly not fuckin' me. See that's the problem with niggas nowadays, y'all mad at me but got a bitch with y'all. I got my boo with me everybody should be good.

The tension was so thick in here that it was crazy. As soon as we walked past them, you could feel it. You know I'm a messy bitch. I was on my good bullshit. I knew I was killing it today. I made sure I was killing these bitches and making these niggas sweat. I had on a gold bikini. It was popping and all eyes were on me. It was gold and shimmery. I had my hair pulled up into a messy bun. Shit, I was ready to swim and not look at these fools. I started singing "I Know You See It." Shaela's was mad as fuck.

She just slapped Tariq because he was looking. I felt the hate dripping from Lucky. I had his stupid ass right where I wanted him. We walked past him. I heard Sonja say,

"Gone back up front, no drama in the house today, Lucky." I wanted to let out a small laugh, but I'll hold that for later. I don't know why he was so fuckin' comfortable running up on me and he had a bitch with him. Have a seat Lucky before I sit your ass down today.

"Hi Tianna," I beamed and smiled. She looked at me and shook her head. I heard Lucky coming behind us. JD got his hands all on my stomach and shit, his cologne was in my clothes. He smelled so good.

"Kaniya, let me holla at you really quick," he stated. I wasn't trying to hear nothing Lucky had to say. Go talk to your bitch and stop making it your business to talk and run up on me. I guess life ain't treating the cheating motherfucka so good.

"Is it a life or death situation?" I asked. I knew Lucky wanted to fuck with me and lay his hands on me. I don't have time to fuckin' talk to him. Go talk to the bitch that's always popping up.

I don't even know why he was pissed because before we made it official or whatever he claimed he didn't want a girl-friend. Every time he saw me in the club posted up with a nigga from my hood he was mad as fuck doing the same shit he's doing now. The only difference between now and then is that you're my EX and ain't shit you can say.

"No," he argued. If it wasn't life or death than he didn't need to fuckin' speak with me. I didn't want to make another scene, but he needs to carry the fuck on with his jealous ass. Everybody wants to tell me what I should and shouldn't do but when this nigga is running up on me like a mad man ain't nobody around.

"It can wait," I argued and sucked my teeth. JD was getting his free feels in. He started biting my neck and whispering sweet nothings in my ear. JD was romantic as fuck. He was telling me all the freaky things, he wanted to do to me. He should stop, fuckin' playing before I take him up on his offer.

"Why doesn't your hot ass have no panty's on?" He asked. He wouldn't know what the fuck I had on if he would keep his hands to himself.

"It's a swimsuit," I explained. We made our way outside toward the beach and grabbed us a beach chair in the shade near the ocean. JD sat me on his lap.

"You feeling him, Kaniya? He's ready for you whenever you ready. But I don't know if I want none because of your OLD nigga act like he crazy. I'm might have to let my gun clap. He can't stop looking over here. What's his issue?" He asked. Lucky is always trying to ruin some shit. Leave me the fuck alone damn. Lucky knew I wasn't a basic bitch. He knew if he cheated, I was done, the next nigga would be on my arm, and he could have front row tickets.

"He can't accept the fact that I moved on," I explained. Why can't he accept it? Melanie can keep him because he's nothing but a fuckin' liar and I don't want to have shit to do with his lying ass. I wish I wouldn't have fucked him a few days ago.

Chapter-23

Lucky

Kaniya thinks she's slick as fuck. What makes her think she can move around with this nigga so freely and it's not any consequences. She must have thought I was playing with her but I fuckin' wasn't at all. She's bold with the shit she's doing and being disrespectful. I needed to holla at her about some shit and she wanted to dismiss me. I got something for all that. I noticed how that nigga was looking at her. I wanted to murk him and her.

She had no business giving that nigga hope. I watched their every move from afar. I can't believe this shit. Kaniya was laid up with this nigga in my fuckin' face like I won't do shit. She plays too many fucking games. What made her bring that nigga over here with her? I'll make a nigga disappear quick. True enough I'm here with Melanie but so what, it's not what it looks like. I didn't know she was seeing anyone. I grabbed my phone out my pocket to send her a text.

Me - You got me so fucked up. You and that nigga must want to die

My phone went off letting me know the text was delivered, she read it and didn't respond back. I sent her two more text messages. My eyes were trained on her. I saw her look at her phone. I'm tired of playing with her motherfuckin' ass. She didn't even want to text me back, but she read that shit. I promise you I'm going to fuck her ass up. I don't give a fuck about any of this shit. I tossed back two shots of Hennessy. I started walking toward where Kaniya and ole boy was sitting. My brother and my dad grabbed me. I pushed them off me and kept walking toward her. I finally made my way toward her. Kaniya was smart as fuck and she knew I would never let any of this shit go down. I heard ole boy ask her,

"How long are we going to be over here at this barbecue?" He asked. He shouldn't even be here because he wasn't fuckin' invited. I don't know who this JD nigga was, but he was about to find out who the fuck I was.

"Not that long. Can we get comfortable?" She asked. I swear I wanted to choke the fuck out of Kaniya for fuckin' playing with me. She's lost her fuckin' mind laid up all on this nigga, putting a target on his fuckin' back.

"We sure can," he explained. She laid on his chest and he was running his fingers through her hair and feeling on her ass. I wasn't about to watch this shit or allow it to go on. Ain't no cuff-ing my bitch in front of me. Kaniya and this pussy ass nigga thought they were about to enjoy themselves. This nigga called himself trying to romance my bitch listening to the ocean and shit. They were talking and laughing and shit. The jokes on them because ain't none of this shit about to go down.

It was just my luck that everybody started to make their way near us. I had to make my move right fuckin' now. Sonja couldn't have been paying attention because she would've stopped me a long time ago. I snuck up on them and made my way near them. They didn't even see me. I snatched Kaniya's ass up off JD's lap. I grabbed her by that little as bra top, she had on. She tried to get away from me. I grabbed her by her neck apply-ing a little pressure but not too much.

"I need to holla at you right fuckin' now," I argued and yelled. JD acted as if he wanted to say something to me about my bitch. I swear he don't want any fuckin' problems. I'll kill his ass right here.

"My nigga, don't you see her fucking relaxing. Don't snatch her up like that. What's your fuckin' problem fuck nigga? You came with a bitch why are you so pressed to speak with her?" he argued and asked. I stroked my beard and let out a hard chuckle. I had to choose my words wisely because I had plans to kill this nigga anyway.

"I don't give a fuck about shit y'all doing. She ain't gone fuckin' disrespect me period. Did she tell you I was balls deep in that pussy before you came and got her? We've been together five years going on six. Ain't shit gone changed that. I need to speak with you Kaniya ASAP and it can't wait," I argued. She stepped away from JD to see what I wanted. Yes, I blew up her spot so what.

"You wanted to speak to me what's up?" She asked, sassed and argued? I don't give a fuck about her having an attitude.

"ARE YOU HAPPY KANIYA? Do you want to die at the age of 24? You keep FUCKIN' testing me. You spared that nigga right now, but he has to go and you fuckin' know that. Don't disrespect me at all," I argued.

"Are you finished Lucky, is that all you needed to say? Are we done here?" She asked. Kaniya walked off pissed off. I don't give a fuck about her being mad. It's levels and rules to this shit and she's breaking them.

Kaniya

I'm so fuckin' tired of Lucky right now. I can't believe he told JD we fucked. He was acting like a real bitch out here. What part of the game is this? He cheated and it ain't no coming back from that. Niggas cheat all the time and bitches go back but I'm not going back. Fuck that shit. I want to have fun just like him. Lucky can't take anything that he's dished out. That's his fuckin' problem. You brought a bitch with you and I brought a nigga with me so we're even. Go enjoy your fuckin' company so I can enjoy mine.

I swear to God if I would've known Lucky would've acted this stupid I would've kept my ass at home for real. At this point, I was ready to fuckin' leave the cookout. Lucky turned me off, he was coming too hard. I didn't want to eat shit. I was ready to fuckin' go. Bitch ass nigga hating on me, let me fuckin' be great. JD knew I was ready to go to. My whole mood changed. I didn't even get to swim. I wanted to take some pictures in the ocean with this swimsuit on. I had to use the bathroom then I'm leaving. That's exactly what I planned to do. I got to get the fuck away from here before I hurt his motherfuckin' ass.

"JD I'm going to use the bathroom and then we can be out," I explained. I knew JD wasn't ready to leave but I was.

Lucky can't stand to see another nigga in my face period. I can see how the longer I stayed here I'll turn into the old me and nobody around this motherfucka would be safe if I did. Yes, it's time for me to keep it moving.

"Kaniya, we don't have to leave because of Lucky bitch ass. I'm not intimidated by him," he explained. I heard everything JD was saying but my vibe was already killed the moment we stepped in the house. We made an appearance and we can bounce, fuck this shit.

"It's not because of him. I just want to get out of here. I'm tired of him seriously," I explained. JD didn't agree with us leaving but we are. He ain't got to prove shit to Lucky because he ain't nothing any fuckin' way but a hating ass motherfucka. I made my way to the bathroom and Quan stopped me. I looked over my shoulder to see what he wanted.

"Hey sis what's up, are you good?" He asked. How come Quan didn't ask me was I good when his fuckin' brother was running down on me like he was fuckin' stupid.

Lucky got one more time to fuck with me and I'm going to give him his fuckin' issue. I swear he's put his hands on me way too many fuckin' times.

"Quan I'm tired of your brother he keeps on fucking with me," I argued. Quan looked at me and laughed what the fuck is so funny? Everybody is laughing but me. I hope they didn't think that I was enjoying Lucky acting like a fuckin' fool because I wasn't.

"He loves you, Kaniya. He doesn't want to see you with anybody else but him," he explained. Lucky has to get over that because every time I see him the same bitch that he says means nothing him she's every fuckin' where. She's something to him and she can continue to be. If he can hide a bitch for three months and I didn't know he can hide anything and right now the only thing he needs to hide is his fuckin' feelings for me.

"On some real shit Quan, if Lucky wanted me like he said he did, then why is Melanie always around? Look she's here now. I left him because he was cheating on me with Melanie. She can have him, shit. I want her to keep him away from me. It's plenty of niggas checking for me. Do you see me on some bullshit when I see them? I'm cool because he cheated on me for her. That's what he wanted," I argued and asked.

"I hear you Kaniya, but listen to what the fuck I'm saying. Lucky can't take seeing you with anybody else. Look that man was about to murk you and old boy. The only reason that nigga ain't dead is that my daddy hid the fuckin' guns. Lucky was ready to make it fuckin' clap. You shouldn't even have brought him over here. Now this man got a target on his fuckin' back because he fell for the wrong chick. I know you and Sonja cool or whatever but stop showing your face.

If you do come around don't bring anybody with you. You're making shit worse by rubbing it up in his face that you're doing you. Do you see him rubbing on Melanie in your face? Stop that shit man before you get somebody killed fucking with you," he argued and explained. I heard what Quan was saying but Lucky knows I'm not that type of bitch. Every time we see each other he'll see somebody in my face. I'm single and I'm dating and I'm looking for some free agents because his spot is open for a replacement.

"Quan, I understand that's your brother and you made some good points, but why do I have to walk on eggshells to spare his feelings? He hasn't fuckin' spared mine. Anything that Sonja has I'm coming. If I bring a nigga with me oh well, it ain't my fault. Lucky knows I'm that bitch and the next man does too. If he wants to show me affection, I'm going to let him.

If Lucky in his feelings oh fuckin' well, so what. That's just some shit he got to deal with. I deal with him and Melanie on the regular. Do you see me fuckin' crying about it and trying to beat her ass every chance I get? Nope. You know why? It's because I've been there and done that," I argued. I walked off on his crazy ass too. I don't need anybody telling me what I can and can't do. Last I checked they're not Killian and Kaisha Miller. I used the bathroom and washed my hands. I looked in the mirror and Lucky stupid ass fucked my neck up. Everybody wants to tell me what I can and can't do. I can guarantee you not one motherfucka told Lucky to send his bitch back where she came from.

I dried my hands off. JD was waiting for me by the door. I grabbed my purse out of his hand. He grabbed my hands and ushered me out of the house. This would be the last time any of these motherfuckas saw me. Melanie and Shaela were standing by the door smiling when we walked off. I swear they should be glad JD is with me because I would've smacked the shit out the two of them. I'm so fuckin' mad and pissed off they for damn sure didn't want to be in my warpath. I just wanted to go back to my room, lay by myself, and Facetime Killany and my momma and tell them about all this crazy shit. JD opened the car door for me. I knew he could tell I was pissed because he didn't say much too me.

"Where to?" He asked. I knew JD wanted to know if I fucked Lucky or not. I didn't have a problem telling him yes if he asked. Lucky only did that because Melanie watched him eat my pussy. It's his fault, he told me to do it.

"My room," I sighed. JD grabbed my hand and I looked at him to see what he wanted.

"Can I come up?" He asked. I really wanted to be alone, but I guess he could come and chill for a few minutes.

"Sure, why not." JD and I made small talk as he zoomed through traffic. I needed my stuff from his condo. "Hey JD, can you swing by your condo? I need my overnight bag and toiletries," JD nodded his head in agreement. After I leave Miami, I'm going to Killany's for a few weeks.

A FEW HOURS LATER

Chapter-24

Lucky

I can't believe this shit but I'm not even surprised. She wanted a reaction out of me. She knew I was going to knock her block off. I'm a street nigga I don't give a fuck about her screaming we ain't together because we are. If she thought, she could bring another man in my face without getting touched she was dumb as fuck and Kaniya is smart as fuck. She got me so fucked up and that's on some real shit. She pulled a nigga hoe card. I can't be mad but nobody but myself. Every time she saw me, Melanie was with me and she kept it cool every time. I know that was a big step for her.

I tell you what though, JD gone regret the day he's ever laid eyes on mine. That nigga was feeling on my bitch in front of me. That shit was so disrespectful and for Kaniya to fuckin' dismiss me when I was talking to her; like my word isn't law. She violated me and to make matters worse, I was just deep in them guts three days ago. I guess that's why I'm pissed because I knew that nigga wanted to fuck her and she'll fuck him just to get back at me.

I was supposed to be enjoying myself in Miami not watching Kaniya and JD. After tonight that nigga will be DOA, he's to pressed for her pussy. I switched Kaniya's phone out a month ago. I had my partner put a chip in it. So, I can screen her calls. I couldn't stop the calls, but I could reroute the text messages. Every time a text came through from him, he was begging for some pussy. I knew it was him because I called his phone. I asked Veno and he said his name was JD. I stopped that shit. The room she had at the Fontainebleau Miami Beach, I had that bitch wired. I could hear everything. As soon as he thought he was about to touch my pussy he would how to see how real this shit gets behind mine.

I'm serious as fuck. I've already told Kaniya if he thought he could fuck her and live to tell about it he was dumb ass nigga. Tonight must be my lucky night. I got action and this nigga was determined to get some of my pussy I bet he won't get any of mine.

I'm doing 100mph down Collins Ave. I valet parked my Audi A8. I grabbed my Louie backpack and I made my way to room 1102. I used the key and I crept inside her room. I sat in the living room for a while. I knew Kaniya wasn't about to give up it like that. The room was dark. The only light you could see was from the beach because the sun was about to set.

"I'm ready JD," she beamed. I could tell her cheating ass was smiling. Kaniya walked out of the room with some lingerie on. It took everything in me not to just shoot and show my ass. She said she was ready. Ready for what she going to make me kill her ass if she tries to fuck this nigga. JD was sitting on the bed motioning with his hands for her to come to join him. She was about to fuck him and give my pussy away. Kaniya was ready to fuckin' die.

"Let me suck on that pussy right before I make love to you alright?" He asked. Kaniya slid her panties down her legs and tossed them to his face. He was sniffing her panties. He picked her up and tossed her on the bed. His head got lost between her legs. She started making the lil sexy noises that she makes let him know that she wants the dick. I couldn't even listen to this shit no more. I'll fuck around and kill Kaniya. That bitch won't make it until Sunday. I walked in the room making my presence known. I started clapping my hands. I wanted her to hear me before she saw me.

"I bet you want to fuck that nigga while I watch!" I yelled. I took a seat at the desk in front of her bed. I lit my blunt and took a few puffs. Kaniya and JD's eyes were trained on me. "I want you to fuck him Kaniya so I can watch. I want to see if that pussy gets wet for another nigga that's not me."

"Lucky, what the fuck are you doing here?" She asked and argued. What happened to the sexy as voice she used a minute ago when she told that nigga, she was ready? She knew why I was here. I wanted to see if she was bold enough to take the bait. I know Kaniya and she won't back down. The question is was JD bold enough to do it while I was here.

"I came to watch you fuck this fuck boy. I had to see it for myself. You want to fuck him go ahead so I can watch. I want to see that pussy pop too," I argued and chuckled. I knew she would take the bait. I heard her suck her teeth. She wasn't about to back down. She was about to prove a point and get this nigga killed in the process. This wasn't a friendly visit.

"Lucky, are you sure this is what you want? I haven't had any new dick in a while so once I hop on this big motherfucker it's a wrap. JD beat this pussy up and put some pressure on it," she sassed and sucked her teeth. JD was looking uneasy as he should. If he was dumb enough to fuck her while I sat here and watched, he deserved to fuckin' die.

"I'm sure. Go ahead Kaniya, I want to watch," I explained. I had to pull on this blunt a few times to stop myself from laughing. I punched myself in my chest a few times.

"Okay Lucky, I'm about that life," she sassed and smiled. Her eyes were trained on me the whole time. She grabbed JD dick and was moving it toward her pussy. I wasn't about to watch that at all. My eyes were focused on rather or not she was going to slide his dick in her pussy. I was about to show her why she doesn't ever want to fuckin' try me. She thought she was about put on a show for me. The moment I notice she was about to slide JD's dick in my pussy I grabbed the silencer out my back pocket and cocked my Mac 11 back.

I emptied the clip in his ass not giving a fuck if I hit Kaniya or not. I let out over twenty shots. His body was slumped over on her body. I walked toward the bed and approached the two of them. I pushed his body out the way. I cupped Kaniya's face roughly. I wanted her undivided attention. She had tears in the brim of her eyes. I killed JD and I don't give a fuck. If she wanted to see how I was coming this is how I'm coming every fuckin' time. Blood was every fuckin' were and guess who was about to clean it up, Kaniya. It's her fuckin' fault. She should've expected it.

"Do you see what the fuck I just did, Kaniya? You see this is what happens when a bitch that belongs to me is hardheaded. Shit gets real. Did you think I was going to let you fuck him in my face and not do shit? Do you like blood on your hands? Clean this shit up before I fuckin' hurt you? Keep fuckin' playing with me Kaniya, This is how I'm coming every fuckin' time you got the balls to even fuckin' disrespect me. Fuck a clean-up crew you can clean this shit up your fuckin' self and dispose of your own body. You're bad right, Kaniya. Stop fucking playing games and disrespecting me. You got that Kaniya Williams?" I argued and asked.

I don't know who Kaniya thought I was, but she got me all the way fucked up. I got to give it to JD, he thought I would let him fuck my bitch and watch. He should've kept it G and got up out the bed and kept it moving. He didn't do that, so he got popped. Kaniya just doesn't get it. I had to leave up out of here quick before I put my hands on her. Why in the fuck would she try me like this?

Kaniya

See Lucky thought he was slick. The game is to be sold not told. You want a bitch so bad you're willing to kill? You wouldn't even have to do all that if you would've walked away from me and started fuckin' with Melanie. See that was too much like right but he wanted me and her. He couldn't have us both, he could only have her. I hate JD lost his life behind me over a nigga that I'm not even with but hey he should've got his ass up and kept it fuckin' moving. Lucky was sneaky as fuck. How did he even know which room I was in? I only beat Melanie's ass twice, both times she got out of line. I don't get it, this man he keeps fuckin' with me and trying me. Every time I see him, he got this bitch in tow. He can't stand the fact that I'm with somebody else and smiling without him. He should get used to this smile because it's not going anywhere.

I was good before Lucky and even after him, I'll be good. I hate Melanie must be a casualty of war because this nigga was on some tick for tack shit. I'll play body for body because that's my fuckin' hobby. Murder she fuckin' wrote and spoke. If Lucky thought, he could kill JD without any repercussions from me he was crazy as fuck. He touched JD so I was touching Melanie, make no fuckin' mistake about it. I swear I didn't want to bring this side out of me, but Lucky passed the fuckin' torch and I'm going to let it fuckin' burn.

I hope he didn't think that I would be scared to dispose of a body. My mother and father taught Killany and me how to do this shit since we were eleven years old. Nigga, blood excites me, and he knew that. I would've fucked Lucky in JD's blood. I don't give a fuck. Disposing bodies is a hobby for me. I do this shit for fun, easy fuckin' water. I told JD to be on point. He was so glad that he was about to get some pussy finally he slipped up. I hope he didn't think that Lucky was going to watch him fuck me and be cool with that shit? Never, no way, not happening.

I'll clean up JD's body. I went to the hardware store and got an ax some bleach and other chemicals that I would need. I chopped his body into small pieces and secured everything in the sheets we slept on and put it in my suitcase. My mother had a few trap houses out here. I pulled up in the hood and used the incinerator in one of the basements. No face no case. I called my lil brother Mook to have his niggas come and get JD's car so they could take it to the chop shop. I need the cameras at the hotel because the last thing I need was this niggas murder coming back to me.

Sleep was the last thing on my mind. I got something for Lucky ass. I had to get him tonight and make it fuckin' count. I pulled up to the beach house. Mook gave me the keys to one of his cars to drive while I was out here. I crept in the house searching for Lucky's room. It took me a minute to find it but I did. He was sleeping so peacefully lying next to Melanie. A devious smile appeared on my face. I couldn't stop smiling. I should smack the fuck out of him but I'm not. I move in silence. He'll feel me and see me when he opens his eyes. His arms were wrapped around her waist too. He comfortable as fuck after the crime he just committed a few hours ago.

He just doesn't get that he's awakened a beast. One that he'll hate to see. Game on Lucky. I swear to God he doesn't want to go to war with a bitch like me, he'll lose every fuckin' time. My mother and father took me out the hood so I wouldn't have to move like this fuckin' with a nigga like him. I sat right in the corner in this nigga room contemplating on my next move watching him and Melanie sleep peacefully. Lucky has me fucked up. How in the fuck does he think he can sleep well every night, but he stays trying to ruin my life. It's not going down like that at all.

I grabbed my Glock 40 caliber and screwed the silencer on. I approached Melanie's side of the bed. I pressed my gun toward her temple. I let that bitch loose six fuckin' times. I shot Melanie in her head. I made sure I got blood on his fuckin' face. I dipped the tip of the silencer in her blood. I wrote CHECK

MATE BITCH in her blood on the sheets right next to Lucky's face. I wanted him to see how I was coming. I can only imagine the look on his face when he wakes up and sees his bitch dead in the bed lying next to him. I whispered in his ear on my way out. "Now you dispose of this bitch." Lucky started stirring in his sleep. As quickly as I came in, I was out like a thief in the night. He should quit playing with me right fuckin' now.

I hope all this little bullshit is worth it. I don't even bother him. I had plenty of opportunities to fuck with him an old girl, but I didn't but now I'm not going to ease up on his pussy ass since he keeps going out his way to fuck with me. Lucky only had one job to do and that was to be faithful, that's it but he couldn't even do that.

Lucky

Kaniya plays a lot of fuckin' games. If I could see her right fuckin' now I swear to God I would lay hands on her. I thought I was tripping last night when I thought I heard her say dispose of this bitch. Imagine my surprise when I woke up this morning and blood was splattered on my face. I wiped my face my with the back of my hand to see what was up. I thought I was tripping. I didn't understand why blood was on my face. I raised up to see what was going on and Melanie was lying next to shot in the head. Blood was every fuckin' where. Right next me to CHECKMATE was written on the sheet. I shook my head and ran my hands across my face. I couldn't believe this shit. How am I supposed to explain this to Shaela, her sister and Melanie's parents?

How did she fuckin' get in here? I swear to God that shit shook the fuck out of me. I'm used to dead bodies, but God damn I ain't never lied next to one or had one lying in the bed with one. Damn Kaniya was cold as fuck with this shit. She just showed me she's tired of fuckin' playing games. I thought Kaniya lost her touch. I guess not but this is a side of her that I didn't want to see. I was praying this right here didn't resurface because it ain't no coming back from none of this shit.

All I wanted her to do was fight for us. That's the only thing I wanted her to fuckin' do. She didn't even want to do that. She wanted to be a hoe this summer. All I wanted to do was talk to her and come to an understanding so we could move past this shit, but she refuses to do that. I had some other shit going on too but it wasn't about nothing. I had plans to dead that shit too. We're stronger together than we are apart. Ugh, I'm so fuckin' tired of this shit with her. What else do I have to do to show her she's everything to me? I've been trying to get us back for almost two months now.

I've been shaking these hoes the best way I know how. I swear these two bodies disappearing is going to look suspect. JD and Melanie both gone, that's not a coincidence. I heard a knock at the door. I peeked to see who it was, and It was brother Quan and my father. My father and brother both looked at me and shook their heads. My father stroked his beard and asked,

"Damn, she did that Lucky?" I nodded my head in agreeance. Kaniya made a fuckin' mess. It's too many motherfuckas in here to dispose of this shit. Damn, Melanie, she didn't even see Kaniya coming.

THE NEXT DAY

Chapter-25

Sonja

I've been the happiest I've been in a long time. My nephew was out of prison from doing two years in prison. My niece was home from college doing great. I had Deuce the love of my life and we were about to get married. The only thing that was bothering me was Kanan. I knew that nigga was out of jail. If he told Kaniya he was getting out 6/16/16, which means that crazy nigga was already out. It was a warning and he wanted her to run it back to me that he was coming for blood. I love Kanan but I'm not in love with him anymore. We had some good times together and we had some bad times. I took the good with the bad. Our bad days outweighed our good days. Kanan and I have been through it all together.

I love Deuce and I'm riding with him to the wheels fall off. He completes me and I complete him. I had one problem though. I knew some shit was coming. I felt that shit in my soul.

Kanan couldn't accept that I moved on. He knows we're not to-gether and we haven't been for a few years. We had business ties but the moment he made his presence known, I'll politely server any business ties we had. I told him if he ever went to jail while we were together it was a wrap.

I kept money on his books. I ran all his businesses and his money was A1. He was still a paid nigga because of me. Killian didn't do shit but collect and distribute. I was up early in the morning cooking up dope and weighing up work. Bitches were still screaming Free Kanan. Just the thought alone made me laugh because I was screaming Fuck Kanan. I was glad that nigga was gone. I was the one that got him locked up truth be told. I hoped and prayed he never got out. Kanan and Killian were some real OG's. They had every judge and DA in their pockets.

Kanan was facing twenty years and they got that shit cut down to six years. He ended up catching another charge in jail and they added another two years to his sentence. I did what I had to do for my sanity. Kanan and I were together for over 20 years.

This man had the nerve to have a baby by the help. The moment he did that it was a smack to my fuckin' face. I lost all respect for him. It was me who helped that nigga get on. I was in the trap with him day in and day out until he sold out. For him to have a baby by that bitch Yasmine was a blow to my fuckin' ego.

I guess those motherfuckas thought the joke was on me. I had something for him and her. She gave that motherfucka two twins boys to be exact, and this bitch had the nerve to smile in face like shit was cool.

You could never play me, but you can bet your fuckin' life that I will play you. I started watching Kanan's move to see what he was up to. The dots finally connected. This bitch was living lavishly like me off my fuckin' money. God is my witness and the lord could take me right fuckin' now, It was going down like that at all. Imagine to his surprise when they got knocked and I had to come and get his stuff and his kids. He was about to shit bricks, but I had the biggest smile on my face.

I will never take Kanan back. I really need to beat Yasmine ass. This bitch thought she could smile in my face and fuck my nigga. I saw right through that shit. I knew what time it was. I knew she was fuckin' him, but you can't run game on a game seeker. I pimped niggas for years and played the game raw. You had the nerve to have two kids by him. You couldn't even keep it real about none of that shit. So, I don't respect you at all. That nigga was so far up Yasmine ass he was fuckin' up big time.

His stupid ass didn't even know I was stealing from him. I stole six million dollars from him and he couldn't even tell. Oh well, I don't give a fuck what bitch or nigga think about me. I helped him build this shit, so it was mine literally. I was the muscle behind his success. I was ready for him. I know he's lurking in the shadows. I stay on go. I got to let Kaniya know what's up because she loves her uncle to death. She doesn't know what's going on.

I know she can relate because she and Lucky are going through some shit right now. I'm rooting for her and Lucky but I wouldn't tell her that. I must admit she's handling her break up very well and serving Lucky every chance she gets. Every time I see the two of them I think about Kaisha and Killian because history was repeating itself. She's giving that man hell and it shows on his face. I think he's sorry. He brings Melanie around for a reaction out of Kaniya, but she won't give him one.

Kanan was too possessive for me. I couldn't piss without him being there to wipe my pussy with a tissue. I could go on all day about him, but I won't. These last eight years he's been gone I thanked God every day while he was gone. I know it sad but oh well. It's about to be war in these streets, I know how Kanan is. It's whatever with me.

If we got to shoot it out in these streets, I'll make time for that. If I got to kill that motherfucka myself I'll make time for that too. Oh well, I'm prepared to do that shit too. He taught me the game and gave it to me for free. I'm not new to boding niggas and bitches. He isn't excluded either. He knows how I get down. I needed to stop thinking about Kanan's trifling ass. He's in my past for a reason and I would like to keep him there. I felt a pair of strong hands wrapped around my waist. I didn't even have to look over my shoulder to know who it was. He started kissing me on my neck and fondling with my breasts. God, I love this man.

"Sonja Harris, I can't wait to marry you and make you my wife," he explained and bit my collar bone. I can't wait to marry him too. Deuce is perfect and I didn't want to lose that because of Kanan. I knew Kanan hadn't changed because if he had he would just leave me alone and own up to his fuck ups. But that too much like right, he doesn't want to see me happy if I'm not with him.

"I can't wait to say I do, Deuce." I beamed and let out a soft moan. Our wedding was scheduled for next month. I wanted a big ass wedding. I had it scheduled for July because I knew Kanan would've been out by now I wanted him to know that I change my last name and it would never be Miller. I knew that shit would've killed him.

"So why are we waiting for Sonja. We could've done that months ago. I'm ready after my birthday. Let's speed this shit up like next week. I'm ready for you to carry my last name. I want to take you on the honeymoon of your dreams," he explained. I turned around to face to Deuce. I rested my hands on his chests. I stood on my tippy toes and placed a kiss on his lips. He gripped my ass and raised my nighty up over my ass. He was trying to find my hole and he did. Deuce always felt so fuckin' good to me.

"I love you so much Deuce. Thank you for loving me," I moaned.

"I love you too," he grunted and continued making love to me.

Kanan

It feels good to be fresh out the FEDS. The only thing missing was Sonja, but it won't be long before she's back home where she fuckin' belongs. True enough we weren't together, but that shit didn't mean anything to an OG like me. She knew what it was between us. I knew she was fuckin' off out here in the streets because I'm behind bars. I'm home now and whatever she has going on, she has to dead that fuckin' shit. I won't allow her to be with another man if it's not me and she fuckin' knows it. I make niggas disappear and Deuce wasn't fuckin' excluded, he had to go. Any motherfucka that had a chance to come in between Sonja and me had to go.

The day I got pulled over my life changed for the worst. I had no clue it was by the fuckin' FEDS. I'm a street nigga and I would've run, fuck that. I got caught up with Yasmine. She was in the car with me. I swore up and down to Sonja that I wasn't fucking with her. My two boys were with us. Sonja had no clue Yasmine and I had kids together. I kept that shit a secret too. I had to call her to come and get my car. I needed her to get the kids too because Yasmine had drugs on her also.

We both went to the FEDS. That shit was reckless as fuck. Can you imagine Sonja's face when she came and got me, she was pissed off? Every lie I fuckin' told bit me in the ass. When she looked at the twins she saw me. They looked just like me. She gave me the nastiest look I'd ever seen. She didn't fold though, and I appreciated her for that. She left my ass high and fuckin' dry. She wouldn't come and see me or accept any of my calls. She wouldn't even write to me. She kept money on my books and she ran my empire while I was away. She made it clear that we weren't together. She said it was no coming back from that. I accepted that THEN. Shit, I'm man enough to admit I was wrong but daddy's home now. I heard all about her and Deuce. The streets talk.

I've seen her and him out a few times. I wanted to snatch her up so quickly because I didn't like how happy she looked with him. I man enough to admit that I fucked up but I never wanted another man to make what belongs to me smile. She got two fuckin' options, she can do it my way or she's going to learn the hard way. She can come back voluntarily, and I'll forgive her for entertaining that nigga while I was gone.

If she doesn't want to do that, I'll kill Deuce. She knows I don't give a fuck about catching a murder charge or violating parole. I will kill that nigga in broad daylight.

I don't care about faces because I can guarantee you any motherfucka that had the balls to tell on me wouldn't make it to court to fuckin' testify. I hope Sonja can deal with it because I'm about to show her how real shit gets when you belong to me. I'm tired of playing games. This shit is about to get ugly quick. She needs to come on back home. I'm heading to Miami. I'll be there in a few hours. I was making some moves out in Fort Lauderdale. A lil birdie tells me Sonja's every move. Sonja has been on my mind the moment they freed a nigga. I thought she would've come to her senses by now.

"Kanan, can we do something other than handling business," she argued and nagged. I looked over my shoulders to see what the fuck she wanted. She had her hands rested on her hips. I was looking for ass because I didn't see it while I was caged. Don't get me wrong, Yasmine is fine as fuck but she isn't wife material. She wanted my bag and I wasn't giving it to her. I taught her how to get it out the mud but she wanted to put miles on her pussy instead.

I've been running these streets for a long ass time and the only thing I regret is letting that bitch ride my dick raw. I wouldn't trade my sons for anything in this world. I don't even know why I brought this bitch with me. She couldn't even suck my dick right. I'm too old to be coaching a motherfucka on how to do my dick.

"What do you want to do?" I asked. Yasmine was still ghetto as fuck. The moment I touched down she was at Black's night club looking for me. I kept my ears to the streets to see what she was up too. She only had one job and that was to raise my fuckin' son's right and she would've been well taken care of, but she didn't want to do that. She still wanted to run the streets and fuck whatever nigga had the biggest bag.

"I want to shop Kanan, of course. Don't you want to spoil me since you left me with your sons?" She asked. I'm a little wiser now and tricking off with Yasmine wasn't worth it at all. I was only breaking bread with my sons and that's it.

"I want you to spoil me. Cash out on your baby daddy. I'm good for it," I chuckled. Yasmine's face instantly turned into a frown. I knew she was broke, as fuck. I just wanted her to tell me she was.

"Are you serious Kanan, right now. You know I don't fuckin' have it. In case you forgot I have your two sons to provide for. That bitch Sonja you were fuckin' with has taken everything except your fuckin' kids," she argued and sassed. I wasn't about to go back and forth with her, I refuse too.

Shaela

I like Tariq but I'm not in love with him. I think I used to love him at some point. When you're in a relationship with someone eventually your love will blossom, but none of that shit is happening with us. The whole two years he was gone I was doing me. All the bread that nigga left me I ran through that shit and balled the fuck out. The only reason my ass came back around was to get knee deep in his pockets. I didn't visit him one fuckin' time. I never wrote a letter or put any money on his books. I just wanted the paper that's it. I promised to hold him down and that was a lie. I was out as soon as those gates shut. I changed my number and everything. Money was always a motive for me. I don't fuck with niggas in jail period. I don't give a fuck how much he did for me.

I was curious as fuck because I couldn't understand how in the fuck, he left Kaniya $200,000.00. That shit bothered the fuck out of me. Do you know how I would've been living if he left me that? Lavish as fuck. He only left me $10,000 but I'm his main bitch and she was his cousin. I wasn't buying that shit at all. I knew it was more than what he said. How in the fuck did he think I felt when that bitch gave him a cashier check for $220,000.00. That was a huge blow for me?

He refuses to discuss that shit with me. For the life of me, I couldn't see why he was pressed for Kaniya's ass, him and Lucky both. She had the two of them tripping hard as fuck. I knew Tariq fucked Kaniya. I don't know how Lucky didn't see it but I did. I don't know how long I can keep doing this shit. The only reason why I was entertaining Tariq was for my mom, the infamous Yasmine. She keeps some bullshit going on and I hate being mixed up with it. She had some beef with Sonja, Tariq's aunt.

I don't like Sonja. She knew Tariq wanted to fuck Kaniya, her play niece. I got something for that bitch. Don't ever try to play me and smile in my face. It's one of the reasons why I pushed Melanie up on Lucky so hard. I didn't like Kaniya at all. Never have and I never will. Yes, I made sure my sister got her fuckin' man. I just didn't know that Kaniya was hood as fuck. I knew she went to college and stuff. Immediately I thought she was a square, but she fooled me.

I've been with Tariq for a long time. I never had any competition when it came to him. When I met Tariq, he was fuckin' with this bitch named Tamia. I pushed her out my way, now I had another fuckin' problem, Kaniya. Now I can't get this nigga to love me for shit.

My mom must come with something better. I'm tired of being with this nigga. He doesn't show me any affection or even looks at me like he wants me. I just can't be a side bitch and not get any attention. That's one of the main reasons why I was fucking his partner John. I will give Tariq credit, he did tell me that he wanted to be with Kaniya on more than one occasion.

He told me that before the dinner that Sonja had a couple of Sunday ago. I refuse to accept that and let Kaniya have Lucky and Tariq both. That bitch got me fucked up. I could never tell him that I was fucking John. No fuckin' way, not happening. I know she done fucked my nigga because ain't no nigga just eating pussy and that sprung. She done came down with some pussy trust me. See unlike Melanie I didn't catch feelings, I was catching checks. I was in my bag if a nigga didn't have it than we couldn't communicate.

My sister was so fuckin' dumb. Every time I would ask her did Lucky give her some money, she would say no but she was steady giving up pussy. Speaking of which let me call her. My sister just up and disappeared and didn't say bye or nothing. The story Lucky gave me that she up and left I'm not buying that. I called Melanie and sent her a few text but she never responded. That's not like her, she always answers on the first ring. I promise you this on my unborn yes, I'm pregnant by John of course, if something happened to my sister I'm coming for Lucky and his bitch, trust me.

I need to call my mom and see if she and Kanan made it. Yasmine better be glad she's my mom because if she wasn't fucking Kanan he would be mine. Sonja and I would have issues. Deuce can get it too. I see the way he looks at me. I still might try and dig my claws into him because he's paid too. My mom answered on the first ring.

"Hey ma, have you made it?" I beamed. I could tell my mom had an attitude, but I wasn't the one for it. I'm doing her a favor and I shouldn't because she never raised us. The only kid's she cared about was the twins because their family was rich as fuck.

"Yes, we made it, Shaela. I told you not to call me I'll call you," she argued and hung up the phone. I don't even know why I tried to have a relationship with this bitch and she was always out for herself. Motherfuckas wonder why I'm so vindictive, I get it from my mother.

Yasmine

I'm Yasmine Carter soon to be Miller. I know a few bitches who would hate to see that. I know Sonja has dragged my name through the mud, but I don't give a fuck. I never liked her since High School. She always thought she was better than people. I couldn't stand that bitch because she had everything. She was pretty, well-kept, and all the niggas wanted her. She was too good to socialize. She wasn't better than anybody because she was giving up pussy just like everybody else. Her momma was a hoe and she was too. What bitch do you know that goes to a TRAP HOUSE to cook up dope, make pills, and bag up weed in a fucking mink coat? I just shook my head and rolled my eyes thinking about it. She was so over the fuckin' top with the shit she did. I hated it and I wanted it. I did everything I could to try and get it. Her sister Tyra, she was cool may she rest in peace. I wanted everything she had starting with Kanan, which I got.

My beef with Sonja wasn't about any dick. Kanan wasn't hard to get. I didn't have to do much but fuck, suck and be on call pussy. Guess what, I did that shit. Everybody knew the Miller Boys was some paid niggas. I wanted to get paid so wherever they were I was fuckin' there too. That bitch wasn't. Any bitch that's about hers was in their faces. I did what I had to do to trap him. I'm never going to beef with a female about a nigga that couldn't be kept.

My beef with Sonja only intensified the day we got pulled over by the FEDS. I had our two boys with us. I was careless as fuck and I regret that shit every fuckin' day running up behind a no-good ass nigga. He didn't take my charge so I could get my boys. Real women do real things and despite Kanan's infidelities, you could've got my kids. Instead of letting them go to foster homes since you were supposed to be his fuckin' ride or die. Nobody in my family would get them. I thought Sonja would step up since she loved Kanan so much, but she didn't.

To be truthful she can have Kanan back if she wanted him. You know how sometimes you do everything you can to get a nigga and when you finally get him, he isn't about shit. Well, that's Kanan. He doesn't even treat me like he should. You would think since I'm the mother of his kids I would still be living lavish but nope, that nigga still had me in the trap cooking and bagging. He told me if I didn't like it I could go and get me a 9 to 5. I guess the saying is true, how you gain them is how you lose them.

He's been keeping company with some young girl. He was so fuckin' disrespectful with the shit he was doing it right in my face. Just dismissing me. I was mad because he wouldn't fuck me, he only wanted me to suck his dick. Like right now he got me riding to Miami with him to chill. I know he's trying to fuck with Sonja, but it's cool though because I've wanted to address her ass for the longest anyway. I had a lot of shit on my chest that I wanted to say to Kanan, but the time never presented itself, but I want him to know how I feel. Kanan had money out the ass and he still was fine as fuck. I could never get enough of him.

He was tall, stood about 6'3, he had to weight about 250 pounds solid. Jail did his body good. His skin was the color of a pecan. Dreads adorned his head and they were freshly twisted. He had them pulled back into a ponytail and they were draping down his back. He was iced the fuck out. He had a few gray strains but not too many. His mustache and goatee were trimmed to perfection. I could tell he was aging because the salt and pepper look was visible in his facial hair but none the less, he still looked good. He was dressed in all Versace. He was a fuckin' boss in every sense. I couldn't stop catching glances at him. I couldn't for the life of me figure out why I could never get him to love me. The music was loud in my ears. I cut the volume down immediately. He looked at me and gave me an evil glare.

"I told you about that shit, Yasmine. Don't fuck with nothing in here that don't fuckin' belong to you," he argued and yelled. He turned his music back up dismissing me. I turned it back down. "Yasmine, what's your fuckin' problem. You've been with the shits since we got here. If you're ready to go back home I'll book you a fuckin' flight."

"Can I ask you a question Kanan and I want you to be honest with me. How come you never loved me? Why wasn't I good enough for you. I always wanted to know why I wasn't your number one?" I asked. Tears filled the brim of my eyes because I wanted to know that. I couldn't stop my tears if I wanted too.

"Stop fuckin' crying. You want the truth, you can never handle the truth. You knew what it was between us the moment you opened your legs and swallowed this dick. It was a fuck. You wanted me to fuck you. I gave you what you wanted. It'll always be Sonja, it was never you. I got love for you, Yasmine, because you carried precious cargo of mine and that's about it. When I did my bid you got out before I did and you were with the next nigga. Loyalty is something that you don't possess and I can't fuck with that."

Chapter-26

Kanan

I couldn't wait to touch down in Miami. I was forty-five minutes away, right outside of Fort Lauderdale. I've been gone for eight years. I couldn't go any longer without Sonja. I hope she's ready because I'm coming hard in the fuckin' paint. She refused my calls and she refused to visit. The house we had in East Lake she moved all her shit up out of there. She didn't even get the mail forwarded. She kept money on my books. I never went without. You can run but you sure can't hide. Let me get straight to the point.

I understand you left a nigga and you wanted to prove a fuckin' point. She cut off all communication and she refused to discuss any of our issues with me. It's my time now and I want her to tell me to my face. that she doesn't want me. I was shoving my dick down Shaela's throat, Yasmine's daughter. I know it's fucked up, but her momma should've raised her better. At least I wasn't fucking her. She was begging for it, so I fed it to her. Call it what you want but I can give two fucks.

I'm coming for mine and I'm not taking no for an answer. What I will say is if I find out that my niece hooked Sonja up with her father in law it was over for her ass too. Your loyalty is with me and me only. My fuckin' blood flows through her. I'm her fuckin' uncle. Deuce and his son ain't shit to her. I heard Lucky was fucking Melanie, Yasmine's other daughter anyway. Kaniya better recognize that shit. Killian will be alright if I kill his daughter, that's why he was blessed with twins. He still had another daughter left. If Deuce even thought he had the balls to interfere with what I and Sonja got going on I was going to shoot that nigga right where the fuck he stands.

I need to shoot his ass anyway because his pussy ass knows me. He knew I was with Sonja. All I can is say is that Sonja better do shit my way. She knows I play for keeps in any and everything I do. I hope she makes her next move her best move. I wonder if she was cheating on me with him, that's why it was so easy for her to throw in the towel. Let me stop because I'm thinking too much and these crazy thoughts of mine, will get a lot of motherfuckas laid down. It will be a fucking massacre at this birthday dinner.

"Yasmine, give me some fuckin' head. I need to relieve some stress and don't use your teeth."

Kaniya

☆

Tonight's the night for Deuce's birthday dinner. I had a feeling some shit was going to pop off. I couldn't seem to shake it for anything in this world. I've learned these past few days to start trusting my instincts because they would never steer me wrong, but I was hard-headed as fuck and I would never listen. Maybe it was something in the air. It was Sunday and anytime Sonja had a gathering or family dinner on a Sunday some shit went down. It always happened like that.

To be safer than sorry I came to Prive early before the place opened and brought my guns up in this bitch. My uncle Kanan was crazy, he was a fuckin' lunatic. I didn't trust him at all. I heard what my father said loud and clear, but I didn't like how Kanan came at me when he called me the other day. I trust my first instincts when dealing with crazy motherfuckas. That old ass motherfuckin' nigga had the nerve to tell me he'll kill me and I should pick the right side. He will never catch me slipping.

It's kill or be killed. I live by and die by that shit. I'll kill your ass today and be at your funeral tomorrow. I will cry and console my dad and grandma like I haven't done shit. I won't lose any sleep. At the end of the day it was you or me, and it for damn sure wasn't going to be me. It was the night of the party. I was keeping it simple but very cute. I went to the Dominicans and got my hair flat ironed bone straight. My hair was flawless I couldn't stop looking in the mirror.

I found a cute all-white fitted dress. I paired it with a pair of gold Gucci open-toed sandals. I wanted to wear all black because I knew I was about to fuck some shit up. I already knew what time it was. I could feel it in the air. I knew my uncle or somebody was coming for me. I hope they're prepared for how real this shit could get for fucking with a bitch like me. The only thing is this shit could be Kosher or shit could go left quick.

I was prepared for the worst anyway. I'll play it how it goes for now. I got fresh Mani and Pedi. I loved my toes painted cocaine white. The only thing that was bothering was I didn't want to catch a murder charge behind my uncle, so I had to make this shit neat and clean, no fuck ups. No faces, no cases, no witness and no evidence. I wanted Killany to come but she couldn't make it. I think she just didn't want Kanan's blood on her hands, scared ass. I had to fuck with her about it constantly. I wanted to call my girls in on this, but I decided not to. I made plans to relax until 7:00 and then it was show time. Lights, camera, action and the smell of gun smoke.

Sonja

Tonight, was the night of Deuce party. Trust me when I tell you it was some bullshit in the air. I could feel it in the air. Guess what I didn't give a fuck! I was still living my life like it was my last. I know Kanan is somewhere lurking in the shadows. Kanan just didn't know I'm ready for his bitter ass. He created a beast years ago. I'm ready for this shit! I know how he is coming but wait until he sees how the fuck I'm coming. Only the good Lord himself could prepare him for this. It was about to get real real quick. I wanted to look good doing it. Like right now I was at the salon getting a vixen sew-in. Fresh Mani and Pedi. My niece Raven and daughter in law Tianna was with me. I called Kaniya stubborn ass and she didn't answer the phone. I didn't invite Shaela. I didn't like her or trust her sneaky ass. For some reason, I thought it was funny Melanie was her sister and she's fucking my niece's man. As long as Shaela has been with Tariq, she has never mentioned her sister and I've never met her mother. That was some strange.

All of sudden your sister pops up and she just so happens to be the side bitch that Lucky is fucking with. Something was up with her, trust me. I was going to get down to the bottom of it. For her sake and not mine, I hope all of this was coincidental and not intentional. Shaela doesn't want to see what I do to bitches that do things intentionally. She'll be dead on arrival wherever I see her I'll drop her right where she stands, seriously.

"Auntie, Auntie," she yelled.

"What child?" I asked.

"I forgot to tell you the other day I overheard Shaela talking on the phone to some lady named Yasmine. She was saying that she needed to come up with another plan quick because she was tired and pregnant for John or Rock one of Tariq's friends, I can't remember which one." Raven revealed.

"Back the fuck up Raven, say this shit again," I yelled and asked?

"Raven, said she pregnant for John or Rock who is that?" Tianna asked.

"You have to be kidding me. Please tell me you are lying? Yasmine? How does she know Yasmine?" I spat.

"What the fuck is going on?" Tianna and Raven said in unison.

"Tianna and Raven get Kaniya on the phone right fucking now?

Tariq

Tonight, was the night of Deuce dinner party. You know I had to get on my fly designer shit. I'm a fly ass nigga. Ain't no way around it. I jumped fresh in a Balmain fit of course. I got my dreads retwisted and pulled back in a fishtail braid. My face was lined up to perfection. I was a handsome ass nigga too and I can have any bitch I want. I had one problem though. I only wanted one female, Kaniya Nicole Miller. She needs to make up her fuckin' mind about what the fuck she wants to do. I think she wants me but I'm not for sure. I'm tired of this high school shit.

These past few days I've been kicking with this badass little jawn from Philly name Jassity. Shawty was right as fuck too. Her skin was brown, the color of cognac. She was thick as fuck too and she was short. Her body was nice and petite. She had a nice edgy haircut. I could fuck with it She was going to be my date to the party. I didn't care that Shaela brought her trifling ass down here. John already told me that she was pregnant for him. I didn't care. I never had feelings for the bitch anyway. I just wanted her to tell me which she has yet to do.

I can't wait to see Kaniya's face when she sees me with Jassity. I know she's feeling me more than what she lets on. I love her though and the feelings are mutual. I can't hide it and I won't deny it but I won't sit in the background and be anybody's side nigga. I wish she would stop fuckin' playing games and be with me. Fuck Lucky, he can get this iron too. I was tired of sparing him anyway. He bleeds just like anybody else. I should just go ahead and kill him and get this shit over with so I could get his bitch.

Love will make you do some crazy shit. I didn't think I would ever get here again but I am. I just finished getting my shape up and twisted up. I was on my way to pick up Jassity so we could go to the mall and get fly together. I know I'm a petty as nigga for doing this shit, but I wanted to see if I could get a reaction out of Kaniya. I can't be the only one fighting for us. She wanted to make it seem to Lucky like I've only eaten her pussy, but she knows I've had her climbing the walls plenty of nights. Shit, my back is still scratched up because she showed her ass. She knows those weeks we spent together. I was 12 feet deep in her guts. I still remember how wet her pussy got for a nigga.

I was digging deep as fuck. I wanted Kaniya to have my child. I made love to Kaniya I never fucked her. I was ready to tell Lucky anyways. I didn't give a fuck.

To make matters worse I watched her fuck that nigga on the bus. She lied to my face and she knew she did. I wanted to hurt her ass for that. I felt some type of way about that shit. I was sick to my stomach because I care about her. On top of that, I was tripping when she brought old boy to the cookout. He was rubbing and feeling her up. I wanted to fuck her ass up bad.

Not to mention the other night I saw when she pulled up and pulled off. I watched her body Melanie ass the other night. I don't want her killing anybody behind Lucky's fuck ass. She's down to ride and that shit was sexy as fuck to me. I'm putting some shit on the table tonight and some feelings will be hurt tonight Jassity's included. I sent Kaniya a text and told her that I missed her, but she never responded. Since she killed Melanie she hasn't been around. I just wanted to make sure she was straight but if she didn't want to be bothered then it was nothing that I could do about that. I tried but she should be willing to meet a nigga halfway and she didn't want to do that.

I sent Jassity a text and told her to come out. Miami has always been good to me even with the little bullshit that was brewing out here, it was cool. Jassity walked her fine ass outside. I was always a gentleman no matter what. I met her halfway so I could open the door for her. She had on a pair of jeans and they were tight as fuck I don't even know how her pussy was able to breathe but it did. She slid in the car and I pulled off.

"Hey Tariq, you look handsome as fuck, if you were an edible I wouldn't mind eating you," she cooed. I know Jassity wanted to fuck me, but I wasn't trying to take her down through there yet. I would let her suck the skin off my dick if she wanted too. I thought she was a good girl. I had no clue she was a little fuckin' freak.

"Is that right, Jassity? I got a few things you can suck on," I chuckled. Jassity ran her hands up my thighs trying to feel my dick. She finally found it. "Did you find what you were looking for?"

"I did hope one day I'll get to see it instead of feeling it through your pants," she stated and smiled. Her eyes were trained on me the whole time while she spoke.

"Play your cards right and I'll see if I can arrange that for you."

"I will. Don't keep me waiting too long Mr. Harris." I nodded my head in agreeance. She knew I wasn't ready for a relationship, but I could fuck her as long as no strings were attached.

DEUCE'S PARTY

Chapter-27

Deuce

Today was my fucking birthday, it was a real niggas holiday. I was coming of age and more than ready to settle down. I lived a life of sin for many years and lord knows I thought I would never make it here. I was turnt the fuck up as my children would say. It's a blessing to be alive in the land of the living. A lot of niggas don't even make it past the age of twenty-five. That alone is a vibe itself. Black lives matter. I guess my ancestors and God had other plans for me. I made it see the age forty-six. I had no fuckin' complaints. Life is great minus the bullshit. "Happy Birthday Calvin Rogan Sr. a.k.a Deuce to the fuckin' streets." I had the woman of my dreams Sonja, and my two sons with me, Quan and Lucky. I was in good health and in my right state of mind. I wasn't broke. I was wealthy as fuck. I had money out the ass, too much money if you ask me.

All of my years of living I've never had a woman who holds me down and caters to me the way Sonja does. For instance, she was throwing me a birthday party to celebrate my life. Not one time has she asked me for a dime and that speaks volumes? She has access to everything, and she hasn't touched anything. Any woman I've ever been with has yet to do the things that Sonja does. I've never had a birthday party before. That's the main reason why she was about to carry my last name. I always knew my first time getting married would be my last time. I want to spend forever with her. I threw my player card two years ago. I knew all about Sonja and Kanan. I knew everything there is to know. I always had security on Sonja. She didn't know it, that's how I knew that Kanan was out a month ago and plotting?

He's been out for over a month and he had his eyes on my wife. The streets talk and my name holds weight out here. I already knew what he had planned. I called Killian the other day and discussed with him what was going on. Of course, he didn't want to hear about his brother getting bodied. He didn't want his daughter touched at all. That was his only concern. I never knew Kaniya Miller was his daughter. She's a reflection of her mother. Kaisha with a K gives it up to the same way as her daughter does.

It's funny because Killian and I were close friends growing up. What are the chances that my son and his daughter were dating? Speaking of which I needed to have a conversation with Lucky and Quan about these streets and the women they chose to be with. I didn't hustle my whole life and avoid the FEDS for them to do the same thing. I didn't want my kids to do the same shit I did. I wanted them to better than me. I knew Quan was in the streets heavy.

Lucky owns a few businesses but he's deep in the streets more than what I would like him to be. He's doing some other shit too that he thinks I don't know about. We needed to have a conversation today. I hated to address it on my birthday, but it couldn't wait. I've called the two of them to come and see me before the party starts. They both walked in the conference room at the beach house and taken a seat. I passed the cigar box and lighter down to each of them. They lit their cigars and smoke started to fill the room. Lucky and Quan both gave me their undivided attention.

"I brought both of y'all here because we need to discuss business. First things first everything is looking good. I couldn't be prouder of the two of y'all than I already am. I've been hustling in the streets for a long as time and I'm ready to sit back and enjoy the fruits of my labor. I have never been to prison and I don't plan on going. I run a tight ship with no fuck ups. If I was to hand y'all my empire can y'all assure me that it would be ran the same," I asked.

My eyes were focused on Lucky because he was the hot head and Quan was reserved like me. "Quan I know you're in a serious relationship with Tianna and Lucky I don't know what the fuck you're doing but you need to tighten up. The shit you and Kaniya have going on is dangerous and if I hand you empire I need you to cut the bullshit and focus because you've been acting real reckless and the last thing I need is for pussy to cloud your judgment and fuck up my business. Do you understand me?" Quan and Lucky both nodded their heads in agreement.

I handed each of them a manila folder explaining which portions of the business they would handle and which lieutenant of mine would help them with their day to day operations. That was my gift to them. The blueprint to a multi-million dollar empire. I wanted things in place in case something ever happened to me God forbid. My sons would know how to move accordingly. I gave them the KEYS to the streets.

Killian

I had to take this trip to Miami. I didn't want too, but I had too. I received a call from Deuce and Killany. I'm my brother's keeper. We shared the same womb for nine months we were identical twins. To know him is to love him. To hate him or become an enemy of his you've signed your own death certificate. I'll lay my life on the line for him any day. I refused to let my brother die behind some pussy or my crazy ass daughter. I heard Deuce loud and clear. I understood where he was coming from but a motherfucka can't threaten my brother's life and live to tell about it. Kanan was wrong and I had his back right or wrong. It didn't fuckin' matter to me.

This situation itself is a mess. Kanan was wrong and he knew he did Sonja wrong. He needs to move on and let her live her life. I was going just to tell him that. I knew all about Kaniya's plan to kill my brother. Killany called and told me everything. I love my daughter to death and she's just as crazy as Kanan. Hell, he named her. When he first laid eyes on Kaniya he said she was the daughter he never had. Kaniya was just like Kanan and Killany was just like me. Ain't no way in hell my brother was about to die at the hands of my daughter. It wasn't going down like that. I had to interfere because I wasn't losing my brother.

I told her to have her uncle's back not killing her uncle. She didn't listen to shit I was saying. It went in one ear and out the other. To make matters worse she wanted Killany in on it with her. It was true that Kanan was coming for her too; he thought she hooked Sonja up with Deuce since she was dating Lucky. Deuce never knew that Kaniya was my daughter until yesterday. Kanan knew not to fuck with a picture of my daughter. That's where he and I would have a problem.

My daughter doesn't have shit to do with your cheating ass and why Sonja left you. To be real he needs to move on. At least Sonja kept money on his books and she made him money. He didn't come home broke. Everything he left behind he came back to it and he had more. It doesn't get any more real than that. You're picking up where you left off. I didn't have to send my brother anything.

All I had to do was visit and answer the phone, that's it. He should be mad at Yasmine. That bitch has been out for two years. She couldn't hold a candle to Sonja. She didn't send him shit or go see him or put money on her phone for him to call. That's what he gets though, the same way you gain them is how you lose them.

Shaela

I wanted to get my hair and nails done too courtesy of John and Tariq. See Sonja is a petty bitch. She never hid the fact that she didn't like me. She made sure she told me every fuckin' time and she made sure I never forgot. At least be cordial with me. I didn't know anyone out here. I wanted to get cute also. Lord knows where my sister is. If she was here, we could have gotten an Uber and I wouldn't even care to be in the company of those bitches. I couldn't call my mom over here to pick me up because our cover would've been blown, and you know I'm saving the best for last.

I can't wait to tell Sonja to pick up her fucking face. Yes, bitch, I'm the product of Yasmine the bitch you love to hate. I made sure to tell my mom that Sonja treats me like crap. My mom couldn't wait to see Sonja and she was going to walk her like a dog, and I was going to help her. I had to call Tariq to come and pick me up and take me to the mall. It was cool because we could get some alone time anyway. He said he would be here in twenty minutes. I've been waiting for forty minutes.

He was going to The Shops at Merrick Park. I figured it was some high-end shit because I've never heard of it. That's cool because he was going be my trick for today. Imagine my surprise when he pulled up, he had some chick in the car with him and it wasn't Kaniya.

"What's up Tariq, are you going to tell your escort to get in the back," I sassed and sucked my teeth. I had to be messy because he shouldn't be with her. He should be with me until we got back to Atlanta. Tariq wouldn't even fuck or kiss me. I tried to suck his dick and he wouldn't even let me put my mouth on it. It's safe to say he's not fuckin' with me.

"Shaela you can go on with that shit. You need a ride or not because we can dip? Her name is Jassity and she's not going anywhere. You can get your ass in the back and shut the fuck up and ride. If you don't want to do either you can keep your ass here," he argued and yelled. He embarrassed the fuck out of me in front of her.

"You know what if I didn't need a ride that bad and your auntie didn't fuckin' leave me, I would've never called your ass. I'm tired of you disrespecting me. First, it's Kaniya and now Jassity. When will it be about me and only me," I asked. I knew I was pushing it but oh well.

"Keep it real with me Shaela? You don't want me, you want my money and what the fuck I can do for you. Answer this one question and don't lie. Are you pregnant?" He asked and yelled? My heart dropped instantly. Where did that come from?

"No, I'm not pregnant," I argued and lied. Tariq knew something. I made John promise he wouldn't tell Tariq, I would.

"The lies you tell," he chuckled. I was so pissed off. I'm mad that I had to even ride with Tariq and this Jassity chick. I'm not even going to call her a bitch. I couldn't be mad because I was doing me. I didn't like how he read me in front of her. I don't need a chick judging me. I wanted to tell him so bad that I was pregnant for John but I couldn't.

I wanted to hurt his feelings about how he has hurt mine. I should've kept my ass in Atlanta at home with my man instead of chasing a nigga that don't want me. I'm tired of trying to destroy the lives of people that hadn't done anything to me. I chose the cards that I was dealt with. I had to carry through with the plan. If I made it through this last bit of scandalous tricks that I had up my sleeve. I promise I was through with the bullshit and I just wanted to focus on John and my unborn.

I promise I would be a better woman. It's just cost too much to keep up with a lie and cause unnecessary drama. I guess you can say I'm tired of the drama. I'm going to let Tariq be and live his life. He thought enough of me to come and pick me up and take me to the mall even though he was keeping company with Jassity. I still didn't want him with Kaniya. Tariq could be with any bitch but her. I just didn't like Kaniya. She acts as if she was God's gifts to men. I sent John a text because I wanted to know if he told Tariq about us.

Me - Did you tell Tariq about us?? He had an iPhone so he was responding back fast as hell.

Him - It's bro's before hoes and my loyalty is with my nigga. Never forget that. He been known, I fucked you. He just never said shit because he didn't give a fuck about you. I know I ain't the only nigga fuckin' you. Don't hit my line until I can get that DNA test. If you'll fuck me and know that was my nigga bitch, you'll fuck anything hoe

Oh my God, I can't believe him. I had to lower my face in my lap. I didn't want Tariq or his bitch to see me crying. I may be a lot of things but John is the father of my child and I would be lying if I said his words didn't hurt.

Tariq

I can't believe Shaela's dumb ass had the nerve to question me about what the fuck I got going on. I'm on to her and I hope she knows that too. To make matters worse she had the nerve to call Jassity an escort. I never had to buy pussy. She of all people should know that. Jassity played it cool even though she was giving me dirty looks like she didn't know all about Shaela. I respected her more for not even going back in forth with Shaela. Jassity is older. She's twenty-eight. I'm digging her. I don't know if I could do the long-distance shit. We'll see though the fact remains the same. I only want Kaniya. I wanted her to be Mrs. Tariq Harris. I couldn't shake this girl for anything.

Here I am with Jassity and she still consumes my thoughts. I needed the answers tonight. If she was rocking with your boy I was done. No, we couldn't be friends. It fucked her and no Lucky couldn't have her either. Straight up if I couldn't have her I would make sure that he couldn't have her. I was letting him know I made love to Kaniya. Fuck keeping secrets I wasn't sparing her anymore. I know what I want and she's it for me. I haven't been sure about a female since Tamia Raye Carter.

I knew Kaniya was the one if I was even comparing her to my first love. I looked at Shaela through my rear-view mirror. She held her head down. I knew she was in her feelings but it's nothing I could do about that. She fucked my nigga and she left me when I went to jail. I don't know what she expected from me but this ride is about as far as gets with me. I care about Shaela. I never wanted to see her down bad, but I don't trust her. I gave her too much of my fuckin' time for her to shit on me how she did. I couldn't rock with that. John sent me a text. I grabbed my phone to see what he had to say.

John Gotti - Aye tell ya bitch to stay off my fuckin' line, the hoe, had the nerve to text me asking me did I tell you? Fuck she thought. I tell you everything. A hoe can never tell her friends she played us. Nah, bitch, we played you and that pussy

I couldn't hold my laugh in if I wanted to now, I know why she held her head down. She thought she was playing us. I already knew she fucked him. I knew she would never have the balls to tell me that.

Me - Good Looking Out

Chapter-28

Lucky

Tonight, was the night of my dad's birthday party. It was my dad's motherfuckin' G-day. It was a fuckin' Holiday. He was born and raised in Miami, Florida. This was his city. Miami raised him but Atlanta paid him, that's just how it was. Deuce's named rung bells in the South. I wanted to follow in his footsteps. I wanted to be the boss of all bosses. People knew me out here just off my father's name. I wanted to make a name for myself. I had a connect out here who I just met with and he wanted me to take over some extra territory. He asked me how my dad would feel about that? He didn't want me to have to choose, but I couldn't run both empires. I understood that but that's a choice that I would have to make when I get there. I wanted to be a fuckin' billionaire.

I knew my dad knew I was involved in some other shit, but he didn't say anything. The meeting we had earlier he was talking to me, I felt it. Enough about business. It was time to turn up and get my dick wet. It's my dad's G-day. I know Sonja had this dope ass party planned, but I wanted to bring some strippers out. I wanted to fuck a few strippers. What better way to do then to bring out KOD's finest? She can be mad all she wants but I don't give a fuck. I wanted some pussy in my face just to keep Kaniya off my fuckin' mind.

I know when she sees me tonight, she's going to be in her feelings. I'm tired of chasing her. I chased her long enough. I was on my dog shit tonight. We weren't together so tonight I was going to show her exactly how I got down. Trust me I was extra fly, and I was feeling myself. These hoes were already choosing. I was draped in all white Versace from my head to my fuckin' toes. I got a fresh cut and line up. My jewelry was on full display. I had a few rings on and two chains adorned my neck. My wrist was flooded with my Audemars Piquet Pink Gold Watch. I was a flashy ass nigga tonight and I was fly as fuck with my designer shit on.

I even had some nice eye candy accompanying me. I was sure to get Kaniya's blood pressure high. All the shit she never saw me do to a chick tonight I was doing it in her face. It is what it is. I knew she would be solo. I made sure I killed JD. I was going to give her the pleasure of watching me do me. Two can play that game. You'll never win going against me. She needs to think seriously about what she's going to do because I'll be the nigga she loves to hate.

I'll show her every fuckin' day what she's missing. I cheated one time that she knows of and she's acting like this. You know how many chicks want these eleven inches of hard dick on a regular?

Kaniya

The party started an hour ago. I wanted to arrive kind of late just to scope out the scenery. I wanted to see if I peeped out anything suspicious, but I didn't. Sonja and Tianna sent me a text and asked me when I was coming. I told them I was on my way. I was making my way toward the VIP section and everybody was there. I wanted to post out here with the general population. I looked around and took in my surroundings. Deuce was making his entrance last because it was his G-day I respected that. I felt good tonight believe it or not. I felt stress-free.

Prive was lit. Sonja had this spot sewed up. As soon as you pulled up the only thing you saw were foreign whips. It looked like a fucking dealership. You know me, I put my money walk on. The baddest bitch was coming through and I'm not talking about Trina but Kaniya. Watch me fuckin' work. I made my way in the VIP section and all eyes were on me. I headed toward the VIP area. Man, this place was lit as fuck. I love the decor in here. It was decorated in red and gold with a few hints of white. It speaks Royalty. Everybody was dressed in white like Sonja requested. I saw Raven and I had to hug my lil boo. She was so cute, and she looked really pretty in her all white.

Tariq was going to be mad tonight about his sister. Niggas were about to be choosing. I saw Tianna and Quan and they looked super cute. Her stomach was poking and she looked super happy. I had to get a picture of them too. We talked, laughed, and kicked it for about twenty minutes. I made my way over to Sonja the body. Yes Lawd, my auntie was showing the fuck out tonight. She had that body on display, a fresh sew in, and her face was beat to the gods. She was draped in a nice white Prada catsuit and Red Bottoms. She was killing it and she knew it. She slays all fuckin' day. I see why Kanan was mad. Sonja was that bitch.

"About time you made it over here. You know I got beef with your hot ass," she beamed and laughed. I swear I'm not beat for Sonja's shit tonight. It's too much fuckin' money in this building. I just wanted to bag me a couple of Miami niggas that's it. More of a reason why I didn't want to be in this VIP section. I didn't want anybody to think I was booed up with anybody up here. I'm single and on the market.

"Save it for another day please," I begged and laughed. Sonja and I were having fun laughing and dancing. Raven came over and joined us. We were having a good time you know.

Speak of the devil, Shaela was making her way over here toward us, ugh. I elbowed Sonja and cut my eyes at her giving her a warning. If she starts that shit, I'm busting her in her mouth.

You know how a bitch that wants to be seen acts. I could already tell she was on some messy shit.

"Hey y'all," she beamed proudly. I couldn't miss the bull shit and mess coming from her. She was giving hugs and shit. I don't do hugs at all. I'm not with the fake shit. She didn't like me and I didn't like her, there's no need to pretend.

"Give me a hug, Kaniya," she said. I looked at that bitch like she was crazy. I know she didn't say what I thought she said. I mumbled under my breath "bitch please" and cut my eyes quick.

"No, I don't want your perfume on me," I beamed proudly and lied. I'm not with that fake shit.

"Did you see our man?" She asked. See here she goes.

"Shaela, me and you don't share a man. I'm single boo," I argued and sassed.

"We share a man Kaniya, be honest," she sassed. She was being messy and I wasn't with it. I paid that hoe no mind. I was not about to argue about a nigga that wasn't mine. I didn't need to get my adrenaline rushed for no reason. She thought she was cute or whatever, so she wanted to be messy. I didn't care to engage in that shit. I had to focus on other shit. I had to be on point for my Uncle Kanan's crazy ass. Not this dumb broad. Low and behold Tariq walked over where we were standing and he had this chick with him. She was alright. She looked better than Shaela but not better than me.

"Kaniya, you see our man?" She asked again. She was trying it. Did she forget that I would beat the dog shit out of her ass. This hoe wants her ass beat seriously.

"What's up, Kaniya?" He asked. I spoke to Tariq.

"What's up, I'm good and you?" I asked.

"You look good, can you take a picture of me and my date?" He asked. Is this fuck with Kaniya Sunday?

"Sure, I'll do it. What's your name, Ms. Lady?" I asked.

"Jassity," she cheered and smiled.

"Pretty name for a pretty girl, you guys look great together. He deserves it." I stated. I'm being honest. I took pictures of them. I played it cool because he wanted a reaction from me. I can't deal with that tick for tat shit at all.

"I told you to leave him alone," Sonja stated. I don't want to hear anything that she is saying right now.

"I did after the dinner at your house," I explained.

"He got you in your feelings now, huh?" She asked. He does but I would never tell her that. What's understood doesn't need to be explained.

"No, he's free to date. We are not together," I explained.

"It's okay if you are Kaniya, Tariq's a great catch," she stated.

"I'm good." The DJ made the announcement that the birthday boy was in the building. The club was going crazy. Deuce made his way to VIP to find Sonja. All of a sudden these strippers popped up. Sonja started going off. "Who in the fuck invited strippers to my shit!" She asked and yelled? Not too far behind Deuce, Lucky walked in right behind him. Damn, that nigga was fine as fuck and on his fly shit. I know this nigga didn't have a bitch with him? If he's doing, this must be fuck with Kaniya Sunday or some shit. These niggas wanted me to murk something bad.

"I brought them here. I wanted to give my daddy a present," he argued and slurred. Lucky was on his level. I could tell he had a few drinks before he made it here. His eyes were trained on me the whole time he was talking to Sonja.

"You need to run shit by me before you do anything. I don't want no hoes popping pussy in my nigga's face. You can keep them strippers for yourself or whoever else but not fuckin' Deuce!" She argued and yelled. She sure read his disrespectful ass.

"Kaniya, you good?" She asked. I didn't even see Tianna standing there.

"Yes girl, I'm cool on Lucky and Tariq."

"Good because you know I can't help you whoop no ass with your nephew," she laughed. Tianna couldn't do shit. Quan wasn't going to let that happen.

"Oh, it's a boy? Girl he's going to be fine just like his daddy and a hot ass mess like his uncle," I stated. I and Tianna were laughing on our messy shit. Lucky walked up with his date. His eyes were trained on me. I sipped my drink. Why does every-body want a reaction out of me?

"What's up Kaniya, you good?" He asked. I sucked my teeth before I replied. Leave me alone because I'm not bothering you.

"I'm good, can I help you with something?" I asked. Lucky was smiling like a fuckin' black bat. I can't stand his motherfuckin' ass. He was up to no good.

"I wanted you to meet my girl Amber," he stated. I swear this nigga was up to no good. I'm so glad I'm fuckin' single. He's really going out his way to fuck with me.

"Hi Amber, I'm Kaniya. Lucky's EX it's nice to meet you. He's a great guy and I wish you guys nothing but the best," I beamed proudly. I killed that motherfucka with kindness. Bitch nigga, I'm not thinking about you.

"Awe, thank you. I know how it sucks to meet your Ex's new girl," she sassed and smirked. I couldn't let that shit slide for one fuckin' minute. I had to read this bitch one good time.

"Oh really, I'm not bothered by it. I don't feel any type of way about it but understand me when I say this, don't let Lucky pump you up to get your ass fuckin' beat because then it'll suck to be you lying on this motherfuckin' floor. I'll slide you these hands quick as fuck. Treat him right he's all yours," I argued and explained.

"Alright Kaniya, I'll see you around," he stated. Lucky was too fuckin' fine to be so messy and petty I swear.

"Tianna, can you believe this nigga? He just fucking tried me. He really wanted me to meet his girl. This nigga wanted a re-action out of me. See folks be wondering why I go so hard. Leave me the fuck alone period. I'm not even tripping on him. Do you see me bothering him? I wear my heart on my fuckin' sleeve because I know that nigga doesn't deserve me," I argued.

"Kaniya, calm down. It's cool, he's a pussy ass nigga. I just don't get him. He was so mad the other day about JD, but you got a bitch today?" She asked. EXACTLY.

"That's why I will never take him back. Trust me when I fuckin' tell you. Girl, I need a stiff one. Let me get out this VIP section and move around. I'll be back," I stated. I hate to leave Tianna. I couldn't wait to text Riley, Barbie, and Ketta. This shit felt like Déjà vu. The only thing is that I knew he was a dog. I already caught him in the act. So, this stunt didn't faze me. You must come harder than that, this shit doesn't faze me. I already had seen the worst.

The only thing you could do at this point would be to have a baby that's about 3 or 4 years old. That would shock me. I made my way to the bar and got me a drink. My next stop was the dance floor. I had to shake this ass that Kaisha gave me. I had to get this mug off my face I was too cute and to fly to be worried about any nigga. I was on my replacements and free agents' shit. Live by and Die by that shit and that's law. Lucky doesn't want to see me on my pimping shit. I was raised by the best, Killian and Kanan Miller.

I promise you Sonja's Sunday events weren't in the cards for me. I haven't even been at this bar for five fuckin' minutes before Tariq and Jasper, I mean Jassity came up and stood beside me. This nigga ain't got no fuckin' chill at all. I had my back turned and he bumped into me on purpose. He was rubbing all on this bitch talking all loud. He was telling her how he wanted to fuck her and eat her pussy. She was begging for the dick. I just shook my head.

It's cool if you wanted to fuck her, but why did I need to know that. To top it off Lucky and his chick made their way over here also. He was already disrespectful by the shit that he pulled off earlier. I knew what to expect from him. He's on the other side of me. He sat right fuckin' next to me on the bar stool. He sat old girl on his lap and started feeling all on her breasts and playing in between her legs.

"Lucky, stop you're making me want to fuck you right here and right now," she moaned.

"I'm ready whenever you are, I'll bend you over right here for a quickie. Payback is a bitch," he chuckled. It took everything in me not to throw my drink in his face. I can't believe I was fuckin' with this clown. I already see what time it is, action speaks louder than words. These niggas wanted a reaction out of me. I wasn't even going to drag these hoes. I was ready to drag these dog ass niggas. Jasper, I meant Jassity she wasn't disrespectful at all. She had no clue what was going on. I wasn't even going to put my hands on her.

But Amber she knew what time it was, she knew me but I didn't know her. She can get these motherfuckin' hands. Lucky is sending her straight out. I was going to give these niggas exactly what they asked for. I hope it was worth it. Ain't none of y'all petty ass niggas for me.

"Excuse me, miss, can I cut in," he asked. I looked over my shoulder to see who it was and it was my father.

"Hey what are you doing here," I asked.

"I came to see my favorite girl. Give me a hug," he said. I was so happy to see my dad. I haven't seen my dad in two months. My dad was a fly a nigga at forty-six. He didn't look a day over thirty-six. I hated going places with him. I made sure I ran every bitch off that wanted him.

"How did you know I was here at this spot," I asked.

"Killany, who else. You know I had to come and see about my brother. I'm my brother's keeper when he's on the gun line. I'm on that bitch front and center too. I wish a motherfucka would cross that bitch too," he argued and explained. Killany talks too fuckin' much. Where's the loyalty?

"OH lord, here you go. I can't with y'all two," I laughed.

"Nah, I can't with you, Kaniya. I raised you better than that. You know why the fuck I'm here, Killany told me everything. Get that stupid look off your face. Yes, I came to stop you in your tracks. If you are busting any guns, it's for your uncle and nobody fuckin' else. Do you hear me?!" He yelled and asked. I heard him loud and clear. My dad was mad at me. I couldn't wait to see Killany and it wasn't going to be via Facetime. I needed to see her face to face.

My dad and I were having a good time. I saw Lucky making his way over here toward us. I hope for his sake and not mine that he wasn't on any bullshit, but if he was it's not a guarantee that he would make it out of here alive. People thought I was bad but my dad, he doesn't ask any fuckin' questions at all. If you got excuses, he got fuckin' solutions.

He will air this bitch out and not give a fuck. I'm like Kermit the frog I'll sip my tea and enjoy the smell of gun smoke. I guess that was wishful thinking. I was Lucky's victim tonight. He stopped at the table. He grabbed my hair.

"You're really fuckin' disrespectful," he argued and stated. Before he could get another word out my dad rushed him.

"Bitch ass nigga don't you ever in your fuckin' life put your hands on my fuckin' daughter. Who is this clown, Kaniya?" He asked. My dad beat the breaks off Lucky. That's what the fuck he gets. He didn't even get one lick in. I told you my dad didn't ask any fuckin' questions.

"He's my ex," I sighed.

"Keep him as your ex too. I don't want you dating a fuckin' jealous ass clown," he argued and yelled.

"I can't believe this nigga had the nerve to put his fuckin' hands on my you. Is he fucking crazy? The only reason why I didn't kill the nigga with my bare hands is that I know Deuce? Other than that, he would've died today. Don't touch my daughter at all. Kaniya, I hope you weren't letting him put his hands on you. You didn't look too fazed at all by him. He made me lose my fuckin' focus and the real reason I came here was for you Kanan," he explained. I know my dad was pissed but I'm glad Lucky got his ass handed to him. My dad and I finished chilling meanwhile keeping our eyes open for Kanan.

Lucky

I had to leave the party early. I got my ass beat and I can admit that. I deserved that shit. I can't believe I came at Kaniya like that in front of her father. I would've done the same thing if that was my daughter. Kaniya could've warned me. No wonder she was cool as fuck about it. Any other time she would've shown her motherfuckin' ass. I'm about to fall back though. I did, I tried one too many times to get back in her good graces and she isn't budging.

I'm going to let her live her life. I need to face it that we are through. Especially after tonight. I was so disrespectful towards her. I was trying so hard to hurt her that I ended up hurting myself. I fucked up good, real shit. She didn't react but I could see the pressure off her body that she was pissed. I'm just going to let it be for now. It is what it is.

If it's meant to be then eventually, we'll get back together. At least I tried. I gave it all I got and I don't have shit else to give. I'm good on Kaniya. I'm going to let her be finally, I promise you that. I'm married to this fuckin' money from here on out. I got her back forever though.

Tariq

I wanted to hurt Kaniya so bad. I didn't need a reaction out of her. Her eyes told it all. She handled that shit like a real woman. She didn't fold one fuckin' time. I feel stupid as shit. I didn't even want Jassity. I was just using her. I don't know what pushed me to do this. Kaniya has been nothing but good to me. This chick held me down and she wasn't even my woman. If I called her, she answered. If I wrote to her, she hit a nigga back.

She never switched up on a nigga. It was me that caught feelings. She told me from the jump she wasn't looking for a relationship. If I had a chance, I'm sure I blew it now acting like a bitch ass nigga. I don't know what the fuck came over me. I'm man enough to admit that I was wrong. I'm going to apologize to her. I can't believe I did this fuck boy shit. What she needs to understand is that I have feelings too.

Has she ever considered my feelings? How does she think I feel? I love her and I wanted to be more than her friend. She gave me the pussy too. I had to watch Lucky fuck her. We have yet to discuss that shit. We needed to have a real discussion asap, no family gatherings, just me and her. I was about to make that shit happened rather she liked it or not. Tonight was going to be the night.

Chapter-29

Kanan

Sonja and Deuce's security wasn't hitting on shit. I walked straight through. Kanan fuckin' Miller these niggas in Miami knew me. They knew I was a fuckin' killer. I was good in every hood. I was sitting in the cut for an about an hour. Yasmine was starting to bore the fuck out of me. I was ready to let my presence be known. I was coming for Sonja and she didn't even have two options anymore. She had only one fuckin' option and that was leaving with me. I made my way to VIP and Sonja and Deuce didn't even see me coming.

See Sonja was falling off hard as fuck. That's another reason why she needs to come home. Number one rule sip water while you out. Be on your P's and fuckin' Q's. A sober mind is the best mind. I would never let Sonja sip any alcohol unless we're at home. I'm standing right behind her and she doesn't even know it. I grabbed her by her neck and told her "Let's fuckin' go right now."

"I tell you one fuckin' thing right fuckin' now Kanan, you better raise the fuck up off me," she argued and yelled. She sobered up quick. We had a crowd now and everybody was looking at us.

"What's your fuckin' problem, Kanan? You and I aren't together. It was over eight years ago. You know this shit. I'm with Deuce and you can't change that shit. After eight years and you're still running up behind Yasmine?" s6he asked and argued. I looked over my shoulder and Yasmine was right on my heels.

"You can keep my name out your mouth," she argued. Yasmine needed to shut the fuck up and stay in her place.

"Mommy, mommy," Shaela cheered. She wanted to be seen. I looked over my other shoulder and it was Shaela.

"I knew there was a reason I didn't like your ass. You were affiliated with this bottom bitch. Let me ask you this Yasmine, after all these years you're still chasing behind a nigga that don't want you? You still want to be me? I'm never imitated but often duplicated. This nigga drove you thirteen hours to come to see about me. It sucks to be you. What's your purpose, Kanan? Say what the fuck you have to say and move on. Let me live my fuckin' life? I want to be with Deuce that's all," she beamed proudly.

"I don't give a fuck about none of that shit you're spitting. I don't give a fuck about what you want to do or who the fuck you want to be with. You don't have options. The only option is me. Please do as I say before all these innocent people make FOX news. You know how the fuck I get down. Let's fuckin' go, your playtime is over. Tell Deuce it was nice knowing him, but your husband is fuckin' home," I argued and yelled.

"Kanan are you fucking crazy. I do not want to be with your ass, truth be told. If you want this shit to get real, I'm the reason why you were locked up. Yes, I set you and your side bitch up," she argued and sassed.

"What the fuck did you just say? Say that shit again bitch?" I asked. I know she didn't say what the fuck I thought she said.

"Yes, I fuckin' set you up. You heard me right the first fuckin' time," she argued and sucked her teeth. I pulled my gun and put the butt of my gun to Sonja's temple. I was ready to push her shit back. She pulled a gun out on me also but her gun was pointed at my chest.

"You know what the fuck I do to snitches. I'm dropping you six fuckin' feet bitch. It ain't no coming back from none of that," I argued and yelled.

"Kanan, shoot that bitch or I will. She doesn't give a fuck about you, that bitch set us up. My boys had to go to a foster home behind her," she argued. I wish Yasmine would shut the fuck up.

"Give me the go pops and I'll drop his ass right now. Fuck that talking," he stated. I don't know who this young nigga thought he was but he better asks about me.

"What's going Auntie Sonja and why does Uncle Kanan have a gun to your head," she asked. It was Raven. She was Sonja's niece and she pulled out a gun also.

"What the fuck is going on Auntie Sonja? Kanan, you need to lower your fuckin' gun. I don't know what y'all got going on. I can see it's some deep shit, but I know one thing you're not about to empty no clip in her while I'm here. Kanan drops the motherfuckin' gun. You raised me and I don't want to fuckin' drop you," he yelled. It's been years since I saw Tariq. I respected him but Sonja knows what it is. I'm not dropping shit.

"Kanan, you heard what the fuck I said. If you gone shoot. Shoot me now motherfucka. We can both go today. I'm prepared for this shit. If you aren't going to shoot me get this shit the fuck out my face. Move the fuck on. I said what I had to say," she argued.

"Sonja, that's how you feel? That's what you had to do to get a nigga back? I laid down for eight years because of you. You know what the fuck I do to snitches. I don't give a fuck about you pointing a gun to my chest. I got shooters in here now. All I got to do is nod my fuckin' head and you're fucking done. The fact remains the same is the shit you just told me hurts worse than death.

Bitch, you ain't shit fuck you. I can't believe I loved you," I argued. I looked at Sonja one last time. My finger was rested on the trigger. I wasn't ready to leave here yet. I came for blood. I felt a pair of hands on me. I knew nobody was bold enough to touch me. I looked over my shoulder while my gun still trained on Sonja, it was Killian. He finally made his way to VIP to see what was going on. Guns were pointed at me and him.

"Bruh, drop that shit man. It isn't that serious. I'm not losing you behind no pussy," he argued.

"It's not about the pussy bruh, this bitch set me up. She's the reason I did the bid," I explained. I hate to even let that shit escape my lips but it was the truth.

"Let that shit go, Kanan. I know you mad under the circumstances but she's a woman scorned. At least she didn't leave you without. She made sure your money was right and your businesses were good. Fuck the time that was lost. Come on man, drop the gun," he explained. I don't give a fuck about any of that shit.

"I'll drop the gun for now, but this shit is far from over," I argued and glared at Sonja on my way out.

Killian

I finally got Kanan to move the gun from Sonja's temple. We walked off but before we got out of VIP good **Fuck Them Other Niggas** by **C-Murder** came on. I looked at Kanan and we already knew what time it was. Them niggas started a war that they weren't prepared for. Deuce didn't say shit when Kanan was in the VIP Section. That nigga was on fuckin' mute.

> **Fuck them, other niggas**
>
> **Cause I'm down for my niggas what**
>
> **Fuck them, other niggas**
>
> **Cause I'll ride for my niggas what**

The club started going crazy and then the lights were killed. The bullets started flying from multiple directions. I ducked and the crowd started moving quickly. "KANIYA SUIT THE FUCK UP NOW and SHUT THIS MOTHERFUCKA DOWN," I yelled. We were all ready by the tables where she stashed the weapons at. It's been a minute since we've laid some shit down but today was the fuckin' day.

Kaniya through her bulletproof vest on. I already had mine on. I'm sure Kanan had his own. It was us against them. I for damn sure was making it out this bitch alive. It's kill or be killed. Kaniya had two AR-15's with the extended clip. She threw me one and she pointed with her flashlight at the other table where Kanan could grab his. It was on from there. "MAKE SURE THE FUCKIN' SCOPE IS ON AND HIT EVERYTHING THAT'S FUCKIN' MOVING. I FUCKIN' MEAN IT." Deuce a hoe ass-fuckin' nigga for him to get at me while my back was turned. That nigga knew he couldn't get at me straight up so this is how he came.

Man, this shit just got real than motherfucka. My daughter has never been on the gun line with me and Kanan. She was trained to do this shit and she was on go. I was on go too. She did every fuckin' thing I asked her too. I told her to clear this motherfucka out and she did. She sprayed this bitch wet. I wanted her to hit everything moving and, that's what the fuck I meant. Don't leave a fuckin' body moving.

I had the AR-15 with the scope and the extended clip. All you heard was that big motherfucker cock back and bullets flying every fuckin' where. We sprayed this bitch wet. Any motherfucka that was against us was fuckin' dying tonight. I noticed Kaniya dropped Shaela. I wonder what that was about. Practice makes perfect and she got right back on task to what we came to fuckin' do.

Kanan

My niece proved me wrong, her loyalty was with me tonight. It was us versus them and we demolished THEM. I don't know how she got these AR's in here, but I thank god that she had them. I was making a fuckin' mess. This shit was gruesome. This is worse than any massacre I've ever done. If Sonja got hit oh FUCKIN' well, that nigga shouldn't have got at me while my back was turned. It was dark in this motherfucka too, but I could smell death and it was lingering something serious. I can't believe how my niece was toting that big ass AR. She was handling that motherfucka well, better than her bitter ass momma ever could. I didn't want my niece involved in this shit at all. I would die if something happened to her.

I had this infrared beam trained on Deuce. I was going to shoot him, but I wasn't going to kill him. I was going to put some hot ass lead in his ass. Killing him was too easy, he needed to suffer. I sprayed his legs with this AR. I'll paralyze his bitch ass. Let's see how good he fucks my bitch now.

"Kill me, pussy ass nigga, because if you don't, I'm at your mammy house in the fuckin' morning," he argued. Deuce is talking a lot of fuckin' shit and he got at me while my back was turned. If it ain't directed it ain't fuckin' respected it.

"Oh, you're ready to die my nigga behind some pussy that never fuckin' belong to you. Today my nigga on your fuckin G-day. Sunrise and Sunset, huh?" I asked. Deuce knew I was a stupid ass nigga. I bent down and opened his mouth up. I cocked the AR back and pushed it in his mouth. "You ready because if you go today this is how the fuck you are going. Your shit will be pushed all the way back. You asked for this shit Happy Birthday, Bitch." I unloaded the AR his brains were everywhere. I heard sirens and I heard the police. I had to get the fuck up out of here ASAP. Whoever killed the lights I hoped they killed all the cameras and street cameras too. No face no motherfuckin' case my nigga.

Sonja

Kanan's words hurt my fuckin' soul. I thought I was hurting him but damn I hurt my fuckin' self and I feel bad. I sat here and watched Kanan and Killian walk out the VIP section backward. Something was telling me some shit was about to pop off. I just knew some shit was about to go down. Just as I thought shots were fuckin fired and guns were fuckin' blazing through the club. Deuce was the cause of all this shit. He already knew what type of nigga Kanan and Killian was, and to be honest with you. I knew he couldn't compare to Kanan because that's a crazy ass motherfucka. I also knew that he wouldn't back down either.

I should've kept my mouth shut and put my feelings back to where they've been hidden all this time. But who am I fuckin' kidding? When Kanan walked into the club and grabbed me by my neck and told me to bring my ass on. My fuckin' heart dropped to the floor? I almost pissed and shitted on my damn self. He was fine as fuck before he left but damn, he was finer than a motherfucka since he had gotten out. His dreads were longer and he had a few nice tats on him. The nigga even had my name on his neck. Where the fuck did that come from? Yes, his fine ass is really on one.

Ugh, I can't believe Deuce had the lights killed at the party. Damn Kanan, looked good after all these years. My pussy still did a dance for him. Jail did his body good. I wanted to jump on him right then and there. I was screaming take me fuckin' now. I did want to leave when he said come on. Let me get my mind out the gutter. Kanan was good and he was leaving, because Killian came to make sure of that. Was he coming back, probably so. As soon as that song came on, I knew shots were about to be fired. I knew some shit was about to pop off and then the lights went off to make shit worse.

It was a wrap. It was game time from there. I pulled my strap up out of my fuckin' purse. I walked up on Yasmine and push that bitches cap all the way back. Close range, bitch. She didn't even see me fuckin' coming. Deuce didn't know that Kanan lived for this type of shit. He gets a rush off this. It's was fuckin' go time for him. I prayed that Deuce made it out safe and alive. I hope everybody was accounted for my niece Raven and nephew Tariq. Quan and Tianna, of course, Kaniya, Lucky and Kanan and Killian. I didn't want to lose anybody tonight. I should've never told Kanan I set him up. What the fuck was I thinking? If something happened to Deuce on his birthday behind this shit I would lose my fuckin' mind. I prayed everybody made it out safe.

The police and ambulance came quick and started helping people out of the club. People were shot and injured. It wasn't too bad they would make it. The news came out because this was a popular spot. The reporters were saying that Miami hasn't seen anything like this before at a popular night spot. I had to make sure that everybody that came with me was accounted for and I needed to get the fuck away from here before the police and news started asking me questions. Since it was my party I started calling everybody's phone to see where the fuck they were at. I saw Tianna and Quan come out and they were fine thanking God. Raven was behind them thank you, Jesus. Tariq came from the back he must have already been out here for a while. Everybody made their way over to me.

"Do you mind telling me what the fuck was that back there? I'm trying to figure out what just happened. Where is my dad and Lucky? Did they fuckin' make it out? If something happened to my dad behind you on my unborn child I will kill your ass. I could've been killed tonight. My wife and I could've been killed. We all could've fucking died. Did you see the type of guns they had in there? Why in the fuck was Kaniya with them niggas? This was a fucking setup. Get Lucky on the phone now. Where the fuck he is?!" He yelled and argued. Quan grabbed his phone to call Lucky. He had his speaker phone on.

"Yeah, bra what's up?" He asked.

"Where the fuck are you? Are you still at the club?" He asked.

"No, I left early. I'm in some pussy," he explained. I just shook my head listening to his disrespectful ass.

"Man, get the fuck over here now. It was shoot out. I can't say too much over the phone bring your ass now!" He yelled. Tianna rubbed Quan's back.

"Calm down baby it's going to be okay. Your dad he's good trust me," she explained.

"Can you promise me that baby?" He asked.

"I can't promise you that, but I have faith and I prayed that he will make it out alive," she explained. Tianna wrapped her arms around Quan and gave him hug. I prayed for better days. I love you, Quan," she stated.

"I love you too," he explained. I prayed for Deuce, too. Lord knows I didn't want his blood on my hand.

Chapter-30

Lucky

I had to jump out this dry ass pussy real quick. This was a fuckin' dub. Shit had to be serious if Quan called me this late. Where is my fuckin' dad and why didn't he call me? I called his phone over ten times no answer. I promise you if something happened to my dad tonight on his birthday, shit is going to get ugly quick. Let me call Kaniya to see if she can tell me what happened. Her number was changed, what the fuck. I had to look at my phone again. I need some fuckin answers and my dad's not answering.

Quan didn't tell me much of anything over the phone. I took a bird bath and made my way out the door. I hopped in my Audi and took off. I was doing 100mph the whole way there with the flashers on. I didn't give a fuck about getting pulled over. Something didn't seem right. My dad wasn't even answering the phone. He never does that. I finally pulled up and jumped out. The police had this bitch swarmed. Yellow tape was every fuckin' where. I didn't even get the chance to cut the car off. I walked over toward Quan to see what the fuck was going on.

"What happened, where is my OG? I see everybody but him and Kaniya, what's up? Did somebody died tell me something damn," I asked and argued. It's like some shit wasn't fuckin' right.

"Calm down, bra. Sonja and some nigga got into it. He pulled a gun out on her she pulled a gun out on him so, we pulled our guns out. The nigga and his twin brother left. The DJ played Fuck Them Other Niggas, bruh when that fuckin' song came on. The club went stupid. The lights were killed and shots were fired. It was a fuckin' massacre. Them niggas made a fuckin' mess in that bitch. To make matters worse your fuckin' bitch has suited up with them niggas and airing shit out. She wasn't with us she was against us!" He argued and yelled.

"Kaniya, I don't believe that shit, Quan."

"Look bra, I recorded her ass just in case you said some shit like that," he argued. He showed me the video.

"That's her and her fuckin' dad. It's more to this story. I don't believe this shit. I need to holla at Sonja now and I want to see the fuckin' tapes," I argued.

Sonja

Deuce still hadn't made it out yet. I was pacing back and forth hoping he would reveal himself. He either made it out early or I can't even say it. I won't say it. I was going back in there to look for him. I don't care. I don't want his blood on my hands. The cops stopped me. I told them I need to find my fiancé. They advised me the only thing left in the club was dead bodies. My heart dropped instantly. If they were able to identify someone, they'll let us know. I waited to see. I needed to make sure Deuce didn't have a body. I wanted to get out of here before the cops came and I had to answer some questions.

It is what it is. I know people wouldn't say much of anything by just looking at what happened they didn't want to be involved. Just my luck the cops were headed this way and my heart started beating extremely fast and I got nervous. I knew this wasn't a friendly visit. I closed my eyes and said a quick prayer. I always pray for the worst but now I'm praying for the best.

"Hi, I'm Officer Stanley. The club manager sent me over. Are you guys the family of Calvin Rogan?" He asked. Of course, we were motherfucka.

"Yes, we are, is everything alright officer?" I asked. I gave the officer a faint smile.

"I'm afraid that Calvin didn't make it tonight. Whatever happened back there, it was something terrible. You can't even recognize him. It was execution style. He was identified by his identification in his pants. I fell to the floor. I screamed. "Nooooooo!" I was so fuckin' loud I damn near lost it.

"Can I see and make sure it's him?" I cried. Lucky and Quan helped me up. I damn near lost it. I couldn't stop crying. I started hyperventilating. I need to see him. "Please officer, please tell me it's a lie. It can't be him, please let me see him," I begged and pleaded.

"Can I ask you a few questions?" The officer asked. This is what I was afraid of. Nigga, does it look like I'm in shape to answer any questions? You just told me my fiancé is dead,

"What happened back there? We heard it was an altercation between you and someone, do you care to explain?" The officer asked. He was looking at me searching my face for a fuckin' lie. No matter what I said he already formed his own fuckin' opinion.

"He was an old friend of mine. We had issues years ago and we resolved them today but after that, he walked off and left. The next thing I know the lights were killed. I don't know what happened after that," I cried and explained. I was laying it on real thick

"May I have his name," the officer asked. I had to think of something quick. I couldn't give them Kanan's name even though I should.

"Mahomadu Olwayen." I made up a fuckin' name.

"Thanks for your time," the officer stated. I got in the car with Lucky, Quan, Tianna, and Raven. I couldn't stop the tears from falling. I couldn't catch my breath even if I wanted too. This is all my fuckin' fault. Oh my God, this is all my fault. Why couldn't Kanan just leave me alone? Once we were riding away Lucky and Quan told me I have a lot of explaining to do. Currently, my mind was on Deuce, not what I have to fuckin' explain. No matter what they think I loved Deuce and that'll never change. I wiped my tears with the back of my hands. I can handle mines, trust me. I knew that in my heart what the officer was telling me was true. I didn't want to believe it. My future husband was gone, and it was my fault. Deuce was everything to me.

I was still in love with another man, and I decided to play a deadly and dangerous game with him, and I hurt him in the process. I ended up getting a man killed tonight that I really loved. I didn't have a choice now but to go after Kanan. He came for me and I never sent for him. I'm sure I'm not on his list of favorites right now but it is what it is though. I'm coming good and hard. He can forgive me, and we can move forward. Or we can go to war because of his bullshit because those are the only options he has right now. I can also play for keeps. He started this shit, now I must finish this shit. Poor Lucky and Kaniya can't catch a break. This right here will really fuck up their relationship even more and Kaniya is in the middle of all of this because of her family.

Lord have mercy on my soul. Lord shine on me. When the police told me they found Deuce and he was unrecognizable. I couldn't fuckin' believe it this shit for real? If not somebody, please wake me the fuck up now. Not my lover, my protector and my soon to be husband. This can't fuckin' be happening right now.

I let out the ugliest cry I ever heard. I loved Deuce so much. He was everything to me. This shit hurts so bad it's unexplainable. My heart hurts for real. I will die of a broken heart. All I wanted to do was throw him a nice birthday party in his hometown to celebrate him, something he said he never had. I wish I could turn back the hands of time, if I could I would.

I didn't want him to die on his birthday. This shit went to fuckin' far and it's all my fault. I got to live with this shit for the rest of my life. I started this shit and seeing Kanan and Yasmine together done something to me. I was trying to show out and hurt Kanan and embarrass him. I hurt my damn self and got my one true love killed. I lost my chance at my happily ever after.

Why me Lord why me? I shouldn't ask why. I know we all must go someday but why Deuce on his born day. Deuce loved me unconditional. We never had any bad days. Life was good. I'll cherish that forever. I pray for his kids, give them the strength to get through this. I pray they forgive me. I never wanted any of this to happen. Please, Lord, tell me this is all a dream. I'm ready to wake up now.

Killian

Miami Police Department had this motherfucka swarmed. They were trying to find whoever lit this motherfucka up. Thank God we made it through the road-blocks. I knew they wouldn't fuck with a church van that's why anytime I committed a fuckin' crime I pulled a church van out. If it wasn't for this church van, I'm sure they would've pulled us over and I would've been serving another fuckin' life sentence.

"I'm glad we made it out of there before the cops came. Kaniya, you did good tonight. I'm proud of you GI Jane. I think Kaisha got some competition," I laughed. Kaniya or Killian didn't find shit funny.

"Whatever old man, take me to my room," she stated. Ain't shit old about me. She saw those young bitches were trying to choose me. I only wanted one though and I can't wait to see her disrespectful ass again. This shit is far from fuckin' over.

"Fuck that room, shit is too hot. We're going back home tonight," I explained. I wasn't going back through Miami period. It was too fuckin' risky. I was ready to get the fuck out of dodge.

"I need to get my stuff," she pouted and whined. I don't have time to be bothered with this fuckin' brat. She heard what the fuck I said, and she needs to respect that. It's not up for debate.

"First we have to dispose of these guns and get all of this shit melted up off us. I have a partner down here that does that. It's too many bodies that dropped tonight. We must get rid of this van. I have a house in Key Biscayne where we can crash and we can dip tomorrow, and you can get your stuff," he mentioned. Killian had houses everywhere just to keep tabs on his wife.

"Daddy, how come I didn't know you had a house here?" She asked. Killian was a secretive ass motherfucka. He wanted to keep tabs on everyone but you never knew what he was up too. I knew he was coming to Miami and he lied like he wasn't.

"He has a house everywhere," I stated. He couldn't tell Kaniya why because she would tell her mother.

"I can't with y'all two," she laughed. Kaniya was cool as shit like her mother. I guess that's why she was my favorite.

"We can't with you," we laughed. Killian and I wasn't beat for Kaniya's shit tonight.

"Kanan, how about I had to beat Lucky's ass today for grabbing Kaniya the wrong way," he argued and explained. I knew it took everything in Killian not kill Lucky because of his daughter or his pride and joy. I hope Kaniya wasn't letting that nigga beat her ass or else I'll lay his ass right next to his fuckin' daddy.

"Oh Lord, daddy it wasn't that serious," she argued and defended that pussy ass nigga.

"Kaniya, why in the fuck is he putting his hand on you? Does he hit you? If so, I'm glad I killed his bitch ass daddy," I argued. I wouldn't hesitate to kill Lucky either.

"No, he doesn't hit me. He was just mad about some things that happened a couple of days ago," she stated and lied. I can smell bullshit from a mile away.

"Good, don't be trying to cover up for that jealous ass nigga. He thought I was her nigga. Nigga that's my fuckin' daughter," he argued. Killian was a crazy ass motherfucka. He didn't care what it was. He wouldn't let anybody touch his child while he was present.

Kaniya

I can't with these two, please get me out of here. They will go on and on all night. I'm going to go ahead and get my number changed. That's the first thing I'm doing in the morning. After that, I'm going back to the hotel to get my shit.

I'm booking me a flight to VA because I can't wait to see Killany. Sister or not you got me fucked all the way up. Everything you told daddy you could've fucking told me if you felt that serious about it. I hoped and prayed that Deuce wasn't dead but knowing Kanan I doubt it. I'll pray for Lucky and Quan, but I can't be there for him physically. I needed to have a conversation with Sonja but now isn't the time. I'll pray for her in her time of need.

Chapter-31

Lucky

I'm not believing this is at all. I'm not accepting this
shit. My dad is dead. My OG died on his fuckin' birthday. I swear to God them fuck niggas gone see me about this shit.
I don't give a fuck about Kanan or Killian or what weight they
name hold in these streets. That shit doesn't intimidate me. To
think that Kaniya may have been behind this shit got me feeling
some type of way. I know we are beefing but it's not something
serious. I knew she wouldn't do this shit to me. Our love is
deeper than that. She just up and got her number changed on a
nigga too.

On the tape, you can see Kaniya, her dad and Kanan.
What's Sonja's relationship with Kanan. They were arguing on
the tape. What's their beef that got my OG killed. Sonja still
hasn't answered that. I can understand Kaniya riding with her
family, that's what she's supposed to do. Why is my OG dead behind that shit and why Sonja's not dead? That's the fucking question. I needed Kaniya and Sonja to answer some fucking questions for me.

I'm blind to this shit. Sonja needs to keep it real and give me the full run down because she's looking, real fuckin' suspect. This can't be life. My daddy died on his G-Day and when I identified his body I passed out. The air I breathed left my body. I wasn't prepared to see that shit. They did my OG dirty. Those niggas played for fuckin' keeps. I guarantee you when I connect the dots on this shit it won't be any identifying bodies. My OG was gone and his niggas were gone.

What type of shit is that? Kanan and Killian are still breathing I must go toe to toe with them niggas. It can't go down like that. My dad wouldn't want that. I live by and die by that, seriously. I'm trying to keep it together but damn every nigga got a breaking point and I'm at mine.

Tariq

Man this shit is crazy I can't believe this shit. Auntie got some shit she needs to explain to me. I heard her tell Kanan she set him up. I don't agree with that shit. I don't know the extent of everything. I walked in on the tail end of the conversation. I need to holla at her ASAP. It was a fucking massacre. The only thing on my mind was my sister, my auntie, and Kaniya. I called Kaniya a couple of times and her phone went straight to voice mail. If something happens to either of them, I'll go crazy.

Tianna

I had to text Kaniya. I don't know what the fuck was going at this party but everybody had guns and shit pulled out. I couldn't believe it, out of all the days I chose not to carry my strap it was today. Soon as the shit popped off I sent her a text quick so she wouldn't miss anything while I was gone. I sent her numerous text and she didn't respond. Am I the only one that's not fucking carrying a strap? These are some crazy mother-fuckers. I should've gotten the fuck up out of there.

Tianna - Kaniya get your ass up to VIP now. Some man just pulled a gun out on Sonja it's going down.

I just can't believe this shit. I've met Deuce numerous times and he was always nice to me. He was excited about the birth of his first grandchild. I hate that he passed on his birthday. This shit is fucked up. I can't believe it we were just celebrating his life now we are about to celebrate his death. Quan is so stressed out and I'm holding him down and I promise to be there for him every way possible.

I can't deal with him talking about Kaniya, it's just too much. He needs to understand that Kanan is Kaniya's uncle and Killian is her dad so of course, she's going to ride with her family. That's what she's supposed to do, and he would do the same thing, let's be honest.

Did she kill Deuce I don't think she would do that despite her and Lucky's bullshit they got going on. She loves him and wouldn't do anything to hurt him.

What I will say is that my bitch wasn't playing any games looking at that video. She was moving quickly and she was slaying doing that shit.

I couldn't say that around Quan because he was in his feelings. I had to let Riley know and she was cracking up. She said we were to hood and she couldn't get down with that shit at all. I'm mad I was pregnant. My heart went out to Sonja though.

She's really going through it. I wanted to be there for her too but Quan and Lucky say, she's suspect.

TWO WEEKS LATER

Chapter-32

Raven

I was supposed to stay in Atlanta all summer, but I just couldn't. Too much shit has happened. I hated to leave my Aunt Sonja and not attend Deuce's funeral. I didn't feel safe at all. Quan and Lucky were making threats accusing my aunt of things I know are untrue. She loved Deuce like no other. I haven't seen or heard from Tariq. I didn't want him to go back to jail for no stupid shit. I needed to get as far away from Atlanta as soon as possible I had to be out the way.

I didn't want to be a casualty of war. I'm going back to California to get me an apartment for the summer until school starts back. Kaniya changed her number. She gave it to me and told me not to give it to anyone. I knew who she was referencing. She told me that she was doing great and she was good. I told her that I was back in Cali for the summer. She said she would come and hang out for a week or so to kick it.

I'm glad I heard from her. I'm glad she's doing good. I hate her and Tariq didn't work out. I chewed his ass out for being so fuckin' disrespectful at the party, him and Lucky too. They found Shaela and her momma dead. I told Kaniya and she busted out laughing.

I don't know what that was about. I can only imagine. I knew Kaniya killed Shaela I watched her fuckin' do it. Shaela deserves everything that came to her. She was messy as fuck anyway. I don't like how she played my brother and her mother was jealous of my auntie, anyway, fuck them. They only came to the party to start trouble.

Kaniya

So much shit has gone wrong these past few weeks. I couldn't even keep up. I stayed out in Virginia with Killany for two weeks. She was surprised to see me. I pulled up on her ass. I wish my mother could've seen the look on her face when she saw me at her front door. I moved her out of my way and made myself comfortable in her house. I told her straight up "Bitch you already know how I'm coming. You set my ass up yesterday. I'm at your front door in the morning. Don't fuckin' play with me. You already know how real this shit get fuckin' with me."

She started laughing and I didn't find shit funny. I was ready to beat her ass. Killany and I haven't fought in a long time. I didn't appreciate her doing that. We had so much fun though. I hadn't seen her in about six months. The time we spent together was needed. I liked Virginia, they had beaches and niggas, so I'm good.

I wasn't checking for anybody at all. I needed to get my life together because May was too fuckin' heavy, and June was the fuckin' worst. Hopefully, July will be better. I can't even call it because it's too early to tell. I got my stuff done for Work Now Atlanta. I hated to leave Killany, but I had to. She didn't want me to leave her. I enjoyed her annoying ass too. She spoiled me rotten and she cooked breakfast every morning, that's how much she missed me. I think she enjoyed the party and bullshit the most. I needed to see what Virginia had to offer. I had her lit though, she was fuckin' with the kid.

She had some dilemmas going on too that she never cared to share. She was dating like three niggas at the same damn time. They were cool as fuck and nice looking. Killany had good taste. It was this one guy named Chad. He was crazy as fuck. I told her I would have to body his ass today and I meant that shit. We were at this bar kicking it. I'm a dancer and I'm going to show my ass anywhere I fuckin' go and I don't care. I'm on the dance floor dancing and this nigga had the nerve to snatch me up talking about Killany, you got me fucked up.

I turned around so fuckin' fast and pushed and mushed that nigga in his fuckin' face so hard. He fell to the fuckin' floor. I told that bitch ass nigga my name is Kaniya hoe and don't you ever put your fuckin' hands on me. I have Red hair and Killany's hair is brown motherfucka.

Don't ever step to my fuckin' sister crazy or put your motherfuckin' hands on her. Killany thought that shit was funny. Bitch, I don't play any games with these fuckin' niggas. Domestic violence is real out here and he got issues that I will gladly solve.

I saw it in his eyes, and he saw it in mine that I will kill his fuckin' ass. I told her to leave him the fuck alone. He isn't hitting on shit.

Bye Chad. I told him to lose my sister's fuckin' number. He knew I was fuckin' crazy. I'll make good on every fuckin' promise, trust me. If something happened to my sister, you'll be the first nigga's doorstep I'm at, then I'm at your mammy house terrorizing her ass. I love my sister to death. I'm my sister's keeper. They think Killian and Kanan are hell. Motherfuckas ain't ready for us.

My time was winding down in Virginia. My flight leaves tomorrow on June 29th. Killany and I were going to do something really fun today.

"Sis, what you want to do today," she asked. I knew Killany didn't want me to leave but I had too. I wish she would just move in with me.

"Not much. What you want to do?" I asked.

"Gun Range?" she asked.

"Yes bitch, you need some new fuckin' guns. I need to pick out some guns to have when I come back here," I explained. Killany is crazy. Motherfucka, she'll cut your ass up and serve you to your family as a fuckin' food sample.

"How about a massage and facial too," she mentioned.

"That's cool. How long is it going to take you to get ready," I asked. She takes forever to get ready.

"Not as long as you," she smiled and hollered back.

"Whatever," I laughed and threw a pillow at her ass. Killany was so pretty you could only tell us apart because she was a little taller than me. She had green eyes that I didn't get. My dad had them but Kanan didn't. She stood about 5'6 and her hair was brown with thick curls. She wore her hair wild and natural. Her shape was cute as fuck. Kaisha blessed us. Killany had a big ass and big titties and some thick ass thighs. She stayed in the gym though.

She was a baddie. I couldn't wait until our birthday party we were having in August in Atlanta. I don't want to give away the theme but just know it's going to be dope as fuck. I handled my hygiene and I threw on something simple. I copped me a few pieces of Beyoncé's Ivy Park clothing line. It was comfortable. I had to make sure my snapper and my grill was extra fresh.

I loved Killany's bathroom. She had a nice loft. Her decor was nice I could fuck with it. She claimed she picked it out herself, but my dad told me she hired an interior designer. You see how bitches lie. I brushed my hair back into a nice ponytail and put my snap back on. I'm waiting on Killany now. I got a text from Raven. That's my lil sister well Tariq's sister. I love her ass to death. I hated that she had to go back to Cali because she was terrified of Quan and Lucky. She told me how Quan was speaking on my name.

Oh well, fuck him. I didn't kill his daddy. I would never do that, but don't threaten my fuckin' sister at all. She's innocent. Nobody knows what was going on but Kanan and Sonja. I don't even care to know anymore. I just wished that Deuce didn't get caught up in that shit. I feel where Quan's coming from. More of the reason why I ran off all of Killian's bitches because my dad won't die behind no pussy but the ones, he created himself and the one he came out of.

I told Raven I would come out to Cali and spend a week with her. I just felt so connected to her. It's like what I have with Killany. Her last name is Miller too. I wonder if she's any kin to me. I need to ask Sonja who's her dad's people.

"I'm ready, quit daydreaming," she laughed and pushed me.

"About fuckin' time. Killany why do you wash your hair every fuckin' day like you're white? You're stripping your natural oils," I asked. I already knew she had something smart to say because she sucked her teeth before she spoke.

"Because I fuckin' can, Kaniya. You put heat in your hair every fuckin' day and guess who ain't fuckin' complaining," she argued and sassed.

"Come on I don't feel like going back and forth with your ass," I sassed and sucked my teeth. Killany locked up her loft. She had a nice ass, Benz. She was a payroll specialist and she had the luxury of working from home. She would be also handling the payroll for Work Now Atlanta.

She helped me with the contracts and stuff also. She was smart as hell too. I appreciated her for that. The things she helped me wish I didn't have to worry about it because she had it. It doesn't get any better than that. Please don't get it confused Killany is worse than me. She's one that I wouldn't push. I'm telling you what the fuck I'm going to do, she's not going to tell you shit. She'll show you. I guess that's why they say I'm Kanan's child and she's Killian's child.

"Can you stop daydreaming!" She yelled.

"Girl, shut up and drive okay. Turn some fuckin' music on or something and quit worrying about what I'm doing," I argued.

"Yeah whatever Kaniya, there's been a change of plans. We're going to have breakfast this morning at this spot. Someone wants to meet you," she beamed and smiled.

"Bitch, what? I'm not looking for anybody. I don't do blind dates and shit. You play too fuckin' much Killany I'm not even hungry," I argued. I was pissed.

"You'll be alright I promise you'll like him, trust me. I have good taste," she explained.

"Whatever Killany," I argued and flipped her off. We pulled up to a nice small breakfast diner. I don't like this shit at all.

"Kaniya, get out the fuckin' car now and quit all that kid shit," she argued and yelled.

"I told you I wasn't hungry," I argued and explained.

"You know what, I can't fuckin' deal with you today. Get out of my fuckin' car now before I get you out my damn self. I'm hungry and I want to eat. Stop being so damn childish and shit, got me acting ghetto like your ass, ugh!" She argued and yelled.

"You love my ghetto ass. Do you think you're better than me or something? Last time I checked we got the same fuckin' blood type and were identical fuckin' twins so Killany the apple doesn't fall too far from the tree lil bitch," I argued.

"Girl come on shit. I'm not playing these ghetto ass games with you. It's just fuckin' breakfast you're not marrying the nigga damn Kaniya. You're so fuckin' childish. You got people looking at me sideways and shit," she argued. I got my ass up out the car. I walked in the diner with Killany. I had to fuck with her ass. I like to push buttons because I'm a messy bitch.

I had my messy boots on. I love the mess. We sat in the far back. A gentleman was waiting for us. He had his menu up covering his fuckin' face.

"About time you brought crazy ass in here. I see y'all two are arguing about what?" he asked.

"Daddy, what are you doing here? If she would've said it was you. I wouldn't have given her a hard time," I explained. That's all she had to fuckin' say.

"You give everybody a hard time hush, Kaniya!" He yelled.

"Well, hey to you too," I sighed.

"I just wanted to spend some time with my two favorite girls, that's all. Can I do that, Kaniya Miller?" He asked.

"Why are you so hard on me daddy? I haven't done anything to you. I was just fuckin' with Killany a little bit. She's your favorite I know it," I argued and sassed.

"Here you go with this shit, Kaniya." She sighed. She knows it's fuckin' true.

"Look shut the fuck up Kaniya, or should I call you K? I don't treat you guys any fuckin' different. Whatever I do for her I do for you too. I don't have to worry about her as much as I do about you. I worry about you more because of your ass always in some shit.

You can't even sit still. I thought you were taking your ass home after Miami but your way in Virginia. I've called you over ten fuckin' times already and you haven't returned any of my calls. Why? If something happens to you, I would go fuckin' crazy.

I called Killany and she said you were in her bed fuckin' sleep. Did you think to call and tell me that? No, but your momma knew where the fuck you at. Quit leaving me out of shit. You're grown Kaniya, true enough but you still must answer to me. I order your fuckin' steps. I always need your fuckin' location," he argued.

"I'm sorry."

"Sorry isn't fuckin' good enough. Actions speak louder than words. Show me and sit your ass still sometimes. When I call you answer the fuckin' phone? Don't have me worried about you," he argued.

"I'm sorry daddy, and I promise I won't do that anymore. I just needed some time to myself, you know with everything," I explained

"I forgive you. I love you Kaniya, don't you ever forget that. If something happened to you I will kill every motherfucka that looked at you," he explained.

Killany

Kaniya is a fuckin' drama queen. Ugh, that's my messy as twin though. Why aren't you answering the phone though when your father is calling? He isn't one of those lame ass niggas you be entertaining. My father is the most real nigga I know. When he calls answer the fucking phone straight up. She's ruined my appetite with her theatrics. We finally ate, talked and caught up with each other. It's been a while since we all have been in the same room together. I cherished moments like this. I had the waiter to take a few pictures of us. Our dad took us shopping, skating, we went to the beach. We had fun just the three of us.

Kaniya

I felt so bad my dad had to chew me a new ass, but he was right though, I should've answered the phone. I just wanted to enjoy Killany and bug the fuck out of her; because I never get to do it. I hated my dad felt he had to worry about me more. I'm in the house a lot. Shit, these streets don't love anybody that's why I'm not in them I'm at home.

It's just these last two months have been crazy. If I could change a lot of it, I would trust me, but I can't it. We're having dinner tonight at Waterman's Surfside Grille. It was on the ocean front. I'm really looking forward to it. We went back to Killany's and watched some movies. I Facetime my mom so she could see us. She was hot. She said we ain't shit. I couldn't help it I had to laugh. I need to check my emails and then after that, I was taking a nap. I checked my emails nothing piqued my interest, so I checked my junk mail to see if anything important was in there.

I had an email from Lucky. I'm surprised he wasn't going in. He was talking with some sense. He had a couple of questions that he wanted to ask me about his father's death. I didn't have a problem clearing up what I did know and what I didn't do. I emailed him back and guess what, he hit me right back. He told me that when he needed me the most, I was nowhere to be found. I felt his words in my heart. No matter what, our bond should've been stronger than any of the bullshit we had going on. I responded back. I'm sorry I should've been there, but I couldn't be there physically.

I was praying for him every day, trust me. I don't know if Quan wanted to see my face with how he's dragging my name through the mud.

Lucky responded back. A small smile appeared on my face. He asked me could I Facetime him so he could see my face.

I wanted to see him too, so I left the room so I could Facetime him. I hit him up on Facetime and he answered quickly.

"Hey Kaniya, what's up baby? I miss you. You're looking good as fuck stand up so I can see you," he chuckled and smiled.

"You look good too Lucky. Stand up and let me see what you are working with," I stated and smiled.

"Go on with that shit Kaniya, you know I look like shit right now. I'm sick without you," he explained. Lucky didn't look like himself. I could tell that he's been going through a lot.

"I need you to get to the barber asap. You need to get cleaned up real good," I stated and smiled.

"Let me come see you? Can I lay with you and hold you? I need something familiar right now?" he asked. I needed Lucky just as bad as he needed me, but we've been at odds for a minute.

"I'm not at home Lucky. When I touch down, I'm going to come and see you, make sure you're looking like the Lucky I know," I beamed and smiled. The last time I saw Lucky damn he looked good. I just wanted to jump on him. I wanted him in the worst fuckin' way.

"Kaniya, you promise? I need you to get me back right," he asked and explained? I'll try that's about it. I'm not making any promises.

"I promise I'll hit you up," I beamed and smiled. It felt good talking to Lucky and not being in an awkward place.

"I love you Kaniya, don't let nobody tell you differently," he stated and explained.

"I love you too Lucky," I smiled. I loved Lucky with everything in me and that'll never change.

"You mean it, Kaniya?" He asked. I don't know why Lucky was questioning how much I loved him, but I did with everything in my heart and that'll never change. We've been through it all together.

"Yes, Jamel I do." God, I love this man. Jamel Lee Williams.

"Kaniya, are you pregnant yet!? He asked. I looked at Lucky as if he was crazy. Hell no I wasn't pregnant yet. I wasn't trying to be either.

"Where did that come from?" I asked.

"I just asked, that's all. I love you Kaniya, goodnight," he explained. I love him too more than he would ever know. Lucky and I hung up the phone with each other. I missed him. It was good hearing from him. Killany just barged in my room invading my fuckin' privacy. I couldn't even smile or blush in peace.

"Bitch, who were you on the phone with? I heard you laughing and smiling," she asked. Can I just have my moment to fuckin' blush damn? I can't stand her ass.

"I was on Face-time with Lucky, nosey." I sassed and sucked my teeth.

"Oh, let me guess, you're trying to pop that pussy when you get back home? So that's why you're leaving your sister, ha. For some dick?" She asked. Killany was with the shits for real.

"Whatever, he emailed me. I'm not trying to give up any pussy. He just wants to see me," I beamed and smiled. I'm sure when we do see each other we won't be able to keep our hands off each other.

"Sure, tell me anything," she sassed, sucked her teeth and rolled her eyes. Killany was doing the fuckin' most.

"Girl, I don't think we could be together especially with Kanan killing his dad. Too much tension," I explained. It'll never happen.

"Y'all don't have anything to do with that," she explained. We don't but everybody would be against it.

"Yeah, let me take a nap before dinner. I have an early flight," I sighed. I wanted to dream about Jamel Lee Williams.

"You're getting ready to have phone sex freak bitch, I know you," she laughed. I swear I can't stand her petty ass.

"Girl bye, leave me the hell alone please," I laughed and ushered Killany to the door. My phone alerted me that I had a text message. It was from Lucky.

Lucky - Somebody misses you. You got me rocked up hard over here thinking about you. Damn Kaniya I want you to ride this dick.

He sent me a picture message of that monster between his legs.

Me - You play too much. Who else you done sent this picture too?

Lucky – Nobody. Why you trying to play me. These chicks aren't weighing up to you

Me - I'll see you soon. I had to send him a pic too.

Lucky - Where the fuck you at

Me - 581 miles away

Lucky - You gone make me come find you and that pussy. Stop fuckin' playing with me

Me - I'll see you soon

I'm all hot and bothered now fucking with Lucky. I can't even sleep now I might as well go ahead and get ready for dinner and pack my bags. I had an early flight. I know Killany is going to miss me something serious. I needed to get back home. Ketta and Barbie are supposed to be home Friday because we made plans to go to Magic City.

I was already thinking about what I wanted to wear. I had to get my hair touched up. I'm thinking Wild Cherry red this time. It was the Fourth of July Weekend. It was about to be a Lit Session in full effect. Yes, it was about to go down. It's been a while since we linked up and made a fucking mess at Magic. I like Onyx and Blue Flame better. We were fucking with Magic for the Fourth of July weekend. I'm looking forward to it. The summer is flying bye.

I had a blast hanging out with Killany. We were on our twin shit. I could tell she was sad to see me leave. It's sad to say but she misses the kid. It's all good though. I miss her ass too. I like Virginia. I could live there maybe, or we should spend six months in Georgia and six months in Virginia that way we wouldn't miss each other so much.

I'll put a bug in her ear to see what she thinks. It's touch-down time for me. I haven't been home in three weeks. It's a party It's a party. I started twerking just thinking about it. Fresh off the plane at Hartsville Jackson International Airport. Ubers were everywhere. I need to call my girl Redd Gal up and tell her to pull up. I can't wait to see my house.

Lucky has been texting me. I'm not trying to see him. I don't want to bust this pussy open. That's the only thing that will be happening. I'll pass. Riley called me and said she was coming down for the Fourth of July. I know Quan isn't going to let Tianna come anywhere near me. It's all good but me and him need to have a conversation anyway. I don't have time for that petty shit. I will be in my god son's life with or without his ap-proval.

I've been so busy with everything I haven't been by the group home to see my favorite girls. I'm going to make sure Saturday or Monday I would go by there to see them. As a matter of fact, I will go by there today. Once I go home and freshen up. I wanted to put some more clothes on. I couldn't really wear this. I'm going to take my girls shopping. I love me some Aubrey, Kirsten, and Natalie. They probably thought I forgot about them. That's not the case. As you can see I've been through a lot these past two months. It's like I've been living in straight hell.

I had plans to adopt them but Fulton County Courts have been backed up, so the process was taking a bit longer. The girls were my god sisters. Their dad was one of my dad's best friends and their dad passed away last year, but I've always looked after them. They never knew they're mom.

I need to go by and see Sonja and see how she's holding up. That's my auntie no matter what. I don't have anything to do with her and Kanan. I don't have anything to do with her and Deuce. The facts remains the same, I don't know shit and I can't speak on shit.

I can't answer any questions. It is what is. I hope Tariq isn't anywhere near.

I still haven't forgotten about how disrespectful his ass was with Jasper I meant Jassity. The only reason why Lucky gets a pass is because my dad beat his ass. I bet he will never forget that as long as he lives. It's been enough bullshit going on these past few months, it's time to get back to some happy shit. That's what I'm praying for.

Let's have some fun. I want to take some trips and have fun. I know I'm going to Tennessee in a few weeks to see my mom and her family and get on Riley's nerves. I don't know when I'm going to California to see Raven. Probably before I go to Tennessee. I wanted my cousin Neshun to make me a strawberry shortcake. That's where I get my recipe from.

I have a lot of things that I need to do before Work Now Atlanta opens because I won't be able to do any of this stuff. My Uber driver finally pulled up. Finally, I'm heading home after a long three weeks. I'll take me a good nap. I can't wait to give my pillows some good head and a wet slob. Then I'll make my rounds. I want some good Jamaican food today. Ox tails, rice, peas cabbage, and mac n cheese. Oops here goes my phone going off already I just want to go home and relax. It was him.

Lucky - You made it back yet

Me – Damn can you smell me or you are tracking me

Lucky - Something like that

M e- I'm in route

Lucky - I'll beat you there

Me-Who said I want company

Lucky - I did you said you'll see me soon

Oh

Oh Lord, what did I get myself in too. I promise you it seems like this Uber driver was driving fast as hell. I promise you I have never rode with an Uber driver who was whipping shit like him. I was at my house in 30 minutes' top. He deserved a tip and I damn sure was going to give him one trust me.

Finally, Home Sweet Home! Lucky said he will beat me here and guess what he's here waiting in the driveway like he ain't got a fuckin' key. My locks were never changed for some reason. The lock smith never came. He's probably been at my house the whole time who knows.

"Hey baby, you happy to see me?" He asked. Of course, I was, I missed him despite the beefing we've been doing for the past few months.

"Always," I beamed.

"Go on with that one liner shit. Give me your bags," he explained. Lucky grabbed my bags and ushered me into the house. I knew Lucky had been in my house because after I talked to him yesterday I seen his on camera raiding my refrigerator.

"Why are you outside waiting like you ain't got a key. Like you haven't been in my shit nigga," I asked and laughed? Watch him tell a fuckin' lie.

"How you know I had been here?" He asked. He knew I knew he'd been here. I just wanted him to tell me. I know he missed me because I missed him.

"I know you," I stated and smiled.

"I sure have, Kaniya. A nigga has been here waiting on you, to bring your ass back home. I don't want to argue. I don't want to talk about shit, but I'm sorry Kaniya," he explained. I knew he was sorry about all the shit he took me through but actions speak louder than words. I need him to show me.

"I'm sorry too." My damn car is still at Sonja's house. I must go and get that. I have been gone for so long shit I forgot.

"Come on Lucky let's go upstairs I'm tired. All I want to do is lay down. What's been up with you? I thought I told you when I saw you, I wanted your hair cut and you looking like the Lucky I know?" I asked.

"I've been waiting on you to come back. I'm on my rough shit. Do you want to go to the barber shop with me?" He asked. I knew Lucky wanted to chill with me but I didn't like going to the barber shop with him.

"No, you know I don't like going to the barber shop with you. I don't want to sit around and look at niggas all day," I explained. Lucky knew he didn't want niggas sitting around looking at me.

"I've been lost without you. I said I was gone fall back but I can't seem to find my way without you," he explained. Lucky was saying the right shit at the right time. He was melting my fuckin' heart. This is why I love him so fuckin' much.

"You will find your way back. I'm here I'll help you get back. I got you," I explained and promised. No matter Lucky and I have been through I will always have his back no matter what. We've been through so much together no one knows the half. Just the minor shit. I'm always one call away no matter who I'm with.

"Promise me you won't up and disappear on a nigga again? Can't nobody relate to me like you. I swear you're the only person that understands me, besides my momma since my daddy gone," he explained. Lucky and I get each other but I got him never question that.

"You got Quan. That's your brother."

"Quan, is really going through it. He can't really relate to me because he got issues with you. So, he and I can't grieve together," he explained. Quan is cool but I don't want to be involved in the things he's accusing me of. I was there but I didn't pull that fuckin' trigger.

"Quan and I are going to have to a conversation because everybody was blindsided by what happen. I never knew that Sonja was dating your dad. Her and my uncle were together for years. I didn't even know they weren't together. I found out at the dinner that she was dating your dad.

My uncle thought that I hooked them up, which I didn't and he was coming for me too. For the record, I didn't kill your dad. I can account for everybody that I dropped. I would never do anything to hurt you in that way. He was always nice to me every encounter that we had. I'm sorry that it was my uncle who did whatever," I explained. It is what it is I didn't mean to throw Kanan under the bus but hey they knew it was him. I just confirmed it.

"I know you didn't Kaniya I seen your GI Jane ass on video. Quan knows that you didn't kill him either. You're like the sister he never had he felt that you should've been laying down everybody except for my father's people. I understand that family shit though," he explained.

"I'm glad you do and I'm glad to get it off my chest," I revealed.

"I just need you to be here for me Kaniya, that's all. I'm not going to pressure you into the relationship shit. I just need you right now. I'm going through some shit," he explained. I had plans to be here for Lucky I know he needed me mentally and physically.

"I got you," I smiled and cupped his face giving him my undivided attention.

Lucky

Out of all the days that passed this is the only thing that seems real. All this other shit is foreign to me. I see why my dad used to always say, you'll have to go through bullshit just to see where you are going. It gets greater later. Fuck the bullshit I rather have the real shit. I haven't been able to sleep or think straight but now my missing piece is back and I'm good.

I learned my lesson. I'm waiting on my blessing. All I want to do is just hold Kaniya and cherish and adore her. Even though I do want something else. I'm going to be good today. I might try her though, she's looking really fuckin' tempting. She ain't gone turn down no head.

Kaniya

I can't believe this shit Lucky and I are in the same room and no arguing. We're not at each other's throat. I must take a picture, it's something to capture. This moment right here felt so right. This is how we use to be. This is how the real Lucky and Kaniya got down. Our good days outweighed our bad days, shit we didn't have any. It was always us against the world.

I don't know how we let so much bullshit come in between us. I don't ever want to go back to that place, but I was having fun. I'm not gone lie. I was doing the damn thang. Shit, he was too. I'm not ready for a relationship though. We must rebuild our foundation.

"Lucky, capture this moment. Let's take a pic and don't post this shit." It's been a minute since Lucky and I laid up and took pics of us and posted it for the world to see, but I just wanted to keep this moment between us.

"I'll post whatever the fuck I want. These bitches know what it is with us, you should let them pussy ass niggas know what's up," he argued. He didn't even need to say anything. This moment was about us and not anyone else. We were moving past the bullshit.

Chapter-33

Lucky

I don't know who Kaniya think she's talking too but I'm not that nigga. She talks to me like I'm some average ass nigga. I have been with this girl for five fuckin' years. I got to remind her I wear the pants around here. If I had hoes by the pound and I wanted to post of us a bitch couldn't say shit because they already know what it is between us.

She doesn't want me to post this shit just in case one of her niggas sees us. See she done got me back already. These niggas know what it is with us. Watch this, I'm about to post this and put this caption on it and tag her ass in it. #I'mComingBackForGoodSoLetThemNiggasKnowIt'sMine

#Daddy's Home Bryson Tiller was on to something when he said that shit. He wrote that song for us. I tagged her ass right in it. I don't give a fuck. These niggas out here in these streets knows she's mine. My name is already tatted on, that we're bonded together for life.

"You play too much. Why you do that shit, Lucky?" She asked. Kaniya knew I was making a fuckin' statement and I don't give a fuck who knows it.

"It's the truth, can I express myself because that's how I feel," I explained. Everybody knows I fucked but a nigga is ready to right all his wrongs and love the hate and hurt out of her.

"Whatever," she sighed and mumbled. Kaniya wanted to be away from me so fuckin' bad. More of the reason why I need to be here and loving up on her so she can get that single shit out her fuckin' mind frame. We're together even when we ain't together. It's a minor setback for a major comeback.

"Look Kaniya we were doing well, just a few minutes ago. Fuck all that arguing and shit okay? Let's fuck and make up. If you ain't trying to do none of that take your ass to sleep," I argued and mentioned. Kaniya has put on a few pounds. I want to bend that ass over a few fuckin' times.

Kaniya

I don't like how he's talking to me. He knows he's wrong for posting that picture. I'm still on my replacements and free agent's shit. Hell, what are you talking about you coming back for good? No motherfucka you're not. Not today or tomorrow either. I like this right here just the way we are with no strings attached. I just want to have fun shit. We can be cool all day, layup, and chill or whatever.

Barbie and Ketta are going to dog my ass out today. Riley too, and please don't let Killany see this shit. I'll never hear the end of it. I'm cutting my phone off right now. I don't want to hear the drama or theatrics. At the end of the day, it is what it is. We gone always be cool though. I should be messy and tag that bitch in the picture that was in Miami, watch this.

"Lucky what's the girl's name you were with in Miami at the party," I asked.

"I don't know, Kaniya. I don't want to talk about shit that happened in Miami. Take your ass to sleep if you can't go on your own, I got some hard dick I can drop in you right now and fuck you senseless until you fall asleep. Cat got your fuckin' tongue now," he argued and explained. I can't stand his cocky ass.

"You're an asshole you know that right," I sassed and sucked my teeth. Since he's calling shots let that bitch know what time it is.

"Go to sleep Kaniya and stop all that fuckin' talking. Do you need me to put you to sleep because I will and you're tempting as fuck right now? Say I won't Kaniya I'm begging you too," he argued and baited med. I didn't even respond at all.

"I don't want no dick," I sassed and lied. I wasn't trying to take it there with him.

"I know exactly what to do to shut your ass up. Threaten you with some dick, you know you fuckin' want it. Stop playing hard to get. Let me see what the pussy looks like. Put that mother-fucka in my face Kaniya. You were teasing me a couple of days ago. You know I need it. I need you to stop fuckin' playing and come on down with that shit," he argued and explained. See that's why you can't be a niggas friend or be nice to his ass.

He takes shit the wrong way. See we can't be cool and hang out and shit. I don't want to fuck or whatever he wants to do. I'm already late anyway. I don't trust this nigga. Hell, he might be trying to trap me. I'll never be able to get rid of him then.

"You're thinking real hard over there ain't you. You re-member this song," he asked. I just shook my head at him while that shit was playing.

You Ain't Gotta Say Too Much

By the Look Your Eyes

I Can Tell You Want to Fuck

You Ain't Gotta Call Me Your Boo

Just as Bad as You Want to Fuck, I Want Fuck Too

"You know what Lucky fuck you. You're full of shit I'm going to sleep on the couch," I argued and laughed. I wasn't about to fuck him as bad as I wanted to sit on his face I'll pass because these past few times as soon as he ate my shit, he was demanding to slide his dick in me. Nope, I'm good on it.

"You don't have to go downstairs on the couch I'm going to leave you alone I promise," he explained and lied. If Lucky was going to let me sleep in peace I must be dying tonight.

"Yeah right," I sassed. I wasn't buying it period.

"For real though, I see you on your ego shit. I'm not going to take your pussy. You'll give it up come take these boxers up off me. Take my shirt off me too and help a nigga up out his clothes, he explained. See two can play that game I'll take all your shit up off you. Play with your dick and all. Take my clothes off too strip naked and flex a lil bit. I'll put my robe on and take my hot ass downstairs where I need to be.

"Where the fuck you think you going?" He asked. He knew he couldn't lay next to me without sliding his dick in me. We're not ready to take it there because the moment he sees me with someone else it's going down and he's going to act a damn fool.

"Downstairs," I beamed proudly. I couldn't even get out of the room good because he was already on my heels.

"No, the fuck you're not. Kaniya, bring your mother-fuckin' ass back here. We're grown as fuck, we can lay here in the bed together naked and acted civilized at least I can," he argued and lied.

"Yeah okay, act civilized and no touching," I stated and laughed. I turned around and got on my side of the bed and before I could snuggle under my covers. He was making his way over here to me. "Back up now. I told your ass no fuckin' touching and you said you could act civilized I can't tell." Lucky didn't give a fuck about shit I was saying. He was lying directly behind me. He wrapped his arms around my waist and started whispering all the good shit in my ear.

"It's cold as shit Kaniya, you know it's freezing like a motherfucka in here," he stated and shivered. I thought I cut the air off when I left for Miami, I guess I didn't. It was freezing in here.

"Well, put your damn clothes on and you won't be so cold," I laughed. Lucky wanted to fuck bad. He kept caressing every part of my body trying to get me to give in. As bad as I want it I knew we didn't need to cross that line.

"I'm so fuckin' tired of playing these games with you Kaniya. It's my pussy why can't I have it when I want it. If you're not giving it to me who are you giving it too? I want to fuckin' know. I'm not about to deal with your smart ass mouth," he argued and asked. Lucky is always trying to flip the damn script on somebody and I'm not with it. Currently, I'm not fuckin' anybody at the moment, but if I was it's my business. I know he's fucked somebody since the last time we fucked but I'm not asking any questions because I wasn't trying to go there with him.

"See, that's the thing you don't have to deal with me. You can take your ass to fuckin' sleep," I argued. Take a nap nigga you worse than kids. You were talking about Tariq and JD being pressed for pussy when you're in the same fuckin' boat. I had to handle his ass. No pussy over here and I mean it. I buried myself underneath the covers. Praying that sleep would take over my body soon.

Lucky

I've been trying to get Kaniya to come down with this pussy for about thirty minutes now and she still isn't budging. I guess I must put that hurricane on her. A few licks and she would be ready to give up that shit. Kaniya ain't never turning down no head. That's her weakness. She can fuck my face all fuckin' day if she wants too. Soon as she gets hers and tap out. I'm beating that pussy out the frame, since I had to wait so long to get. You don't believe me just fuckin' watch.

I waited until she got good and sleepy. I knew if she was too tired, she wouldn't put up a fight. I moved right between her legs and she didn't budge. I threw her legs over my shoulder and started finger fuckin' her wet. I had some shit to prove so I was going in. I put that hurricane on her, and she started moaning and rubbing her hands through my hair and riding my face.

The only thing she said is "Lucky what are you doing?" She asked. She knew what the fuck I was doing. I was taking what was mine. She didn't tell me to stop. She knew what fuckin' time it was. Once I was between her legs it wasn't no stopping me. I was doing me. I knew she was about to cum, I made sure of that. I raised up she opened her legs to give me easy access. I tried to slide my dick in but she was tight. She better be. I had to play with the pussy for a minute. I started stroking Kaniya long deep and hard. I pulled out and she looked at me with wide eyes.

"Lucky, why you stop?" She asked and moaned.

"Because you ain't ready," I chuckled. She grabbed my dick and shoved it in. I went in because she gave me the fuckin' okay. She already knows what time it is now. A fuck session is about to go down and I'm dropping some twins off in her ass tonight. I hope she's pregnant already. It's time for her feisty ass to have my kids.

Kaniya

☆

Ketta and Barbie finally made their way back to Atlanta. It was about fuckin' time. I missed the shit out of them. My life has been like a fuckin' movie these past few months. I went from being in love to being in lust. I've been chin checking bitches Monday through Thursday about Lucky. I was catching bodies Friday through Sunday. Running from crime scenes and changing the forecast frequently. I went from fuckin' one nigga to adding another body to my hit list and to top it off I haven't even had the Grand Opening for Work Now Atlanta yet. It was good to be in the presence of my girls finally. We had to catch up on everything.

"Bitch, you got some explaining to do. I saw the picture that Lucky posted of y'all on Instagram. That nigga said **I'm Coming Back for Good So Let Them Niggas Know It's Mine! Daddy's Home** what's up with that? You done finally let Keith Sweat come back home," she asked and laughed? Barbie was on that good bullshit. I'm here for it though. I knew it was coming.

"Girl don't fuckin' play me. You of all people know he's fucking messy and we aren't back together. We're just cool. We lay up, chill, and we've been fuckin' from time to time. That's it, no strings attached," I explained. Lucky and I are cool I can't fuckin' complain.

"And he's cool with that shit, Kaniya?" She asked." Ketta knew Lucky and she knew he wasn't going for that, but I've made it clear that we're not together.

"Yes girl, he's cool with it but I'm not dating anybody else," I explained. I've been too busy to even entertain anybody else. If I'm not with him I'm getting things together for Work Now Atlanta.

"Girl, what had happened to Tariq old fine ass?" She asked. Ketta and Barbie knew all about Tariq. They knew I was crushing hard as fuck on that man.

"Girl who knows. I haven't heard from him. I'm going to see Raven in two weeks. Hell, he might still be in Miami with Jasper I meant Jassity, the bitch he was trying to make me jealous with. On everything I love I wanted to murk that nigga when he was talking about how he wanted to fuck her. He had me climbing the walls every time we made love," I laughed and explained. I didn't mean to let that slip. Busted oops.

"Girl you been showing the fuck out. Bitch, you didn't tell us that you fucked that nigga. Bitch, you can keep a fuckin' secret I don't even want to know how good it was because you've said enough. I pray Lucky never finds out, because if he does bitch let me get my fuckin' black dress ready. I'll give the Eulogy. Ketta, bitch we've missed too much shit being in New York," she laughed and explained. Barbie wasn't lying. Man, I missed them.

"Yes, y'all have. Y'all hoes booed the fuck up on a bitch quick and dipped on me. I haven't even been invited to come and visit. I need me some New York dick. Nah I'm going to Chicago Sonja and I. We're going to go find us some thug ass niggas like Mz. Lady P be talking about in all her books. I've packed my hoe bag already," I laughed and slapped hands with Ketta and Barbie.

"Girl, you in them damn books. Those books are going to get your ass killed," she laughed. Barbie is crazy as fuck. God, I missed them.

"Reading is fundamental. You might learn some new tricks or two. Don't knock it till you try it," I beamed proudly.

"Some new tricks. Kaniya, I see you've been learning a lot," she laughed too. Ketta and Barbie ain't shit.

"I'm not about to fool with y'all about my books. What's the move for tonight. Are we going to Magic City or y'all got some couples shit planned?" I asked and laughed? I know bitches must run shit by their man first. I'm the only one that doesn't have to answer to anybody.

"We're going shit we need to go to the mall and get suited and booted you know," she explained. Barbie knew she didn't need any fuckin' new clothes. Ketta said she's been fuckin' up a check every week in the mall.

"Remember the last time we went to the mall together all the shit unfolded about Lucky. It isn't July Day but it's Independence Day. Do y'all got some shit to tell ya girl or nah? I'm just saying what's the tea," I asked. I'm just saying.

"Bitch, we ain't got no tea for your ass shit. You got all the tea," she explained. If they had they drop on Lucky. I wanted to know because Barbie knew it all.

"Alright let's make a move and turn a corner. Low and behold I hope don't no drama unfold. Anything can happen fuckin' with y'all two." We decided not to go to Lenox this time. We were headed to the Perimeter. I wasn't going to show my ass tonight. I sent Riley a text to see if she was still going, she said she was and to pick her up from the Westin at 11:00 p.m.

That bitch loves the Westin Hotel. I promise you they should name a suite after her. I really didn't need to much from the mall. I went into Victoria Secrets and got me some pink fits and bathing suits they had on sale. I was ready for tonight. I already knew what I was wearing was Lucky approved. I can't believe these chicks picked out some shit quick and was ready to bounce. They're moving like New Yorkers now. These chicks done switched up on my country ass.

"Kaniya, you full of shit now and you know it," she laughed and mentioned. I'm not fooling with Ketta today. Go play with Don and not me.

"Umm hum y'all hoes are too. Y'all motherfuckas still haven't invited me to New York yet. That's cool, just know when I get good and god damn ready, I'm at your fuckin' front door with my fuckin' bags looking for the guestroom," I laughed and explained.

"Girl come on now. You know you're welcome to come anytime but leave that bullshit here. I don't need Lucky popping up at my shit showing his black motherfuckin' ass," she laughed and explained. I slapped hands with Ketta. Everybody knows Lucky was a fool and he'll show his ass any fuckin' where.

"Are y'all coming to my birthday party next month?" I asked. I've been planning this party for months and I really want them to come.

"Yes bitch, we wouldn't miss that shit for nothing, and I mean NOTHING in the world. I already got my fit ready. The theme is fuckin' bananas," she beamed and cheered. I'm glad, I miss my turn up queen Barbie. I just knew this summer me and her would've been on tour living it up.

"Okay, let's go. I need to go home and lay down for a few hours. What time do y'all want to meet up. I'm picking Riley up at 11:00 p.m.," I asked. I don't know why I've been so tired lately, but I am. I need some fuckin' energy.

"Ok cool, we can meet at 12:00 a.m.," she explained. That's the perfect time. That gives Barbie and Ketta both plenty of time to get ready. I'm glad Barbie said that.

"That's perfect," I beamed proudly. We left the mall and headed toward my house. We laughed and bullshitted the whole way. I missed they ass something serious. Ain't No Bitches Like the One's I Got. It's crazy, the whole five years I was with Lucky none of them were in a relationship. They were doing boss shit and having fun. Now the tables have turned, it's all good though because they deserve that shit. I was happy for they ass.

I hoped they ass got pregnant and married before me since they up and moved to New York on my ass. I made it to my house and checked my mailbox, but nothing was in there. I didn't go through the garage I went through the front door. There was a vase on my porch with something in it. I'm nosey as fuck. I started walking fast as hell to see what it was. I finally approached my porch and it was filled with roses. I counted them and it was twenty-four white roses with a card attached. I tore open the envelope to see what the card read. I was curious to see what the card said. I opened it and it read.

I've been watching you and I'm coming for you, see you soon Kaniya!

Oh shit, I knew this wasn't Lucky because he was here earlier. I don't know who this could've been, but they should know how real shit gets if they want to fuck with me. I hope they ready because I stay fuckin' ready. I appreciate the roses. I'm not going to dwell too much on it. I'll see their ass soon too. I needed to get ready because 11:00 p.m. was rolling up on me and I was nowhere near ready. Everybody knows how impatient Riley's ass is.

☆

I jumped in the shower and handled my hygiene. I was gone thug it tonight since I got that card and roses. I wasn't about to let a motherfucka catch me slipping. I found a cute pair of shorts and a tank top that read **Hustle & Heels** I copped that from **Chyna L**. I laced up my Chucks. I was on go and ready for some bullshit. I brushed my hair back in a ponytail. I threw my fitted hat on and sprayed some perfume on. I locked up my house and was heading out to meet Riley. I made it to the Westin in about twenty minutes. Riley took her precious time coming out. I toyed with my phone texting Lucky until she came out.

"What's up bitch, you look cute," I asked. We exchanged a hug before I pulled off into traffic.

"What's up with you girl? Long time no see. I see you on your thug shit. Did I miss something?" She asked. Riley was always on point. I don't give a fuck she stayed ready.

"No, are you strapped the fuck up incase shit get ugly," I asked. I always wanted her to be able to protect herself just in case some shit pops off.

"Fuck yeah, that's all that matter. Let's roll," she beamed proudly.

"That's my fuckin' girl, you already know what time it is. If some shit pop off. Shoot first and ask questions later. That's why you're my right hand," I explained. Riley and I slapped hands with each other. We made it to the Blue Flame. Ketta, and Barbie were waiting on us inside already. This shit was lit already. I parked my Corvette up front and tossed the valet my keys. I sent Barbie and Ketta a text and told them to come on and I'm headed inside.

We made our way inside and this shit was lit. These niggas were making a fuckin' mess in here. Bitches were getting paid tonight. The only thing I saw on the floor was a fuckin' blue face. I guess theses niggas said fuck these old hundreds the new ones are on display. Now it was time for us to do the same. I didn't mind fuckin' up a check on a few strippers. The DJ was playing some new shit too. It was about to be a good night. One for the books.

Unknown

I've been watching Kaniya for a minute and the moment she stepped foot back in Atlanta she was on my fuckin' radar. She knew I was coming for her ass. Ain't t no fuckin' way around it. We got unfished business and I'm ready for my new beginning. I'm just getting started though. Let the games begin. She's been playing them and now it's time for me to get it in. She always screaming she plays for keeps and shit. Let's fuckin' see.

"Any word on the subject yet," I asked. They've been trailing her for the past few days and have yet to bring her back to me. What the fuck am I paying these niggas for and they can't snatch one motherfucka up? Tonight, is the night and I don't want any fuckin' excuses just solutions.

"Not yet boss, we just got a notice from a third party. They spotted her at Magic City with some friends, her car is parked up front on Forsyth St," he explained.

"Go over there and case that shit out. Put her tires on a flat. I don't give a fuck what you got to do but as soon as she leaves grab her and bring her ass to me. Don't put a fucking scratch on her. She may put up a fight, and I can guarantee you she's fuckin' holding. Don't put no fucking scratches on her and move with caution you know the fuckin' police are hot in that area," I argued and explained.

"I got you boss," he explained. I hope he does because that's what the fuck he said the last time and she's still moving around fuckin' freely.

"Do exactly what the fuck I said no fuckin' deviation. Can you handle it, or do I need to give someone else the fuckin' job?" I asked. I'm tired of paying a motherfucka with no results.

"I got you, boss I'll see you soon," he explained.

"This is the subject you heard what fuck our boss said. No scratches and move with fuckin' caution that's it," he explained.

Kaniya

Man, these past three weeks have been crazy. I can't change the past; I can only shape the future. I can't believe some of this shit, but hey when life throws you lemons make dirty lemonade. That's why I live my life to the fuckin' fullest. I've been stunting, balling like it ain't no tomorrow. Ketta and Barbie came in from New York to pick up Ketta's truck. Riley's here for a few days. We came to Magic City to kick it and turn the fuck up and its Monday too. We just blew a fuckin' check.

Monday Night Magic City

Throw Them Grands on Them Hoes

We were making a fucking mess. The niggas in here couldn't believe we flooded this bitch with some stupid cash. We've been here for about three hours. I was ready to go now. I'm tired and I'm not spending any more cash. I was tipsy and I wanted Lucky. Everybody agreed and we paid our bar tab and made our way outside to where we were parked. Tonight, was a good night. I can't even complain.

"Man, we had some much fuckin' fun. The drinks were extra fuckin' stiff. Gawd damn I love Atlanta. I missed this shit," she slurred and mentioned. Barbie was fucked up. I must admit we did have a fuckin' ball. We continued walking and talking doing our bald-headed hoe shit. Girl, we didn't have a care in the world. I've been living my life in the fuckin' fast lane. We weren't paying attention to shit. We were staggering and all sudden three masked gun men jumped out of nowhere. "What the fuck?" The masked men told us to,

"Drop every fuckin' thing and don't bust a fuckin' move!" He yelled. I wanted that motherfucka right there that's calling the shots.

Aye y'all know what the fuck to do right?" I asked. If a motherfucka had the balls to try us, then tonight they were fuckin' dying. I was on my level, but I wasn't fucked up. We dropped our purses and sprayed them niggas fuckin' wet. They weren't expecting that we laid them motherfuckas out.

"You tell that fuck nigga or bitch that sent you, we ain't laying shit down. We're laying mother niggas down. Who fuckin' want it?" Ketta yelled. She let that shit be known. That's my fuckin' bitch.

"Call the police Barbie," I yelled.

"Sis, why I got to call the fuckin' police?" She asked and yelled? Barbie was being fuckin' difficult. We're already on fuckin' camera, I wasn't about to flee the scene. I caught a body and its self-defense.

"Oh my God, here we go again. Riley call the fuckin' police please," I argued and asked. I knew Riley would do it without a doubt. "We can't leave these bodies out here. If we leave these fuckin' bodies here. All APD got to do is pull these fuckin' street cameras and we're going to fuckin' jail because they'll come looking for our asses and they have no reason too. We ain't done shit," I yelled and explained. I felt a tap on my shoulder. I looked over my shoulder to see who it was. It was another fuckin' mask man pointing a fuckin' AK-47 at my head and to make matters worse another masked gunman was behind me. "Man, what the fuck is this?"

"Don't say shit bitch. Don't fuckin' move and don't breathe to fuckin' hard. Look bitch don't you try no fuckin' bullshit. Don't click your fuckin' heels to fucking loud. I know your kind motherfucka, you just killed three of my niggas. We got her boss but three dead," he explained and said to the person on the other end of his phone.

"Tell your fuckin' boss with his pussy ass Kaniya, said fuck him," I argued and spat in his fuckin' face. He wiped the spit off his face and laughed.

"You better be glad I can't fuckin' touch you. Last I checked bitch I didn't tell you to fuckin' talk. Get your hard-headed ass in the mother fuckin' car," he argued. The other masked man that was with him took a picture of me. I guess he was sending it to his boss.

"Is that her," he asked.

"That's definitely her." I heard the other motherfucka on the end of the phone say.

CHECK MATE

Pushing Pen Presents now accepting submissions for the following genres: Urban Fiction, Street Lit, Urban Romance, Women's Fiction, BWWM Romance Please submit your first three chapters in a Word document, synopsis, and include contact information via email Nikkinicole@nikkinicolepresents.com please allow 3-5 business days for a response after submitting.

CONTEST ALERT

E-Gift Card or CashApp Contest! I Wanted to Announce It Here First. Read, Review on Amazon and Goodreads! Post Your Review or Thoughts in Your Favorite Reading Group on Facebook or Instagram. Tag Me in It (Nikki Taylor) on Facebook or Instagram (WatchNikkiWrite) Twitter (WatchNikkiWrite) Email Your Entry to NikkiNicole@Nikkinicolepresents.com.

If You Don't Have A Favorite Reading Group Request the Book at Your Local Library Send Proof. The First 60 Reviews I Get I'm Going to Draw A Name. You Pick the Gift card or CashApp It'll Be For $40.00 for The First Drawing. Once the Book Reaches 100 Reviews It'll Be A Drawing for Another $40.00 Prize. Give Me Your CashApp Name I'll CashApp You $40.00. I Do Things in Real Time! I'm Not Holding It Until the End of The Month.

If I Get 60 Reviews on Day 1 Of This Release. I'll Draw A Name the Next Day and You'll Get The E-Gift Card of Your Choice or The CashApp. For Each 50 Reviews I Get I'll Draw A Name. You Can Get A 40.00 E-GIFT-CARD or 40.00 CashApp. I'm Giving Away 3 prizes.

CPSIA information can be obtained
at www.ICGtesting.com
Printed in the USA
LVHW051553020819
626317LV00001B/130/P

9 781075 740572